THE LOST CAUSE

Other books in the
Randy Lassiter & Leslie Carlisle Mystery Series

An Undercurrent of Murder

A Nasty Way to Die

A Piece of Paradise

The Lost Cause

A Randy Lassiter & Leslie Carlisle Mystery

JOE DAVID RICE

ISBN (paperback): 978-1-7362391-6-2
ISBN (ebook): 978-1-7362391-7-9

Cover and book design: H. K. Stewart

Printed in the United States of America

This book is printed on archival-quality paper that meets requirements of the American National Standard for Information Sciences, Permanence of Paper, Printed Library Materials, ANSI Z39.48-1984.

Dedicated to my many friends
in the tourism and advertising communities

~ ONE ~

How much can you learn, really learn, about a person or a workplace in a single hour-long conversation?

That's why I've never been a big fan of job interviews whether I'm being interviewed or doing the questioning. In my opinion, the interview is, with rare exceptions, little more than a temporary ceasefire between two competing entities. Both parties are wary of the other, often trying to keep little secrets tucked away. And perhaps some larger ones as well.

But there are times when the interview dance is unavoidable. So it was when my executive assistant at Lassiter & Associates received a well-deserved promotion within the agency. Given our organization—me, in particular—functioned far better with someone filling the position, it was important we find the right person. And necessary, alas, for us to conduct a round of interviews.

As for Lassiter & Associates, it's an up-and-coming advertising firm in Little Rock now entering its second decade of service. A dozen and a half or so of us rub shoulders in a cramped office between the downtown skyscrapers a quarter mile to the east and the State Capitol five blocks in the opposite direction. We work hard to keep our existing clients prosperous and happy and make the occasional pitch to bring in a new account.

My name is Randy Lassiter. I'm the primary owner, although I've instituted a profit-sharing plan giving each of my colleagues equity in the company after 18 months on the payroll and then more as their tenure advances. Through trial and error, I've come to endorse an uncomplicated theory of personnel management: having skin in the game improves one's attitude and performance. And adds to the agency's bottom line.

I'd established Lassiter & Associates after graduating from the University of Arkansas and putting in months of eye-opening and character-building grunt work for other agencies in town. To be sure, our billings aren't yet approaching those of our top competitors. But the good news is we're trending in the right direction, eking out a small profit while trying our best to disrupt the status quo, and even upsetting several of the industry's old-timers along the way. Bringing in a new top-notch team member will contribute to our positive momentum.

The selected candidate will become a key player on the Lassiter team, operating across all facets of the organization with a full load of responsibilities. He or she will maximize use of my time, schedule and set agendas for staff meetings, handle travel arrangements and expense reports, participate in strategy sessions with current and potential clients, and serve as our unofficial director of corporate culture. For those who assume this position is little more than a glorified secretary, think again. I figure bringing onboard a top applicant is going to run at least $85,000 a year. More if you include insurance, retirement, and other perks.

We'd advertised the vacancy for four weeks, both in professional outlets and the local media. Some 25 individuals responded. Of those, eight looked to have the desired combination of education and experience to invite in for interviews. When we called to schedule the meetings, two declined, having already agreed to other offers. Six, however, accepted our requests to meet with me and two of my colleagues to discuss the position and its duties.

Over the years, I've found questioning by a three-person committee seems to yield the best results, helping to achieve a balanced evaluation. An entire day—Wednesday, April 19—had been set aside for the series of hour-long meetings with the prospective employee. I'd spent a good deal of time the previous afternoon and evening reviewing résumés of the six finalists. Although dreading the process, I felt encouraged with our prospects.

The first contender, a pleasant man with an undergraduate degree in communications, made a favorable impression. Favorable, but not great. He had a fair grasp of the field of public relations, maintained decent eye contact, and asked germane questions. My chief concern was he displayed no understanding whatsoever regarding the agency or our clients. Once he'd left the room, I complained to my fellow committee members I suspected he hadn't bothered to spend any time on the company's website.

"Maybe the next one will be better," said Abigail Ahart, one of my veteran employees and a member of our interview team. "She has one heck of a résumé."

I, too, had high hopes for this applicant. She had almost 10 years of relevant experience, including a lengthy stint in a similar position with a prominent advertising outfit in Houston. Her husband's transfer had brought her into the Little Rock job market in recent weeks. But ten o'clock, the hour of her confirmed appointment, came and went without an appearance. After 15 minutes had passed, I stepped outside our conference room and asked the receptionist if she'd received a call from a late-running prospect. She hadn't.

At 10:25, the door opened and the woman was ushered into the room. She introduced herself with a broad smile and shared updated copies of her CV before occupying the seat at the head of the table. She thanked us for the opportunity to visit about the job and provided more than satisfactory answers to our queries. Yet she never bothered to explain her late arrival and never apologized. The three of us went through the motions, asking the same questions we'd posed to our first applicant. However, my colleagues knew I had no interest in hiring anyone who didn't respect the time of his or her peers.

Unlike our first two candidates, the next—a female in her late 20s or early 30s—failed to wear what I'd call job-appropriate attire. Her dress, a provocative bright red number, might have been fine 10 hours later in another venue altogether.

Megan Maloney, the third member of our team, shook her head after the lady had left the room.

"I have no real objection with a woman taking her girls out for a walk," she said, "though parading them in the River District this evening would have been a smarter choice."

Remembering the stern sexual harassment warnings I'd heard time and again from my lawsuit-conscious attorney, I refrained from any remarks and pushed away from the table. Likewise, I resisted the temptation to comment on the woman's perfume, the musky aftereffects of which lingered well past her departure.

We had an hour until the next applicant was scheduled to arrive. I darted into my office, grabbed a handful of almonds and an apple for lunch, and checked telephone messages and e-mails. None of the phone calls were urgent, but I opened a text from Leslie, my bride of six months. A magazine's photo editor had sent her into the Ozarks of north Arkansas to shoot the spring waterfall season in the Buffalo River country. An accomplished professional photographer, she'd been away most of the week on this assignment.

"Hiking down into Hemmed-In Hollow; will be out-of-service for four or five hours," she wrote. "Day going well. Wish me luck!"

"Interviews have been underwhelming so far," I replied. "Would rather be with you. The Buffalo's special!" I added a pair of heart emojis for good measure.

We'd met on the banks of the Buffalo River a year and a half earlier. I was on a camping trip with Dr. Gib Yarberry, my annoying brother-in-law, and Leslie had been pulled from her home base in Texas with an assignment to capture the peak of fall foliage for *Southern Living* magazine. A quirk of fate had thrown us together in the middle of a vast wilderness and the rest, as they say, is history. And, so far, we've compiled a fine history.

Our fourth interviewee was an intense young man who'd relocated from Seattle to Little Rock so he and his wife could tend to her elderly parents. During the course of his short career, he'd held responsible positions with two Fortune 500 companies, accumulating an admirable track record. And he'd done his homework, surprising us with his sense of Lassiter & Associates. But one of his mannerisms unnerved me: the man kept fiddling with his cell phone. He'd placed it in front of him on the conference table and every five minutes or so glanced at the screen, seemingly waiting on an urgent message.

Noticing the same thing, Megan cut to the chase.

"Are you expecting an important call?" she asked.

Embarrassed, the man slipped the phone into a pocket. Too late; the damage was done.

When time came for the next session, our receptionist informed us contestant number five on the day's schedule had telephoned, cancelling the interview without any explanation, and freeing an hour of our afternoon. I again retreated into my office and began returning missed calls. The last was to a reporter with *Arkansas Business*, a weekly newsmagazine headquartered a few blocks down the street.

"Mr. Lassiter," she began, "how would you react to news the advertising account for the Arkansas Department of Parks, Heritage, & Tourism will be open for review?"

Her question left me dumbfounded. Like most of my competitors, I'd fantasized for years about landing this account. Not only did it involve a considerable amount of money—something on the order of $25 million annually in billings—the department was among the most visible and prestigious clients in the state. And it would be a "feel good" account, too, promoting positive things like state and national parks, tourist attractions, festivals, musical events, restaurants, museums, and such. Even the most dedicated and creative folks can grow weary producing ads pitching used cars and vinyl siding and furniture closeouts, not to mention bankruptcy filings or cremation services.

And then there was the matter of the incumbent advertising agency, a powerful institution holding the account for much of my life. Established almost half a century ago as Andrews Bingham Carter, it was known by most of us in the industry as ABC. Its principals had developed exceptional political instincts throughout the past couple of decades, cultivating valuable personal relationships and currying favor as the state shifted from blue to red. Although I'd never heard any hints or allegations of improprieties, it was understood ABC held a solid lock on the account. Other advertising firms, mine included, no longer wasted any time responding to the state's official "Request for Proposals" landing on our desks every two years, realizing we had no chance in hell of unseating the agency of record.

"Mr. Lassiter," she asked, "are you still there?"

I cleared my throat. "Yes, but I'm rather curious. Do you have this on good authority?"

"You could say so," she replied. "I heard it from Governor Butler herself less than an hour ago."

Governor Patricia Butler had been in office not quite three months. A moderate Democrat with no prior involvement in politics, she'd run an aggressive campaign, promising voters she'd use her knowledge of the commercial world to transform state government. And her private sector experience was indeed remarkable. Butler had started an organic-based cosmetics company in her basement a decade ago, a business now employing over 1,200 folks in a sparkling factory in her hometown of Jonesboro.

Along the way, Butler had become something of a Wall Street favorite. She'd breezed through the Democratic primary without a runoff and had walloped her Republican opponent by a three to two majority in the general election. While I'd never met her, I felt comfortable with Butler's platform, especially her commitment to public education, and had no qualms voting for her. And for the first time in recent memory, I wrote a personal check—modest, to be sure—in support of a candidate in a statewide race.

"To tell you the truth," I said to the reporter, "I'm speechless. Have you gotten a comment from ABC's management?"

"Nothing official," she said. "I believe there'll be a statement released in the next day or two. Needless to say, this had to be a shock. As you know, Andrews Bingham Carter has held the account for more than 30 years."

"Has anything been made public regarding the review process?" I asked.

"I was told a schedule will be made available next week," she said. "Will Lassiter & Associates be making a pitch?"

"We'll take a look at it," I said, "although it's too soon to say for sure."

That was an outright lie. I'd been coveting the account most of my adult life and would make every effort to land it. I couldn't wait to share this development with my colleagues. Like me, they'd be stunned by the news.

As the call ended, the door opened and Abbie stuck her head inside my office.

"Our last candidate has arrived if you're ready," she said.

I trailed her down the hall toward our conference room.

"Let's hope this one is superior to the others."

"She looks competent on paper," Abbie said. "And I recognized a name among her references: Leslie Carlisle."

I stopped in my tracks, surprised by this revelation. I pay little attention to references shown on résumés, unwilling to put much stock on the biased recommendations of an applicant's close friends or acquaintances, preferring instead to call previous employers.

Abbie handed me a copy of Erin Askew's résumé. Sure enough, in black and white at the bottom of the last page, was this listing among four other references: Leslie Carlisle, professional photographer, followed by a familiar telephone number and e-mail address.

* * *

Days before our wedding last fall, Leslie had pulled me aside. Something was troubling her.

"I have a serious question," she said, "and I want an honest answer."

"Let's hear it," I said, wondering where this conversation might be headed.

"After the wedding," she said, "I can remain a Carlisle or become a Lassiter. I've been worrying over this for weeks."

My dad and his dad would have insisted on her taking my last name. Times, though, had changed.

"The decision is yours," I said. "We both know how strong traditions can be in this state."

I recalled reading about the public outcry in Arkansas when Hillary Rodham initially chose to retain her maiden name rather than becoming Hillary Clinton. But she had yielded to the pressure.

Leslie nodded, her eyes locked onto mine.

"My view is you've worked hard establishing your career. You've spent years building valuable equity into your name, which is essentially your brand," I said. "If I were you, I'd stick with Carlisle."

She smiled and gave me a kiss. "I was hoping you'd say that."

"Of course, I'll still expect you to love, honor, and obey me."

Leslie had punched me on the shoulder. Gently.

"You'll have to settle for two out of three."

* * *

When Erin Askew and I shook hands, I noticed her tailored navy-blue pantsuit, thinking Leslie had one similar to it. Or maybe it was because of the startling contrast with the attire of the previous female applicant.

As our interview with Ms. Askew progressed, it became obvious she was head and shoulders above the others we'd seen. Despite her youth—she appeared to be in her mid- to late-20s—she displayed an unexpected level of maturity. Ms. Askew had a fine sense of humor and demonstrated an amazing familiarity with Lassiter & Associates and its clients. Taking notes as we talked, she handled our inquiries with refreshing candor. In fact, she had as many questions for us as we did for her, one of them regarding the office environment at the agency.

"I have no desire to be just another person in a tense and stuffy business," she said. "I want to look forward to coming in daily and developing friendships among the staff—with the possibility of advancing through the ranks."

A burst of raucous laughter in the hallway partially answered a portion of her concern.

Megan provided further elaboration. "I've been here half a dozen years after having been employed at three other companies, two in Dallas and one local. Without question, this place is the best of the lot," she said. "We put in the hours, but have fun, too."

"And Randy's sincere when he says Lassiter & Associates believes in career development and promotion," Abbie added, chiming in. "Take this position we're discussing today. Of the past four executive assistants, three have advanced within the agency. The other moved to Tulsa with her husband. As for me, I've received several promotions since joining the firm, and the same goes for Megan."

When the interview came to an end, we stood and shook hands. I thanked Ms. Askew for her time and promised she'd hear from us soon.

As she started to turn and leave, I said, "Oh, I have one more quick question. What's the relationship with one of your references, this Leslie Carlisle person?"

I noticed a subtle exchange between Abbie and Megan.

"I've been working another job as a model through one of the local talent agencies," she said. "During evenings and weekends for the most part."

Her second career wasn't hard to imagine, I thought. Given her tall and trim physique, sparkling eyes, and ready smile, she had the classic "girl-next-door" look.

"I've participated in photo shoots with Ms. Carlisle on a number of occasions in the past six months," she said. "We seem to have developed excellent rapport, and she agreed I could list her as a reference."

I grimaced and shook my head. Megan and Abbie tried to hide their snickers.

Ms. Askew's face fell.

"Do you have problems with Ms. Carlisle?"

"Each and every day," I said, giving her a smile. "Leslie Carlisle is my wife."

~ TWO ~

Thursday was a busy day, start to finish. For one of the rare occasions in the history of Lassiter & Associates, I assembled the entire team in the conference room for a meeting. It was a tight fit. A handful of my colleagues, especially the newer ones, seemed anxious, as if downsizing was on the morning's agenda.

Energized about the day's prospects, I'd stopped at Starbucks on the way in and splurged on a tall caffè latte. I set my cup on the table and glanced around the room and smiled. I was surrounded by an exceptional collection of talent, an amazing group of dedicated, hardworking folks who relished challenges. Today I was going to give them one, the biggest opportunity I'd encountered since founding the agency over a decade ago.

My "Good morning" was met with a chorus of similar words.

"Thanks for showing up on such short notice. This will be a quick meeting, although I hope it's the first in a remarkable journey leading to a fulfilling experience for everyone here."

The looks of apprehension vanished. Many of my associates scooted forward in their seats and others got notepads ready, pens in hand. For once, no one was staring at a cell phone.

"Those of you who've been here a while know one of my long-term goals is to add the Arkansas Department of Parks, Heritage and Tourism to our client list," I said. "In fact, several of you might suggest my interest in this account is more like an unhealthy obsession. I might be inclined to agree."

Three or four of my veteran employees exchanged grins as their heads bobbed up and down.

"This morning I have interesting news to share. The state tourism account will be on the street soon," I said, resorting to the advertising industry's vernacular.

I heard a couple of gasps from the back of the room.

"In other words, open for bids," I said. "Media coverage of this unexpected development should appear in the next day or so. In the meantime, please rest assured landing this account will be a top priority for Lassiter & Associates. I want our organization to be the Department's next agency of record."

I pointed to a waving hand.

"Randy, any scuttlebutt involving ABC? Will it be in the running?"

It was a good question. Everybody in the state's advertising community knew of the long and involved history between the Andrews Bingham Carter firm, one of the oldest ad agencies west of the Mississippi River, and Arkansas state government.

"I'm rather curious about that myself," I said, getting some chuckles. "From what I've learned, it will be a legitimate review, an open and objective process. I'm told Governor Patricia Butler herself directed the contract be put out for bids."

Another arm went up.

"Any word on a schedule?"

"Nothing so far," I said, "but I expect details will be released within a week."

I took a sip of coffee, my eyes moving from face to face. I was delighted to see my gaze met with one nod after another.

"Let me summarize by reminding each of you we'll have a chance to showcase the incredible creativity and resourcefulness of this group. Things will grow hectic over the coming months. We'll be putting in extra hours and tempers may grow thin. However, if we work together and stay the course, the rewards could be mindboggling."

Megan gestured to get my attention.

"Randy, will our relationship with Isla del Sol be a problem?"

She was noting the fact Lassiter & Associates represented one of the largest casinos in the South across the river in Tunica, Mississippi. Competitors might argue having a prominent tourism-related client in another state was a conflict of interest.

"It's an interesting point," I said. "I'm hopeful such issues will be addressed in the official Request for Proposals. We'll have to wait until the RFP's released."

I paused, scanning across the attentive faces.

"If there are no more questions, let's return to work and keep our current clients happy."

I then asked my department heads to convene in my office for a follow-up session. We spent an hour discussing research needs, possible creative strategies, media mixes, and other factors likely to be involved in a bid for the state account.

Megan mentioned ABC's current advertising contract with the Department of Parks, Heritage and Tourism.

"We could file an FOI to obtain a copy," she said, referring to Arkansas's Freedom of Information act. "It'd be helpful to know something regarding their scope of services, rates, and staffing."

"Let me work behind the scenes to acquire a copy," I said. "I'm not ready for the media to connect Lassiter & Associates with a formal FOI request. Let's convene here in my office on Monday morning following our regular staff meeting."

Once everyone left, I called Joan Pfeiffer, a longtime friend and member of the Arkansas General Assembly now serving her second term as a state representative.

"Joan," I said after she'd picked up. "Any chance I can buy you a drink this evening?"

"There's an excellent chance you can do that," she said, her voice lacking its usual warmth and enthusiasm. "I was thinking about calling you."

"Same time, same place?"

"Capital Hotel Bar," she said. "Six o'clock."

I found my copy of Erin Askew's résumé and began making calls. Rather than dealing with the individuals she'd listed as references, I chose to speak with former employers. Two of them gave me the predictable spiel concerning the confidentiality of personnel matters and refused to entertain my questions, although both noted she was eligible for rehire, a bureaucratic way of stating she'd departed on positive terms. A previous supervisor at a local radio station said she'd been the best worker on his staff. "Friendly, punctual, dependable, and intuitive" were the words he used to describe her job performance. And her current boss, a man in the insurance business I'd met a time or two over the years, realized Erin was seeking a new job but still hoped to retain her, claiming she was the finest employee he'd ever had. Ms. Askew seemed almost too good to be true.

Leslie surprised me with a phone call mid-afternoon.

"I marked off the last shot on my waterfall list 15 minutes ago. With a major storm system predicted to blast through the Ozarks early tomorrow morning, my timing couldn't be better."

"You'll be headed home soon?"

"Within the hour," she said. "So, if you've made plans with another woman this evening, you might want to reconsider."

"Well, I am scheduled to meet Joan late this afternoon at the Capital Hotel Bar," I said. "We'll limit our rendezvous to the libations portion of the institution."

"Outstanding answer," Leslie said, giggling. "I'll see you tonight."

"One more thing," I said. "Do you know a woman named Erin Askew?"

There was a short pause.

"She's participated in various shoots," she said. "Erin's been professional in every way. I've always had an enjoyable experience working with her. Why?"

"Erin's the top candidate for our vacancy," I said. "She listed you as a reference."

"Now that you mention it, she e-mailed a couple of weeks ago asking permission to use me as a reference," Leslie said. "I can vouch for her without reservation."

"Thanks," I said. "Travel safely."

* * *

Arriving a few minutes before 6:00, I snagged a table in my favorite drinking establishment next to the window facing Markham Street. One of Little Rock's popular watering holes, the Capital Hotel Bar has a long and storied history. Tycoons, journalists, politicians, and celebrities have gravitated here for over a century. I spotted the mayor dining with her husband across the room and waved, but the remainder of tonight's crowd looked to be everyday customers. Joan strolled in minutes later and greeted me with a hug and a kiss to the cheek.

"Did I detect a touch of distress in our earlier conversation?" I asked. "A tone hinting you might need a relaxing beverage?"

"You did, indeed. A pair of my legislative cohorts have staked out territory well to the right of Attila the Hun," she said. "I had to listen to their disgusting vitriol all morning."

When the waiter asked for our order, Joan skipped her usual glass of Chardonay and shocked me by requesting a bourbon. Neat. I opted for a mug of a local IPA.

"Even worse," she said, "is both of these moronic imbeciles have aspirations for higher office. And given today's misinformed and misguided public, they might well succeed."

We watched a streetcar trundle past our window. On the sidewalk, a quartet of animated conventioneers ambled by, their shiny nametags giving them away.

"I remember when we met here not quite a year ago," she said. "You were trying to track down J.J." She sniffed and wiped a tear from her cheek.

Days later, we later learned Dr. J.J. Newell, my former college roommate and best friend and her one-time lover, had been murdered.

"I miss him," I said. "It's hard to believe he's no longer with us."

After the waiter delivered our drinks, Joan lifted hers and held it midway over the table.

"To J.J. May he live on in our memories."

I touched the rim of my mug to her glass of bourbon.

"To a fine human who left us far too early."

A tall, handsome Black man appeared behind Joan. With his nicely-trimmed gray beard, lustrous skin, and lively eyes, he would have been an intriguing subject for one of Leslie's photographic portraits. Giving me a wink, he leaned toward Joan and kissed her lightly on the side of her face as she lowered her glass.

Startled, Joan twisted around to identify her admirer.

"Somer," she said, her eyes sparkling. "What a pleasant surprise."

Looking to me, he extended a hand.

"Good evening," he said with a radiant smile. "I'm Somer Smith."

I stood as we exchanged a firm handshake.

"Randy Lassiter. Will you join us?" I asked, gesturing to an empty chair

"I'd love to," he said, "but I have a table of impatient constituents expecting me at the other end of the room."

Joan took his big hand in hers.

"Senator Smith," Joan said, nodding over her shoulder, "is my best friend, some days my sole friend, in the entire Arkansas legislature. He's the unofficial conscience of the General Assembly."

Smith shook his head and patted Joan on the back.

"What she means is we're often two lone voices deep in the wilderness of Arkansas politics. Nice to meet you, Mr. Lassiter."

Turning to Joan, he said, "I have an appointment to keep. See you tomorrow in Joint Budget."

I returned to my seat as Senator Smith slipped through the noisy throng gathered around the bar and disappeared into the crowd.

"You've now met Senator Somerset Spartacus Smith," she said. "He's from Osceola in northeastern Arkansas. Working two and sometimes three jobs, his mom raised him and his three older sisters without a husband in a two-bedroom shack. Her parents traced their roots back to slavery, and she named her only son after two of the most famous slaves in history."

"Spartacus, I understand," I said. "I believe he led a rebellion against the Roman Republic two thousand years ago. But Somerset?"

"Somer explained it to me on the morning we were both sworn in for the first time," Joan said. "Although his mother lacked a formal education, she taught herself to read. One of her heroes was James Somerset, a young man from Africa who was sold to slave traders at the age of eight. He was bought by a merchant in colonial Virginia who took him to London prior to the American Revolution. After Somerset escaped from his owner, he was recaptured and put on a ship bound for Jamaica to be sold again. Abolitionists filed a Habeas corpus case with the courts, challenging the legal basis of slavery in England. In a landmark decision, the judge ruled in favor of Somerset."

"Wasn't the senator profiled in a recent edition of the newspaper's weekend edition?" I asked.

"He's the one," she said. "Graduated with honors from Harvard Law, had the highest test score ever recorded for the state bar, and parlayed a successful legal career back home into the Arkansas Senate."

"Future gubernatorial candidate?" I asked.

She shook her head.

"He'd be a great governor. Unfortunately, some of his colleagues in the General Assembly feel Somer asks too many questions and raises too many issues. One or two on the extreme right think it's just a matter of time before he introduces a bill establishing a reparations program for Black Arkansans."

"And making cash payments to descendants of former slaves is not gonna fly with our current group of legislators?"

"Not with this session or any I can imagine in my lifetime. However, he's determined to at least begin the conversation dealing with lynchings, Jim Crow laws, and decades of inequities and injustice."

Joan sighed, took a sip, and then placed her drink on the table.

"I believe you're the one who suggested this get-together," she said. "What's on your mind?"

"I've heard rumors the state's advertising contract with the Andrews Bingham Carter agency may be coming to an end."

Tilting her head, Joan gave me one of her clever smiles. "I can confirm it's more than a rumor."

She enjoyed another sip of her bourbon.

"What I'd like is to review the state's contract with ABC," I said. "Without going to all the trouble of filing an official FOI request. I thought maybe you could … uh … help."

Joan grinned again, set her glass aside, and retrieved her phone. She scrolled through her directory, found a name, and began typing. A minute later, she slipped the phone into her purse.

"I've requested a copy," she said. "I should have it in your hands by noon tomorrow. My position does come with certain perks."

I raised my beer. "To State Representative Joan Pfeiffer. May she continue to serve her appreciative public."

She shook her head, but nevertheless tapped my mug with her glass.

"Politics isn't much fun anymore, Randy. Too mean. Too vicious. Too many people in it for the wrong reasons."

"What's the inside scoop on our new governor?"

"Governor Patricia Butler is one of the rare bright spots in Arkansas government these days," Joan said. "If she can only manage to work with the misogynistic misfits running the General Assembly. She's been in office less than four months and they're already doing everything they can to sabotage her agenda."

Joan glanced at her watch before swallowing the rest of her drink. "The sorry bastards."

"I'm thinking she might have initiated this unexpected ABC development."

Joan gave me a subtle nod. "Let's just say Governor Butler is ready to make changes. Long overdue changes."

When she stood and grasped her purse, I got to my feet and wrapped an arm around her shoulders.

"Sorry; it's time for me to run," she said. "Let's do this again soon. And please tell your lovely bride I said hello."

* * *

I'd been home 15 minutes when Leslie pulled into the driveway. I met her on the porch and was rewarded with a tight embrace and a lingering kiss.

"Welcome home," I said. "It seems like you've been gone forever."

"Next time I need to bring you along," she said. "You could lug my camera gear around like you did in the Bahamas."

We'd combined our honeymoon this past fall with her assignment to photograph Cat Island, Eleuthera, and a couple of other nearby Caribbean isles. I'd earned my stripes as her assistant. And the fringe benefits weren't bad either.

"I take it you're pleased with the waterfalls shots," I said, grabbing her tripod and camera bag.

She reached for the duffle containing her clothes.

"I should have a good assortment of quality images. Maybe some exceptional shots," she said. "The Hemmed-In Hollow trek came close to killing me, but the falls were spectacular. I can't wait to show you the pictures. First, though, I want a nice hot bath."

Once inside, I stored Leslie's photography equipment in her office while she headed upstairs. I then prepared a platter of crackers, cheeses, and fresh fruit, poured a goblet of her favorite Pinot Grigio, and met her in the bathroom. She was up to her neck in bubbles when I arrived.

"Your interview with Erin Askew," she said. "How'd it go?"

"She did a fine job, impressing all of us. Erin had done her homework on the agency and asked pertinent questions regarding the position's workload and responsibilities. I think she'd be a strong addition to our team."

"Unlike several of the other young women I've worked with," Leslie said, "there's nothing of a prima donna in Erin. I enjoy being around her."

"I called her former employers and, from those willing to talk candidly with me, got rave reviews across the board."

"It sounds like you had a productive day," Leslie said following another sip of wine.

24

"There's more. Joan confirmed the advertising contract with state government's biggest account will be up for review."

"Isn't it the tourism client you've coveted most of your adult life?"

"The very one. My colleagues realize Lassiter & Associates will be in an 'all-hands-on-deck' situation for the next few months."

"And how is our favorite state representative?"

"Joan said hello, by the way. But she's discouraged with the current political climate, feeling barbarians are storming the gates."

"Her worries are easy enough to understand. Some of the bills they've passed this session are awful, leading the state in the wrong direction."

She took another sip. "Back to Erin. Why don't we meet her for dinner tomorrow night? It'll give you a chance to see her in a less formal, non-work setting."

I considered Leslie's suggestion for a moment. It'd be somewhat unorthodox, taking a job applicant to dinner, yet it'd provide a pleasant opportunity to get to know her better. And I couldn't think of any hiring practices such an encounter would violate. As luck would have it, Erin's phone number was in the file I'd brought home.

When Leslie emerged from the tub, I handed her a thick towel.

Groaning as she bent to dry her legs, she said, "That long, uphill hike out of Hemmed-In Hollow was brutal. My quads may never be the same."

"Can I talk you into a relaxing rubdown?" I asked. "Perhaps a full body massage would interest the lady."

I put on my most innocent expression.

"It sounds appealing," Leslie said, shooting me a grin. "Though I will admit to a certain curiosity regarding your motives."

"One hundred percent ulterior."

"I'd be stunned if you'd said otherwise. And disappointed," she said. "Make your call, and then meet me in bed."

~ THREE ~

I received a thick hand-delivered package midmorning on Friday from State Representative Joan Pfeiffer. It was a reprint of the 118-page contract between Andrews Bingham Carter Advertising Agency, Inc., and the State of Arkansas. Handing it to one of my associates, I asked him to make half a dozen copies and give one to each of my department heads. I next sent e-mails to this same group, reminding them to review the forthcoming document and to be prepared to discuss it in depth at our Monday morning meeting. And I then forwarded a quick note to Joan, confirming the copy of the contract had arrived and thanking her for the help. I'd take the original home and read it over the weekend.

The remainder of the day flew by, much of it spent with my senior management team discussing an account the agency was considering. Cannabis is now legal in Arkansas for medicinal purposes, and Lassiter & Associates had been invited by one of the largest suppliers to submit a proposal for a multi-million-dollar statewide marketing campaign. I personally didn't have any problem with business of this nature, but had heard rumblings from a couple of my longtime colleagues. While they claimed to have no objection themselves, they reported considerable pushback from vocal members of their churches. Priests and pastors, in particular.

And then Meagan raised an interesting point.

"If we were to get this," she said, "there's a chance it might have a negative impact on the agency's likelihood of landing the state's tourism account later this year."

Someone asked her to explain.

"Although voters approved cannabis dispensaries a decade ago, a faction of key legislators continues to voice their strong opposition to medical use of marijuana," she said. "They're convinced the vote was a step toward its full legalization in the state."

"And your concern," I continued, "is these same legislators could be involved in the determination of which advertising agency is awarded the state's tourism contract?"

"Bingo," she said.

I glanced at my watch. It was a quarter past four.

"It's been a long week," I said. "We'll take this up on Monday. In the meantime, enjoy your weekends."

* * *

When I'd phoned Erin Askew on Thursday evening, she'd readily accepted our invitation for dinner on Friday night.

"Would Heights Taco & Tamale be okay with you?" I'd asked.

"It's one of my favorites," she said, "and is convenient, located a few blocks from my apartment."

Our reservation was for seven o'clock. Mere minutes after the three of us had been seated, our order for a trio of frozen Margaritas appeared. We shared a friendly toast.

"I want to tell you how much Megan, Abbie, and I enjoyed our interview with you earlier this week," I said.

"To be truthful," Erin said, "I was nervous and had trouble sleeping the night before. Yet I felt comfortable with you and your associates throughout our conversation. Leaving your office, I couldn't believe how quickly the hour passed."

"I should add your former employers, or at least those willing to talk, gave you high marks. As for your list of references, I only checked with one of them," I said, turning to Leslie.

Leslie shrugged.

"I told Randy you were borderline psychotic, but otherwise okay," she said, breaking into a grin

Erin almost choked on her Margarita.

"So, I'm pleased to offer you the position of Executive Assistant at Lassiter & Associates," I said, "consistent with the terms we discussed Wednesday afternoon."

Erin held her drink high and we clinked glasses.

"I am delighted to accept."

I took a peek at the calendar on my phone.

"Will Monday, May 1, work? It's a week and a half away."

I figured that would give her ample time to sever ties with her current job and deal with any loose ends.

"It'll be easy to remember," she said. "It's May Day. And my late father's birthday."

I felt a tap on my shoulder. Turning around, I was surprised to see my sister Ellen Yarberry, her aggravating husband Dr. Gib Yarberry, and their cute and soon-to-be-one-year-old son Jimmy. Actually, surprised isn't the right word, given my tormented relationship with Gib. He was an incorrigible punster, and the gods had somehow determined my unfortunate fate was to be his foil. Distressed would have been a better choice for my immediate reaction.

"We were leaving when Gib spotted you," Ellen said.

By now, Leslie and I'd risen, and I'd introduced Erin to them about the time Jimmy reached for me. I held this squirming dynamo for maybe 15 seconds before he decided Leslie was his favored destination and stretched his chubby little arms in her direction, squealing in delight as she took him.

"What's keeping the Yarberrys busy these days?" I asked.

Ellen winked at me.

"My agency intends to go all out for the state tourism account," she said.

She'd cut her professional teeth at Lassiter & Associates before jumping ship and joining the staff of a competing outfit 15 months ago.

"May I assume the Lassiter team is interested?"

"We're considering it," I said, not willing to tip my hand just yet.

"Speaking of advertising," Gib said, "when we visited earlier this spring, you mentioned something about a potential new client. A promising start-up to be based here in Little Rock if my memory's correct. Maybe an automobile painting company?"

"We chose not to pursue it," I said, both amazed and bothered by his recollection of our brief discussion. "The staff was stretched too thin at the time, and billings would have been small."

"Too bad," Gib said. "I'd come up with the perfect name for it."

Following what seemed to be an interminable delay, he smirked and said, "Fifty Shades of Spray."

He cackled and smacked his hands together, unable to contain his delight with this alleged cleverness.

The loud slap startled several nearby diners.

It also scared Jimmy who broke into a piercing wail.

Leslie returned the frightened infant to his mom who'd giggled at Gib's lame effort at a literary allusion. Leslie rolled her eyes and Erin managed to hide most of a smile.

"There's the signal it's time for us to go," Ellen said. "Nice to meet you, Erin."

I sucked down half of my Margarita as they waved their good-byes and headed for the exit.

The waiter reappeared, eager to hear our requests, and I gestured for Erin to go first.

"I'd like the spinach and zucchini enchiladas," she said. "But no cilantro, please."

Leslie laughed as the waiter took notes.

"Randy feels the same way," she said. "If he had his way, it would be outlawed."

Once Leslie had ordered, I told the waiter I'd like the shrimp and brie quesadillas.

"And, as you might have heard, I'll also need a cilantro-free serving."

"I'm ending this week on a very good note," Erin said after the waiter departed. "Minutes ago, I accepted an exciting job offer from Lassiter & Associates. And I learned this morning Erica, my identical twin sister, is coming to town in the next week or so and plans to stay for a short while."

Erin caught us off-guard, tearing up and patting the corners of her eyes with a napkin.

"I'm sorry," she said, "but this upcoming visit was unexpected."

She took a deep sip of her Margarita.

"Are you okay?" Leslie asked.

Erin flashed a tight smile and again wiped her eyes.

"Three years ago, Erica and I had a hideous falling-out. Far and away, the worst 24 hours of my life. I didn't think I'd ever see her again."

"What happened?" I asked, ignoring the fact it was none of my business.

I felt the toe of Leslie's sandal bounce off my shin.

Overlooking my inappropriate and boorish question, Erin sniffed and shook her head.

"As I mentioned, we're identical twins. Even our parents had trouble telling us apart. We shared clothes, sat in for each other during college classes, and, unbeknownst to them, went out with each other's dates on rare occasions."

She glanced first at me, then to Leslie.

"Looking back, I realize we did some rather foolish things."

Our waiter appeared with three heaping plates of food.

"I believe two of you ordered extra cilantro," he said, placing a plate in front of Erin with a grin. "Just kidding," he added, and then served Leslie and me.

I asked for another round of Margaritas.

"Anyway, to make a long and sad story very short," Erin said, "Erica decided to play a horrific trick on me and my fiancé."

She looked to Leslie.

"You can probably imagine where this is going."

Leslie bobbed her head.

"I'm so sorry."

Erin pulled a tissue from her purse and dabbed her nose.

I stared at Leslie, hoping for a clue regarding their cryptic exchange. She gave me a subtle shake of her head, apparently amazed at my inability to figure things out. I opted to keep quiet and listen—an approach I've learned over the years that's seldom a bad choice.

"Three years later, Erica and my ex are no longer an item," Erin said. "Although I will never forget what happened, surely I can forgive her."

Leslie again tapped my shin with her foot. Gently, this time. I nodded, eager to let her know I was back in the loop. Sort of.

Erin took a bite of her enchilada, chewed on it for a moment, and then gave me a thumbs up.

"Good news, Randy," she said, forcing a weak smile. "No contamination."

During the meal, Leslie described several of her upcoming photo assignments to Erin, stating she hoped they could work together again in the days to come. And, keeping my voice low, I shared a few stories involving the agency's weirdest and most unreasonable clients, avoiding names and organizations to protect the guilty. You never knew who might be sitting at a table within earshot. When the waiter returned to clear our dishes, he gave us a bright grin.

"We have a special dessert this evening, the first strawberry shortcake of the season. Fresh Arkansas berries from Bald Knob," he said, referring to the state's strawberry capital an hour north of town.

We each succumbed to temptation, and I requested a round of coffee to complete the dinner.

Leslie, who'd spent her formative years in the barren plains of west Texas, had never been exposed to fresh strawberry shortcake.

"This may be the best dessert I've ever had," she said.

She took another bite.

"It's amazing."

Erin and I agreed with her assessment, scraping the last of the tasty morsels from our plates.

After I'd paid our tab, Leslie and I escorted Erin to her car, an older model Honda Accord. We waved as she drove away.

When we turned toward my truck, Leslie linked her arm with mine and gave me a mischievous grin.

"Those Margaritas seem to have aroused my libido," she said. "Would you like to keep your lucky streak going?"

It proved to be a fine suggestion.

~ FOUR ~

At our Monday morning staff meeting, I shared the good news about hiring Erin Askew, noting our new executive assistant would report for work the next week. The announcement generated a short burst of applause.

I also updated my colleagues on the bid situation regarding the state's tourism account. Earlier in the day, I'd received a fax from the Arkansas Department of Finance & Administration detailing the schedule for the official bid process. The formal RFP—or Request for Proposals—would be issued by July 1, some 10 weeks away. Responses from interested companies would be due on September 1. State officials would evaluate submissions, inviting the three top-scoring advertising agencies to prepare full-fledged bids for the account.

The actual presentations—the notorious dog-and-pony shows—would take place on November 1 before a five-person committee of independent judges from outside the state. The winning agency would be announced later that day, with detailed negotiations with departmental representatives to begin following legislative approval.

I reminded the staff the state's current contract with Andrews Bingham Carter would end on December 31, with the new agreement going into effect the next day. The ABC firm, of course, could participate in the bidding process, and was expected to pull out all the stops with an aggressive proposal. In fact, one of ABC's owners, in a news article over the weekend, had expressed confidence her company would retain its long-standing relationship with the State of Arkansas. "If it ain't broke," she was quoted as saying, "there's nothing to fix." The statement didn't set well with me or several of my associates.

Next on the agenda was a spirited debate regarding the pros and cons of the cannabis account. Once the dust settled, we decided to decline the invitation to pursue the business. The billings would be modest, and getting it might jeopardize our chances for landing the far more prestigious—and lucrative—advertising account with the Arkansas Department of Parks, Heritage and Tourism.

"Anything else to discuss?" I asked.

Chantille Huxley, the agency's longtime billing coordinator, raised her hand to speak.

"When I attended the parent-teacher meeting at my children's school last week, the principal asked if the good folks at Lassiter & Associates might be interested in mentoring a group of kids who need help with their reading skills," she said. "I promised her I'd check."

"I'm game," someone said, and other heads in the room bobbed up and down.

"What school?" another person asked.

Chantille grimaced and then muttered, "Dodd Elementary."

It took a moment before I realized the cause for her embarrassment. Chantille was a Black and so were her two children. And their school, David O. Dodd Elementary, was named in honor of a teenaged boy hanged by Union troops in downtown Little Rock during the Civil War, convicted of spying for the Confederacy.

"Chantille," I said. "It's a cause the agency could support. When you get a chance, assemble the details and you and I can discuss it."

* * *

The rest of the week sailed by. I must have attended a dozen meetings, to include a stressful presentation before the legislature's

34

Joint Interim Committee on Revenue and Taxation where a panel of competitors and I spoke against a scheme to impose a sales tax on services provided by advertising agencies. A trip to Tunica to meet with our Isla del Sol clients took a full day, as did a visit to Pine Bluff to review a proposed contract extension with the board of directors for the Arkansas Entertainers Hall of Fame, a small yet rewarding account.

Meanwhile, Leslie's photography assignments kept her busy. She spent hours shooting interior and exterior views of historic Little Rock Central High School, the best of which she forwarded to the photo editor at *Garden & Gun* magazine. On Wednesday, she drove to Murfreesboro in southwest Arkansas for shots at Crater of Diamonds State Park for another editor. Her Thursday and Friday were devoted to photographing microbreweries in the greater Little Rock area for a feature in *Arkansas Times*.

Soon after lunch on Friday, my phone rang. It was our receptionist, informing me she was transferring a call from a Ms. Erin Askew. Erin, I remembered, was scheduled to begin work with Lassiter & Associates the following Monday. I assumed the worst, fearing she'd received a last-minute proposal surpassing the agency's offer. My stomach tightened as I thought about tackling yet another round of interviews.

"Randy," she said. "Good afternoon."

The warmth in her voice surprised me. Maybe this wasn't going to be bad news after all.

"And to what do I owe the pleasure of your call?" I asked, trying my best to sound cheerful and upbeat.

"Can you and Leslie meet me at Samantha's Tap Room this evening?" she asked. "Say, six o'clock? My treat."

I had nothing on my calendar and remembered Leslie mentioning her evening was open. We hadn't been to Samantha's in months, but following our last visit we'd promised ourselves a return trip.

"Certainly! Looking forward to seeing you again."

* * *

Leslie and I arrived at the top of the hour, spotted Erin waving from the rear of the crowded restaurant, and joined her. We'd hardly finished with our greetings when a waiter appeared and placed three glittering Champagne flutes on the table. After extracting the cork from a bottle of Veuve Clicquot Brut, he filled our glasses as we watched, spellbound by the streams of tiny bubbles rising to the top.

"I hope you're hungry," Erin said. "Queso, cremini mushrooms, and roasted shishito peppers are on the way."

To say I was confused wouldn't explain my frame of mind. Leslie's discreet sideways glance indicated she felt the same. Erin, I knew, seemed to have been pleased with the job offer from Lassiter & Associates. Yet tonight's display appeared a tad excessive. Perhaps even bordering on ostentatious.

Erin's sparkling eyes and big smile provided some sense of comfort.

"I suspect you're a bit curious with all this," she said.

Our nods confirmed her assumption.

"I won the lottery," she said, her voice not much more than a whisper. "One million dollars."

"You what?" Leslie and I asked the same question at once, loud enough to have caused a pair of nearby diners to turn our way.

Surely, we hadn't heard her correctly.

Erin shrugged and shook her head, still grinning from ear to ear.

"It's unbelievable," she said, "yet true."

She leaned over the table and gestured for us to do the same.

"I've been buying a $20 scratch-off lottery ticket every month for a couple of years now," she said, her voice low. "While I've won a handful of prizes, it's never been anything more than $50. This morning's stop at a local C-store, though, produced the big winner. One million dollars."

We stared at her, our mouths gaping. Seconds passed.

"You're not kidding us, are you?" I finally asked. "You're serious?"

She reached down, grabbed her purse, and removed a stiff piece of paper.

"Here it is," she said, handing it to me. "See for yourself."

I'd never even bought a single lottery ticket, unable to ignore a particularly apt observation shared by the agency's comptroller half a decade ago: "Lotteries are for people who didn't do well in math."

Leslie leaned across the table and gazed at the colorful item in my right hand. It was about 4 inches wide by 8 inches tall, printed on a medium-weight stock. In bold type at the top of the page were these words: **$1 MILLION SPECTACULAR**. Erin had rubbed away the layer of coating in the center of the sheet, revealing a row of winning numbers: **25 40 39 2 32 11 19 21**. Right there in the lower left corner, a cleared space exposed her instant treasure:

11

ELEVN

$1 MILL

ONE MIL

"If there's ever been an occasion for a toast," I said, "this is it."

We raised our flutes and clinked them above the table. Erin, we discovered, had selected a fine Champagne.

Our waiter reappeared, carrying three platters of appetizers. He glanced at the lottery ticket in my hand.

"Somebody here gonna cash in?" he asked as he arranged the food before us. "I got lucky and won $100 two weeks ago."

Wary of his prying eyes, I flipped the ticket to the other side. Erin had filled in her name, address, and telephone number and had signed the back of the card.

"Could be," I said. "However, it's no hundred-dollar winner."

Something more on the order of 10,000 hundred-dollar winners if my mental gymnastics were right.

"Maybe next time," he said, and began refilling our flutes.

I returned the winning lottery ticket to Erin and she slipped it into her purse. We passed the appetizers back and forth in between sips of Champagne. I'd never tasted more flavorful mushrooms, and the peppers were nothing short of exquisite. Now and then I got one a bit too spicy, but the Brut provided a cooling antidote.

Leslie slid the queso in front of me.

"Try this," she said. "It's exceptional."

She was right; the dip was delicious. Although unsure about the propriety of pairing queso and tortilla chips with topflight Champagne, I found the combination worked for me.

Once the waiter had left our area, Erin motioned for us to gather closer over the table.

"I called the lottery office earlier today and was instructed to bring the ticket in first thing Monday morning, making sure to keep it safe. In the meantime, I've taken most of the actions they recommended. I've changed my telephone number and e-mail address and deleted my Facebook account. In fact, I'm no longer a party to any social media platform. Facebook, Snapchat, X, Instagram—they're all history."

"Those changes seem pretty extreme," Leslie said, taking another sip of her Champagne.

"When I reacted in a similar fashion," Erin said, "they warned me to expect an onslaught of bizarre requests from friends, relatives, former acquaintances, and total strangers. 'There'll be all kinds of people wanting all kinds of money' is how they put it."

"You may have to hire an appointment secretary," Leslie said.

Erin chuckled and shook her head.

"But I did call my favorite uncle, an attorney living in Fayetteville. He's going to help steer me through this mess."

I noticed a little liquid remaining in my flute and took one last swallow. Erin got the waiter's attention and ordered another bottle of bubbly.

"Let me confirm something," I said, setting my empty glass aside. "A week ago, you accepted my job offer, right?"

"I intend to keep working," she said, meeting my gaze. "I'd prefer to retain as much normalcy in my life as possible."

That, I thought, may be easier said than done.

"Unless you object," Erin said, "I'd like to move my start date to Tuesday. As I mentioned earlier, I have an appointment with the lottery folks on Monday."

"May 2nd it is," I said. "We'll have your desk ready and your computer prepared to go."

"Perfect," she said. "I hope the hoopla regarding this windfall is short-lived."

"So," Leslie said, "no new Porche, lake house, or six-week junket to Bali?"

"Not likely," Erin said, shaking her head. "When I visit with the lottery officials on Monday morning, they'll validate my winning ticket. I'll be asked to choose between a lump sum distribution or a series of annual payments spread over many years. In any event, hundreds of thousands of dollars in state and federal taxes will be siphoned off before I ever see a penny."

Anticipating my next question that, again, was none of my business, Erin said, "I'm leaning toward the lump sum disbursement. I can close out my remaining student loan, make a down payment on a small house, and perhaps travel a bit."

She looked at me and grinned. "Once I accrue some vacation time, of course."

"That won't be a problem," I said, taking another plunge into the queso.

"I plan on making substantial contributions to several deserving organizations," Erin said. "First will be my church. In fact, I intend to see my pastor Monday afternoon to make a pledge. And I'll be proud to support the Susan G. Komen Foundation. My mother died of breast cancer four years ago."

I nodded sympathetically and Leslie reached across the table and patted her hand.

"I'm so sorry," she said.

"It's a good outfit," Erin said. "And I also hope to assist Habitat for Humanity and a handful of other groups."

"You'll be pleased to know Habitat for Humanity is a pro bono client for Lassiter & Associates," I said.

"Habitat is how I got this," she said, elevating her left arm.

I'd spotted a bandage on her hand earlier.

"I smashed the heck out of my thumb this afternoon while working on one of Habitat's construction projects."

"But it's for a good cause," Leslie said.

"I needed a break and figured pounding nails for two or three hours would do me good," she said. "Unfortunately, my thumbnail took the pounding."

"I think you might be a fine choice for our official Habitat for Humanity account representative," I said.

Erin smiled, but it was a brief one.

"I agreed to a request from the lottery's marketing department," she said, "although I'm having second thoughts."

"What's the problem?" Leslie asked.

"On Monday, they want to an announce my good fortune at a news conference. Later, they plan to feature me in a promotional campaign. My photo will be on billboards, their website, television commercials, and Lord knows where else."

"Any chance you could claim you changed your mind?" I asked. "Fall back on the woman's prerogative thing."

"Don't think I haven't considered it," she said. "But the lottery serves a worthy cause, providing college scholarships for thousands of students a year. Besides, I'm already a part-time model, paid to pose for pictures, and will soon be a member of the state's advertising community. I'd feel guilty reneging."

After she'd settled with our waiter, we walked Erin to her car. I noticed her specialty license plate supporting the Susan G. Komen Foundation. The women hugged and I got a firm handshake from my future colleague.

"This has been a lot of fun," I said. "Congratulation on your winnings."

"Let's plan on getting together again in the near future," Leslie said. "You'll have to tell me what kind of boss Randy is."

However, Erin's mind seemed to be elsewhere. She took in a deep breath and then sighed.

"As I mentioned last week, Erica, my estranged sister, arrives tomorrow morning. Wish me luck!"

Stepping into her car, Erin Askew didn't project the appearance of a million-dollar lottery winner. Hardly. Her strained face had a look of grim determination.

Given all we'd learned during the evening, her "wish me luck" request seemed rather unusual.

~ FIVE ~

I blamed my sluggish and painful start Saturday morning on the generous supply of Champagne from the previous evening. Those countless flutes combined with nonstop servings of heavy appetizers exacted an unfortunate toll, chiefly a pounding vise-like clamp on my brain. But in due time, I got the gear packed and food and water organized for our initial canoe outing of the season. In fact, it'd be our first float trip since our original Buffalo River adventure a full year and a half earlier.

"You've brought sunscreen, right?" Leslie asked as she stowed her tripod and waterproof camera bag in my Toyota pickup. "And your hat?"

Of course, I'd failed to include either. So, I made a quick return foray into the house, found those essential items, and locked the front door once again.

We were on the road by 9:00 a.m., an hour later than I'd hoped. By the time we arrived at the outfitter, he'd have launched most of his other customers. Maybe all the loud and obnoxious paddlers would be well ahead of us. That was my hope, at least. I'd called yesterday to make reservations, thinking Leslie would enjoy a second visit to the Buffalo River under less trying circumstances.

"Tell me again about the stretch of stream we'll be floating," she asked once we were on the road.

"The drive will take a bit over two hours," I said. "We'll begin at Tyler Bend. It's the National Park Service campground we floated past with Gib months and months ago before we passed under the Highway 65 bridge. We'll paddle six scenic miles today, start to finish."

"And I believe you said we'll take out at Gilbert, right?" she asked. "Isn't Gilbert the town where you, Gib, and I ended our earlier journey in, shall we say, a borrowed canoe?"

"The very same," I said.

Gib Yarberry, my irritating brother-in-law, and I had stumbled into Leslie that fall in the middle of a vast wilderness area deep in the Ozarks. We'd been backpacking along the Buffalo River and she was photographing autumn foliage for *Southern Living* magazine. A near-disastrous encounter with a vicious band of drug-running thugs had forced us to flee for our lives down the river using a National Park Service canoe we had commandeered during an especially difficult time. Stolen, if you want to know the gospel truth. Luckily for us, everything worked out in the end. Particularly the relationship Leslie and I had established, a closeness blossoming into marriage this past October.

"Today's trip should be much more relaxing," I said. "Plus, we won't be pestered by Gib and his penchant for puns."

My brother-in-law, an unrepentant quipster, was never at a loss for words and then more words. To this day, I'm still not sure why my little sister Ellen married him.

After an hour or so into the drive, Leslie turned to me and said, "I enjoyed our time with Erin last night. I think she's going to be an excellent addition to your staff."

"But I wouldn't want to face the exposure she's going to be subjected to in the weeks to come," I said, shaking my head. "One million dollars. People will be appearing out of the woodwork, desperate to latch onto a share of her windfall."

"Speaking of her good fortune, what would Randy Lassiter do if he were lucky enough to win a mega-sweepstakes?"

"I've given thought to such a question," I said. "First, I'd pay off the mortgage and begin the landscaping project we've discussed. Next, I'd invest a large portion of the proceeds in low-risk mutual funds or bonds. You know me, conservative options. And I might splurge and buy us a small vacation cabin deep in the Ozarks."

I paused and looked to Leslie.

"And where would your million-dollar prize go?"

"I'll confess to having done a bit of daydreaming as well," she said. "There's a wonderful shelter for battered women in Little Rock. It's always desperate for funds, and I'd do something to assist the women and children clients. As you know, I'm a volunteer at Stewpot, the organization feeding the homeless in town. I'd send money their way, too. And I'd contribute to Planned Parenthood. The last thing our society needs is women who depend on Planned Parenthood for basic health care services like mammograms and other routine tests having no place to go."

Comparing my choices with hers, I hung my head in shame. I'd been self-centered, while Leslie demonstrated an abiding interest in helping her fellow humans. I gave her hand a squeeze.

"How 'bout a do-over," I said. "I'd ask for your help and would share a good portion of my new wealth. Following your example and finding an assortment of worthy community-oriented groups to support."

Leslie laughed and shook her head. "You're giving me way too much credit, Randy," she said. "I'm not altogether altruistic. I'd upgrade my photo gear, to include investing in a commercial-quality drone. But the truth is, the very first thing I'd do is buy a dozen or so new pairs of uncomfortable yet dazzling designer shoes with killer heels!"

* * *

As he shuttled us to the launch area at Tyler Bend, our friendly outfitter said he'd already placed over 50 canoes and kayaks on the river.

"Take your time paddling down to Gilbert," he said. "Just make sure to get in before dark."

"Not a problem," I said. "We'll see you late in the afternoon."

We slathered on the sunscreen, tied our gear into the canoe, and slipped on our life preservers. A storm in the headwaters area had caused the river to rise earlier in the week. It had fallen a couple of feet since and the crystal-clear stream now flowed at an ideal level. Enough water to make the shoals noisy and interesting, yet not so much to send us crashing through the willow strainers.

Leslie climbed into the bow and took a seat, paddle at the ready. I gave the canoe a shove, and then hopped into the stern as the current grabbed our boat and pulled us downriver in the general direction of Gilbert.

With temperature in the mid-70s and white puffy clouds scudding across a deep blue sky, Mother Nature had provided a perfect day for a float trip. A slight breeze rustled through the millions and millions of limbs now showing every possible shade of green as the first leaves of spring reached for sunlight. The dogwoods, in full bloom, captivated Leslie, and we made three stops before we'd paddled 500 yards for her to photograph the brilliant foliage.

Thirty minutes into our trip, Leslie quietly got my attention and extended an arm, pointing downstream at the far shore. It took some time before my eyes settled on what she'd spotted: a massive log lodged in the shallows and bedecked with turtles. Seven of the riparian reptiles, ranging in size from tiny to enormous, had crowded onto the long piece of driftwood, basking in the sun's warmth. I repositioned my paddle and began angling us closer to the log. We soon had 14 wary eyes staring at us as our canoe neared. Aiming her camera at the lineup, Leslie took picture after picture. The largest turtle, the size of a dinner platter, decided we might pose a threat and slid into the water. By the time we'd closed to ten feet, five others followed suit, disappearing into the depths, leaving a single representative not much bigger than a silver dollar.

"He's so precious," Leslie said, her voice low. She fired off another shot.

The confident pocket-sized turtle held his ground, never moving, as we drifted past.

We paddled under the U.S. 65 bridge and waved to a small crowd of folks gathered at the Grinders Ferry access point. Leslie took photos of a cute toddler splashing in the shallows. Half an hour later, we stopped on a sprawling gravel bar, stretched out in the sun, and enjoyed the picnic lunch I'd prepared earlier in the day: ham and cheese sandwiches, chips, cookies, and sliced apples.

After we'd put away our leftover food and loaded our gear into the canoe, Leslie wrapped an arm around my waist.

"I have a request," she said. "I want a lesson on skipping rocks."

Given Leslie's athleticism, her appeal didn't surprise me. She ran a couple of half-marathons a year, practiced yoga on a regular basis, and had played softball in high school and later in college intramurals.

"The first thing," I said, "is to find a handful of suitable rocks. They should be thin, roundish and smooth, more or less resembling a small pancake."

I was still searching for ideal rocks when Leslie stepped to the shoreline. She reared back and chucked one of her stones over the water much like an outfielder throwing a ball to home plate. We watched as it plunged into the river with a splash. No skips.

"I think my approach could use some work."

"You hold it like so," I said, showing her how I gripped the stone between my thumb and middle finger. "And rather than the traditional overhand motion, you have to change your throwing method—using a sidearm delivery. When you fling it across the water, make sure to snap your wrist, adding a strong backspin as you release the rock. Something like this."

Leaning to my right and relying on the sidearm technique I'd developed over years of practice, I gave my near-perfect stone a mighty heave. It smacked against the surface of the river 25 feet out, bounced off the water, and skipped one more time before sinking. Not a good start.

What was worse, though, was I'd felt something pop in my shoulder. It was not a pleasant feeling.

"Sidearm, huh?" she said. "More like a throw from shortstop to first base."

46

Leslie again stepped to the water's edge, adjusting her grip a time or two. Rearing back, she hurled the stone toward the river with a vigorous sideways motion, her throwing arm more or less parallel to the ground. The rock skipped once, then another time, and another. Three skips altogether before it sank from view.

She turned to me, her eyes sparkling. "It worked!" she said. "Changing my technique and snapping my wrist made all the difference."

Leslie planted a big kiss on my lips. "You are the best instructor!"

Noticing I was carefully rotating my arm, she glanced at my face.

"I don't like your expression," she said. "Are you okay?"

"I should've loosened up my shoulder," I said. "A few stretches would have been a good idea."

I winced as I gave my arm another painful rotation. "I'm done with skipping for the day, but you go ahead."

She reluctantly returned to the shoreline and threw another rock. Skimming across the river's surface, it did even better than her previous try.

I discarded my remaining stones and got our canoe ready to launch. Meanwhile, Leslie continued to refine and perfect her throwing method.

"Ready to go?" I asked.

"One more," she said, and flung her last stone.

It skipped two-thirds of the way across the river before vanishing from sight.

I got another kiss, and we then climbed into the canoe and resumed our downstream journey.

"How's your arm?"

"Feeling better," I said. "Paddling isn't a problem."

Along the way, Leslie took dozens of photographs, to include images of a solitary great blue heron wading in the shallows, multicolored bluffs towering into the sky, and a bald eagle perched high on a cottonwood limb 50 feet above the stream.

The outfitter was waiting when we beached in Gilbert late in the afternoon. As we drove through town on the way to his outpost, we passed the historic Gilbert General Store.

"I remember this place," Leslie said, nudging my ribs with an elbow. "I bought you a moon pie here."

I thought back to our narrow escape from the drug traffickers, realizing how lucky I was to be married to the woman of my dreams. Even if she had assumed the title of rock-skipping champion.

At the outfitters', we transferred our gear to my truck and headed south, pulling in at the Daisy Queen in Marshall for a pair of ice cream cones dipped in chocolate. As we climbed the steep hill on the south side, Leslie patted me on the knee.

"This has been a great way to spend a Saturday," she said. "At the same time, I'll admit to wondering about our friend Erin. I hope she and her sister are getting along."

"I'm still not sure I understand what happened between those two," I said. "Based on the rather cryptic remarks we heard last night, my assumption is her twin seduced Erin's boyfriend and stole him away. Can you fill me in?"

"I reached the same conclusion," Leslie said. "In fact, I recall a situation with Erin which puzzled me at the time, but makes sense now. Sort of."

"When was this?" I asked.

"It occurred two, maybe three, months ago. I was shooting Dillard's fall sweater collection, and I had Erin and two other young women working with me. One of them said she had some great news, and then stuck out her left hand. We oohed and aahed over a beautiful engagement ring."

"But there's more to your story, right?"

"A few minutes later," Leslie said, "I noticed Erin had stepped aside and was wiping tears from her cheeks. When I asked if she was okay, she admitted the ring brought back a flood of unpleasant memories. And that was all she said."

Before ramping onto I-40 at Conway for the final 30-mile leg into Little Rock, we stopped at a C-store to buy gasoline. As I filled the tank, Leslie darted into the shop and purchased a $20 lottery ticket.

"I know it's a long shot," she said, "but it'd sure be nice to join Erin's elite little club."

I watched her expression as she scratched away the coating on the front of the card. Her sagging shoulders told me this purchase didn't entitle her to membership in that exclusive group.

And the charming frown was temporary. Leslie stretched across the front seat, pulled me close, and gave me a lingering kiss.

"This has been a fine day," she said. "I won the lottery when I met you."

~ SIX ~

When we returned home, I cleaned and put away our picnic supplies while Leslie stored her photography gear.

She walked into the kitchen as I began preparing dinner and extended an arm. I noticed a pair of pills in her open palm.

"Take these for your shoulder," she said. "They're a painkiller prescribed by my doctor."

"Thanks," I said. "My arm's already feeling better."

"As for your bruised ego," she said with a wink, "they're good, but not that powerful."

I swallowed the pills.

"I'm going to call Erin," she said, picking up her cell after we'd eaten. "To tell her again how much we enjoyed last night."

Seconds later, she set the phone aside. "All I got was a recording. Her telephone number is no longer in service."

"I believe she mentioned during our dinner she'd switched numbers and had also established a new e-mail address," I said. "To ward off the mooching masses."

"So, how do we reach her?"

I shrugged. "I guess we'll have to wait until she shows up at Lassiter & Associates early next week."

"But that's such a long time off," Leslie said. After a moment's pause, she gave me a clever grin. "The truth is, I'm eager to know how the reunion with her sister is going."

On Sunday morning, we attended the eight o'clock service at church. Later in the day, Leslie began editing the photographs she'd taken last week on her waterfall expedition while I tried to make sense of the state's current advertising contract with the Andrews Bingham Carter firm, reading one boring bureaucratic page after another.

"Randy," she said, "got a second? I want you to see these latest images."

That was all the excuse I needed to set aside the tedious document. Entering her office, I leaned over Leslie's shoulder. She clicked her mouse and an amazing collection of thumbnail shots appeared on the screen. I'd never seen so many waterfall scenes in my life, a vivid assortment of small cascades, wide drops, rocky cataracts, and raging torrents. The spring rains had come through, doing their job in fine style.

"Your pictures are spectacular," I said, scanning the images.

Leslie clicked again and a striking vertical photograph of a towering waterfall filled the monitor. Standing at the base of the falls, almost lost in the spray, was a diminutive trio of hikers. I recognized it as Hemmed-In Hollow Falls, at over 200 feet the highest waterfall between the Rockies and the Smokies.

"How did you get the water to look so silky smooth?" I asked. "It's stunning."

"A slow shutter speed," she said, "combined with a neutral density filter. Does it appear too gimmicky?"

"That may be the best photograph of Hemmed-In Hollow ever," I said. "And I've viewed dozens of them across the years. I've even tried to take a few myself."

* * *

Late in the afternoon, I washed a couple of potatoes and placed them in the oven. After an hour or so had passed, I went outside to the patio and lit the charcoal. While Leslie prepared a salad, I grilled rib eyes for dinner. Medium rare for both of us.

Prior to eating, I opened a special bottle of Cabernet Sauvignon we'd received as a wedding gift.

"What's the occasion?" Leslie asked.

"We have two things to commemorate," I said, filling a pair of goblets. "The completion of your waterfall assignment is alone worthy of celebration."

"And the other?"

"Hiring Erin Askew as my executive assistant at the agency," I said. "Lassiter & Associates will be fully staffed come Tuesday."

We lifted our glasses and shared a toast. I ignored the twinge in my shoulder.

* * *

At the Monday morning staff meeting of Lassiter & Associates, I reminded my associates the executive assistant position had been filled and they'd meet their new colleague the following day. I didn't mention Erin's good fortune with the lottery, figuring they'd learn of it soon enough via the media. While I convened my department heads for a discussion on the key takeaways from the ABC contract, Chantille invited those interested in mentoring students at Dodd Elementary into her office where they received instructions and a schedule for the summer session.

A delegation from the Little Rock Zoo appeared 15 minutes past the 1:00 p.m. scheduled appointment. Lassiter & Associates had adopted the zoo as one of our pro bono accounts last summer, and today's meeting was to review accomplishments of the past months and to finalize plans for a fall/winter promotional campaign.

I met Constance Engstrom, the zoo's executive director and chronic late-arriver, in the agency's lobby.

"Sorry we're running a little behind," she said. "It's good to see you! And your team has done such exceptional work."

"The zoo is one of our favorite accounts," I said, "and we've all been looking forward to today's meeting."

It was more or less true.

Booker Arrison, my bizarre uncle and part-time employee of Lassiter & Associates, opposed the concept of caged animals and had shared his long list of concerns by e-mail with me. But he was outvoted by a wide margin when I polled the staff regarding the zoo as a potential pro bono project. Not a good loser, Booker had complained more than once about our new client. My reaction was to change the subject. A question about his vegan lifestyle usually did the trick.

I led Constance and her entourage into the conference room where four of my colleagues had been waiting. Once the hand-shake and greeting ritual was completed and everyone had coffee, we sat around the big table and got down to business. I nodded to Constance, indicating the ball was in her court.

"First," she said, getting to her feet, "we cannot thank Lassiter & Associates enough for your efforts in our behalf." She referred to a printout in her hand. "Visitation at the zoo is up 28% since you signed on as our partner, and our revenues have increased 32%." She beamed as a round of applause greeted her numbers. "The mayor was ecstatic when I shared these results with her ear-lier today. Needless to say, we're excited to hear your proposals for the fall and winter season."

She smiled at me and took her seat.

I stood and gazed across the room, making eye contact with every member of my team. The agency received not a single nickel for our many hours devoted to this account, but it provided an excellent opportunity to contribute to the community. I'd encoun-tered no problems recruiting volunteers to participate in our efforts.

"The fact we're working with quality people and a wonderful product makes our job easy," I said. "The zoo is important to the people of Little Rock. It's a strong indicator of the city's quality of life, and we're pleased to have a role in making it an even more vital attraction."

I turned and gestured to Megan Maloney, who coordinated the agency's work for the zoo. "Megan, why don't you lead us through the recommendations?"

Megan and her coworkers used the next half hour to share their suggested marketing strategies. Constance and her group seemed enthusiastic about a proposed wildlife art contest for youngsters. Another client, a local bank, had agreed to sponsor the competition, providing $2,500 in cash prizes for the winners and hosting an ice cream party at the zoo for all contest participants. We concluded the session by signing a one-year extension for the pro bono arrangement between the Little Rock Zoo and Lassiter & Associates.

* * *

When I got home that evening, Leslie sat in front of the television.

"You're just in time to watch the six o'clock news," she said. "Let's see if there's any coverage of Erin and her winning ticket."

As the first segment of the broadcast came to a close, a chyron materialized on the screen: "Next: Central Arkansas Woman Hits Million-Dollar Jackpot!" After what seemed like an endless stream of commercials (one, I noticed, had been produced by Lassiter & Associates, and it was the best of the lot), Erin appeared grasping one of those oversized checks often accompanying such announcements. She stood on one side of a reporter and an older man, evidently affiliated with the lottery office, was on the other.

"Little Rock resident Erin Askew claimed a one-million-dollar sweepstakes today with the Arkansas Scholarship Lottery," the reporter said, turning to face Erin. "Congratulations! Will you share plans for your winnings?"

Flashing a big grin, Erin said, "First, I'll repay my college loan and consider buying a small house. And I'll be sure to support a handful of my favorite charitable groups."

"No fancy car?" the reporter asked. "Or perhaps a month-long tour through Europe?"

Erin laughed and shook her head.

"I hope to continue living a normal lifestyle."

Good luck with that, I thought.

"Again, our congratulations to Erin."

The reporter then turned to her other guest.

"We also have the director of the Arkansas Scholarship Lottery Commission, Wit Davenport, with us. Mr. Davenport, can you highlight the importance of the lottery to our viewers?"

"Thanks to the thousands of people like Erin who buy lottery tickets, we've been able to provide 700,000 scholarships to students representing every county of the state," he said. "It's been a game-changer for higher education in Arkansas."

The camera then closed in on the reporter.

"I've enjoyed meeting my first millionaire," she said with a bright smile. "I'm off to buy a ticket! Back to you."

"Erin did a fine job," Leslie said. "Let's hope she isn't hassled too much by the jealous hordes."

* * *

I fired up my iPad over breakfast Tuesday and found a photo of Erin and her large symbolic check in the online edition of the *Arkansas Democrat-Gazette*. Offering a few more details than the television broadcast, the article stated Ms. Askew had accepted a job offer in central Arkansas, and had no plans to abandon the workforce. For once, I was glad Lassiter & Associates wasn't mentioned in the piece.

Placing a hand on my shoulder, Leslie stood behind me and read the story.

"Not bad," she said. "No hints of where she lives or where she works."

"But I'm sure the hardcore internet trolls will ferret out all kinds of information," I said. "Erin's address and employer. Her new telephone number and e-mail account. Privacy no longer exists in America."

~ SEVEN ~

Tuesday morning, May 2nd, found me unlocking the front door to the office at 7:15. Sticking to my usual routine, I got a pot of coffee going and switched on my laptop. In that order. Although our website stated the hours for Lassiter & Associates extended from 9:00 a.m. through 5:00 p.m., most of my colleagues arrived between 8:00 and 8:30. So, I wasn't bothered to soon notice voices and the occasional laugh down the hall.

But I was caught off-guard when I heard a "Mr. Lassiter?" coming from our reception area. The voice sounded like a woman's. I stepped from behind my desk and into the hallway and saw Erin Askew standing in the lobby.

"Erin," I said. "Good morning, and welcome! It's nice to see you again."

"And it's good to see you as well, Mr. Lassiter," she said as we shook hands.

Her rather formal greeting took me aback. She hadn't had any problem addressing me by my given name during our earlier get-togethers. Perhaps, I thought, it had been the Margaritas or multiple flutes of Champagne talking at those times. Or maybe she didn't want to appear too familiar on her first day on the new job.

"It's Randy, please. Let me show you to your desk."

I led Erin to her work station located adjacent to my office.

"Our IT guy has your computer ready to go," I said. "I believe all you'll need to do is select and confirm a password."

I then pointed to a stack of folders I'd placed near her monitor.

"Those files contain information dealing with current projects for a handful of clients, things you'll soon be involved with. I hope you can review them in the next few days. And please feel free to ask me any questions which may arise."

"Of course," she said, setting her purse on the desk. "I spent several hours scrolling through the agency's website over the weekend, hoping to become accustomed with the staff and their responsibilities."

"If that's the case, you realize we'll place your portrait on the website to join those of your new colleagues."

"I hope this outfit will be appropriate."

"Yes," I said, "it's perfect."

However, I will confess to being a bit surprised she had on the same attractive blue pantsuit she'd worn for the job interview week before last.

"I'll get someone by later this morning to take your picture."

"I thought your wife might be the agency's official photographer."

"Ha! I wish, but we can't afford Leslie's exorbitant rates."

As I started to step back into my office, I remembered another item I wanted to mention.

"We saw your interview on television last night and also the short piece in today's newspaper. You did a great job. What's it like to be an official lottery winner?"

Erin grinned and shook her head.

"It's still hard to say," she said. "Almost too good to be true. I've shared my new contact information with three or four close friends, although I'm trying to maintain a low profile. So far, I've not been besieged by any out-and-out wackos. The lottery director warned me to be careful, though, and to not let my guard down."

I returned a few phone calls, and then spent the next hour escorting Erin through the building and introducing her to her new associates. I'd distributed an e-mail yesterday afternoon again reminding the staff of Erin's arrival, and had attached her résumé, hoping it might help her get established. There was at least one other University of Tennessee graduate in the office, and they enjoyed a good five minutes together exchanging war stories from their college days in Knoxville.

When Erin spotted a photograph of a pair of twin boys at the desk of one of the administrative assistants, she stated she had a twin sister herself who was visiting this week. A third or so of her colleagues noted they'd seen the announcement regarding her success with the state lottery and congratulated Erin. After two brazenly asked how she planned to use her windfall, she smiled and shrugged, stating she'd depend upon recommendations from her financial advisor.

At the conclusion of the office tour, I guided Erin back to her desk.

"There's one other thing I'd like to ask," I said, "if it's not too personal."

"Sure," she said. "What is it?"

"When Leslie and I last talked with you this past Friday night, you said your sister's arrival worried you. Did things go okay with Erica?"

For a moment, Erin seemed surprised, almost startled, by the question. Yet I knew the outcome of their visit would be the first thing on Leslie's mind when I got home this evening.

"Oh, yes," she said. "Our reunion went fine."

"And did I understand Erica will be staying with you for a while? I believe you indicated she might remain in Little Rock for a couple of days."

Erin paused for a moment, seemingly searching for words.

"She's ... uh ... still uncertain of her plans," she said. "My guess is Erica will be in Little Rock for another week at the most. She hopes to explore the city, checking out museums and so on, during my working hours."

The rest of the day flew by. On the phone and gazing through my office window late in the afternoon, I was alarmed to see a unique yet recognizable vehicle squeezing into a parking space along the curb in front of the agency. The driver was Booker

58

Arrison, my notoriously eccentric uncle and part-time director of technical services for Lassiter & Associates. His car was a museum-worthy 1959 Cadillac DeVille coupe. After months of searching, he'd purchased the distinctive automobile a decade ago from an elderly collector, immediately christening her "Cruella DeVille." Almost half as long as a city block, festooned with layers of chrome, and known for its extravagant tailfins, the car never failed to attract attention. In other words, the perfect vehicle for my peculiar relative. Like a magnet, it drew two men from the sidewalk across the street, and Booker was soon chatting them up. Last time I looked, he was leaning against the massive grill and posing for a photograph.

Five minutes later, Booker stepped into my office and closed the door behind him. He seldom made an appearance during regular hours, preferring instead to perform his magic on our computers and the rest of the electronic gadgetry late into the evenings when the place was deserted. Much of the staff had never laid eyes on him and the few he'd met knew him only in passing. Thank God.

"My heavens," he said. "Who is the angelic beauty I encountered in the hall?"

Booker, the black sheep of the family, was an unrepentant womanizer. He'd been married no less than four times, but the number was suspect given we remained clueless regarding the years he'd been employed in Europe following his college graduation.

Booker also had a fascinating element buried deep in his lifestyle. He was a frequent cross-dresser, performing almost every week at one of the city's private clubs. Over the years, he'd acquired an astonishing collection of gowns, shoes, shawls, and wigs. A crowd favorite, he was known by his stage name, Monique Monét.

"She's Erin Askew," I said. "My new executive assistant."

"It was love at first sight," Booker said, patting his heart. "She is Aphrodite personified. You must introduce us. At once."

"She's young enough to be your granddaughter," I said, shaking my head. "Besides, I thought you said something last week concerning a new engagement."

Booker rolled his eyes and gave me a dismissive wave.

"A brief and unfortunate misunderstanding," he said. "She has resumed her profession in the arts."

I knew he was referring to her work at a local tattoo parlor, but I let it pass.

"Erin's off limits," I said. "I don't want you bothering her. Now, why is it you're here?"

"You'd requested my keen insights on a bid proposal for the state tourism account."

I nodded, glad to see Erin had been dropped from the conversation.

"I've spent untold hours reviewing the official tourism websites for the other 49 states," he said as he handed me a thumb drive. "Here are the best dozen ideas from around the country. In addition, I took the liberty of examining travel and tourism websites from selected foreign countries. As you'll observe, I found examples from Australia, Iceland, and Turkey quite impressive."

I slipped the drive into a pocket. "Perfect. I'll be eager to study your notes."

I stepped toward my office door, directing him along. "I appreciate the time you devoted to this."

"I must beseech you to introduce me to this refreshing exemplar of femininity."

"Perhaps at a more opportune time," I said, lying through my teeth.

Grabbing him by the elbow, I steered Booker past Erin's desk and through the front door.

"Maybe you can join me and Leslie for dinner soon," I said, desperate to divert his attention.

"By all means," Booker said. "I am delighted to accept your kind offer. I trust you'll honor my dietary requirements."

Convincing my bride to host Booker for a vegan meal would take serious work. And some luck.

* * *

When I arrived home from the busy day in the office, Leslie was in the kitchen. She'd opened a bottle of wine and had placed a pair of crystal goblets on the counter.

"What's the occasion?" I asked, thinking I could come to enjoy to these spontaneous celebrations.

"I got our tax returns submitted," she said. "It's two weeks later than I'd hoped, although I'd filed extensions earlier. We're good."

She filled the two glasses.

"And if my memory's correct, we should get refunds."

"A modest one from the state," she said, "but enough from the IRS to consider ideas for our landscaping project."

While Leslie enjoyed living in our older home in the city's historic Quapaw Quarter District, she'd been frustrated by both the front and backyards. Embarrassed might be a better word. Flowerbeds were overgrown, the aging Bradford pears were in sorry shape, and the ancient and cracked concrete patio lacked, in Leslie's words, "charm and appeal." After agreeing with her assessment, I'd asked colleagues from work and neighbors for recommendations on landscaping firms. I received five replies: three businesses worth approaching and two to avoid.

She handed me a goblet.

"It's a beautiful afternoon. Let's take these outside. I refilled our hummingbird feeder this morning and hope we'll entice a visitor to stop in."

I followed her through the front door and sat beside her in the porch swing.

"Sounds like it's time to call in the landscape professionals for their estimates," I said.

"My schedule is flexible in the coming weeks," she said. "With a little notice, I can meet the experts at their convenience."

"I'll begin making calls in the next couple of days."

We tapped the rims of our glasses together.

"To a successful home improvement project," Leslie said.

"And may it come in under budget," I added, knowing the futility of that.

Leslie gasped and pointed to the feeder. A hummingbird flitted around the bright red container before settling in for a nectar break. For a minute or more we stared at the tiny creature, watching the aerial acrobat get its fill.

"How was the first day with Erin?" she asked as the hummer departed. "And how did the reunion with her twin sister go?"

"Today was a little strange," I said. "I'm not sure what it was, but Erin seemed a tad different. She appeared a bit reserved. A little distant or distracted."

"Maybe it was the setting, the change to an office environment. Things got pretty informal during our visits with her. After all, a quantity of liquor was involved."

"You might be right," I said. "Yet I was a little perplexed when Erin made no reference of supporting those three or four noble causes when several of her new colleagues noted her lottery winnings. She had seemed so excited when she shared those possibilities with us."

"My guess is she's trying to protect her privacy."

"Even so, Erin wasn't as outgoing and chatty as I remembered."

Leslie took a sip of wine, and then turned and gave me a wink.

"Perhaps the Askew twins resorted to one of their old tricks. It wouldn't be that difficult for them to switch places."

"You've got to be kidding," I said, shaking my head and finishing the last of my wine. "Impossible."

"So," Leslie said, "just how many Lassiter & Associates did Erin meet during her interview?"

"Four of us," I answered. "Our receptionist, Megan, Abbie, and me."

"All Erica would have to do is spend five minutes on the internet to become acquainted with those four smiling faces."

She was right. Photographic portraits of every Lassiter & Associates employee were displayed on the agency's website along with their job titles. Hadn't Erin mentioned she'd devoted an hour or two over the weekend to the internet and reviewing the agency's personnel?

Leslie shot me a sly grin.

"Don't you remember those Bette Davis classics where one twin sister impersonated another?" she asked. "The first movie was *A Stolen Life* and the other was …" She rubbed her chin with a hand for several moments and then snapped her fingers. "The second was called *Dead Ringer*."

I'd never paid much attention to old black and white movies until Leslie entered my life. In recent months, she'd introduced me to films of Humphrey Bogart, Joan Crawford, Fredric March, and, of course, Bette Davis. I vaguely recalled the movies Leslie mentioned.

"Those are clever Hollywood plots," I said. "Don't tell me you're suggesting Erica could be posing as Erin."

"Nothing of the sort," she said, laughing. "But it's still entertaining to think about."

~ EIGHT ~

The next morning, Leslie poured herself a cup of coffee, added a dollop of half-and-half, and sat across from me at the kitchen table. She nibbled on blueberries and a bran muffin while I finished my banana and a slice of whole wheat toast. Disgusted by the embarrassing antics of the Arkansas General Assembly, I'd skipped the front page and had been reading the sports section in the electronic edition of the *Arkansas Democrat-Gazette*. With college basketball season over and football months away, the pickings were rather slim, given I'm not much of a baseball fan.

"You look a little bleary-eyed," I said, shutting down the iPad. "Didn't rest well?"

"I woke up at 3:30 and couldn't go back to sleep."

"Worried an IRS hardliner might call us in for an audit?"

A meticulous record-keeper, Leslie would like nothing better than to be questioned by a self-important but unsuspecting federal tax examiner. In fact, I think she'd relish the challenge. And I could enjoy the dynamics unfold from a safe distance.

She gave me a sleepy smile.

"Bring 'em on!" she said before taking a small bite from her muffin. "My mind kept returning to your interactions yesterday with Erin. Can you think of anything else she said or did?"

"Are you still imagining the Askew sisters have swapped identities? Thinking they've pulled the old switcheroo on a naïve and gullible Randy Lassiter?"

"I'm not saying anything of the sort," she said. "Yet based on what you've told me, things don't seem quite right."

"I'm not sure I understand."

"Here's an example," she said. "When we saw Erin Friday night, she had a bandage on her left hand."

I nodded.

"She'd injured her thumb working on a Habitat for Humanity project."

"How did her hand look yesterday?"

"I don't recall paying any attention to it," I said, shrugging. "We shook hands on her arrival, although I don't remember seeing a bandage anywhere."

"Was her nail discolored?"

"I didn't see it," I said. "But she'd smashed her thumb last week. Couldn't it have pretty much healed by now?"

"Try to check it out today," Leslie said. "If you can avoid being too obvious."

Thinking back to my conversations with Erin, I remembered something that had caught my attention.

"Well, another matter comes to mind, but it's probably nothing."

Leslie's eyes met mine. "Let's hear it."

"No doubt I'll sound like an insensitive and unsympathetic male dolt," I said, already regretting my decision to share the thought. I took a deep breath and then averted my eyes. "Erin wore the same outfit to work yesterday she had on during her job interview."

"The very same outfit?" Leslie asked, her eyes wide. "You're sure? Absolutely positive?"

"I noticed her pantsuit on the day she interviewed because it appeared almost identical to one of your favorites. So, yeah, I was surprised to see her in it again."

Leslie shook her head.

"No woman would ever wear the same clothes twice in a row. At least not to work. It's simply not done."

"Well, there are times I'll wear my navy sport coat twice in the same week."

"Randy, it's not the same," she said. "You'll mix and match a variety of shirts and ties and slacks with it. Besides, men have different … rules or standards or whatever."

"I think you're reading way too much into this. Maybe she forgot."

"Women don't forget stuff like that," she said. "I still remember the clothes I wore the day we met."

I stared at Leslie.

"You're kidding, right?"

"A pair of Madewell denim jeans and a checkered cranberry shirt from Eddie Bauer," she said, recounting our initial encounter in the Ozark wilderness a year and a half ago. "And you had on Levi's and a worn blue chambray shirt. With sleeves wet to the elbows, I believe."

I continued to gaze at her, dumbfounded. She was right regarding my sleeves. I'd tripped and stumbled forward into one of the Buffalo River's shallow pools, breaking the fall with my arms and soaking my shirt in the process, moments before chancing upon Leslie. This was yet another thing I couldn't understand concerning women. How can they store and recall such trivia?

"Have you considered maybe Erin doesn't have many wardrobe options?"

"Ha!" Leslie snorted. "With her lottery winnings, she could've bought half the women's department at Dillard's."

* * *

I showed up at work at the usual time and brewed a pot of coffee. Erin arrived half an hour later, and I tried to sneak a peek at her left hand as she sat at her desk. No luck.

"I'm off to get another coffee," I said. "Would you care for a cup?"

"Yes, please," she said. "No cream, no sugar. Straight caffeine."

As I handed her the cup, I got a good look at both hands, paying special attention to the left. No visible bandages, but polish covered every nail. Even if her left thumbnail had been discolored, it remained hidden under a shiny red gleam.

I pushed aside any concerns about Erin and her fingernail and spent the next couple of hours sequestered in our conference room with my department heads and our new executive assistant where we discussed options for approaching the state's tourism account. It was a productive brainstorming session, one yielding a dozen and a half or so pages of ideas I recorded on a flip chart, careful to use my best penmanship.

I assumed Erin might feel inclined to hold back, given it was just her second day on the Lassiter team. However, she participated like a veteran from the outset, adding her thoughts on several occasions and expanding on those contributed by others.

When we broke a little before twelve for lunch, I found a text message from Leslie on my phone. "Any problem with me stopping by Lassiter & Associates later this afternoon?"

"See you soon," I replied.

My gut told me something was up.

I was standing in the entrance to my office, proofing a second notice to a delinquent client, when Leslie walked through the agency's front door. She was making a beeline for Erin's desk, a determined look on her appealing face. I realized she was going to put her theory to the test. Either Erin would recognize her or not. Never making eye contact with me, Leslie had closed to within five feet of Erin's desk. Glancing up, Erin had opened her mouth to speak as Megan rounded a corner in the hall.

"Leslie!" Megan shouted. "I haven't seen you in weeks."

She and Leslie hugged for a moment and then spent a few minutes catching up on things since their last visit. They belonged to the same fitness center and often worked out together.

As Leslie stepped away from Megan, Erin stood and extended her hand.

"Good afternoon," she said. "It's so nice to see you again."

"Likewise," Leslie said. "I hope you're pleased with the new job. And Randy and his colleagues are treating you well."

"Everyone has made me feel right at home."

"If you'll excuse me," Leslie said, "I've got to talk with this notorious taskmaster."

I stepped into my office and Leslie followed, closing the door behind her.

"Damn," she said. "So much for springing a surprise on your newest employee. Megan's timing couldn't have been worse."

"As you might have observed," I said, "there's no chance of examining the thumbnail on Erin's left hand."

Leslie nodded. "She looks the same, although that's to be expected from an identical twin, right?"

"And I've not become aware of any changes in her voice, mannerisms, or gestures."

"Have you checked her car?"

I walked to the window and pointed to the lot outside our building. "It's the one we saw earlier with the Susan G. Komen license plate."

Rubbing a hand across her forehead, Leslie stared out the window.

"Call me crazy," she said, "but my female intuition tells me something peculiar is going on."

Tousling my hair, she gave me a quick kiss on the cheek and stepped toward the door.

"I'm off to photograph the Big Dam Bridge," she said. "One of the national bicycling magazines is running a feature on the Arkansas River Trail. You can cook tonight or take me to dinner. Your choice."

Leslie then left, saying goodbye to Erin as she departed.

That evening we dined on the outdoor deck at Brave New Restaurant, one of our favorites, and watched a long tow of barges inch upstream against the strong current of the Arkansas River. I opted for the seared scallops while Leslie chose the house special, broiled walleye.

When I asked for details on the day's photo shoot, she displayed an uncharacteristic grimace.

"I'm afraid it's time to bite the bullet and purchase a drone," she said. "I got a selection of acceptable shots, but aerial images of the bike path across the bridge would have been spectacular."

"How big's the bullet you're going to have to bite?"

"Amazon has dozens of low-end models for less than a hundred dollars," she said. "One meeting my needs will run in the $3000 range."

"You buy a drone and I'll guarantee Lassiter & Associates will send additional business your way."

"I might even let you learn to fly it," she said.

"Out there?" I asked, pointing to the river.

She grinned and shook her head.

"Over dry land," she said. "At low altitudes for very brief periods."

We concluded a fine evening by splitting a ramekin of chocolate crème brûlée. The subject of Erin Askew never came up during our conversation.

* * *

Lunch the next day found me seated next to Stephanie Briles, executive director of the local Habitat for Humanity chapter, at our weekly Rotary Club meeting.

"Randy, thanks so much for your agency's work in our behalf," she said. "I don't know where we'd be without the help of Lassiter & Associates."

"The entire staff enjoys dealing with your account," I said, and it wasn't far from the truth. "Which reminds me. We've hired one of your volunteers."

Stephanie lowered her glass of iced tea to the table.

"Who's that?"

"Erin Askew," I said. "She's the agency's new executive assistant."

"She's a delightful young woman," Stephanie said. "One of our most active volunteers. Erin injured a hand not too long ago and I've not seen her since."

I wanted to determine if Erin had followed through with her plans to make a sizeable donation to the organization, but wasn't sure how it could be done tactfully. Those thoughts were interrupted when the club's president introduced the day's speaker, State Senator Somerset Spartacus Smith, noting his rise from abject poverty in northeastern Arkansas to Harvard Law and on to his leadership in the state Senate.

Senator Smith spoke for 15 minutes, easily the quickest quarter hour in my recent memory. His remarks were upbeat and encouraging, the energetic delivery reminding me of an old-time revival preacher. Using himself as an example, he reflected on how the state's emerging work force could advance with the right opportunities. He challenged everyone in the audience to serve as role models for Arkansas's youth, and to pass this vital message on to our colleagues. As a society, he said, "We have an obligation to pay it forward.

"Let me conclude with an observation from anthropologist Margaret Mead," Smith said. "'Never doubt that a small group of thoughtful, committed citizens can change the world; indeed, it's the only thing that ever has.'"

As Smith returned to his seat, the 125 people in the audience rose as one, giving him a standing ovation. I was among the many who migrated to the front of the room afterwards to thank him.

When Senator Smith got to me, he stuck out his hand and said, "Randy, it's great to see you again."

Stunned he was able to recall my name after meeting me the one time weeks ago, I struggled to reply.

"The pleasure is mine," I stammered. "Your comments were perfect."

I stepped away from the throng surrounding Senator Smith, hoping to spot Stephanie Briles so I could ask if Erin had surprised her with a major donation to Habitat for Humanity. But she was nowhere to be seen.

~ NINE ~

Following the Rotary Club lunch, I'd climbed into my truck for a return trip to Lassiter & Associates when my cell rang. It was Leslie.

"Don't forget to call those landscaping outfits," she said.

I found names of the three recommended firms and phoned them from the cab of the pickup. The first had more business than it could handle and begged off, the second went to voice-mail, but I had luck with the final call. A representative would be at our house at eight o'clock on Saturday morning.

I then drove to the office, determined to get to the bottom of this weird situation involving my executive assistant. Perhaps I could begin by investigating the other possible charitable donations Erin had mentioned to Leslie and me during our dinner days ago. Had she followed through with them? If I remembered correctly, her church was the top priority. The question, of course, was which one was hers? The city was blessed with all sorts of houses of worship, dozens upon dozens of them.

I parked in my reserved spot (one of the few perks I'd granted myself) and walked through the front door, smiling as I neared Erin. How would she react if I requested the name of her church? How would she respond if I asked with whom I was speaking? Was she Erin? Or Erica?

"How was Rotary?" she asked. "My dad attended meetings in our hometown for years."

"Tolerable food," I said, giving her a shrug. "Today's speaker, though, was exceptional. Maybe the best talk I've ever heard from a politician."

She handed me a thin stack of papers.

"There are a couple of calls you might want to return."

Closing my office door, I looked at the messages. None were urgent and two of the callers were annoying nuisances, both of them aggressive sales reps from national social media organizations. Tomorrow would be soon enough.

Getting answers regarding my executive assistant was what I wanted. And needed. But how could I identify her church?

I knew Erin lived in an apartment in Little Rock's Heights neighborhood, so I did an internet search to determine those congregations within a two-mile radius of her address. Of the ten churches located in the area, I eliminated half at the outset, feeling their hidebound elders wouldn't condone Erin's affinity for playing the lottery, not to mention partaking of the occasional Margarita cocktail or flute of Champagne. Five were left, and I begin the tedious process of reviewing their websites. Fortune smiled on me an hour later on my next-to-last option.

While browsing through the monthly e-newsletters of Forest Heights United Methodist Church, I spotted a small announcement stating a Ms. Erin Askew was coordinating the formation of a "Young Adult" Bible study group. Then, in the subsequent issue under a standard feature called "Birthday Club," I found a listing for Erin Askew, and the date coincided with the information shown on her job application.

Pleased with my resourcefulness, I shot a fist into the air above my keyboard. If this advertising gig didn't work out, maybe I could become a private investigator.

I phoned Leslie with news I'd discovered Erin's church and told her of my hope to make an immediate appointment to meet with the pastor.

"Let's make sure I've got this right," she said after several seconds had passed. "You plan on showing up out of the blue and quizzing a man of the cloth about a young and very attractive female member of his congregation?"

I noticed a touch of sarcasm in her voice. Perhaps more than a touch.

"Hmmm …" I began.

"Is he going to reveal anything to a perfect stranger? You could be just another total pervert. Well," she said following a moment's pause, "maybe not total."

She had a point.

"Why don't you come along?" I asked. "Your presence might reduce the pervert anxiety."

"I have a three o'clock call," she said, "and it'll take half an hour at most. See if you can schedule an appointment around four."

Although I was rather vague concerning my request, the minister's secretary confirmed he'd be pleased to meet with Leslie and me at 4:15. I texted her this information along with the church's address and said I'd see her soon. I searched through back issues of the *Arkansas Democrat-Gazette* on the internet and reprinted a copy of the short article on Erin's good fortune with the Arkansas Scholarship Lottery.

In mid-afternoon, I telephoned Stephanie Briles, the Habitat for Humanity director.

"Hello again," I said. "I meant to ask you something earlier today during lunch and forgot to bring it up until after you'd gone."

"How can I help?" she asked.

"I don't know if you realize Erin Askew, my newest employee and one of your volunteers, won a substantial prize with the Arkansas Scholarship Lottery within the past week or so."

"That's wonderful," she said. "I recall seeing something in the newspaper noting her good fortune."

"When my wife and I had dinner with her over the weekend, Erin mentioned the possibility of sharing her lottery winnings with the local Habitat chapter."

"Wow! Our board will be thrilled if this happens."

There was my answer. Stephanie had not yet been informed of a forthcoming bonanza.

"So," she said, "you had a question for me?"

"Well," I muttered, scrambling to find a suitable response. "It's not really a question. I … uh … wanted to let you know as a … uh … bonus for your pro bono arrangement with Lassiter & Associates, we'll match Erin's contribution on an in-kind basis. Dollar for dollar."

"You have made my day, Randy Lassiter!"

And a commitment costing the agency a good deal of money. If, that is, Stephanie ever received the pledge.

I phoned Leslie.

"Two calls from my sweet hubbie in one afternoon," she said. "What's going on?"

"My friend at Habitat has not heard a peep from Erin regarding a donation."

The line was silent for a moment.

"Can you remember the other group Erin brought up?" she asked.

I drew a blank. Leslie, however, answered her own question.

"It's come to me," she said. "The Susan G. Komen Foundation. Do you have a contact there?"

"I can track one down," I said, "although I'm not sure it's worth the trouble. Based on our earlier results, I'd say there's zero chance of any knowledge concerning a windfall."

"But I recall Erin stating her mother died of breast cancer. She might've approached the Komen Foundation first."

"I'll check it out," I said.

"Thanks! Wish me luck on my call. I'll be negotiating with an editor about a potential assignment."

One of my former employees had been lured away by the Komen organization within the past year to serve as director of development. I phoned her and asked for an update on the new job and her young daughter. Once those pleasantries were out of the way, I noted the possibility of a recent lottery winner coming through with a major

74

donation for the Komen Foundation's Little Rock office. Her response was similar to what I'd heard earlier from my acquaintance at Habitat for Humanity. She was unfamiliar with it.

* * *

Within a minute of my arrival at Forest Heights United Methodist Church, Leslie wheeled in next to me in the "Visitor's Section" of the parking lot at the base of the enormous red brick structure. We followed "Church Administration" signs through the quiet halls, and at the appointed hour Leslie and I were escorted into the spacious office of Dr. Jerome Schroeder, the congregation's senior pastor. His secretary closed the door as she left and we introduced ourselves.

"Welcome," he said, standing to greet us with a what might have been a genuine smile. "It's so nice to meet you. As you may know, we're a growing church, and I hope you're considering Forest Heights as your place of worship. We have many fine young couples such as yourselves in our congregation."

"Actually," I said, "we're here on another matter. It involves one of your parishioners."

His smile faded as he motioned for us to take seats while he settled behind a huge and suspiciously clean desk, its surface free of everything except a large and worn leatherbound edition of *The Holy Bible*.

I handed him one of my business cards.

"My advertising firm, Lassiter & Associates, has hired Erin Askew as our executive assistant."

"I know Ms. Askew quite well," Dr. Schroeder said, "and have a high opinion of her."

I detected a glint of fire in his eyes.

"As do we," Leslie said, her voice calm. "I'm one of her friends, and also have had the pleasure of working with her regularly in recent months as a freelance photographer."

"Is there a problem?" Dr. Schroeder asked. "I cannot imagine Erin causing trouble."

"We're worried about Erin," I said, giving him the copy of the newspaper article. "It seems to have started soon after this was published."

"Oh, yes," he said. "I saw this in the past week, I believe."

"We had dinner with Erin a few days before this announcement made the news," Leslie said. "She told us the first action once her winnings were validated would be to go to her church and make a sizeable pledge."

Dr. Schroeder's mouth opened.

"Well," he stammered, "it wouldn't surprise me in the least. Erin's a generous member of our congregation." He cleared his throat. "And I must confess after reading this same piece, I was quite hopeful she might devote a portion of her new wealth to our divine mission. In fact, I have included this very matter in my private morning prayers."

"Our question is this: has Erin made her pledge?" I asked. "She verified her winning ticket with the state lottery office earlier this week."

Dr. Schroeder blinked.

"Not yet," he said. "However, I'm sure Erin will honor the commitment she shared with you."

"When did you last see Erin?" Leslie asked. "Did she attend service this past Sunday?"

We watched as Dr. Schroeder thought back to the weekend.

"I don't recall spotting Erin. Normally she would have greeted me as she departed the sanctuary following my sermon."

He scratched his head for a moment before reaching for the phone.

"I'll have to ask our choirmaster to confirm she wasn't here."

Seconds later he had his answer. Much to the surprise of the choirmaster and her fellow singers, Erin had not appeared for the Sunday service.

"I'm sure there's an explanation," the pastor said. "People have unexpected things arise every day. Especially this younger generation."

"Has Erin spoken to you regarding the difficult situation with her sibling?" Leslie asked. "Her twin sister, Erica?"

Surprised by the question Dr. Schroeder looked first to Leslie, then to me.

"Any consultations we had, of course, occurred in confidence."

He cleared his throat again.

"But I can state Erin was worried enough about this ... uh ... reunion with Erica she came to me and we discussed it."

"And you haven't seen her since?" I asked.

He looked at the ceiling for a moment before nodding and making eye contact.

"That is correct."

I stood and extended my hand.

"Thanks for your time. We appreciate your willingness to visit with us. You've been a big help."

"Is Erin missing?" Dr. Schroeder asked. "Do you think we should notify the authorities?"

"We don't believe there's a reason to panic," Leslie said. "We're a bit concerned and are trying to make sense of the circumstances. I'm certain there's a logical explanation for our confusion. My guess is she's taken a few days off to clear her head."

"Let's hope that's the case," he said. "In the meantime, we'd be delighted for you to consider Forest Heights as your spiritual home."

"I'm a member of the downtown Episcopal Church," I said. "My family's belonged for years."

"And he's kind enough to let me attend with him," Leslie said. "But I was active in MYF during my younger days."

Her statement elicited a slight smile from Dr. Schroeder.

"Erin served as our MYF sponsor last year."

He led us through his office and into the reception area.

"Thank you for stopping by," he said. "And I will keep Erin in my prayers."

As I walked Leslie to her car, I turned and said, "MYF?"

"Methodist Youth Fellowship," she said, grinning. "Where I got my first real kiss."

* * *

We prepared a pair of chef's salads for supper, placed them on trays, and adjourned to the den and switched on the television.

"Anything in particular you'd like to watch?" Leslie asked.

"Something mindless."

A rerun of *Seinfeld* did the job.

~ TEN ~

I got up an hour earlier than usual on Friday, May 5, to prepare a batch of homemade guacamole, using my own secret recipe. In the interests of full disclosure, I'll admit to discovering the original list of ingredients and directions in an old *Southern Living* cookbook. However, I've made enough tweaks over the years to claim a modest degree of ownership without feeling too guilty. Bringing this tasty dish to the office was my traditional contribution to Lassiter & Associates' annual Cinco de Mayo lunch celebration.

Coffee cup in hand, Leslie stepped into the kitchen as I pitted the last of half a dozen avocados, scooped out the flesh, and placed it in a large bowl.

"Let's discuss Erin," she said, taking a seat at the counter. "I've given a lot of thought to this situation we've manufactured. Way too much, if you want to know the truth."

I shrugged, and began mincing ten cloves of garlic.

"Same here. Have you reached any conclusions?"

"As you know, I've been a dyed-in-the-wool Bette Davis fan ever since theater class my senior year in high school. I'm ready to acknowledge I let my emotions override common sense. We are not involved in a Hollywood-like scenario based on switched identities. It's ludicrous to think otherwise."

"So, you have complete confidence the young woman sitting outside my office is none other than the authentic Erin Askew?"

Leslie bobbed her head.

"When you get right down to it, all we have to go on are a few spontaneous comments Erin shared hours after learning she'd won a million dollars. Remarks, if you'll remember, made with a flute of Champagne in her hand."

"Along with one or two already in her belly," I said with a nod. Her conclusion made sense.

I then started my least favorite part of the guacamole process: dicing a red onion.

"Everything else," Leslie said, "is pure coincidence."

"You're saying she simply changed her mind from the initial thoughts she disclosed during dinner with us?"

"That's my theory," Leslie said. "Think back to the conversation you and I had on our drive to the Buffalo River in the past week. When I asked how you might handle a sudden financial bonanza, you gave me one set of answers."

"And five minutes later, I came back with a different response," I said, my eyes burning.

I combined the chopped onion with the minced garlic.

"I now believe Erin had ample time to reconsider her choices over the weekend," she said. "Just because she hasn't yet talked with her minister doesn't mean she's not going to give the congregation a sizeable donation. Likewise for those other organizations she referred to."

"What do you suggest we do?" I asked.

"We pretend we never heard Erin mention those possible gifts, washing those words from our memories."

"That may be one of those things easier said than done."

Next, I added lemon juice, kosher salt, black pepper, a cup of diced tomatoes, a deseeded and minced jalapeño pepper, hot sauce, and a tablespoon of cayenne to the garlic/onion bowl.

"So be it," Leslie said. "Anyway, how she uses her winnings is none of our business. You've hired your executive assistant, and I hope Erin will continue to do the occasional freelance modeling for me."

I poured the smaller bowl of ingredients into the container holding the avocado and stirred the mixture. Leslie snuck a spoon into the dip and took a sample.

"It's perfect," she said before giving me a kiss. "I've got to run; see you later."

I decided informing Leslie of my dinner invitation to Uncle Booker could wait until another day.

* * *

The Cinco de Mayo festivities at Lassiter & Associates had started a decade ago at the suggestion of our staff artist, a talented young woman whose family hailed from Guadalajara. Years later, it's grown into a full-fledged luncheon potluck with mariachi music in the background and the sporadic sombrero. So far, we've been spared a piñata experience. And despite a few less-than-subtle entreaties, the boss—that would be me—has outlawed Margaritas.

A handful of phone calls, an annual performance review with the agency's senior media buyer, and a lengthy but productive visit with representatives handling the agency's health insurance coverage consumed most of my morning. When the lunch hour rolled around, I brought up the end of the line, as was my custom, and found myself standing behind Erin. My plastic plate soon neared capacity, holding refried beans, Spanish rice, a beef taco, and a chicken enchilada.

As we approached chips and dips at the end of the long serving table, I heard Erin question the woman ahead of her about the guacamole.

"Why two bowls?" she asked.

"You'll notice the one to the left of the chips has a label," the woman said. "A big C with a slash through it—meaning it's cilantro-free, Randy's specialty. The bowl of guacamole on the right is rich with cilantro. I know, because I made it."

Erin smiled and thanked her colleague. As I spooned a heaping scoop of the pure, unadulterated dip onto my plate, I watched Erin add a hearty portion of the other version to hers.

I almost dropped my food. Surely, my memory was correct. Erin, like me, had a strong aversion to cilantro. Hadn't she indicated as much when Leslie and I took her to dinner a few weeks earlier?

Joining several of my associates at a noisy table in our crowded conference room, I ate my lunch, deep in thought. Troubling and confusing thoughts.

"Randy, your guacamole is even better than last year's." It was Megan. "Did you switch recipes?"

"The only change," I said, "is I used a bit more cayenne."

"The extra kick is perfect."

"Make sure to get seconds."

Once I'd wandered through the crowd and thanked everyone for their culinary contributions, I slipped into my office, closing the door behind me, and phoned Leslie.

"How goes your day?" I asked.

"I spent the morning shooting azaleas," she said. "I've never seen them so rich and full, and the colors are magnificent. But tell me about your morning. Did your dip survive the Lassiter & Associates taste test?"

"Totally gone," I said. "The bowl was scraped clean."

"What's up, Randy?" she asked following a long pause. "You're not calling to be sociable."

"Any chance you could meet me at home?" I asked. "I have a personnel matter and need your advice."

I'd asked her for guidance a time or two earlier in the year, so my request wasn't out of character.

"My afternoon's clear," she said. "I can be there in 15 minutes."

Stepping from my office, I told Erin something unexpected had come up and I'd return in an hour. I'd been home a couple of minutes when Leslie arrived.

I met her on the porch and gave her a hug before we sat in the swing.

"Let me guess," she said. "There's a torrid office romance causing tension among your staff. Inappropriate and disruptive PDA."

I chuckled and shook my head, using my feet to give the swing a gentle push. A pair of aggressive hummingbirds zipped around the feeder, much to our amusement.

"Then my second guess is this: there are complaints regarding a persistent colleague who's taking up too much time selling those awful chocolate bars for a school's fundraising project."

I gave my head another shake.

"It's been an issue in the past," I said, "but not today."

"The annual sales blitz for Girl Scout cookies?"

"Nope," I said. "Not even close. It's … uh … it's Erin."

"I got the impression you were pleased with her performance, feeling she was working out just fine."

"She is," I said after a moment's hesitation. "The problem is I'm not sure she's … Erin."

"I don't understand." She lowered her feet, bringing the swing to a stop. "I thought we'd resolved this at breakfast."

"Me, too. But at today's luncheon, she took a big serving of guacamole."

"So?"

"She ignored my bowl, and chose the contaminated version."

Leslie stared at me.

"By contaminated, you mean—"

"Yes," I said. "The bowl of guacamole laced with cilantro."

"You're sure?"

"I overheard her telling our receptionist how delicious it was. And I then saw her get a second helping."

Rising from the swing, Leslie turned and reached for my hand.

"Come with me," she said, leading me toward the front door. "I have a scathingly brilliant idea."

I recalled her using the same phrase once before, months and months ago, with good results.

We entered her office and Leslie switched on the computer.

"Want to let me in on your plan?"

"It's time to examine some pictures."

She got on the internet, located the website for Lassiter & Associates, and clicked the "Our Team" button. With staff portraits arranged in alphabetical order, Erin Askew was third, following Abigail Ahart and Perry Anderson, a veteran account executive. Leslie moused over Erin's recent photograph, saving it.

"We're going to compare this to a shot of Erin I've taken in recent months for a Dillard's campaign."

She scrolled through file after file of photographs and found the collection she wanted. She opened it, and I saw a pleasing array of images featuring young women wearing jewelry. Lots of pretty necklaces and an assortment of earrings, too. I recognized Erin in many of the pictures.

Leslie studied several of the images and then selected one, saving it.

"This pose," she said, "is very much like the one on your website."

She closed her program. Next, she retrieved Erin's official agency portrait and positioned the two photos—side-by-side—on her monitor. With a few clicks of her mouse, Leslie manipulated the heads so they were about equal in size, filling most of the screen.

The photographs were remarkably similar, no surprise given the same woman was ostensibly featured in both. In each picture, the slight smile was almost identical. The one real difference, at least to my untrained eye, was a minor variation in the hairstyles.

With a series of clicks, Leslie enlarged the pair of images, cropping out the neck, ears, and much of the hair from both shots. Extreme close-ups of two faces stared back at us.

Leslie gasped.

"Oh, my god."

I leaned in closer.

"What is it?"

She pointed to a small mole above and to the left of the mouth of the woman in one of the photographs. I then looked at the second shot. The mole was in the same place, but on the opposite side of her face. I felt the hair rise on the back of my neck.

"Maybe one of these pictures has been flipped," I said. "It could explain—"

"No way," Leslie said. "Notice how she parts her hair."

She zoomed in on both images, studying them intently.

"This photo on the right is the real Erin," she said. "Look closely at the mole."

I did as she instructed. Dark and solid, it appeared three-dimensional.

"Now," she said, "look at this other mole."

I stared at the small facial imperfection. At this magnification, it appeared flat and faded in comparison, with little definition.

"This is the mole on the face of the woman at your office," she said. "You'll note it's not a real mole, but has been drawn on. I've seen a YouTube video on adding these simulated beauty marks with an eyebrow pencil."

Stunned, I continued to gaze at this unsettling image.

"Not only is it fake," Leslie said, shaking her head, "it's on the wrong side of her face."

~ ELEVEN ~

I stared at Leslie's computer screen, still not believing the images in front of my own eyes.

"You're telling me Erin Askew is not my executive assistant? It's her twin sister Erica who's sitting outside my office?"

"That appears to be the case," Leslie said, her gaze shifting from one enlarged photo to the next.

"Where is Erin?"

"I think, my dear, you've hit on the operative question."

"What should we do?" I asked.

"My immediate inclination is to call the police."

I pondered her suggestion for a moment.

"But there's one critical question to consider," I said. "Has a crime occurred?"

"It appears Erica is pretending to be Erin," Leslie said. "Seems to me I remember reading in a novel it's a felony to impersonate a police office. Beyond that, though, who knows?"

She opened her phone, selected an app, and typed in a string of characters.

"Let's check with the almighty internet."

I watched as she scrolled down the device.

"My cursory review indicates there's substantial vagueness in the laws, depending on the jurisdiction," she said half a minute later. "Yet there's one constant. If an individual impersonates another and causes harm, a crime has been committed."

She placed her phone beside the monitor and looked to me. "Has Erica caused harm?"

I mulled her question over for several seconds.

"Not really, unless you can factor in a cost for my mental anguish. As for financial fraud, she's not yet been paid. And her health insurance won't kick in for another two weeks."

"Maybe we should contact the police regarding Erin. You know, file a missing person report."

I shook my head, remembering a conversation I'd had with a captain in the Little Rock Police Department not quite a year ago. Dr. J.J. Newell, my best friend and former college roommate, had vanished without a trace, and I'd gone to the LRPD for assistance. While sympathetic, the police captain had responded with a statement I've been unable to forget. "Mr. Lassiter," he had said, "it's no crime to disappear."

"I have an alternative idea," I said. "Let's confront Erica. Face to face."

* * *

Leslie trailed me in her car as I returned to the agency. We'd agreed it was time to get to the bottom of this situation, to question the person posing as my executive assistant. As I passed Erin's desk, I invited her to join Leslie and me in my office, asking her to shut the door once she walked in. I was amazed she displayed no surprise or curiosity as she entered the room. I sat behind the desk while the women claimed a pair of captain's chairs facing me.

"Erin," I began, and then paused. "Or should I say Erica?"

Following a moment's delay, a knowing smile emerged on her attractive face.

"We've been caught," she said. "What let the cat out of the bag?"

"A couple of things," I said. "Your enjoyment of cilantro was one."

"And you and Erin aren't quite identical," Leslie said. "She has a small mole—a real one—on the left side of her face. Yours is fake, and it's on the opposite cheek."

Erica gave us a telling nod.

"After realizing I'd placed my new mole in the wrong spot on my first day here, I told myself it wouldn't be noticed," she said. "However, I'd forgotten Erin's one of those weird people who can't stand cilantro."

"Why don't you bring us up-to-speed?" I asked. "Is this another of your foolish pranks? I believe you owe us a full explanation."

"It's a long and involved story," she said. "I think coffee might be advisable."

"Please wait here," I said. "I'll bring a cup for each of us."

Fact was, I didn't want Erica out of our sight, worried she might bolt for the door and we'd never learn the truth. After a hurried visit to the coffee station, I returned with a tray carrying three steaming cups, Leslie's fortified with a shot of half-and-half. Erica and Leslie seemed to be discussing Erica's shoes as I handed them their coffees.

"Why don't you start at the beginning," I said. "When you arrived in Little Rock."

"Or, better yet," Leslie said, "perhaps you can go back to the original incident leading to the falling-out between you and your sister."

"You know about that?" Erica asked, her eyes wide.

She took a sip of her coffee.

"Please assume we're clueless," I said. "Completely and entirely clueless."

Erica set her cup aside, dabbed at her eyes with a napkin from the tray, and took a deep breath.

"You might have read the accounts describing the unusual closeness of some twins," she said. "Erin and I were remarkably attuned from birth, reflecting similar moods and often completing each other's sentences, not to mention our uncanny physical resemblance. Until they died, our parents had trouble telling us apart."

Leslie and I exchanged glances, recalling Erin's comparable remarks.

"When we went to the University of Tennessee, we roomed together in one of the dorms our freshman year, then at a sorority, and later in an apartment. We majored in business administration, sometimes one of us attending a class for the other and sharing notes. We both made the dean's list every semester and were selected to the pompon squad. Things were going so well."

Erica dabbed her eyes again.

"What happened?" Leslie asked.

"As we grew up, neither of us had a serious boyfriend. Oh, sure, we went out with lots of guys, and two or three times took each other's place on dates, but we never got serious about a boy."

She hesitated and then cleared her throat.

"Until our senior year at Knoxville, that is, when Erin met a student in graduate school. Alex was his name."

Erica reached for her cup and took another sip of coffee.

"He attended college on a ROTC scholarship," she said, "and majored in mechanical engineering."

"He sounds like a serious young man," I said.

"Even so," she said, "Alex had a great sense of humor, always making everybody around him laugh. Although he wasn't drop-dead handsome in the traditional sense, he had this infectious personality. People gravitated toward him, both men and women."

"Let me guess," Leslie said, "Erin fell in love."

"And Alex was smitten with her," Erica said. "They were such a beautiful couple, always happy."

She wiped away a tear.

"And then something happened?" I asked.

Erica slowly nodded her head.

"One Friday afternoon, just a few days prior to graduation, Erin was running late. She'd agreed to take one of our sorority sisters to pick up her car at a repair shop. Alex arrived unannounced at our apartment—and I happened to be wearing one of Erin's favorite shirts, a sexy little Tennessee Volunteers crop top. Alex grabbed me by the hand, and said we were going to Nashville for the weekend."

"And you didn't object?" Leslie asked. "You didn't try to explain?"

"I laughed, and pushed him away, saying I couldn't," she said. "I tried to buy some time and told him I had to pack a bag, positive

Erin would return at any second. But Alex was insistent, dragging me into his car, saying he'd brought everything I needed and it wasn't necessary for me to pack anything."

We stared at her, waiting for the rest of the story. Erica looked beyond us, her eyes locked through the window on some point she alone could see.

"I thought I'd go along for a few blocks before telling Alex he'd made a terrible mistake," Erica said.

She sniffed, removed a tissue from a pocket, and wiped her nose.

"But I'm the one who made the terrible mistake. Those few blocks turned into 15. And then 20 miles had passed. The farther west on Interstate 40 we drove, the less inclined I was to divulge the truth."

"You spent the weekend in Nashville?" Leslie asked. "With Erin's boyfriend?"

"You see," Erica said, "although she didn't realize it, I was envious of my sister. Erin had met this wonderful man. I had no one."

"When did the truth come out?" I asked.

"Erin tried calling me numerous times during the weekend," Erica said, "but I'd turned off my phone. So she wouldn't contact the police, I'd texted her, said I was taking a little break, and would see her Sunday."

Erica paused and shook her head.

"I finally told Alex on the way back I was Erica. Confessing he'd spent the weekend with his girlfriend's twin sister."

"And how did he react?" Leslie asked.

"He enjoyed a good laugh, sure I was joking," she said. "When I at last convinced Alex I was serious, I wasn't Erin, he flew into a rage, slamming his fist against the steering wheel. Soon after, he began crying. The one time I've seen a grown man cry. He was devastated, utterly devastated. I burst into tears and sobbed the rest of the way into Knoxville."

As Erica took another sip of her coffee, Leslie and I made eye contact. I caught a subtle shake of her head.

"When Alex got me back to our apartment, Erin was so confused. Initially, she was overjoyed to see Alex, but couldn't understand why he'd ignored her calls. Still in tears, he explained he'd muted his phone for the weekend. Only then did Erin realize I'd spent the past two nights with Alex."

This was even worse than anything I'd imagined.

"I will never ever be able to forget the expression of total betrayal on my sister's face. First as she confronted Alex, and then as Erin turned to look at me. I've never seen a person in more pain."

"What happened next?" Leslie asked.

"Alex honored his commitment to serve in the Army and went to the Middle East for a yearlong tour of duty. I'm not certain if Erin ever talked to him afterwards. She moved out at once and somehow ended up here in Little Rock. We'd not spoken since until I saw her this past Saturday."

"Where is Erin now?" I asked.

"That's just it," Erica said. "I have no idea where she is."

~ TWELVE ~

"What do you mean you don't know?" I asked.

"I believe she may have gone with Alex to inspect a piece of property in the Ozarks," Erica said, shrugging her shoulders. "I have no idea where it's located."

"You're telling us this Alex dude is back in the equation?" Leslie asked, incredulous. "I think there's more to this story than we've heard."

"It's still confusing," Erica said. "On Saturday, I posted a photograph on Facebook of Erin and me having dinner at a restaurant here in Little Rock. Alex must have seen the picture."

"In other words," I said, "you and Alex have stayed in touch?"

"Not really. I just never made the effort to 'unfriend' him."

"Okay," Leslie said, her impatience showing. "Let's assume Alex spotted your photo. Did he contact you?"

"Out of the blue, I got a text from Alex stating he's involved with a construction project in a nearby town—Conway, I think—and he'd like to see us. Erin is against it. One hundred percent."

"And then?" I ask.

"I reply to Alex, telling him it's not a good idea," Erica says. "But he's persistent, begging for a chance to see us. Erin eventually relents."

"The three of you get together," Leslie said. "That must have been awkward."

"Alex met us at Erin's apartment the next day, Sunday afternoon. And you're right; things were uncomfortable in the beginning. None of us had seen the others since that awful day in Knoxville," Erica said. "He'd brought a bottle of Chardonnay—Erin's favorite—and we began to relax a bit. Not like the old times, of course, but we were cordial, all things considered."

"What did you discuss?" I asked.

"Alex spent a little time recounting his overseas tour of duty, but thank God he avoided specifics. I got the distinct impression he didn't enjoy his days in the army, that it didn't meet his expectations. He's now a supervisor for a company which renovates schools, hospitals, and other public buildings, in the South for the most part," Erica said. "By sheer coincidence, he was staying near Little Rock inspecting one of their projects when he saw my Facebook posting."

I realized my coffee was gone. I stood, said I'd be right back, and soon returned with a pot of the sacred elixir, refilling our trio of cups. I remembered to bring cream for Leslie.

"The three of you knocked off a bottle of wine," Leslie said. "Then what happened?"

"I noticed Alex isn't the same man he used to be," Erica said. "He's much more serious, even sounding bitter on occasion."

"Bitter?" I asked. "Why?"

"I knew he'd always been conservative, but Alex now seems to have moved farther away from the mainstream, complaining time and again how the country's going in the wrong direction."

"Did he cite any examples?" I asked.

"An invasion of illegal immigrants, to use his words, worries Alex," she said. "And he kept referring to something he called the Lost Cause of the Confederacy."

Leslie and I exchanged glances.

"How did Erin react to this conversation?" Leslie asked.

"She remained distant at first, clearly uncomfortable around Alex," Erica said. "Over time, she warmed to his presence and began talking. As the evening wore on, things almost seemed normal between them. She's always been like a sponge, absorbing his every word."

"I assume Alex returned to Conway?" I asked.

"Not exactly," Erica said, shaking her head. "We'd opened a second and later a third bottle of wine, all of us enjoying a slight buzz. We knew better than to let him drive, and called it a night. Erin and I slept in her bed and Alex crashed on the sofa."

I didn't like the way this tale was unfolding.

"At breakfast, Alex told us about a group he's now affiliated with," Erica said. "He and several of his former army buddies have signed on with an outfit in the Ozarks, joining others holding similar political beliefs and values. They're restoring an old farmhouse with acreage, calling it a retreat. Erin refers to it as his 'hunting club' but there's much more to it than that."

"What do you mean?" Leslie asked.

"Erin had stepped out of the room at some point when Alex was talking about this project. He was so enthusiastic, describing their monthly training maneuvers at length. And mentioned a sniper school they plan to establish."

"Training?" I asked. "And a sniper school?"

Erica bobbed her head up and down.

"Alex said they'll be prepared when our society breaks down."

Leslie took a peek at her watch.

"I hate to abandon this fascinating conversation, but I have a photo-shoot scheduled in a quarter of an hour."

She stood, leaned over my desk, and gave me a peck on the cheek.

"I'll see you at dinner," she said.

She turned and walked to the door, making eye contact with Erica as she passed, before stepping into the hall and going to her appointment.

"Are we done?" Erica asked.

"Not even close," I said. "After your breakfast at Erin's apartment, did Alex leave?"

"Alex drove Erin downtown for her session with the lottery people. I believe it was to be followed by the news conference."

"Am I to understand Erin brought up her winning ticket to Alex?" I asked, for some reason surprised by this revelation.

Erica nodded.

"While we cleaned breakfast dishes, Erin said she had a meeting later in the morning at the state lottery office to redeem a ticket. When Alex kept asking questions, she finally admitted she'd won a million-dollar sweepstakes, acting as if it was an everyday occurrence. Alex, on the other hand, seemed thunderstruck, and badgered her, wanting more information."

"Such as?"

"Like when was she getting the money, and how she planned to use it," Erica said. "And then he went off on a tangent, sharing details about a summer youth camp his group plans to build on their property."

"Did you go with them to meet with the lottery staff?" I asked.

"While they drove downtown to deal with the state officials, I went to Kroger and bought groceries for lunch and dinner," Erica said. "When I returned to Erin's apartment, they were gone."

"Erin and Alex?" I asked. "Gone together?"

"And they left a note," she said. "Erin wrote she'd be away for a day or two with Alex, and begged me to cover for her at Lassiter & Associates, promising she'd make it up to me later. She'd already filled me in on her interview with you and your colleagues, and she'd explained the job and its duties. Realizing I hadn't brought work-appropriate clothing, she told me to feel free to wear anything in her closet."

"And this scheme didn't bother you?" I asked.

"Quite the opposite," she said, massaging her temples with both hands. "It's been bothering me a great deal. But after I hurt Erin so badly a few years ago, I figured I owed her. Big time."

"Is there anything else you'd like to disclose?" I asked.

"Two things," she said. "Alex's last name is Motherwell. That might be useful down the line."

"And the other?"

"This arrived in Erin's mail yesterday."

After reaching into her purse, she handed me a thick manila envelope from the Arkansas Scholarship Lottery Commission.

"What is it?"

Erica shrugged. "I figure it might give us an indication of what's going on."

"Do you want me to open it?"

Although not well versed in the law, I had a vague recollection opening another person's mail was a crime. A federal crime, if my memory was correct. On the other hand, I'd illegally acquired and examined a stack of Dr. J.J. Newell's mail less than a year ago while searching for him, and nothing ever came of it. Not yet, at least.

"I won't tell," she said, "if you won't."

I used my pocketknife to slice open the envelope, and removed a collection of documents. I began leafing through them, handing each to Erica as I went to the next.

"These are copies of tax forms, aren't they?" she asked.

"For the most part," I said. "It appears your sister took the lump sum payment instead of asking for an annual distribution."

Which was consistent with the tentative plan Erin had revealed to Leslie and me regarding her winnings.

"The federal government claimed its share and the state took out another chunk," I said while examining the last form. "Erin netted an even $565,000 in the form of an electronic check. Still, not a bad return on a $20 investment."

"Where's the money?" Erica asked as she reassembled the stack of papers and stuffed them into the envelope.

I pointed to her hands.

"Those papers include a document indicating it was deposited directly into her checking account at First National Bank here in town."

"I wonder if it's still there."

"You've just asked the $565,000 question," I said. "I don't suppose you have access to Erin's accounts?"

Erica shook her head.

* * *

I got home half an hour ahead of Leslie and had the pasta boiling when she stepped into the kitchen. After giving me a hug, she went straight to the pantry and removed a bottle of Pinot Noir.

"Care for a glass?" she asked.

It was a silly question.

I warmed a pot of marinara sauce and placed a pan of rolls in the oven while Leslie prepared a salad. I refilled our glasses as we sat down for dinner.

"This has to be one of the strangest days in my entire life," Leslie said. "I've been wondering all afternoon if you fired Erica."

"I should have, yet in all the confusion, I failed to do it."

"During our conversation, Erica alluded to Alex Motherwell's interest in the Lost Cause of the Confederacy," she said. "Are you familiar with that?"

"It's a myth claiming the Civil War had nothing to do with slavery, insisting the South was defending states' rights," I said. "Proponents have argued slavery was actually a good thing in many respects. These are the same folks who erected dozens of Confederate monuments over the years, attempting to put their own spin on history. Many white supremacists have now taken up this banner."

"Any other items to add to this already bizarre situation?" Leslie asked, reaching for her wine.

"According to Erica, we saw the real Erin on television. Alex drove her downtown to the lottery office for her meeting with state officials. The media event occurred a bit later."

Leslie set her wine on the table, her eyes wide.

"Am I hearing you right? Alex Motherwell was with Erin when she made her decision on the payout?"

"Yes," I said, giving her a nod. "Alex was there."

"His presence may explain why Erin never approached her pastor at the Forest Heights church," Leslie said. "And those other two organizations she'd noted."

"Are you suggesting Alex, her former lover, might have influenced Erin, causing her to change her mind?"

"That's it in a nutshell," Leslie said.

"And Erin Askew might now be subsidizing a paramilitary group in the Ozarks with her lottery winnings?"

Leslie stared into my eyes.

"Do you have a better theory?"

~ THIRTEEN ~

"Unable to sleep?" Leslie asked, her voice low, from the other side of the bed.

I'd been tossing and turning for the past 30 minutes, fearful I was keeping her awake. Our troubling conversation from earlier in the evening kept circulating through my addled brain.

"My mind must be racing 90 to nothing," I said. "It won't let go of this Alex Motherwell character."

"Maybe it's time to ask your Uncle Booker for help. As you've told me many times, he's always eager for new challenges."

Booker was the most tech savvy person I'd ever encountered. If information was out there on the internet, anywhere, he could track it down. Although Booker's methods were often, shall we say, unorthodox and no doubt illegal on occasion, he never failed to get results.

"You haven't said anything concerning Booker in weeks," she said. "What's the old curmudgeon up to?"

"He made one of his rare appearances at the office a day or two ago," I said. "Booker noticed Erica first thing, told me he'd fallen in love with her on the spot, and begged for an introduction."

"Oh, my gosh," she said, bolting upright in the bed. "You didn't, did you?"

"I said in no uncertain terms she was off limits, stating he was to have nothing to do with her."

I chose not to mention the likelihood of Booker joining Leslie and me for dinner in the near future. At some point, though, I'd have to tell her.

"Let's hope he behaves himself," Leslie said as she once again reclined. "To keep him occupied, you might encourage Booker to investigate those paramilitary groups operating in the state in addition to checking out Alex Motherwell."

"Now that we have a plan," I said, "perhaps we can get to sleep."

When I scooted over to give Leslie a goodnight kiss, my hand grazed a bare shoulder. This was a good sign. Beyond good, in fact.

"It seems you forgot your nightgown," I said, sliding my hand down her naked torso.

"Oh, darn. I kept thinking I'd forgotten something."

Her skin was silky smooth. With nice curves in all the right places.

I felt Leslie's hand against my chest.

"You know," she said, "there's another long-standing option for helping us fall asleep."

She proved to be right. Later, we slept very well.

* * *

Leslie and I met a landscape architect at eight o'clock sharp Saturday morning on the sidewalk in front of our house. She and Leslie hit it off from the outset, and I trailed them around the yard as they debated various options. They agreed the aging Bradford pears had to go, to be exchanged for native redbuds and maples near the curb, with a butterfly garden below the front porch. An arbor and water feature were discussed for the backyard, along with a flagstone patio in place of the deteriorating concrete slab. Our new friend promised to provide an estimate within a week.

Leslie gave me a quick kiss after the woman drove away.

"Thank you, Randy," she said. "This means a lot to me."

"I like her suggestions," I said. "I'm thinking our new patio might be ideal for a pair of hammocks."

"Maybe even a hammock for two," Leslie said, giving me a wink.

When we returned inside, I dialed Booker. He despised calls before noon, and this one would surely irritate him—if he bothered to answer.

"Uncle Booker!" I said when he picked up on the eighth ring. "Top of the morning to you!"

"My god," he mumbled. "It must still be the middle of the night. Haven't I beseeched you to respect my daily rituals?"

Booker's typical routine was to arise around noon and enjoy a hearty cup of chicory coffee. A strict vegan, he'd then partake of a breakfast of an egg-free chickpea omelet, avocado toast, and a flute of prune juice before interacting with another human. Unless, of course, he had somehow managed to lure an unsuspecting female into his abode for an overnight tryst.

"I have an important job for you."

"Whatever could it be this time, dear nephew?" he asked, sounding a bit less put out. "Let me guess: Lassiter & Associates has been chosen to represent the Dallas Cowboys and you've selected me to serve as your account executive."

Early in his career in the world of cutting-edge technology, Booker had accepted a job posting in Europe where he'd developed a keen appreciation for soccer. Still a rabid fan of the sport, Booker detested what he contemptuously called "American football," with a particular animosity directed toward the Cowboys for reasons unknown to me.

"Something a little closer to home," I said. "Will you set your investigative sights on a man named Alex Motherwell, and check for ties between him and paramilitary groups in the state?"

"Are you referring to the talented Canadian actor by that name?" he asked.

Over the years, Booker had amassed an encyclopedic collection of obscure factoids on Hollywood personalities.

"This Alex Motherwell is a University of Tennessee graduate involved in the construction industry," I said. "And he may have connections to a militia outfit operating in the Ozarks."

"My investigation shall commence at a more reasonable hour," he said. "And I shall keep you apprised of my findings."

"Have I told you lately you're my favorite uncle?"

Booker, needless to say, was my sole uncle.

"Must I again implore you to demonstrate a modicum of respect for your elders? Your entire generation is nothing more than a wasted, self-absorbed embarrassment to humanity. And furthermore—"

He was still going strong when I hung up.

* * *

The telephone rang soon after lunch, and it was Booker.

"Good news, my dear nephew," he said. "I have obtained limited information on our Mr. Motherwell."

"Leslie's also interested in this matter," I said. "I'll put you on speakerphone."

"Hello, Uncle Booker," she said, stepping closer to the phone. "We haven't seen you in a while."

"A ghastly situation to be rectified in the near future," he said. "Your thoughtful husband has invited me to your home for dinner. I trust you'll honor my vegan philosophy."

Leslie's head jerked and she gave me one of those withering female expressions all men have come to dread.

"Later," I whispered.

"It sounds wonderful," she said, her glare intensifying. "Would tomorrow evening work? Say, six o'clock?"

"Splendid!" Booker said

"Back to Alex Motherwell," I said. "Is he on the up-and-up?"

I made sure to stay out of Leslie's reach.

"He seems to have compiled an exemplary record," Booker said. "Mr. Motherwell graduated with honors from the University of Tennessee, earning a master's degree in mechanical engineering several years ago. Next, he served a stint in the U.S. Army, including a yearlong deployment in the Middle East. Motherwell received an honorable discharge within the past year and a half, and continues to serve in the Army Reserves, devoting one weekend a month to training."

"Any idea of the skills or expertise he might have acquired?" I asked.

"It appears he was involved in the construction and maintenance of facilities such as supply depots and airfields," Booker said. "And he acquired more than a cursory introduction to explosives."

Leslie looked at me, raising her eyebrows.

"What's kept him busy in recent months?" I asked.

"For over a year now, Motherwell has been employed by a prominent engineering firm headquartered in Memphis," Booker said. "The company specializes in designing or renovating major institutional structures—hospitals, schools, dormitories, airport terminals, and the like. The majority of its clients are based in the southeast."

"Anything else to add?"

"Mr. Motherwell is licensed to work in Tennessee, Mississippi, Kentucky, Missouri, and Arkansas," Booker said. "He's been quite active in the professional engineering associations. Also, he received his private pilot certificate in the past six months."

"Any details on his personal life?" Leslie asked.

"Despite an extensive search, I located nothing of substance," Booker said. "He's not been married, divorced, arrested, sued, or had any liens filed against him. I discovered a few photographs of Motherwell in business settings, but his Facebook page is almost anonymous. Nary a trace of him on other social media platforms."

"Anything on those paramilitary groups operating in the Arkansas Ozarks?" I asked.

"I suspect I'll be forced to delve into the netherworld of the internet for this information. Some of the websites are easily accessible, while others are on what's known as the dark web and—"

"The dark web?" Leslie asked, interrupting. "Did I hear you correctly?"

"Allow me to explain, my dear," Booker said. "There's an enormous internet universe out there—called the deep web—beyond Google, Yahoo, Bing, Dogpile, and the other search engines. Medical records, membership websites, and confidential corporate websites are a few examples."

"But I thought you referenced the dark web," I said.

"Patience, my dear nephew, patience," Booker said. "The dark web can be explained as a subset of the deep web. Much of the deep web is populated by legitimate businesses. However, the dark web is an altogether different story. It's where the most disgusting members of our society wreak their havoc, purchasing stolen credit card numbers, counterfeit currency, illicit drugs, firearms, child pornography, and programs for ransomware. Among other revolting commodities."

"And these secret militias rely on the dark web?" Leslie asked.

"It appears the dark web is ideal for many of the groups," Booker said. "If they wish to schedule meetings they would prefer the world to not know about, the dark web is exceedingly useful. If they're seeking to purchase, say, prohibited weapons or outlawed ammunition, the dark web provides the desired cover."

"And you're going to venture into this den of wickedness later tonight?" I asked.

"Have you forgotten what night this is?"

I thought on it for a moment, and then realized Booker had a point. I'd failed to remember his regularly scheduled Saturday evening performance at Little Rock's top drag revue. If his Facebook following was a reliable indicator, he was among the most popular cross-dressers in the South.

"But I will enter the perilous recesses of the dark web in the wee morning hours after entertaining my fans," Booker said. "I never cease to be amazed at how low we humans can go."

~ FOURTEEN ~

After giving my lunch time to settle, I took a short run through the neighborhood, waving to a couple of neighbors tending to their lawns. Returning home, I found Leslie sitting at the dining room table. Surrounded by an array of open cookbooks, she didn't bother to glance my way when I wandered into the room. Not a good sign.

"How is my beautiful bride on this delightful afternoon?"

My effusive greeting failed. She looked up for a moment, reached for another book, and began halfheartedly began flipping through its index.

"Wonderful," she said, her icy voice a perfect monotone. "Couldn't be better."

As is the case with most men, I often have trouble deciphering a female's moods. This was not one of those occasions.

Leslie shoved herself away from the table, stood, and wrapped her arms around me.

"I'm sorry," she said. "I'm just not sure I can prepare a respectable meal for your Uncle Booker. As you know, he's the consummate vegan."

"How can I help?" I asked. "I'm somewhat handy in the kitchen."

She pointed to a legal tablet on the table.

"There's our grocery list. You can begin by accompanying me to the store."

Only the yellow margins of the top sheet were visible, with hand-written words and phrases and numbers covering the rest of the page.

Following an expensive hour-long trip to Kroger, we spent the remainder of our Saturday afternoon and most of the evening in the kitchen. While Leslie mixed ingredients and experimented with a dozen or so recipes of various sorts, I stood over the sink, struggling to keep pace with a never-ending parade of dirty bowls, cutting boards, measuring cups, knives, platters, spatulas, pots, and pans. I must've washed several of the items four or five times over the course of the exhausting day.

"I'll never serve a dish I've haven't already tried," she, hovering beside the stove and stirring a pot. "It's a lesson I learned the hard way years ago."

We took infrequent breaks to sample the assortment of salads, sides, entrees, and desserts. At the end of the long run of trials, Leslie settled on a vegan menu for our Sunday dinner with Booker: an avocado salad, sauteed broccoli, glazed carrots, an artisan bread, and an entrée of spinach-artichoke lasagna. Dessert would be a homemade banana cream pie.

* * *

I switched off the lamp on my nightstand once we climbed into bed a few minutes before 1:00 AM.

"Don't we have something to discuss?" Leslie asked.

I noticed her voice lacked its usual warm and friendly tone. Not a good sign. Again.

"I'm not sure what you're referring to."

"Your dinner invitation to Uncle Booker. Without my knowledge or input."

I felt myself sink even lower into the mattress.

"My invitation occurred in a weak moment," I admitted. "My motives were commendable. I was trying to divert his attention from my new executive assistant."

"I appreciate honorable intentions as much as anyone," she said. "However, in the future, let's consult on such matters."

I heard a heavy sigh.

"If you choose to say a prayer this evening, you might as well go ahead and ask for divine assistance with tomorrow's dinner."

I got a goodnight kiss, but it wasn't one for the ages. Before going to sleep, I mumbled a short though quite sincere prayer.

* * *

The next day following church, we ate a hurried lunch and then returned to the kitchen to prepare the evening meal. I began washing and peeling carrots while Leslie worked on the pie and made the bread and the lasagna. Afterwards, I put in another long stretch at the sink, scrub brush in hand. By 5:30, the table was set and all the dishes were either on the stovetop, in the oven, or ready to serve.

As Leslie headed upstairs to change into what she called a cuter outfit, she turned and gave me a faint smile.

"Thanks for your help," she said. "This is going to be a fine dinner."

"I owe you."

"Yes, you do," she said. "In a big way."

Booker arrived at six o'clock on the dot, parking Cruella DeVille on the curb and drawing the appreciation of a pair of joggers passing through the neighborhood. I watched from the porch as my uncle fielded their questions about his stylish vehicle, first directing their attention to the massive grill and later to its flamboyant taillights. One of the runners handed a cell phone to Booker and he took their photograph posing with the classic car.

I met Booker on the front steps and escorted him inside where he commented on the wonderful aromas wafting through the house. I gave full credit to my blushing bride as she came down the stairs.

"May I get you something to drink?" I asked.

I knew the answer, but went through the motions. My teetotaling uncle was particular regarding his beverage of choice. Leslie was already well into her vodka and club soda while my hand held a half-empty bottle of craft beer, my second for the afternoon.

"Spring water," he said. "Evian, of course."

While Leslie steered Booker to an attractive appetizer platter of nuts, vegan crackers, and fruits, I stepped into the kitchen and found the Evian bottle I'd set aside for his rare visits. Holding it under the tap, I filled the bottle and twisted on the cap. After placing it and a goblet on a serving tray, I returned to the living room.

"Thank you, dear nephew."

He poured the water into his glass and raised it toward the ceiling.

"To Leslie and Randy. And their vegan future."

I almost choked on my beer while Leslie came close to spilling her cocktail. Nevertheless, we joined Booker in his toast.

"Let me bring you up-to-date on a few rather provocative discoveries I've made since we last talked," Booker said. "I started with a search on the website of the Southern Poverty Law Center."

"That sounds like a radical outfit," I said.

Booker actually snorted.

"Goodness no. It's a distinguished institution based in Montgomery, Alabama, and has been ferreting out one hate group after another for decades now. I'm proud to state I support its worthy cause by contributing a modest sum to the center on an annual basis."

"Hate groups?" Leslie asked. "Like the Klan?"

"The Ku Klux Klan is but one of hundreds of such organizations operating in our fine country," Booker said. "The Center has identified at least 14 hate groups active in Arkansas alone."

"You've got to be kidding," I said.

Booker shook his head.

"I noticed the name Alex Motherwell on the membership list of one of them."

"The same Alex Motherwell we're interested in?" Leslie asked.

"That seems to be the case," Booker said. "Known as the Flyover Family, the group is based near Ralph, a community in Marion County."

I remembered Marion County was two or three hours north of Little Rock. Located in the heart of the Ozarks, it was sparsely populated with large areas of remote and rugged countryside.

"Flyover Family?" Leslie said, a questioning tone in her voice. "What an unusual name."

"It's not an actual surname," Booker said. "As you may recall, much of the middle of the United States is referred to as 'flyover' land by certain segments of our society."

"I've heard the term used disparagingly on late-night television talk shows by some of the arrogant coastal elites," I said. "I suspect the organization is making a statement with this name."

"My thoughts as well," Booker said. "The regular search engines yielded nary a trace of information on this group, but the dark web was a different story. This Flyover Family assemblage has developed an illuminating home page, complete with its history, mission, and—"

"Mission?" I asked, interrupting.

"Oh, yes, indeed," Booker said. "I believe I can quote it verbatim: 'To restore, defend, and perpetuate the White Christian culture of the United States of America.' The word 'white,' I should add, is capitalized." After a brief hesitation, he continued, "I found the section on 'Legacy' to be quite revealing."

"Tell us more," Leslie said.

"A key requirement of this august group is every member must demonstrate a viable connection to the Confederacy. If not by blood, then by marriage."

"No doubt Alex Motherwell made the cut," I said.

"Ha!" Booker said, almost shouting. "Motherwell's great, great grandfather served under the command of Confederate General Nathan Bedford Forrest."

The name sounded vaguely familiar.

"And Forrest—" I started, before Booker interrupted me.

"—was the founder of the Klan," Booker continued.

"You're telling us Alex Motherwell is a direct descendant of a Civil War veteran who fought under the very man who founded the Ku Klux Klan?" Leslie asked.

"You are correct," Booker said. "It's an exclusive group."

"Is it only for men?" I asked.

Booker surprised me with a chuckle.

"Strangely enough, the Flyover Family is remarkably enlightened with its membership requirements. Blacks, Jews, Asians, Hispanics, Hindus, Buddhists, gays, and trans need not apply, of course, but women are allowed."

"As long as they're white and Christian with valid links to the Confederate States of America," Leslie added.

"Well, yes," Booker said. "There is that."

"I believe we can set this topic aside for a while," Leslie said, leading us to the dinner table. "Let's enjoy tonight's food."

The meal was an outstanding success. My scrawny uncle took a second helping of every dish and a third serving of lasagna. I still don't know where he managed to put it. He normally was careful with his diet, wanting—as he put it—to keep his "girlish figure." Which reminded me.

"Uncle Booker, how was last night's soirée?" I asked.

Booker performed almost every Saturday evening in one of the town's bars featuring talent contests for cross-dressers. Leslie, who was familiar with his fetish, had once been invited to inspect his walk-in closet. She later told me his collection of evening gowns alone was worth tens of thousands of dollars, and his selection of women's heels far outnumbered hers.

Smiling, he gave me an exaggerated wink.

"Well," he said, "I was honored to be chosen as the crowd favorite. Again. I happen to have a series of delightful photographs I'll be pleased to share."

As he began scrolling through the pictures on his phone, Leslie stepped away from the table and asked, "Could I interest anyone in dessert?"

~ FIFTEEN ~

Returning from the kitchen, Leslie carried three large servings of her homemade banana cream pie and placed one before each of us. She watched Booker slip a small bite into his mouth, his eyes shut in anticipation.

"My dear Leslie," he said after a long pause, "this is without a doubt the most exquisite culinary creation I have ever had the pleasure to sample. C'est magnifique!"

Upon learning Leslie had minored in French, Booker had developed a habit of working in a few French words and phrases when she was around.

"Merci beaucoup," she said, giving him a faint smile.

I noticed a look of relief on her face.

"Back to our Flyover Family friends," I said. "What do you know about the members?"

"The membership roster lists 55 men and 20 women," Booker said. "Two-thirds have mailing addresses in Arkansas, most from the northern half of the state. Another dozen or so live in Missouri and Oklahoma, with others from Tennessee and Texas. And there are a couple of outliers, one man from Idaho and another living in Montana."

"Have you had any luck on the money front?" I asked.

"Indeed," he said, and I detected a rare note of excitement in his voice. "I have exceeded even my own ambitious expectations."

"Should I resurrect one of your favorite quotes from American history?" I asked.

He'd brought it up over the years while dissecting whatever political scandal was current in the country at the time, instilling it in my memory.

Booker actually chuckled. "As you know, those are three of the most important words uttered during the 20th century."

Confused, Leslie looked to me for help.

"Booker's referring to 'Follow the money,' the cryptic message from Deep Throat to an intrepid duo of *Washington Post* reporters."

She bobbed her head in recognition.

"That was the brief exchange leading to the downfall of President Richard Nixon in the infamous Watergate caper, right?"

Booker nodded. "'Follow the money.' There's no better advice when researching unscrupulous individuals or groups."

"I assume you've found money to track?" I asked.

"Outside of a pair of timber sales providing funds for a generator and construction of a firing range, the Flyover Family has operated under a modest budget," Booker said. "Their annual dues cover little more than routine expenses such as property taxes and insurance."

"Have things changed?" Leslie asked.

"A check for $100,000 appeared in their bank account within the past few days."

My thoughts went to Erin Askew's windfall.

"Have you identified the source of this deposit?" I asked.

Booker reached into his shirt pocket and removed a folded piece of paper, handing it to me with a flourish. I examined it for a moment before passing it to Leslie.

"The $100,000 deposit was, as you can see, a personal check from one Erin Askew, made payable to the Flyover Family," Booker said. "I printed this image of that very check in the wee hours of the morning."

"Did this cash infusion generate any notice?" Leslie said.

"More than you can imagine," Booker said. "Crediting a generous but anonymous donor, the president sent a brief e-mail to the membership announcing its receipt. Comments about the gift spread through the group like wildfire," he said. "Yet there was a strange uniformity to the reactions, often referred to as Stage 2."

"Any idea what Stage 2 refers to?" I asked.

"I am convinced the members were alluding to a major purchase or activity of some sort," Booker said. "Several of the replies noted the compound had plenty of space. But so far, I've been unable to ascertain how they might propose to use these funds."

I looked again at the copy of the check. The memo line caught my attention. I noticed Erin had written: **Special Project**.

"This is interesting," I said, pointing to the words on the check.

"I'm hopeful to make progress on that particular item later this evening," Booker said. "The phrase also piqued my curiosity."

"What's next?" Leslie asked.

"Upon returning to my humble abode, I plan to probe further into the financial intricacies of the Flyover Family organization. Perhaps we can determine how the $100,000 might be used." After a pause, he added, "I have serious doubts it will be for the common good of the American people."

Following the last bite of his dessert, Booker wiped his mouth, and set his napkin aside. "Don't I recall an Erin Askew as a recent addition to the staff at Lassiter & Associates?" he asked. "Could she be the delightfully luscious young woman stationed outside your office?"

Before I could reply, I felt Leslie's hand on my shoulder.

"At the risk of offending our distinguished guest, I will politely but firmly remind him Ms. Askew was hired on the basis of her professional merits," Leslie said, glaring at Booker. "'Delightfully luscious' is no way to refer to one of your colleagues. End of lecture."

Booker seemed to realize he'd overstepped his bounds, something he'd done most of his life, although I couldn't remember anyone ever having called him on it. Looking at Leslie as his face reddened, Booker nodded.

"Point taken," he said after several long seconds had passed.

He glanced at his watch and then got to his feet.

"I believe it's time for me to initiate the next phase of my discreet investigations into the Flyover Family."

As we made our way to the front door, Booker took Leslie's right hand into his own.

"I cannot remember a more marvelous dinner," he said. "Thank you for an absolutely delightful evening." After a moment's hesitation, he added, "And please absolve me for my insensitive description of Ms. Askew."

Leslie pulled her hand back, wrapped her arms around Booker's neck, and gave him a hug.

"All is forgiven. We'll have to do this again!"

Booker shook my hand and reached for the door, mumbling something about the dark web as he left. Leslie collapsed against me, giggling into my chest, as he marched across the porch and down the steps to his car.

"Did you get a look at his face when I came back at him regarding Erica?" she asked. "Priceless!"

"Until tonight, I'd never seen Booker speechless," I said, leading her into the kitchen. "Let's put our leftovers in the refrigerator. We can tidy up in the morning. That was a kick-ass dinner!"

"It was pretty good, wasn't it?" She gave me a smile and waggled her eyebrows. "You do owe me, you know."

"I've already accepted my fate."

"I'm thinking something along the lines of a nice piece of jewelry might be appropriate."

"Maybe something in silver?" I asked. "Or perhaps gold?"

She shook her head.

"I had something in mind featuring carbon."

Carbon? If my memory from high school chemistry was correct, it was among the most common elements in the universe. Graphite was a familiar example of carbon, and carbon exists in everyday ashes. Atop a slice of burned toast, for instance. And then I remembered yet another configuration of carbon. Something a bit more precious than graphite or ashes: diamonds.

Her eyes sparkling, Leslie watched as I tried to make sense of her puzzling wish. When my jaw dropped, she nodded with an even bigger smile.

"Yes," she said. "An extremely beautiful form of carbon."

* * *

After we climbed into bed, I leaned over Leslie and gave her a good night kiss.

"Is something the matter?" she asked. "You seem distracted."

"I'll admit to feeling a little confused," I said. "We have solved the compelling mystery of the Askew twins, right? Case closed. Why are we pursuing this paramilitary thing with the Flyover Family?"

Leslie turned to her side and faced me as one of her clever smiles appeared. "Do you really want an answer?" she asked.

"Can you provide one?"

"You're bothered by thoughts of these zealots inflicting harm on our democratic society and its values. Remember how apoplectic you got when those insurrectionists stormed the U.S. Capitol in early 2021? The angry mob attempting to overturn a national election and topple our federal government?"

"I'll never forget those images," I said. "Like you, I was beyond irritated. Incensed might be a better word."

"You see something similar happening here. And we're taking steps to prevent it."

I reached across the mattress and caressed Leslie's face.

"I love you."

~ SIXTEEN ~

First thing Monday morning, Leslie and I spent a busy hour in the kitchen dealing with the remaining mess from last night's vegan extravaganza for Uncle Booker. That job complete, I drove to the agency. While perched behind my desk relishing the calm before the daily storm and reading the latest edition of *Arkansas Business* on my computer, I heard someone say, "Good morning, Randy."

The voice sounded familiar, although it didn't sound quite right. Something a tiny bit different. I looked up and saw Erica standing in my doorway.

"Hi," I said. "I trust you had a nice weekend."

She gave me a pleasant smile. But a second closer look confirmed the small mole had migrated again and was now on the other side of her face. The correct side.

"Please come in, close the door, and have a seat," I said. My pulse had kicked into overdrive. "Today, I believe we have Erin starring in the continuing 'Erin & Erica Askew Saga' at Lassiter & Associates. Am I correct?"

"You're good."

After shaking my hand, she claimed a chair.

"I owe you an explanation. And certainly an apology."

"An understatement if I've ever heard one."

"Any chance we can carry on our conversation over coffee?"

"Black, I assume?"

"Of course."

I soon returned with two cups of the morning brew.

"First," she said, "I should let you know Erica's fine. She'd taken a few weeks off before beginning her new job as a webmaster for an online retailer in Fort Worth, starting today, in fact. She asked me to mention how much she appreciated her time at Lassiter & Associates."

Erin went on to tell me she'd given Erica her driver's license and a voided check to share with our personnel manager on her first day at the agency. Since we hadn't yet run payroll after Erica started, Erin said she'd reimburse her sister for her wages equal to the forthcoming direct deposit into Erin's checking account.

I raised my palm, hoping to redirect this monologue.

"I'm not too interested in details of your financial gimmickry," I said, "as long as the agency comes out unharmed and I get honest answers to a few questions."

Erin nodded and took a sip of her coffee.

"However, I am interested in how your reunion with Erica went. And how your meeting with the lottery folks worked out." After a moment's pause, I continued, "Also, I might add, I'm quite eager to hear your thoughts on why I should even consider retaining you on the staff at Lassiter & Associates."

"Let me start with our reunion."

She said Erica had arrived as scheduled and they had a big cry before composing themselves and going to dinner. Erica had posted a photograph on Facebook of them enjoying their meal, and then Alex Motherwell, her former fiancé, saw it and contacted Erica. He informed her sister he was in the area and said he hoped to see them the next afternoon. At first, Erin opposed any contact with Alex, and begged Erica to refuse. But Erica convinced her a brief meeting would be harmless, and afterwards Alex could be sent on his merry way.

"That's not how it played out, is it?" I asked.

Erin shook her head.

"I couldn't stand to look at Alex at first," she said. "As the evening wore on, though, my attitude began to change. Maybe the wine helped. We talked and laughed and reminisced for hours, reliving many of the wonderful times we'd shared in Knoxville. I'd already forgiven Erica, and I decided I could do the same with Alex."

"Did he accompany you when you met with the staff at the lottery office?"

"Following breakfast, I mentioned my appointment later in the morning to redeem a lottery ticket. Erica chimed in, noting I was going to collect a substantial prize. Alex kept pressing for details, and I finally admitted I'd won a million-dollar sweepstakes."

"How did Alex react to this?"

"He was amazed, as you might expect, not believing me at first," Erin said. "Alex began telling us about a special group he belongs to, a collection of everyday men and women working together to restore the American dream. They're operating out of an old farmstead in the Ozarks."

I opted not to comment, but nodded, encouraging her to continue.

"He explained how they hope to develop an ambitious outreach program for the youth of the South. One of their primary aims is to construct a summer camp for kids, complete with a dormitory, kitchen, dining hall, and classrooms. They'll bring in girls for one session, and boys for the next, to help perpetuate our southern heritage. Also, they've reserved booth space at this fall's Arkansas State Fair, aiming to recruit new members."

I'd make a point of asking Booker if he'd found any details on these proposals.

"Go on," I said.

"The more Alex talked, the more excited and animated he became regarding their long-term educational goals. He said he'd volunteered to chair a fundraising committee for the summer camp."

I had an uneasy feeling where this was going.

"I told him I'd soon have more money than I could spend," she said, "and would be pleased to give $100,000 toward the camp. So, to answer your question … Yes, Alex went with me to the meeting in the lottery office. I arranged to have my lump sum payment deposited into my checking account, and wrote a $100,000 personal check that afternoon for his project."

"Do you still intend to help those charitable organizations you mentioned to Leslie and me?" I asked, as if her personal donations were any of my concern. "Your church, Habitat for Humanity, and the Komen Foundation?"

"Checks to all three will be mailed later this week," she said, showing a flash of anger in her eyes and confirming the allocation of her winnings was none of my business.

"Back to the proposed summer camp. Have you had a chance to visit the farm?"

"That's why I asked Erica to temporarily take my place here at the agency," she said. "Alex insisted I see the property, and we drove to it once the news conference ended. I'd planned to be gone for a single day, but he and I spent several days … uh … touring it."

She looked away as a blush crept up her face.

"It's fabulous, and so remote. Rolling hills covered with trees. There's a beautiful spring flowing into a small lake, and an enormous cave under a bluff on one of the hillsides."

I realized her description corroborated what Booker had learned.

"Alex showed me the site where they'll construct the building to house the dorm, cafeteria, and classrooms. He and I devoted two afternoons to flagging a pair of hiking trails. I never anticipated Erica having to cover for so long, but time just got away from me. I'm very sorry."

"Your former fiancé," I said. "Alex Motherwell. Is he a full-time resident at this farm?"

I wanted to see if her information was consistent with Booker's other findings.

Shaking her head, Erin said, "He's an engineer based in Memphis. One of his jobs brings him to the Little Rock area on occasion. Right now, though, he's trying to spend every other weekend or so at the farm. It's a couple of hours from Memphis, closer if he rents a plane and flies. They call it the Flyover Family compound."

118

"What an unusual name," I said, wondering if she might validate our suspicions.

"Alex said it's a jab at the snobby elites who look down their noses at the real America," she said. "A primary objective of the youth camp will be to instill a sense of pride in the participants, to remind them of the South's many contributions to this country."

"So," I said, "where does this leave us?"

Rubbing her chin, Erin met my gaze.

"If I were you, I'd fire me on the spot."

"I've been thinking the same," I said. "Unless you can convince me otherwise."

Erin rose to her feet and gave me a faint smile.

"If you're willing to listen, I've prepared a five-minute speech on why you should keep me."

I glanced at my watch.

"Go."

Four minutes and 45 seconds later, Erin returned to her seat. In the interim, she apologized once more for the deception she and Erica had perpetrated, guaranteeing it would never happen again. She then outlined what she hoped to accomplish with her position at Lassiter & Associates during the next six months and how she could add to the agency's bottom line. Erin closed with half a dozen strategic ideas aimed at helping the agency land the state's tourism account, a list she handed to me before she sat down. Every one of them, I had to admit, was on the mark.

"Are you willing to give me another shot?" she asked. "Please."

My professional instincts said no, definitely not. Yet her pleading gaze and my gut told me Erin seemed genuinely contrite. She brought a lot of energy and talent to the table, I realized, and could be a valuable colleague. And, of course, I wouldn't have to go through a dreaded round of interviews.

"You made your case," I said, "with one caveat. No more of these Bette Davis scenarios. Ever."

"Thank you!" She left my office, giving me a firm handshake on the way out. I thought I saw tears in her eyes, but perhaps I was imagining things.

Leslie would call me lazy. Maybe she was right.

* * *

I met Leslie at home for a delicious lunch of vegan leftovers.

"My appointment to photograph the grounds of the Governor's Mansion was cancelled at the last minute," she said. "Governor Butler's entertaining a trio of federal bigwigs from D.C. and the security is tight. How was your morning?"

"Guess who appeared today in the office?"

Leslie smiled and waggled her eyebrows. "Emma Watson?"

I'd shared my longtime crush on the actress during a weak moment months ago, much to my regret.

"My original hire, Ms. Erin Askew, arrived at eight o'clock on the dot."

Leslie gasped. "Erin's back? You're sure?"

"Her little mole was a dead giveaway."

"I hope you fired her."

"Well, not exactly," I said, recounting the highlights of our conversation and concluding with my decision to keep her on the agency's payroll.

Leslie shook her head. "You are such an easy mark, Randy Lassiter." She sighed. "But you know what worries me deep down?"

"My sanity?"

"Besides that," she said, rolling her eyes. "It's the summer camp for kids the Flyover Family is organizing. The one Erin's donation is making possible. With this new facility, they can indoctrinate hundreds of kids every summer with their anti-democracy, white nationalist propaganda."

I looked at the kitchen clock. It was 12:45.

Way too early to drink, I thought.

~ SEVENTEEN ~

I kissed Leslie goodbye and made a mad dash for the office, arriving just in the nick of time to conduct our regular Monday afternoon meeting about the agency's forthcoming bid for the state tourism account. Today's schedule called for a decision on cities for our focus groups. We'd listed over a dozen candidates—places such as Chicago, Dallas, Memphis, Oklahoma City, Tulsa, St. Louis, Kansas City, Birmingham, New Orleans, and others—within what was considered Arkansas's primary marketing region, but Lassiter & Associate's budget could only accommodate sessions in two.

"Given that 40% of Arkansas's tourists come from Texas," Abigail said, "I think we'd be foolish not to include at least one city from The Lone Star State."

The murmurs and nodding heads in the conference room indicated a consensus. We spent an hour comparing the pros and cons of including residents of Fort Worth, Houston, Waco, Austin, San Antonio, and, of course, Dallas, in our research. Because of its large population base and due to its proximity to Arkansas, Dallas won out.

Determining the second city for the focus group exercise proved more difficult. Noting Dallas lay west of Arkansas, Meagan suggested we go in another direction for the next selection. Her recommendation got universal approval, eliminating Tulsa and Oklahoma City from the mix. One member of the staff made an argument to include Jackson, Mississippi, but a handful of his colleagues felt the metropolitan area was too small. Springfield,

Missouri, and Shreveport, Louisiana, were excluded for the same reason. Following an animated conversation, the choice was reduced to either St. Louis or Memphis. After a thorough review of the demographics of each, the staff voted by better than a three to one majority to go with Memphis. I was pleased Erin took an active role in the discussion.

Now all we had to do was to hire a facilitator to conduct the focus groups. And for the Lassiter team to execute a series of fabulous creative concepts to share with the participants. We still had several months to do those things.

* * *

Between a pair of conference calls, participating in a marketing presentation to the owner of the city's largest pawn shop, and consulting with my banker to review a potential expansion of the agency's profit-sharing plan, the remainder of the afternoon was little more than a blur. The day ended on a positive note when the pawnbroker called minutes before 5:00 and stated Lassiter & Associates had won his account. It took an effort, but I managed to talk him out of scheduling a news conference to announce the deal. Bringing his business on as a client wouldn't add much to our bottom line and even less to our prestige, although it'd help keep a couple of employees on the payroll.

* * *

When I returned home for the day, Leslie waited on the porch, purse in hand. She dashed down the steps and met me before I had time to climb from my truck.

"We're going out for pizza," she said. "You're driving."

"Any particular place?" I asked as she slid into the passenger seat.

"Pizza Café," she said. "In the Riverdale neighborhood. One of the women who models for me claims it's the best in town. After last night's vegan jamboree and today's lunch, I need something less healthy."

It was a good pizza, an excellent pizza, in fact, and not terribly harmful, at least by my standards. There was a fine assortment of vegetable matter in the form of green peppers, onions, and marinara sauce, fruit via chunks of pineapple, and a bit of protein courtesy of the Canadian bacon. We curbed our carb intake by opting for the thin crust variety. And in a remarkable show of restraint, we limited ourselves to a single beer each.

"What's next on our quest to get to the bottom of this Flyover Family situation?" Leslie asked.

"Based on my chat with Erin earlier today, I'm inclined to ask Uncle Booker to continue his investigations into the organization's plans. And maybe to take a deep dive into the membership, with a close look at the officers."

I paused to enjoy a sip of beer.

"Any other thoughts?"

"If they're serious about a summer camp, I'm sure there are plenty of governmental hoops to jump through," Leslie said. "I developed a contact in the Secretary of State's office while getting my LLC established last year. I'll nose around a bit."

We declined the waiter's offer for another round of drinks, and Leslie asked for the check.

"Tonight's on me," she said, handing him a credit card.

"Thanks for dinner," I said as we stepped outside and walked to the truck. "Your friend was right. That was a fine pizza."

"Tomorrow night," Leslie said, "we'll eat the last of the vegan leftovers. Thank God."

* * *

We'd been home an hour when Booker phoned.

"If your lovely bride's available," he said, "could you please put me on speakerphone?"

I got Leslie's attention, motioned for her to join me, and engaged the speaker function.

"She's present," I said.

"My dear Leslie, thank you again for last night's spectacular feast. It was by far my best culinary experience of the year," he said, then paused. "Also, I want to provide an update on my discrete surveillance of our Flyover Family friends."

"Any new breakthroughs?" I asked.

"Ms. Askew's $100,000 contribution served as a catalyst, resulting in a flurry of additional donations. None as large, of course, but $10, $50, and $100 gifts are flooding into the organization's coffers. In the past 24 hours alone, better than $5,000 has arrived."

"Have you spotted any references to a summer camp for youth?" I asked. "Any announcement, plans, or programs?"

"Interesting you should mention a camp, lad," Booker said. "An e-mail from this Motherwell chap touting that very topic seems to have instigated the onslaught of contributions. His message states their large anonymous gift will be used as a kick-start for the Francis Marion Memorial Camp for Southern Youth."

"But Marion wasn't from Arkansas, was he?" I asked.

"If my memory of American history's correct, he was a South Carolinian who fought during the American Revolution," Leslie said. "Wasn't Marion the war hero known as the 'Swamp Fox'?"

"Right you are," said Booker. "I suspect Marion was selected because Southern heritage is paramount with this group."

"Since Arkansas wasn't a factor in the Revolutionary War, we have no local champions from those days," I said. "I guess Francis Marion is a logical choice, all things considered. After all, the Flyover Family's compound is based in Marion County, and odds are it was named in his honor."

"Speaking of history," Booker said, "I've uncovered an unexpected footnote regarding the Flyover Family's property. Years ago, the deed was held by one Ardis Thomas, a powerful man who ran Marion County like it was his personal fiefdom. He started out as a deputy sheriff, vanquished his boss in a bitter election, and served as county sheriff for decades. Thomas was a staunch ally of former governor Orval Faubus, and Faubus appointed him to the Arkansas State Police Commission, one of the most coveted patronage positions in the state."

"Faubus?" Leslie asked. "As in the notorious segregationist?"

"The one and the same," Booker said. "Subsequent governors reappointed Thomas to the Commission time and again. That is, until Bill Clinton was elected in 1978. He refused to consider Thomas, instead favoring a prominent supporter from northwest Arkansas who'd hosted a major fundraising event."

"How did Sheriff Thomas react?" I asked.

"The old newspaper accounts indicate Thomas was beyond livid, vowing to exact revenge. When the next election rolled around, Sheriff Thomas made certain Marion County went to Clinton's opponent by a landslide. And that, mind you, was the year Bill Clinton lost the governorship."

"Basic hardball politics," I said. "An Arkansas tradition."

"There's more to this mesmerizing story," Booker said. "Until her death a decade ago, the sheriff's late wife, one LuAnne Thomas, served for 38 years as director of the Arkansas Division of the United Daughters of the Confederacy."

"Is the group still active?" Leslie asked.

"With 22 chapters in the state and over 600 members, it remains a potent force," Booker said. "And Hutch Thomas, the grandson of Ardis and LuAnne Thomas, is now serving his third term as Marion County Sheriff. He's also the long-standing president of the Flyover Family."

"No doubt he has the necessary credentials," I said.

"Soldiers of the Confederacy hang from his family tree like apples," Booker said. "More than you can imagine."

"Where do we go from here?" Leslie asked. "I'm intrigued by our progress so far."

"I, too, am quite taken with this project," Booker said. "My recommendation is we persist in our digging. Few things can equal the satisfaction I get from perusing the latest atrocities on the dark web."

"I agree we should continue our efforts," I said. "Uncle Booker, could you unleash your investigative skills on the group's leaders beyond Hutch Thomas, paying particular attention to their backgrounds? Education, jobs, military service, police records, and so on. In addition, you might take a serious look at any affiliations they might have with other organizations."

"My thoughts exactly," Booker said. "If my suspicions hold true, we'll make some fascinating discoveries."

"Meanwhile, I'll take a look at how to establish and license a summer camp in Arkansas," Leslie said.

Following a long period of awkward silence, Booker said, "And, my dear nephew, what will be your responsibility?"

"The usual," I said. "I'm simply trying to keep an advertising agency solvent."

~ EIGHTEEN ~

Keeping Lassiter & Associates afloat meant recruiting new clients at each and every opportunity. Therefore, I was encouraged the next morning when Erin handed me a note to call Delmar Boddington, president of Hillcountry Marine, a boat manufacturer based in Yellville.

"He was rather vague," she said. "But I think he might be interested in having the agency represent his company."

Prior to returning Boddington's call, I did a bit of online research on Hillcountry Marine, learning the outfit had been producing fiberglass runabouts and fishing boats for the past decade. Under private ownership, it employed between 15 and 25 workers.

I then spent three-quarters of an hour examining the company's website. Appalled might be too strong a word to describe my reaction, but it was, at best, an ineffective sales tool. The half dozen or so featured boats appeared attractive, yet a quarter of the photographs were poorly composed or out-of-focus to varying degrees. Likewise, descriptions of the boats left a lot to be desired; I counted at least 15 typos before giving up. My click on "Testimonials" rewarded me with an "Error" message, and a hot link supposedly connecting the viewer to a state-by-state list of dealers didn't function.

Following this review of the website, I called Mr. Boddington and introduced myself. After a couple of minutes of introductory chitchat, he got down to business.

"Mr. Lassiter," he said, "for a little better than ten years now, I've overseen the design and fabrication of our line of boats. We offer good quality products, and have built our business for the most part on word-of-mouth marketing, never giving much thought to promotion. My daughter has now convinced me we need to bring in professional help, and she is somehow acquainted with your agency's work. Any chance you'd be willing to come to Yellville and talk with us?"

I'd taken a peek at my calendar before making the call. "Certainly," I said. "I'm available tomorrow or Thursday of—"

"Tomorrow it is," he said. "It's a three-hour drive from Little Rock to Yellville. Would eleven o'clock work?"

"Sounds great."

"Tell me how many of you there'll be and we'll provide lunch."

"Count on three of us," I said.

Megan often accompanied me on visits with prospective clients, and I figured this meeting would also give Erin a valuable learning experience.

Upon completion of my conversation with Mr. Boddington, I invited Megan and Erin into my office and told them about our plans for tomorrow. And I asked Erin to assemble a file containing everything she could find regarding Hillcountry Marine.

* * *

The three of us met at 7:45 the following morning in our parking lot and headed north toward Yellville with Megan driving. Once we were underway, Erin passed me a folder, saying, "Here's the information you requested on the company."

She'd tracked down the same Dun & Bradstreet material I'd uncovered, along with six or eight news articles to include a detailed cover story on Hillcountry Marine from a recent issue of *Arkansas Business*. She had also reprinted several pages from the company's website.

As I glanced through the latter, Erin said, "They need assistance with their online presence. It's not very well done."

"And you're being kind," I said.

We discussed our options as we twisted and turned our way into the Ozarks. I expressed hope the agency's years of promoting one of the state's largest automobile dealerships might resonate with Boddington while Megan suggested our successful relationship with the Tunica casino could illustrate our competence in the recreation industry.

Erin had been quiet during most of the drive, but spoke up during this portion of the conversation.

"Junior Judson, an all-star second baseman, played for the New York Yankees back in the day," she said. "Unless I'm mistaken, he was from Yellville. Maybe we could get him involved in a promotional campaign."

I felt Megan ease up on the accelerator as she turned to glance at Erin.

"How in the hell did you know that?" she asked.

I wondered the same thing.

"Our dad was a big major league baseball fan and it rubbed off on my sister Erica and me," Erin said. "Although he loved the St. Louis Cardinals, which was the closest professional team, we preferred clubs in the American League. Erica adopted the Red Sox as her favorite, and, of course, I picked the Yankees. My dad took us to New York after our senior year in high school to see those two teams battle in a classic double-header in Yankee Stadium. Much to my sister's dismay, the men in pinstripes won both games."

"Was Judson still playing then?" I asked.

"He'd already stepped aside," Erin said. "But he was recognized between games when they retired his jersey in a memorable ceremony."

"Bringing in Junior Judson is a brilliant thought," Megan said. "It might help seal the deal."

I looked over the seat at Erin and gave her a nod.

"When we return to Little Rock, I want you to track down his contact information. My guess is he's like many other retired players, living either in Florida or Arizona."

Megan steered us into a visitor's parking space at Hillcountry's plant on the north side of Yellville with ten minutes to spare. Boddington, a short balding man probably in his mid-60s, met us at the front door and led our trio into a conference room where he introduced his daughter Tabitha.

"And please," he said, "call me Del."

Over coffee, the five of us spent an hour getting acquainted with each other and our respective operations. Del brought us up-to-speed on the history and growth of Hillcountry Marine, from its humble origins in a decrepit century-old barn to its current state-of-the-art manufacturing plant. In turn, we shared a quick introduction to Lassiter & Associates with our hosts, highlighting the agency's experience in the recreational field. We were all surprised to discover the two organizations had been established within months of each other.

During the discussion, I asked Tabitha about her familiarity with the agency's work.

"Earlier this spring, two of my girlfriends and I were considering a weekend getaway," she said. "We'd noticed the TV commercials for Isla del Sol, the casino resort in Tunica, and went there a few weeks ago. We had a great time, and I asked the general manager for information on her advertising agency. She's the one who mentioned Lassiter & Associates."

"Until now," Del said, "we've built our reputation on runabouts and fishing boats. Tabitha's convinced her mom and me we need to add pontoon boats or party barges to our mix. Bringing on a new line represents a substantial investment, and we want help launching these products."

At noon, two young men delivered a fine lunch of pulled pork barbecue and side dishes of baked beans, fried okra, slaw, and potato salad. Afterwards, we toured Hillcountry Marine's factory, a sparkling 45,000-square-foot facility capable of manufacturing 10 to 12 finely-crafted boats a day. Boddington introduced us to three of his employees who explained their roles in the assembly process and answered our questions.

He also pointed to a fresh concrete slab at the end of the massive building. "This is where we'll expand to build the party barges. Five units a day if we can meet our goals."

At the conclusion of the tour, the group returned to the conference room where we discussed how Lassiter & Associates might be able to assist Hillcountry Marine. It was a cordial conversation, ending with the agreement we would forward, within two weeks, a draft contract for Mr. Boddington and his daughter to review. At a minimum, it would address: compiling research on past and potential customers; improving and expanding the company's website; development of a print campaign to be placed in selected trade publications; production of a four-color promotional brochure; and design and purchase of a portable exhibit booth to be used at trade shows. Recalling Erin's comment on our drive to Yellville, I suggested we'd also check into identifying a celebrity spokesman who might be willing to work in behalf of Hillcountry Marine.

"This has been an enjoyable time," I said, shaking Boddington's hand as the meeting adjourned. "Thanks for inviting us to Yellville. I had no idea touring a boat factory would be so fascinating. And congratulations on your plans for expansion."

"It's been our pleasure," Del said. "We appreciate your interest in our little venture, and look forward to getting your proposal. Maybe we'll be working with y'all in the future."

* * *

As we left the Hillcountry parking lot, I asked my colleagues for their impressions of our visit with the Boddingtons.

"I think it went well," Megan said. "I like them and am eager to work on the proposed contract. My take is the agency's strengths match nicely with their needs."

I turned to Erin.

"This was my first experience, but they asked relevant questions and seemed pleased with our answers. Thanks for letting me tag along."

"I believe several of our colleagues take their fishing seriously," I said, making eye contact with Megan. "Be sure to involve them as you begin working on the draft contract."

As we drove back through Yellville, Erin pointed to a small diner surrounded by pickup trucks.

"That's where we ate when I was here last week."

I looked to Erin. "When you were exploring the Flyover Family compound?"

She gave me a slight nod.

"It's a few miles south of here if you'd like to see the place," she said. "It's not too far off the main highway. Alex gave me a set of keys so I could drop in and inspect the camp's progress."

"Sure," I said. "You'll have to guide us there."

Once she got Megan pointed in the right direction, Erin gave her a brief explanation of how she'd accompanied a good friend to see a piece of land that will soon house a summer camp for kids. She didn't note her financial contribution to the project. Nor did she mention her good friend was a former fiancé.

As we passed through the community of Ralph, I realized we were approaching the Buffalo National River, a popular outdoor recreational mecca operated by the National Park Service.

"How close is your land to the Buffalo River property?" I asked.

"It's immediately to the north of the park," Erin said. "In fact, we're bordered on three sides by federal holdings."

After we'd gone another couple of miles, she tapped Megan on the shoulder and said, "Turn at the next right."

We'd left the state highway and had driven almost a mile down a narrow, graveled road when Erin gestured ahead.

"There's the entrance," she said. "Park in front of the old mail box."

A pair of corroded **Posted: No Trespassing** signs hung from trees on both sides of a rusty steel gate. Erin inserted a key into the thick padlock. It fell open, and she removed a heavy chain and pushed the gate aside.

"Given the rough road," she said, "I'd recommend we leave Megan's car here. We won't have time to explore the whole tract, but I can show you the house. It's just ahead."

We walked less than a hundred yards down a dusty rutted track before stopping in front of a substantial two-story wood frame house. While its siding was weathered and needed painting in places, the building looked to be in good shape. The windows were all intact, the metal roof appeared to be new, the fieldstone chimney stood tall and straight, and the steps and railing on the front porch had been replaced.

Erin led the way onto the big porch with Megan and me at her heels. Again using her keychain, she unlocked the front door, flipping on a light switch as she entered. With a classic stone fireplace filling much of one end, this must have been the living room at one time. The sole furnishings were a long oak table surrounded by eight to ten mismatched wooden chairs. An American flag stood on a pole on one side of the fireplace. The Confederate battle flag occupying the opposite side wasn't unexpected, but still unsettled me. Hanging from the wall adjacent to it was a large framed portrait of Confederate general Robert E. Lee.

"This is where members meet," she said. "The small room off to the left, once the master bedroom, is what they refer to as the office, although it also serves as a library. The kitchen and dining room are ahead. Beyond them are two bedrooms for female members to share. Upstairs has been reconfigured to barracks-style sleeping quarters for men."

I angled off to the left to inspect the office. A Formica table held a survey of the property. Above the table was a handsome framed engraving of a man on horseback. A closer look at a small nameplate along the bottom of the old artifact confirmed it was Brigadier General Francis Marion. A vintage four-drawer metal filing cabinet sat in one corner of the room. An assortment of volumes filled a built-in bookcase, with titles ranging from *A Long-Range Shooting Handbook* to *Building Your Own Water System* to *Retrofitting Your Cabin for Solar Power*. I noticed a manila folder on one of the shelves was labeled, "Licensing Requirements for Overnight Camps: Arkansas Department of Health."

Next on my tour was a visit to the kitchen, and it was far more spacious than I expected, with equipment that wouldn't have been out-of-place in a restaurant. Erin and Megan caught up with me as I examined the six-burner stove and warming oven.

"There's a commercial-size freezer in the basement," Erin said. "The property is served by a rural electric co-op, plus there's a new emergency generator near the rear door. They hope to install solar panels soon."

"I think you mentioned the group plans to establish a camp for kids on the property," I said. "Any idea when it might open?"

"Maybe later this summer if they can fast-track things," she said. "The new building will be a short distance down the hill."

As I peeked into the enormous refrigerator, Erin and Megan left the kitchen and climbed the stairs to check the men's barracks. I opened a narrow door on the far side of the kitchen, and found myself gazing into a deep pantry filled with shelf after shelf of canned goods.

Shutting the pantry door, I came face-to-face with a bulky man holding a pistol 15 inches from my nose. His face an angry red and his lips glistening with spittle, he gave the barrel of the gun a little wave.

"You know I every right to kill you on the spot!"

~ NINETEEN ~

A cold sweat broke out over my face and my pulse skyrocketed. I stared at the man who held my life in his big hands. He was tall and wide, a generation or so older than I, and his wrinkled khaki uniform included a shiny badge above his left breast pocket. His eyes were mere slants, boring into me.

"Give me one reason why I shouldn't go ahead and shoot you," he muttered, his breath reeking of garlic and onions. "You might want to make it a good one."

We heard the clatter of footsteps coming down the stairs.

"Who's that?" he hissed.

He grabbed my elbow and yanked me next to him, the end of the gun barrel digging into my temple.

Erin and Megan stepped into the kitchen, both sliding to a stop when they saw me and the man holding a pistol aimed at my head.

"Miss Askew?"

The man lowered the gun as he stared at Erin.

"Why are you here? And who are these two?"

He waved its barrel first at me and then toward Megan.

"Sheriff Thomas," she said, her voice a pitch or two higher than normal. "These are my coworkers. We came to Yellville earlier today and I wanted to show them where we're building our summer youth camp."

Seconds passed. The man released my arm and slipped his handgun into the worn leather holster dangling from his belt.

"I reckon that's all well and good," he said. "But how'd you get in here?"

"Alex gave me a set of keys," she said. "He encouraged me to drop in now and then to check on the construction progress."

The sheriff took a step back, cleared his throat, and nodded to Erin.

"If it's not too much trouble, maybe you could introduce me to your friends."

"Yes, sir," she said.

She pointed to Megan.

"This is Megan Maloney, one of my colleagues."

Megan and the sheriff shook hands.

"And the poor man you almost shot is my boss, Randy Lassiter."

"Mr. Lassiter," he said, "I'm sorry we got off to such a poor start. We've had a bit of trouble with trespassers, vandals, and thieves, and I suspected the worst. I hope you'll forgive me."

Our handshake was about what I expected from the sheriff: firm and long-lived. I wondered if I'd ever get my arm back.

"No harm, no foul," I said, forcing a smile when he finally relinquished his grip on my fingers.

"Let's go into the conference room," he said and led the way. "We can visit for a couple of minutes before I've got to leave. I was on the way to serve a warrant when I spotted a strange car parked out front. Naturally, I had to make sure things were okay."

Erin and Sheriff Thomas sat on one side of the long table, and Megan and I found seats on the other.

"What brings y'all to Yellville?" he asked, his face framed by the Confederate flag standing behind him.

"We're in the advertising business," I said. "We had a meeting this morning at Hillcountry Marine with Del Boddington."

"Del and I went to high school together, played on the same football and basketball teams. He runs a good outfit. I've owned one of his boats for must be five years now."

"He and his daughter invited us up to discuss development of a marketing plan," Erin said.

136

"Del's hinted a time or two he and his wife are getting ready to turn the business over to Tabitha," the sheriff said. "Seems to me I heard they're considering a week or two of foreign travel. His wife mentioned something to mine regarding a Caribbean cruise when Christmas rolls around."

"Tell us about this summer camp," I said. "When does construction begin?"

"It's already underway," the sheriff said. "The slab was poured day before yesterday. Our architect, a local man, found a line of pre-fabricated structures which will speed things up, allowing us to hold the first two camps in August if the weather cooperates."

He pushed away from the table, got to his feet, and walked into the room Erin had called the office, talking over his shoulder as he went.

"The architect left us a set of drawings if I can find them."

Erin caught my attention from across the table with a subtle bob of her head. She shrugged and whispered, "Sorry."

Moments later Sheriff Thomas reappeared with a long cardboard mailing tube in his hands. After removing several rolled-up sheets of paper, he unfurled the one on top and spread it over the conference table in front of us.

"This here is a rendering of the new building from the front," he said.

We all learned forward to better see the illustration. It portrayed a single-story metal structure with a deep porch extending across the front. Neither overly ugly nor especially attractive, it was—in a word—utilitarian. Above the double-door entrance and under the gable were the words: **Francis Marion Memorial Camp**. Erin was quite interested in the rendering, no surprise since she'd made a major contribution for the project. She lifted the page and studied it for seconds, her eyes skimming across the paper.

"It's plain yet practical," she said, "but I like it. Are there interior sketches we can see?"

Sheriff Thomas sorted through the remaining sheets, removed one, and placed it before Erin.

"This shows three different views," he said. "Here's the lobby," pointing to a corner of the paper. "You'll also see one of the three classrooms along with a small lecture hall which will seat 40 guests."

Thomas then showed us a drawing of the sleeping quarters.

"We can host 30 campers at a time," he said. "Girls one week, followed by the boys. Each camper will have a bed, desk, and locker. Next summer, we'll schedule multiple sessions."

The final illustration Thomas spread in front of us was a detailed architectural schematic for the kitchen. Erin reviewed it, nodding as she went.

"If my memory's right," she said, "one of the classrooms will double as the cafeteria."

"That combination will save us a chunk of money," Thomas said.

At my request, the sheriff led us outside and a short distance down a slight incline to the freshly-poured concrete slab. Surrounded by stakes and forms, its surface was interrupted by a series of short vertical stubs allowing the plumbing to be finished at a later date. A large assortment of material on pallets had been placed to the side.

Sheriff Thomas noticed my gaze.

"Those are the prefabricated walls," he said. "We'll give the concrete another 48 hours to cure, and the crew will begin installation. I'm told it'll be in the dry in a matter of days. Less than a week for sure."

On the horizon beyond the foundation, the deep green forests of the Ozark Mountains seemed to be stacked in layers, the most distant disappearing into the afternoon haze. The distinctive "bob white" calls of northern quail could be heard from a hillside behind us. It was, I decided, a fine place to build a camp.

"The pasture to the left will serve as a septic field for the new building," the sheriff said.

He pivoted and pointed across the slope in the opposite direction toward a large earthen berm.

"There's the dam for our five-acre pond. It'll provide a perfect swimming hole for the campers. The fishing's pretty good, too."

Once we returned to the house, the sheriff locked the doors.

"Thanks for the tour," I said. "It's time for us to head back to Little Rock."

We closed the gate behind us, and Erin secured it with the padlock.

As he neared a pickup with a "Marion County Sheriff's Department" decal on the door, Sheriff Thomas stopped and faced Erin.

"There's something I want you to see."

He opened the passenger-side door, reached for an envelope, and handed it to her.

"I think you'll find this interesting. It arrived in the morning mail."

Erin removed the contents and began examining what appeared to be a page of correspondence. As her eyes widened and her chin dropped, she looked to the sheriff.

"Is this for real?" she asked.

She waved a slender piece of paper at him.

"This cashier's check?"

He gave her a big grin.

"Yes, ma'am. An anonymous donor from Kansas heard about our plans for the Francis Marion Memorial Camp and pledged to match the fundraising campaign dollar-for-dollar. The check in your hand is the first installment."

My immediate thought was someone in the Koch family, the ultra-conservative and politically active clan based in Wichita, had forwarded the donation.

"It's for over $125,000," Erin said, still shaking her head in amazement.

"That's equal to your original donation combined with other contributions," the sheriff said. "Together they give us in excess of a quarter of a million dollars to get the building up, furnished, and put in operation."

Megan looked at me, her eyebrows raised, when Erin's gift was mentioned.

"Later," I mouthed.

"A quarter of a million dollars," Erin said, shaking her head. "It's unbelievable."

I was thinking the same thing.

After another round of handshakes, the sheriff slid into his truck and drove off, waving from the open window as he left. We climbed into Megan's car and followed his trail of dust to the state highway where Megan turned south toward Little Rock.

~ TWENTY ~

I phoned Leslie once we were on the highway and told her I'd be home around seven o'clock.

"I'll have a special dinner ready when you arrive," she said. "Also, our landscape architect e-mailed me her estimate for the job we discussed."

"How bad is it?"

"She came in $500 under our budget."

"That's welcome news."

"I felt the same," she said, "and have already replied, accepting her bid."

The smell of frying bacon greeted me as I stepped inside the front door a couple of hours later. I found Leslie in the kitchen hovering over a skillet, and kissed her on the back of the neck.

"BLTs made with heirloom tomatoes, the first of the season, are tonight's surprise," she said, giving me a wide grin. "I was shooting at the farmers' market this morning and snagged a sack of them."

She knew I'd been salivating at the chance to sample the deep red, meaty, and incredibly delicious tomatoes. The sandwiches were perfect, worth the long wait. Wonderful enough I opted for a second.

During dinner we shared our day's activities. I learned she'd photographed the latest exhibits inside the Historic Arkansas Museum in addition to her work in the farmers' market. I updated her on the trip to Yellville, concluding with the nerve-wracking experience we'd had at the Flyover Family compound.

"You're serious?" she asked, her mouth gaping. "The local sheriff held you at gunpoint?"

"Only for a short time," I said. "Erin came to my rescue. And Sheriff Thomas apologized."

"What about their facilities?"

"The group's headquartered in a large two-story frame house," I said. "Men sleep upstairs; women down. I couldn't overlook a Confederate flag in standing in one corner of their main meeting room."

Leslie rolled her eyes.

"Any progress on their summer camp for kids?"

"The foundation's been poured, and the exterior work begins soon," I said. "It's a prefabricated building and will go up in days. If things proceed according to plans, they'll host their first batch of campers before the summer's over."

"We need to get Booker back in his search mode."

"Erin also learned her original donation has been matched by an anonymous source from Kansas," I said, "bringing the total contributions to over a quarter of a million dollars."

"That's scary," she said. "Very scary."

Since Leslie had prepared dinner, I volunteered to clean the kitchen and load the dishwasher. When I returned to the dining room ten minutes later, she was seated at the table facing a large open cardboard box. Various pieces and parts were spread in front of her, and she appeared to be skimming a manual of some sort.

She turned to face me, her eyes sparkling. "My drone arrived this afternoon."

I looked over her shoulder at the strange array covering much of the table. I spotted what appeared to be plastic propellers, several batteries, a pair of landing skids, an antenna, a frame, something resembling a control box, and a multitude of smaller items of an undetermined nature.

"It's still daylight," I said. "Want to step outside and give it a spin?"

Leslie shook her head.

"It'd take an hour to assemble everything and charge the battery pack. I'll watch a tutorial—maybe two or three—on YouTube before taking it for a test flight."

"Isn't a federal permit required to operate a drone?"

"Hobbyists can get on the internet and register for a nominal charge," Leslie said. "Folks like me, using drones for commercial purposes, operate under different rules."

"Does this involve a test or exam?"

"It's going to require serious study," she said with a nod. "I've read the online test takes half an hour, and, once I pass, I'll receive my official certificate."

Leslie handed me a piece of paper.

"Here are the basic regulations."

I scanned down the sheet. It was a list of common-sense rules: flying at 400 feet or below; keeping the drone within sight; not operating in restricted airspace, near airports, or over stadiums or other sporting events; not flying near emergency response situations; and, of course, not flying while under the influence.

"The exam worries me a bit," she said, flashing a rare grimace. "I haven't dealt with a real test since my senior year in college."

"If you flunk it," I said with a wink, "I'll buy the entire package for $500. Cash. I've always wanted to be a pilot."

Leslie was not amused.

* * *

I'd been in the office almost an hour the next morning when Erin walked in and gave me a thin sheaf of papers.

"Here's the contact information you requested on Junior Judson, the former major league baseball player," she said. "I've also included his entry from Wikipedia. Not a true Yellville native, Judson was born a short distance to the north in the community of Summit, not too far beyond Hillcountry Marine's factory."

"Was I right?" I asked. "He's retired and living in Florida or Arizona?"

143

"Somewhere about halfway in between," she said, giving me a grin. "His home's in Hot Springs Village, less than an hour from here."

Surprised with this news, I thanked Erin. As I reviewed the material she left with me, my cell rang. It was Leslie.

"My afternoon's clear," she said. "What would you think if I threw a rack of baby back ribs on the grill?"

"Sounds like an ideal way to get a jump start on our weekend."

"Why don't you call Joan Pfeiffer and ask her to dinner tonight? I haven't seen my favorite state representative in weeks."

Two minutes later, I was on the phone with Joan, apologizing for the late notice while inviting her to our home for barbecue ribs.

"I'm delighted to accept," she said, "if you'll let me bring a guest. Senator Somer Smith."

"Of course! Leslie's been wanting to meet him."

"Somer agreed to a speaking engagement in town tomorrow evening, and we'd discussed getting together for dinner tonight. Your invitation is perfect!"

"We'll see you sixish. And this is backyard casual," I said. "No suits, ties, or heels."

Next, I called Junior Judson, explaining I owned a Little Rock advertising agency and hoped to visit with him regarding a potential endorsement deal involving Hillcountry Marine.

"Sure," he said without the slightest hesitation, surprising me. "I'd be pleased to discuss it with you. Strangely enough, I was born within a stone's throw of their headquarters, but seldom get back since my parents died twenty-odd years ago. In fact, I've never met the owners."

"It's owned by the Boddington family," I said. "Good folks from the area."

"Any chance you can come down Saturday morning?" he asked. "My wife and I leave soon for a two-week vacation in South America."

I entered Judson's address into my cell phone and took notes on dealing with the guards at the entrance to Hot Springs Village.

"Make sure to arrive through the East Gate," he said. "It's the closest one to Little Rock, off Highway 5. I'll alert the guardhouse to expect you around nine o'clock."

I left the office a couple of hours earlier than usual, figuring Leslie would appreciate my help getting the place ready for dinner guests. She was removing a blackberry cobbler from the oven as I stepped inside. When I mentioned I'd be going to Hot Springs Village first thing Saturday morning for an appointment with a baseball all-star, she suggested we make a day of it.

"While you're negotiating with your famous athlete, I'll take stock shots in the Village," she said. "Once your meeting with Mr. Judson's done, let's drive into Hot Springs. There's a brewpub I want to shoot. I'll photograph the establishment and you can sample the products."

It was an offer I couldn't refuse.

After changing into more comfortable clothing, I began preparing my homemade baked beans and setting the table. Leslie tended to the ribs, made a potato salad, and sliced two of the huge heritage tomatoes.

Joan and Senator Smith arrived a little before six, smiling and carrying a paper bag as they climbed the steps to the front porch. I led them through the house to the smoky patio where Leslie stood at the grill, basting the ribs. Once Leslie and Joan finished their hugs, I introduced Senator Smith and Leslie which resulted in another round of warm embraces.

"Your ribs smell wonderful," Somer said, presenting us with two bottles of wine.

One was an Oregon Cabernet Sauvignon and the other a Syrah from Chile. I opened both. Never much of a believer in the practice of allowing wine to breathe, I poured four glasses, the women opting for the Oregon vintage while Somer and I sampled the Syrah.

Swirling the beautiful ruby-red liquid in my goblet for a moment, I offered a toast: "To Joan and Somer: two shining stars in the Arkansas legislature."

We clinked our wineglasses together. I then motioned to the quartet of patio chairs upwind from the grill and we took seats.

"Your analogy is flattering," Joan said, taking a sip. "However, to carry it a bit further, I fear your two so-called stars—shining or not—are about to be swallowed by a black hole."

"Much as I hate to admit it, our state seems to be regressing," Somer said. "In my short time serving in the General Assembly, I've seen a disturbing decline in human civility. Bipartisanship is a thing of the past."

"It's not just among our fellow members in the legislature," Joan said, "but across our culture in general. 'Social media,'" and at this point she made quote marks in the air with her fingers, "may be the undoing of our country. Earlier this afternoon, Somer received a particularly vile message."

Leslie and I turned to the senator.

"All members of the House and Senate are provided official e-mail addresses so we can stay in touch with constituents," he said. "It's not unusual to get negative feedback and much of it can be quite harsh, even vicious. But the item Joan referred to ..." He paused, swallowed a sip of wine, and shook his head.

"Can you elaborate?" I asked.

"First, let me give you a bit of background," he said. "You may have seen the occasional piece in the national news concerning reparations for slavery. Certain members of Congress have broached this controversial subject now and again, and task forces in two states—California and Illinois—are looking into the issue."

"This isn't a new topic, is it?" Leslie asked. "Don't I remember from my American history classes the newly-freed African-American slaves were led to believe they'd get '40 acres and a mule' at the end of the Civil War?"

Somer nodded. "Those words can be traced back to a field order issued by General William Sherman upon completion of his infamous march to the sea from Atlanta. His order was reversed by President Andrew Johnson after Lincoln's assassination. Then came Reconstruction, to be followed by decades and decades of discrimination and even worse during the Jim Crow era."

"And the question of reparations went by the wayside?" I asked.

"For the most part," Somer said, "although a handful of my constituents have asked me to propose a reparations bill for consideration by the Arkansas Senate."

He took another swallow of his Syrah.

"But I haven't, and I won't."

"Somer and I've spent hours discussing this situation," Joan said, "and he's developed what I believe is a reasonable position."

"Reasonable to a few, maybe," Somer said with a chuckle. "It seems to me financial compensation would have been appropriate for those actual slaves who were freed well over a century and a half ago. In effect, paid for their years of labor."

He paused and ran a hand over his beard.

"Giving government handouts to their descendants six, seven, or eight generations later is something I can't support."

"And it certainly wouldn't be accepted by our fellow legislators," Joan said. "We'd be laughed out of the State Capitol chambers."

Noticing the four wine glasses were nearing empty, I refilled them all.

"Don't get me wrong," Somer said. "I remain convinced we can take productive measures to counter the pervasive injustices in society. Things such as targeted educational opportunities, workforce training, and small business development grants, to name three."

"Before we hear details on the disgusting message you mentioned," Leslie said, "I believe our main course is ready to be served."

While Leslie removed the ribs from the grill, I led our guests inside. Next, Leslie and I placed the dinner dishes on the table.

As we gathered in the dining room, Somer asked, "May I give thanks?"

Following his short but sincere prayer, we sat around the table.

"Bon appetit," Leslie said, passing the platter of ribs to Joan.

"Now, where were we?" I asked before spooning a serving of baked beans onto my plate.

"It appears a small group of vocal malcontents in my district has placed me in their sights," Somer said, shaking his head. "They've given me a nickname—'Reparations Smith'—and have posted my home address, e-mail address, and telephone number on the internet. I've been inundated by dozens of hateful calls and notes, to include the one Joan referred to."

"Even though you haven't introduced legislation dealing with reparations?" I asked.

"And I have no intention of doing so," he said. "I'd have a better chance of the Vatican naming me Pope Somerset the First than I'd have getting a reparations bill passed in Arkansas."

He paused and looked to Leslie.

"These may be the best ribs I've ever eaten," he said. "And I've put away more than my share over the years."

"The meat is falling off the bone," Joan said. "They're wonderful."

"Looks like it's time for more," Leslie said, passing the platter.

"Back to the faction targeting you," I said. "Have you been able to identify it?"

"I suspect the ringleader is the same man I defeated in the primary election three years ago. A local ne'er-do-well named Buck McFadden," he said, sliding another serving onto his plate.

"Do you know for certain he's responsible?" Leslie asked.

"I haven't caught McFadden with his hand in the cookie jar," Somer said with a shrug. "During the last election, though, his campaign materials were filled with typos. And the matter Joan mentioned earlier continues his tradition, misspelling the word 'reparations.' Twice."

~ TWENTY-ONE ~

"Back to your favorite reprobate," I said, looking to Somer. "What's McFadden's latest act?"

Somer placed his fork beside the plate, reached into a back pocket, and removed his cell phone. He scrolled down the screen for 10 to 15 seconds and then stopped and handed it to me. "Here it is." His jaw was clinched and his eyes were moist.

I gazed at the image on his phone, noting it resembled a primitive editorial cartoon. A large tree, its limbs leafless, stood alone on a barren slope. Tacked to the thick trunk was a sign reading "Repparations Tree," misspelled as Somer had mentioned. A black-and-white photograph of State Senator Somerset Spartacus Smith had been crudely inserted onto the illustration. The man in the picture was unmistakably Somer, although a label identifying him as "Senator Repparations Smith" had been attached to his torso to make the point clear. A rope noose circled his neck, and his body dangled from a massive limb. The photograph of Somer had been altered, leaving his head tilted at an awkward angle to show what could only be a broken neck. I grimaced and felt the hair on my neck rise.

"My god," I said. "This is disgusting."

Leslie extended a hand over the table.

"May I see it?"

I passed her Somer's phone, shaking my head.

Leslie gasped, her chin dropping.

"I can't believe this," she said as she returned the phone to Somer. Her hand was trembling. "I'm so sorry …"

"Somer shared it with the security team at the Capitol and the Arkansas State Police," Joan said. "We're not sure if there's anything else we can do."

"One thing we can do is change the subject," Somer said. "To something a bit more positive."

"Would a homemade blackberry cobbler fit the bill?" Leslie asked. "I bought a quart of berries at the farmers' market yesterday."

"I cannot think of a better idea," he said, with a big grin. "Please feel free to make mine a generous serving."

While I cleared the table, Leslie prepared our desserts, topping each bowl of cobbler with a scoop of vanilla ice cream. Somer's was the largest of the lot.

After his second or third bite, Somer turned to me.

"Randy," he said. "You are one lucky man. Your beautiful wife grilled the best ribs I've ever eaten, and then produced this amazing cobbler."

"No argument there," I said. "She often reminds me of my good fortune."

"As well she should," Joan added.

"I understand you're also a professional photographer," Somer said to my blushing bride. "Randy pointed out a collection of marvelous shots as we walked through your home."

I'd surprised Leslie months earlier by having a dozen of her favorite magazine covers framed, hanging them in the hallway. A trio from *Southern Living*, a pair from *Garden & Gun*, and one from *Outside* were among the impressive display.

"She also takes fabulous portraits," Joan said. "Leslie's the source of the photograph of me you admired in my office."

"I'll need a new head shot before the next election," Somer said, looking to Leslie. "Would you be willing to do it?"

"Of course," Leslie said. "We can take a portrait and maybe get an assortment of candid photos of you talking with constituents."

Once the desserts were eaten, we adjourned to the living room for coffee. Somer and Joan took turns regaling us with stories involving experiences with their fellow legislators.

"I recall a trip to Washington during my first term," Somer said. "Three of us in the Senate had gone up for a national energy conference. After dinner on the second day, we decided to visit Georgetown where we wandered into a popular pub for cocktails. We'd been there 30 minutes or so, enjoying the music, and were well into our second or third round of drinks when we realized we'd entered a gay bar."

"It took you half an hour to figure that out?" Joan asked, incredulous.

"Needless to say, we weren't at our sharpest," Somer said. "Anyway, I feel a tap on my shoulder. I turn around and there's this tall, handsome white man. He looks at me and says, 'Would you care to dance?'"

There was a long and awkward pause.

"What did you do?" Leslie finally asked for all of us.

"Well, I'm shocked and look to my colleagues, both of whom had heard the invitation. One of them is dumbstruck, but the other, a known homophobe, is itching for a confrontation. You could see it in his face."

Somer shook his head and took a sip of coffee.

"Go on," Joan says. "Let's hear the rest of this story."

"I get to my feet, look this well-dressed stranger in the eye, and say, 'Why, yes, I believe I would.'" Somer laughed and slapped his thigh. "And that was that; one brief dance with a gay guy for this straight man."

"The bigot didn't create a scene?" I asked.

"He muttered something under his breath and stormed from the bar."

Somer took another swallow of his coffee.

"Yet the most memorable part of the evening happened after midnight as my fellow senator and I made our way back to the hotel. We instructed the cabbie to stop at the famous reflecting pool. My colleague, who shall go nameless, was quite intoxicated by this time, and tumbled face-first into the water."

"My gosh," Joan said. "Was he injured?"

"With the help of the park police, we fished him out. He ruined a suit, trashed his heirloom pocket watch, and lost his phone but was otherwise unharmed."

"Is this unnamed individual still in the legislature?" Leslie asked.

"He's now serving as president pro tempore of the Arkansas Senate."

I thought about the prestigious title Somer had just mentioned and connected it with a prominent name.

"Isn't he the very senator who professes to be a righteous tee-totaler?" I asked. "And chairs the legislature's Christian caucus?"

"Right on both counts." Somer smiled and nodded his head. "The one and the same."

"Believe it or not," Joan said, "he and Somer have become good buddies."

Somer chuckled. "She's right. Despite our differences, he's my closest friend in the entire state senate."

Before Joan and Somer left, Somer pulled a business card from his wallet and gave it to Leslie. "Drop me a note when you have time and we'll schedule those shots."

* * *

As I drove to the office a little after 7:00 the next morning, I crossed Capitol Avenue, spotting the marble dome of the State Capitol gleaming in the bright morning light. Recalling the previous night's conversation with Joan and Somer, I wondered for a moment about the future of our state, the future of the entire country. Was the democracy envisioned by our founding fathers at peril?

But those troubling thoughts vanished once I stepped inside the front door to Lassiter & Associates and worried instead over the continued solvency of my advertising agency. When Erin and Megan appeared an hour into the work day with smiles on their faces, my mind relaxed a tad. Erin handed me a folder, explaining it contained everything I needed to know concerning Junior Judson's highlights in the major leagues. And then Megan reported she and our staff artist had finalized a suggested design for Hillcountry Marine's portable booth. All we needed was a signed contract with Del Boddington and his approval, and the booth would be delivered in time for use at the national trade show later in the year. Two tidbits of good news. Not a bad way to start the day.

Constance Engstrom, director of the Little Rock Zoo, called mid-morning and surprised me with an invitation to lunch.

"Let's meet at the Arkansas Museum of Fine Arts," she said. "The new chef at their Park Grill is amazing."

Although wary of Constance's motives, I accepted her offer, having heard rave reviews regarding this newcomer to the city's culinary scene.

As was her usual M.O., Constance ran late, 15 minutes on this occasion. I was making a second pass through the gift shop when I felt a hand on my elbow.

"Sorry for the delay," she said, giving me an air kiss. "I'm starving."

After we'd been seated, Constance said, "Thanks for fitting me into your schedule. I've been wanting to visit with you for several days now."

I studied the woman sitting across the table from me, wondering why she'd requested this meeting.

She must have read my mind.

"The sole purpose of today's lunch is to thank you for all the time and effort your agency has invested in the zoo. No ulterior motives. None whatsoever."

I managed to hide my shock.

"It's our pleasure," I said, stumbling for a reply. "Most of the staff who are involved with your account have young children, and it provides them with a way to explain their jobs. They say they work for the zoo, and the kids beam."

The waiter took our drink orders and left copies of the lunch menu with us.

"Any insights you can reveal on this chef?" I asked. "Is he a local?"

"First," Constance said, "the chef is a young woman. She's African-American, hails from Dumas in southeast Arkansas, and her name is Althea Etienne. She got her start with the CIA."

I set the menu aside and looked to my host.

"The CIA? You're kidding, right?"

"I had the same response," she said, enjoying my reaction. "Until learning CIA refers to the Culinary Institute of America. Ms. Etienne's training also includes stints in Chicago and San Francisco and more recently in New Orleans where she was sous-chef at one of the city's most famous restaurants."

"In that case," I said, "I'll ask for the Creole catfish."

It proved to be an excellent choice. And my lunch conversation with Constance proved to be quite productive, much to my surprise. I learned her younger brother owned a large resort on Lake Ouachita outside Hot Springs and had been involved with the state's hospitality community for years. When I mentioned Lassiter & Associates might bid for the state's tourism account, she volunteered to introduce us.

"I'm sure Charlie will be delighted to disclose his insights on the travel industry," she said. "It often seems he'd rather talk about nothing else."

In fact, after she presented her credit card to the waiter, Constance pulled out her phone and e-mailed her brother, copying me in the process. I felt my phone vibrate.

Thanking her for lunch, I escorted Constance to her car and got another air kiss next to my cheek.

* * *

When I returned to the office, I saw a young man perched on the side of Erin's desk, engaged in a conversation with her.

Erin saw me approaching and stood.

"Randy," she said, "I'd like you to meet my friend, Alex Motherwell."

As he got to his feet and extended a hand, I noticed he was tall with a thick head of dark brown hair and a full beard and mustache. His grip was solid.

"Randy Lassiter," I said. "Pleased to meet you."

"Alex was in the neighborhood doing research at the State Archives," Erin said, "and decided to stop by for a quick chat."

"Doing some genealogical investigations?" I asked. "I've always been afraid to discover the secrets lurking in the branches of my family tree."

He shook his head.

"Simply looking at old architectural drawings of the State Capitol Building."

"Erin mentioned you work for an engineering outfit," I said. "Is your firm bidding on a job involving the Capitol?"

There was a moment's hesitation in his response.

"It's not business-related," he said. "I've always … uh … had a strong personal interest in historic buildings, especially iconic structures such as the State Capitol."

"It was good to meet you," I said and stepped into my office, closing the door behind me.

Something about my brief conversation with Alex Motherwell bothered me, and I decided to phone Uncle Booker. He answered at once.

"Another call from the dear nephew," he said. "Whatever could it be this time?"

"Alex Motherwell is in our building," I said, "talking at the moment with Erin."

"Why has this young man entered our fair city?"

"He claims to have spent time earlier today in the State Archives."

"The archives would seem to be an unusual destination for an engineer involved in the construction industry," Booker said. "You'd think he might gravitate toward the Arkansas Building Authority or the Office of State Procurement."

"My thoughts exactly."

"Did he offer details on the rationale for his visit?"

"Motherwell said he was looking at the original architectural renderings for the State Capitol Building. He implied it was a hobby of sorts."

Booker responded with a protracted, "Hmmm." After a long pause, he said, "Let me contemplate on this matter a while, and I'll get back to you."

~ TWENTY-TWO ~

At 7:30 the next morning, Leslie and I were on our way to Hot Springs Village with a later stop planned for Hot Springs itself. We'd been on the road less than five minutes when Leslie turned to me.

"Are Joan and Senator Smith an item?" she asked.

"You're curious if they're dating?"

She nodded.

"Hmm," I said. "That thought's never occurred to me. I assume they're good friends, and nothing more. Why do you ask?"

"Although I saw no outright signs of affection, I caught the occasional significant glance between them. My female intuition tells me something is going on."

I considered Leslie's comments.

"They're both single, have similar political beliefs, are close in age, and make a handsome couple," I said. "Maybe you're right. I'll quiz Joan next time I see her."

"Randy Lassiter," Leslie said, shaking her head. "You will do nothing of the sort. We'll observe things from a respectable distance, letting them share the news—if there is any—when they're good and ready."

The friendly guards at the east gate to Hot Springs Village were expecting us, waving us through after providing directions to Junior Judson's home.

"It's a beautiful place made of native stone," one of them had said. "Mr. Judson's house sits on a large corner lot overlooking Lake Balboa."

"There's the answer to your earlier question about my plans as you make the sales pitch to the baseball star," Leslie said. "As you know, I brought my camera gear. I'll take photos around the lakeshore."

Lake Balboa was bigger than I expected, several hundred acres at least, and its deep blue surface was dotted with fishing boats, a handful of canoes, a couple of sailboats, and even a few youngsters on paddleboards. The steep green ridges of the Ouachita Mountains could be seen rising in the distance beyond the marina.

"This is perfect," Leslie said as I parked on the road in front of the Judson home. "I'll wander along the shoreline while you two visit."

I trudged up the lengthy, steep sidewalk leading to the house and rang the doorbell. Mr. Judson met me on his front porch with a welcoming grin and a firm handshake.

"Come in, come in," he said, steering me inside and past a pair of oversized suitcases placed near the door. "As you can see, my wife and I are packed and ready to head out first thing this afternoon. We've been waiting for years to tour the Galapagos. A trip of a lifetime, we're told. I'd introduce you, but she's having coffee with a neighbor."

Judson led me through the spacious home into what he called "my personal retreat." Maybe 15 feet by 20 and lined with display cases, the room housed an enormous collection of baseball memorabilia—uniforms, caps, cleats, pennants, autographed balls, gloves, an assortment of bats, numerous trophies, and dozens of framed photographs, articles, and posters.

"My favorite glove and bat are on display at Cooperstown," he said, referring to the National Baseball Hall of Fame in upstate New York.

He reached into a rack mounted on the wall, removed a black bat, and handed it to me. A Louisville Slugger, it was battle-scarred with countless scuff marks along the barrel.

"I used this bat to drive in five runs when we swept the Red Sox during the playoffs my final year."

I thought back to the information Erin had given me on Judson's career.

"I believe you had a pair of doubles to go along with a tape-measure home run that weekend," I said.

Judson smiled and slapped me on the back. "You've made an old man happy, young feller!"

I took a couple of easy swings with it, remembering my glory days as a Little Leaguer.

"This is the first bat I've held in the past 20 years," I said.

Judson looked me in the eye. "Feels pretty good, doesn't it?"

"Yes sir," I admitted. "It feels damn good."

After we'd made a cursory tour through his other mementos, he took a seat in a recliner opposite a large television and pointed me to a nearby easy chair.

"Mr. Lassiter," he said, "the floor is yours. Let's hear this proposal."

"Please call me Randy," I said, handing him a business card. "My advertising agency hopes to land Hillcountry Marine as a client, and we'd like you to be a celebrity spokesman for their brand of boats."

"A spokesman," he said as a frown appeared. "Would this involve giving speeches?"

I shook my head.

"Maybe a better choice of words would be 'celebrity representative.' You'd appear at trade shows, signing autographs and posing for pictures."

"I'm not sure what you mean by trade shows."

"The recreational boating industry has two main exhibitions for consumers each year," I said. "One every spring and the other in the fall. They rotate these national shows among major convention cities. Dallas and Minneapolis hosted the last two; Las Vegas and Chicago are next on the schedule."

"So, I'd be mingling with baseball fans, to include parents and their kids?"

"And doing the infrequent media appearance," I said. "We'd try to book radio interviews on the local drive-time sports shows when that's an option."

"Let's cut to the chase. What's in it for me?"

"We'd fly you and your wife to the shows, business class coming and going, and place you in nice hotel suites. Plus, we'll give you a $2500 cash stipend per show for meals and other incidentals."

Judson shrugged, plainly not impressed.

"To be honest, the cash and travel arrangements aren't much of an incentive. It seems I've spent half my life in hotels and eating restaurant food."

"We thought that might be the case," I said. "To sweeten the deal, we'll trailer a new Hillcountry Marine boat to Hot Springs Village for your exclusive use, docking it at the marina you can see from your front porch. In addition, we'll cover insurance, licensing, and the slip fee. We'll furnish a new boat every January as long as you're under contract. Take your pick: a fishing boat, runabout, or party barge. And—"

"You had me at party barge," he said, waving his hands and interrupting me, his eyes alive and sparkling. "Now you're talking. We moved here from Florida a year ago, and my wife's been pestering me to get us back on the water. Throw in an ice chest and a pair of life vests with the party barge and we have a deal."

We stood and shook hands.

"It's been a pleasure getting acquainted," I said. "Once the agency finalizes its agreement with Hillcountry Marine, we'll send you a contract to sign. It should be in the mail when you return from your trip."

I followed Judson through the house and out the door onto the front porch. He stopped and pointed toward the street.

"Good lord," he muttered. "There's a young woman breaking into your truck!"

He yanked his cell phone from a pocket and began dialing 9-1-1 before I could react.

"No need to call anyone," I said, touching him on the shoulder. "That's my wife."

After he cancelled the call, Judson stared at me, waiting for an explanation.

160

"She's a professional photographer," I said, "and chose to take pictures around the lake while you and I talked."

He sighed and slipped his phone back into his pants.

"Thank God," he said. "We've gone 17 days in the village without an incident on the police log, and I didn't want to break our streak."

We shook hands again, and I then trotted down the long sidewalk and caught up with Leslie.

"How'd it go?" she asked.

"Mr. Judson's onboard," I said. "Now all we lack is a contract between Lassiter & Associates and Hillcountry Marine. And I hope to have it signed in the next ten days."

As we climbed into the truck, I turned to Leslie. "What about you?"

"I got a useful assortment of stock shots, including a nice portrait of a great blue heron. Once I gain experience flying my new drone, this'll be a great place to revisit."

"Any timeframe for its inaugural flight?"

"Maybe tomorrow," she said, giving me a wink.

Twenty minutes later, we'd found a parking space on Central Avenue in downtown Hot Springs across from the Superior Bathhouse Brewery. While Leslie interviewed the owner and took a series of photos, I sampled a flight of beers before settling on a fine pale ale to go with my steak sandwich. I also texted a note to Megan, explaining I'd enjoyed a productive session with Junior Judson and our proposed partnership with the Major League All-Star was a done deal.

Leslie joined me as I put away my phone.

"I had no idea this is the world's only beer brewed with thermal spring water," she said. "Or it's the sole brewery in a national park."

I held up my half-empty glass.

"I can vouch for the pale."

~ TWENTY-THREE ~

Following our Sunday morning church service, Leslie and I enjoyed a fine lunch of leftover barbecued ribs.

As we put away the dishes, Leslie asked, "Are you ready to witness Amelia's maiden launch?"

Staring at my bride, I shook my head.

"I'm sorry, but you've left me clueless. Who is Amelia?"

"Amelia is the name I've chosen for my drone," she said, giving me a wink. "In honor of Amelia Earhart, of course. After reviewing the manual backwards and forward and watching three YouTube videos, I'm eager for a test flight. The batteries charged overnight and current weather conditions are perfect: clear skies and no wind."

Half an hour later found us on the manicured grounds of MacArthur Park, an urban oasis in our neighborhood that includes the historic Little Rock Arsenal where General Douglas MacArthur was born almost 150 years ago, the Arkansas Museum of Fine Arts, and acres upon acres of open space.

I suggested a vacant picnic table near the center of the park, but Leslie favored a remote bench along its eastern edge.

"There are no people or pets in the immediate vicinity," she said, leading us to it where she placed the box holding Amelia.

While Leslie spent a couple of minutes studying our surroundings, taking in the vegetation, power lines, pavilions, and park visitors, I gazed at the arsenal building, noting the massive oaks standing to its sides. I remembered reading about spectators climb-

162

ing trees around the ancient brick structure many decades ago to witness the hanging of David O. Dodd, the young Confederate spy, and wondered if limbs of these old trees had provided vantage points for that terrible spectacle.

"This should work," she said, interrupting my strange reverie, "as long as I can avoid the big pond."

She nodded toward a body of water some 50 yards away. Leslie then opened the carton and began assembling her small aircraft. I watched her install batteries and insert a memory card. She next checked the camera settings and made certain all four propellers were securely attached.

Taking a deep breath, she smiled at me and said, "We're good to go."

"How can I help?" I asked.

"Two things," Leslie said.

She tossed me a long cardboard tube she'd removed from her box.

"First, unfurl this landing pad and position it 10 to 12 feet in front of our bench."

"Landing pad?" I asked. "Are you serious?"

The bright orange pad, 30 or so inches in diameter and made of a thick plastic material, was weighted along its edge. In the center was a large black H—no doubt for Helicopter—enclosed by a circle. I started to ask if a big D for Drone wouldn't be more appropriate, but opted to remain silent.

"I caught your hint of a smirk," she said. "But the pad keeps twigs, grass, dust, and other debris from damaging the propellers or smudging the camera lens."

"That makes sense," I said, giving her a nod. I arranged the mat on the ground as directed. "You said two things. What else?"

"Your primary job is to be my spotter," she said. "You're my second set of eyes."

Leslie placed Amelia in the center of the landing pad. She returned to the bench and reached for what I assumed was a control box.

"This is the remote transmitter," she said. "Wish me luck."

I stood behind her as she powered up the drone. With the four propellers spinning feverishly, it rose above the ground, pausing as it reached chest high where it remained for maybe 15 seconds. After Amelia rotated once, Leslie guided her down where she settled on the pad. She repeated this exercise three more times without incident, increasing the drone's elevation a few feet on each occasion.

"So far, so good! This is amazing!"

Her eyes were as bright as I'd ever seen them.

"See the trash can over there," she said, nodding toward it. "My goal is to fly around it twice."

Concentrating on the controls, Leslie piloted Amelia from the pad to a height of eight feet or so before directing her toward the litter barrel. The drone circled the can once, then again, and turned toward us. Halfway back, it jerked sideways for a few feet before hurtling into a sidewalk.

"Dang!" Leslie dashed to the downed drone and retrieved it, examining Amelia from top to bottom.

"I got confused, pushed the wrong lever, and caused the crash, snapping one of the propellers."

She held the aircraft so I could see the broken part.

"Good thing I have a sack of spares."

Trotting back to the bench, Leslie removed the busted piece, replacing it in less than a minute.

For the next hour, Leslie gained experience and confidence, flying Amelia higher and further, while I kept a close eye on the drone. Her landings and takeoffs were things of beauty—smooth, controlled, and gentle. She had two more minor mishaps, neither of which caused any damage. She guided the drone above my truck and then up and over the Little Rock Arsenal building, laughing in delight, as she returned it to the landing pad.

"Amelia will transform my business," she said. "I'm watching video footage on the transmitter's screen, and it's spectacular. I can't believe I've waited this long to buy one."

"Are you ready to pilot Amelia over the pond?" I asked, pointing behind her.

Leslie halfway turned and looked past her shoulder. She rubbed her chin for a moment, met my gaze, and broke into a big smile.

"Heck yeah!"

"You're sure?" I asked. "Didn't Amelia Earhart crash somewhere in the Pacific, never to be found?"

"But she didn't have you for a spotter!"

I jogged across the lawn to the edge of the water and flashed Leslie the A-OK sign. A moment later, the drone lifted from the ground and flew my way, a good 12 to 15 feet above the grass. When Leslie added some altitude, I could scarcely hear the faint buzz. I gazed upward and watched Amelia soar over the middle of the pond where she hovered for a few seconds before returning to the landing pad.

Leslie had placed her drone in the carton and was storing the pad by the time I joined her. She tossed the cardboard tube aside, wrapped her arms around me, and kissed my cheek.

"This is so exciting," she said. "As soon as we get home, I'm getting online and will take the exam. And I should have my official certificate within a week!"

"Assuming, of course, you pass the test." I waggled my eyebrows.

Leslie grinned, mumbled what sounded like a disparaging comment on my ancestry, and pounded my chest with both fists. Tenderly. Sort of.

"Watch it, buster," she said. "I now have a personal air force at my disposal."

* * *

Monday morning found me at Lassiter & Associates bright and early. During the staff meeting, I mentioned the agency would be submitting a proposal to represent Hillcountry Marine. I saw Megan raise her hand from the back of the room and gave her a nod.

"Several of us worked together and knocked much of it out on Friday afternoon," she said. "I got inspired over the weekend and made a first cut at a draft," she said. "I've sent the file to you."

"I'll read it before the day's over," I said. "And thanks to all for the quick work on this."

Chantille got my attention and rose to speak.

"Our first session with students at David O. Dodd Elementary will be tomorrow afternoon. There'll be five of us participating, and we can carpool in my van, leaving at 1:30 on the dot. We'll return around 4:45."

I asked those who'd signed on as weekly tutors for the Dodd students to raise their hands and then thanked them for their civic-mindedness. Their colleagues gave them a warm round of applause.

Next on my morning agenda was the routine meeting with the agency's department heads to discuss progress on our future bid on the state tourism account. Abbie reported she'd located facilitators in both Dallas and Memphis willing to handle the focus group sessions for us later in the year.

"They'll rent facilities, conduct sessions, and submit detailed analyses along with video tapes of each gathering," she said. "Our responsibility is to provide the demographic profiles of the groups we want in the rooms along with questions regarding travel habits and preferences we'll need answered. And, of course, the artistic concepts we choose to test."

"What about the costs?" I asked.

"They came in under our budget in both cases," she said.

This was unexpected news. Maybe we had a chance at landing the account.

Following lunch, I spent a couple of hours reviewing the comprehensive marketing and brand development proposal Megan and her colleagues had prepared for Hillcountry Marine. As expected, she'd done a thorough and professional job. She and our chief media buyer had assembled a short list of trade publications to target with print ads. Working with the agency's art director, Megan had included information on producing an eight-panel promotional brochure and purchasing a portable exhibition booth for use at trade shows. Most of her efforts, though, had been directed at improving and expanding the company's website, with two-thirds of the recommended budget allocated to this category. My sole change was to add a page explaining the rationale for bringing in Junior Judson as a celebrity spokesman along with a list of his responsibilities and costs for his services.

In mid-afternoon, I forwarded the revised proposal to Megan for her comments. An hour later, I got her reply.

"Looks great! Who'd be a good account executive for Hillcountry Marine?"

"I'm leaning toward Harrison Davies," I replied, referring to one of our recent hires. "He's eager for new challenges, loves his work, and gets along well with everyone. And I suspect the large-mouth bass mounted on his office wall indicates he knows something about fishing."

"My thoughts exactly!" she replied. "He was a big help in preparing the draft. Let's send it."

After composing a compelling cover letter, I e-mailed the Lassiter & Associates proposal to Del Boddington at Hillcountry Marine.

* * *

Leslie was perched in our swing porch reading a magazine when I got home.

"This came in today's mail," she said, handing me a small envelope.

Our address had been written in fine penmanship.

"What is it?"

"A kind note from Joan."

I removed the card and began reading:

Dear Leslie & Randy,

Somer and I had a wonderful time at your home this past Friday. As we drove away, we agreed that Leslie's ribs were the best we'd ever eaten.

In fact, Somer and I had such a good time together, we've decided to start "dating"! Our enjoyable evening with you will go down in history as our first "official" date. Thanks so much!

Love,
Joan

P.S.—dinner next time will be at my place.

When I slipped the card back into the envelope and returned it to Leslie, I noticed her clever grin.

"Is there something you want to add?"

She gave me a slight nod.

"You may remember I spotted signs of this blossoming relationship Friday night."

"Some sort of woman-to-woman telepathy, if I recall."

"I believe 'female intuition' is the correct term."

~ TWENTY-FOUR ~

When I arrived at work Tuesday morning, I was surprised to see an e-mail from Del Boddington.

"Received your proposal," he wrote. "My wife and I met with Tabitha last night over dinner and discussed it. We're ready to sign the contract. Drop me a note and we'll schedule a meeting. Maybe Friday morning of this week?"

Once I'd confirmed both Megan and Harrison were available, I sent Del a message we'd be at Hillcountry Marine at 10:00 AM Friday.

"Looking forward to seeing you again," was his immediate reply.

Late Tuesday afternoon, Chantille and her fellow tutors returned from their initial mentoring session at David O. Dodd Elementary School. She stepped into my office, closing the door behind her.

"How'd it go?" I asked as we took our seats.

"The Lassiter team would have made you proud," she said. "Everybody was so patient and understanding and helpful. And the kids seemed genuinely attentive and grateful."

I studied Chantille's face. Something was bothering her. "What is it?"

"Call it a mother's insight," she said, "but I'd swear those kids are hungry, Randy. Not just for attention and knowledge but for bodily sustenance. You know, something to eat. Food."

I gazed at Chantille. A single mother working hard to raise her two cute kids. A woman who'd overcome one adversity after another. A person devoted to her community.

"What if the agency supplied snacks for the students?" I asked.

"You're serious? Lassiter & Associates could spring for healthy munchies?"

"We could commit, say, $5000 a year. Or $100 a week for a full year, minus the two weeks they get off for Christmas. Would this help?"

Chantille rose to her feet, scrambled around my desk, and wrapped her arms around my neck.

"It would make a huge difference," she said. "You have made my day."

I noticed tears in her eyes as she returned to her chair.

"We can get by with much less. A third or at most half of that will be plenty."

"I appreciate you taking the reins on this," I said. "It's for a good cause."

"I guarantee we'll provide nutritious snacks and drinks," she said. "No processed sugary stuff. I've found recipes for blueberry muffins, cinnamon chickpeas, and veggie pinwheels—treats my own picky children have sampled and approved."

"I'll let the folks in accounting know about this," I said.

"Tell 'em I'll be around every Friday with receipts."

Chantille gave me another heartwarming smile as she left my office.

* * *

Wednesday was not a red-letter day in the short history of Lassiter & Associates. Not even close. One of the agency's employees was identified by the *Arkansas Democrat-Gazette* in a front-page article as Little Rock's leading scofflaw for unpaid municipal parking tickets. And, of course, her place of employment was noted in the lede's first sentence.

Soon after she and I concluded our brief yet intense heart-to-heart discussion regarding this matter, I learned the compressor in our building's AC system had ceased to function. The repair was scheduled for later in the day. That was the good news. The bad news was the job could run in excess of $10,000.

And then I took a call from our newest client, the supremely confident owner of the city's premier pawn shop. He'd gotten married over the weekend, and his new bride had convinced him she could handle the promotional work of his business, making the arrangement with Lassiter & Associates unnecessary. I started to ask if he routinely allowed his customers to tear up their contracts without consequences. But I chose the high road and brought the frustrating conversation to a welcome close. I thanked him for the notice and hung up.

* * *

I'd completed a tedious call with a persistent media rep late Thursday morning when Erin stuck her head into my office.

"Don't you have a Rotary Club meeting to attend?"

I peeked at my watch and realized I had 13 minutes to get there. I made it—barely—although the one vacant seat I spotted was at a table dominated by competitors from the Andrews Bingham Carter agency. That's strange, I thought, settling into the chair. Until today, I'd never seen more than one or two of the firm's employees at these meetings.

A glance at the program solved the mystery. Today's speaker was Ms. Steele Parker, the state's tourism director. The ABC folks were here in force to show their respect. And protect their turf.

I hadn't paid much attention to the announcement at the beginning of the year when Governor Patricia Butler appointed one of her sorority sisters from college to this coveted position, figuring she'd repaid some long-overdue favor. Patronage wasn't unknown in Arkansas politics.

However, as I read Ms. Parker's biographical sketch, I realized my initial impression was incorrect; she brought an amazing résumé to the job. A theater major in college, she'd worked summers as a cast member and then supervisor at Walt Disney World in Orlando. She'd parlayed her Disney experience into an extended upper management stint at Marriott International, and from there was recruited to lead Google's hospitality division. She and her husband had taken early retirement, moving back to Arkansas less than a year ago. Asked to join the Butler administration, Ms. Parker signed on without a second thought.

I'm not sure which was colder: my glass of iced tea or the reception I got from the ABC quintet. Lucky for me, the other two individuals sitting at our crowded eight-top were realtors, always a friendly and gregarious tribe. And our lunch of chicken-fried steak was tolerable.

Ms. Parker's introduction was short and concise, and her comments were interesting, informative, and amusing. If she had an ego, it was held in check by her self-deprecating remarks. Speaking without notes, she demonstrated a thorough command of her topic, and by the end of her talk she seemed to have convinced everyone in the room tourism was the single most vital cog in the complex machine comprising the Arkansas economy. I realized working for this woman would be both a challenge and a delight.

At the conclusion of her talk, the moderator announced there was time for a couple of questions. I stood and raised my hand. Once Ms. Parker had responded to a query from the other side of the room, I was given a microphone.

"Can you provide insights on the selection process to choose the state's next advertising agency?" I asked. I could feel five sets of eyes from the ABC contingent boring holes into my back as I returned to my seat.

"An excellent question," she said. "First, let the record show my staff and I appreciate the fine work the Andrews Carter Bingham group has done over the years."

Upon hearing that statement, three of those from the advertising community at my table burst into vigorous applause, but sharp glares from their two senior colleagues silenced the celebration. It was no coincidence the last names of those two stern individuals were included in the ABC acronym. I recalled the third member of this unholy trinity had died during the past spring, collapsing on the 18th green at Little Rock's most exclusive country club after missing what should have been a gimme putt during a charity pro-am event. Gossip had it he was dead before hitting the ground.

"Governor Butler told me, and I agree, the state's hospitality industry is in the initial stages of a vast transformation," Parker said. "The governor also said if Arkansas tourism is to reach its potential, we must increase our promotional budget, and she's prepared to recommend additional funds. Yet she's firm in her belief we must have the absolute best team working for the state's taxpayers. An all-star panel of high-profile marketing experts from across the country will make its recommendation on the advertising agency to be awarded the department's next contract. I'd be very surprised if the ABC wasn't among the finalists."

Ms. Parker sat down to an enthusiastic ovation. Upon the meeting's adjournment, she was approached by a dozen or so members from the audience, five of whom had been seated at my table. As I considered walking to the front of the room and joining the conversation, I felt a tap on my shoulder. I turned and saw Stephanie Briles, executive director for the local Habitat for Humanity chapter, standing at my side.

"Randy," she said. "Good news! Erin Askew came through with the donation you mentioned a couple of weeks ago."

Habitat for Humanity was one of the agency's pro bono accounts, the other being the Little Rock Zoo. I remembered something about making a rash offer to match any contribution Erin made to it.

"With your generous help, her $10,000 gift will mean a big boost for our work this year," she said. "Thank you so much."

"The team at Lassiter & Associates is always happy to assist," I said as we shook hands. "We'll look forward to fulfilling our commitment."

I made a mental note to share this tidbit with the agency's comptroller.

* * *

When I got home, Leslie met me at the front door. With a purse hanging from her shoulder, she seemed to have a destination in mind.

"I was worried you'd overlooked our dinner with Ellen and Gib," she said following a kiss. "I know how much you look forward to visiting your brother-in-law."

I bit my tongue, did an about-face, and followed her across the porch and down the steps toward my truck. Leslie was right. Dr. Gib Yarberry, my sister Ellen's unfortunate choice for a husband, irritated me to no end. While I usually managed to ignore his arrogant and condescending attitude, I had trouble tolerating his penchant for puns.

I put those thoughts aside as we climbed into the Toyota and instead wondered if my mind was already starting to slip. Surely, dementia was still decades away. Yet without Erin's last-minute reminder, I would have missed my Rotary Club meeting earlier in the day, and tonight's dinner invitation had fallen through my memory banks leaving nary a trace.

"It'll be fun to see Jimmy," Leslie said. "No telling how much he's grown since we last saw him."

Jimmy was their cute and cuddly son. Although he'd entered this world not quite a year ago, I'll always remember his birthday. It was the day after the murdered body of my best friend and former college roommate, Dr. James Joseph Newell, had been discovered. Known to everyone as J.J., he was also close to Ellen and Gib, and they'd named their newborn after him.

When we arrived at the Yarberry's palatial home in one of the city's trendy western suburbs, we learned Jimmy still hadn't taken his first step. Nevertheless, he was a crawling fiend, scampering on hands and knees from one doting adult to the next. But following an hour of non-stop movement, Jimmy ran out of energy. As Gib carried their sleepy boy upstairs to his bedroom, Ellen brought serving dishes from the kitchen to the dining room.

We'd hardly begun our meal before Gib mentioned the prominent article in yesterday's newspaper concerning my embarrassing employee.

"You know," he said, "the one who's been flouting the city's parking regulations for years on end. The flagrant scofflaw, as she was described by the reporter."

"I'm well aware of this awkward situation," I said, feeling a warm flush work its way up my neck. "I've given her 60 days to pay her fines in full and set the record straight."

"What's her role at your agency?" Gib asked.

His interest puzzled me.

"She oversees our social media department," I said.

A familiar smirk appeared on Gib's annoying face.

"I hope you'll consider a new title I've developed for her."

I ignored him and grabbed my gin and tonic.

Ellen, though, took the bait. "Share it with us."

"My suggestion is she should be publicly crowned and recognized as," and he paused a beat for effect, "the 'Queen of Scoffland'!"

His attempt at a Scottish brogue was worse than pathetic.

Gib howled in pleasure, and both women chortled at his wit. Lowering my head in defeat, I waved my empty glass in Ellen's direction, hoping she would take pity on me and quickly bring another G & T.

~ TWENTY-FIVE ~

Early Friday morning found Megan, Harrison, and me on the road to Yellville, Megan at the wheel, to meet with Del Boddington and his daughter Tabitha at Hillcountry Marine.

"I've never participated in a contract signing," Harrison said. "What should I expect?"

"It's little more than a formality," I said. "We'll use today as an opportunity to introduce you to our new client. As I noted earlier, your main responsibility is to go over the proposed contract point by point. The three of us should be able to handle any questions they have."

"It'll be a good experience, with fresh-made pastries if we're lucky," Megan said. "The real work begins when we return to Little Rock."

I peered into the backseat and saw Harrison open a folder and begin reviewing the seven-page document. Not only had he helped draft it, he'd taken the final version home with him last night and probably had it memorized by now.

Several hours later, as Megan steered us onto the Hillcountry Marine property, we met a pickup headed out. I was certain I'd seen the driver's face before.

"Wasn't Sheriff Hutch Thomas in that truck?" I asked Megan.

I gazed over my shoulder and saw a long trailer loaded with a pair of aluminum pontoon tubes behind the pickup.

"Sorry," she said, "but I didn't notice."

The truck rounded a curve and soon vanished.

As he'd done on our first visit, Del Boddington met us at the front door of his establishment, greeting us with a warm smile.

"And this must be the young man who'll be our day-to-day contact," he said as he and Harrison exchanged a handshake.

"This is Harrison Davies," I said. "Your account executive."

"Pleased to meet you, Harrison," he said.

"My pleasure, sir," Harrison said. "I've been an avid bass fisherman since I was a kid. Working on an account like yours is a dream come true."

Tabitha was in the conference room arranging a tempting tray of doughnuts next to the coffee machine as we entered.

I looked at Megan, wondering how she knew about the pastries. She caught my glance, shrugged, and gave me a subtle smile.

"Good morning," Tabitha said, "and welcome back. Please make yourselves at home."

Once Harrison and Tabitha had been introduced, we took seats around the table. Megan was right; the doughnuts were delicious.

"We appreciate your prompt attention to the contract," I began. "Here are copies for everybody. If it's okay with you, we'll let Harrison provide a quick review."

"Please proceed," Del said as he took a copy.

Like Tabitha, he'd placed a notepad and pen in front of him.

Although Harrison was a bit nervous at first, he settled in and did a fine job covering the details and answering the occasional question or clarifying a point. The Boddingtons were pleased with the idea of bringing in Junior Judson to serve as a celebrity spokesman.

"Tabitha and I think he'll draw good crowds at trade shows," Del said. "I might even want an autographed picture myself."

After mentioning the need for new photography, Harrison suggested scheduling a photo-shoot later in the summer, perhaps at nearby Bull Shoals Lake.

"That sounds perfect," Tabitha said. "We'll have examples from our new line of party barges ready by then."

"Did you notice anything in the contract you'd like to revise?" I asked after Harrison concluded his remarks.

"There's another matter I want to bring up," Del said, "One of my longtime employees heard we're considering a marketing plan and came to us with an idea."

"This particular gentleman's family has been affiliated with our local 4-H Club since its inception," Tabitha said. "For generations now, they've traveled to Little Rock every October for the annual Arkansas State Fair & Livestock Show. Over the years, the family's children have entered livestock in the various competitions."

"According to him, there's a large building on the fairgrounds where vendors rent space to promote their products," Del said. "He wondered if Hillcountry Marine might be an exhibitor."

Megan and Harrison turned to me.

"I believe your colleague is referring to the Hall of Industry," I said. "It's a favorite with fair-goers, always attracting a big throng. I'm sure the fee is reasonable, so your main cost would be staffing it."

"My employee indicated he and his wife would volunteer," Del said.

"They'll be down there anyway," Tabitha said. "We're told their grandchildren will show rabbits and ducks this year, and they'll be in Little Rock to support them."

I nodded toward Harrison.

"And I suspect your new account executive would be willing to help."

"You bet," Harrison said. "I grew up going to the state fair with my family every fall. And we might be able to recruit Junior Judson to work the booth."

After amending the contract on the spot to reflect the state fair addition to the scope of services, Del and I each signed a copy, confirming Lassiter & Associates was the advertising agency of record for Hillcountry Marine, Inc. The brief ceremony was followed by a round of smiles and handshakes, and, in my case, another blueberry cake doughnut.

As Del led us from the conference room toward their lobby and exit, I remembered something I'd meant to ask him an hour earlier.

"Was Sheriff Thomas driving away as we arrived?"

"You know Hutch?" he asked.

"I've met him," I said, an admission bringing a wry grin to Megan's face.

"Hutch called a few days ago, asking if we had any surplus pontoon tubes we'd sell him at a discount," Del said. "As luck would have it, we had two units damaged in shipment and I told him he could have them at no cost. They're still watertight but we couldn't use either because of the blemishes."

"Will he put them to use at the new summer camp?" I asked.

Del shrugged.

"That'd be my guess, maybe for a small dock or swimming platform at the big pond on their property."

"He must be one busy man," I said, "between being sheriff and dealing with their ambitious camp project."

"And he's going to get even busier," Del said. "In fact, you might be seeing more of him in Little Rock in the future."

"He's moving to the big city?" I asked, surprised.

"Not quite," Del said with a grin. "Hutch announced earlier this week he's running for the state legislature."

"Seems way too early for a campaign," I said, wondering if I'd managed to hide my shock. "The election's not for at least another 15 months."

"Hutch claims our current state representative is too close to Governor Butler," Del said. "Calls him a 'tax and spend socialist' and says this district needs somebody with true conservative values."

I looked at Del in surprise. "A so-called socialist from up here? You've got to be kidding."

Del touched me on the elbow and steered me to the side of the room.

"Our current state representative is a decent church-going, God-fearing Navy veteran who's a lifetime member of the National Rifle Association," he said, his voice low enough only I could hear him. "But he supported the governor's proposal to expand health insurance coverage for pre-school children which the legislature passed by a wide margin, a program Hutch maintains is a liberal scheme."

"Aren't most of those funds helping families in rural areas like this district?" I asked.

"Hutch has also promised to introduce legislation requiring public schools to teach the Ten Commandments," Del said. "Now, don't get me wrong. I'm a staunch Southern Baptist and try to follow them every day. But I also believe in separation of church and state, and feel our founding fathers would have a problem with this."

I stared at Del, trying to keep my jaw in place.

"And there's more," Del said. "The incumbent's wife had the audacity to buy an electric vehicle. You can be damn certain Hutch will make her purchase an issue in the campaign."

Del put a hand on my shoulder and leaned in close.

"Randy, there's one thing to remember if you ever cross paths with Hutch Thomas," he said. "He operates by his own rules."

I'd come to the same conclusion a couple of weeks earlier.

* * *

Leslie greeted me with a beaming smile and a tight hug when I walked into our home late in the afternoon.

"I received my test results less than an hour ago," she said, squeezing my hands. "I passed and am now certified to fly Amelia for commercial purposes."

"And Lassiter & Associates has a signed contract with a new client. I'm thinking tonight might be a good occasion to uncork the bottle of Champagne we've been chilling for a while."

"My thoughts exactly!"

My cell phone rang as we entered the kitchen. The screen indicated my favorite uncle was on the line.

"Booker! And a pleasant good evening to you."

"I have gleanings from my latest assignment to share," he said. "Is your lovely bride available?"

"Leslie's here," I said, "and you're now on the speaker."

180

After Booker and Leslie exchanged greetings, he said, "If you remember, I agreed to investigate the Flyover Family's officers. As you know, accessing the dark web is like opening Pandora's Box."

"Did you discover anything of interest?" Leslie asked.

"Indeed," Booker said. "I'll begin with the lowest elected position, the sergeant at arms, and advance through the ranks."

"A sergeant at arms?" I asked. "Do they need such a post to keep order during their meetings?"

"In this instance, it appears to be little more than a ceremonial role," Booker said. "The office holder is a former state police captain who enjoys carrying a sidearm. As you might expect, his record is clean. No arrests, no warrants. In fact, he and his wife celebrated their 50th wedding anniversary last month."

"Is he an Arkansas resident?" I asked.

"As are the other officers," Booker said. "This man's from Cave City in the northern part of the state."

We heard the shuffling of papers in the background.

"Our next individual for this organization is the secretary, and, to no one's surprise, it's a woman. A retired nurse, she, too, has a spotless record."

"Does she also live in the Ozarks?" Leslie asked.

"She's one of few members from southern Arkansas," he said. "Her mailing address is in the small town of Smackover."

Again, we heard rustling noises.

"We'll now move along to the next position, the role of treasurer."

"An ever more important job," I said, "given the recent influx of funds."

"Right you are," Booker replied. "The treasurer is a 29-year-old man from Ravenden Springs who has compiled a rather checkered career despite his age. A former youth minister in Harrison, he left the fundamentalist congregation under rumors of sexual misconduct involving an underage female parishioner, although charges were never filed. He's now a clerk at a convenience store and also operates a seasonal lawn-service business."

There was a long pause.

"Is there more?" I asked.

"Only that he was among the hundreds of rioters participating in the infamous January 6 insurrection at the U.S. Capitol years ago. He was convicted of interfering with police, obstructing an official proceeding, and trespassing. As a result, he served two years in a federal prison."

"And this dude's in charge of their money?" Leslie asked.

"Evidently so," Booker said. "As for the vice president, he, too, is a piece of work. He's had restraining orders filed against him by both ex-wives and has been held in contempt of court for failure to make child support payments. His trout fishing guide service on the White River is based in Cotter."

"Which brings us to the Hutch Thomas," I said. "The Flyover Family's president."

"Sheriff Thomas seems to have kept his nose clean," Booker said. "Nothing untoward on his official record. In fact, he's a former president of the Arkansas Sheriff's Association and last year taught a course at the Arkansas Law Enforcement Training Academy."

"Anything else you can tell us about him?" I asked.

"The deeper dive on the honorable sheriff yielded no red flags," Booker said. "He lives within his means, drives a late-model Dodge Ram pickup, and paid off the mortgage to his house eight years ago. One wife, three grown children, and a 40-acre farm near Pyatt where he maintains a small herd of cattle. For a decade now, he's served as an elder in their rural evangelical church. Outside of a minor balance on a VISA card, he's debt-free. Not the slightest hint of financial improprieties."

"Do any members of the Flyover Family have connections with other far-right clubs or groups?" Leslie asked.

"At various times, several of them have participated in out-of-state events organized by the Oath Keepers, Proud Boys, and similar outfits," Booker said. "They've been arrested in Montana, Idaho, Oklahoma, and the District of Columbia on an assortment of minor charges."

"I can add one interesting item to our file on Hutch Thomas," I said. "I learned this morning he's running for a seat in the Arkansas House of Representatives."

I heard a gasp at the other end of the conversation.

"Tell me you're joking," Booker said. "Please."

Leslie and I never got around to opening our bottle of Champagne.

~ TWENTY-SIX ~

A loud and incessant knocking on our front door at 7:00 AM Saturday interrupted my coffee ritual and reminded me this was the morning for our landscaping crew to arrive. A couple of noisy hours later, a truckload of offending vegetation had been removed, and by mid-afternoon the place was looking damn good, especially the cascading water feature in one corner of the new flagstone patio. When the last vehicle pulled away at 6:00 PM, our lawn—both backyard and front—had been transformed.

Leslie, who'd launched Amelia to film portions of the work, was ecstatic with the outcome.

"Maybe we should celebrate with the champagne we failed to open last night," she said.

We did just that. After I filled our flutes, we adjourned to the patio and were reviewing her drone footage when my cell phone rang.

"It's Uncle Booker," I said, taking a peek at the screen. "I think I'll let it go to voicemail."

"There's a chance he might have found something important," Leslie said. "Maybe you should answer it."

"You're sure?" I asked.

She nodded.

I reached for the phone.

"Good evening, sir," I said. "How's my favorite uncle on this fine spring night?"

That he was my only uncle was not unknown to Booker.

He mumbled his usual refrain about the disrespectful, self-indulgent, and wasted younger generation to which I belonged before asking if Leslie was available.

"She's right here," I said. "I've activated the speaker, so be careful with what you say."

"Salutations to you, Ms. Carlisle," he said. "I trust you're enjoying the weekend."

"I'll be feeling better about it if you have useful news to share," she said.

"My exploration on the dark web continued well into the wee hours of the morning," he said. "And I can report on several intriguing discoveries."

"More insights concerning the Flyover Family's officers?" I asked.

"I rather feel I've exhausted the subject, at least for the time being," Booker said. "I directed my latest inquiry into the group's summer camp."

"Their Francis Marion Memorial Camp for Southern Youth, right?" Leslie asked.

"Correct," Booker said. "If you're not otherwise engaged, I'd hoped to stop by and update you on my discoveries regarding this particular endeavor."

I pushed the mute button on my phone and turned to Leslie.

"What do you think?" I asked.

"Sure," she said. "And we can show him all this."

She swung an arm across the new patio.

"Come on over," I said after clearing the mute function. "We're out back."

While I brought a third chair onto the new flagstone, Leslie refilled our Champagne flutes.

"I suspect we'll need this," she said.

As Booker strolled through the gate to our large backyard a quarter of an hour later, his appearance reminded me of the occasion a little over a year ago when he'd arrived unannounced at our May Day Party soon after Leslie had moved to Little Rock. She must have been thinking much the same.

"I believe he wore the same outfit on the afternoon I met him for the first time," Leslie said, her voice low, as Booker closed to within 100 feet.

Terrified of over-exposure to the sun, Booker covered as much of his body as possible if spending even a short period outdoors. He wore loose cotton slacks and a billowing long-sleeved shirt buttoned to the neck, both in white, with shiny black leather boots and a matching belt. A wide-brimmed Panama hat and an emerald green scarf wrapped around his thin neck completed his look.

"Almost the same," she whispered. "Last year's scarf was a vivid fuchsia."

"You sound pretty sure."

"It's the same color as my favorite bikini."

I turned to stare at Leslie, once again amazed at her ability to recall the slightest details.

"How can you remember this stuff?" I asked.

"I'm a photographer," she said. "Observing things is how I make a living."

We stood to greet Booker as he stepped onto the patio. I noticed he'd smeared zinc oxide down his nose and beneath his eyes. He took note of our shorts and tank tops, his expression indicating something less than approval.

"I see you remain oblivious to my admonishments dealing with solar radiation," he said. "Mother Nature is not forgiving."

"We've been in the house until the past half hour," Leslie said, "and have remained in the shade while outside."

It wasn't far from the truth.

Shaking his head, Booker took a long look around our new outdoor space, his disdainful gaze pausing on the burbling fountain.

"Which reminds me," he said. "I'm quite parched. Any chance I can partake of a liquid refreshment?"

He slipped into a lawn chair and set a manila folder on the small table at his side.

"One revitalizing beverage coming up," I said and trotted to the kitchen.

Using water straight from the tap, I refilled the same Evian bottle we'd shared with Booker during his recent visit to sample Leslie's vegan dishes. Placing it on a serving tray with a glass, I returned to the patio moments later. I then filled the glass and presented it to him.

"Thank you, dear nephew," he said, taking a sip. "Now, on to the Flyover Family's camp. The preliminary schedule was posted on the dark web last night for the members' approval. The girls' session will be held the first full week of August; boys will convene the next week. Campers are to arrive for check-in before noon on Monday, departing the following Friday afternoon."

He opened his folder and removed two sheets of paper, handing one to Leslie and the other to me.

"If my memory's correct, the new facility can accommodate 30 campers at a time," I said.

"The group's gone mainstream," Booker said, "and will soon display this application form on its new Facebook page, noting the 30-camper maximum. They're urging parents to submit their paperwork and deposits at once."

Leslie examined the information Booker had given her.

"$195 per camper sounds high," she said.

"My initial reaction was quite similar," Booker said. "However, upon further reading, I learned the fee includes lodging for 4 nights, 13 meals, and a host of activities all under the supervision of an experienced camp director and a trio of trained counselors. A registered nurse will be stationed on the premises 24 hours a day. And thanks to a generous donor, a handful of scholarships are available."

"Did you notice the age requirements?" I asked, staring at the sheet of paper. "Can that be correct?"

"I, too, was puzzled at first," Booker said. "Requiring campers to be between the ages of 12 and 16 eliminates the younger set. But then I studied the list of activities you'll find on the opposite side."

"You sound surprised by your findings," I said as I flipped the page over.

"Many are the predictable summer camp pursuits you might recall from your youth," Booker said. "Canoeing, archery, pottery, horseback riding, swimming, and so on. At least for the afternoons. On the other hand, the morning sessions—"

"What?" Leslie said, almost shouting as she interrupted Booker. "You've got to the kidding."

She waved her sheet of paper at us.

"Read down their list of morning activities."

I studied the page in my hands. I'd located the **Typical Morning Schedule** heading when Leslie gasped.

"Just listen to these classes," Leslie said, her eyes were wide.

"'Slavery in the Bible.' 'A Southern Manifesto.' 'The Actual History of America's Founding Fathers.' 'Reclaiming States' Rights.'"

Booker chuckled, something I'd seldom heard him do.

"Settle down, my dear," he said. "You'll discover other topics a bit less reactionary. There's one on the Bill of Rights and another on the Arkansas Constitution."

But Leslie had yet to settle down.

"Oh my God," she said. "There's one titled 'The Real Truth Behind the War of Northern Aggression.' And another on 'Honoring the Legacy of the Lost Cause.' Whatever that is."

I read further down the page.

"I suspect these classes explain the age requirements," I said. "The kids need to be old enough to participate in discussions."

"Or maybe old enough for the Flyover Family's political indoctrination to take effect," Leslie said.

"According to this overview, the camp also offers opportunities for skits and games," I said. "And it claims each camper will be expected to recite the preamble of the Constitution of the United States by the end of the week."

"Another item catching my eye," Booker said, "was the 'flag competition.'"

Leslie and I both glanced up.

"A game?" I asked. "Something on the order of flag football?"

"Evidently, the Flyover Family has determined their new camp needs its own distinctive pennant or banner," Booker said. "Art classes will be held during both sessions where campers will have an opportunity to design one. The winner will get free registration for camp the following year."

"I have a couple of ideas for a flag," Leslie said with a mischievous grin.

But Booker was not amused.

"There's one last matter I must speak to," he said. "I've given considerable thought to Alex Motherwell's recent trip to the State Archives."

"His interest still puzzles me," I said. "Motherwell's engineering firm doesn't have a contract to do any work on the building. The Secretary of State is responsible for the Capitol's upkeep, and a spokesman for the office confirmed they have no plans for any major maintenance or renovation projects in the next biennium."

"Randy mentioned Motherwell's little expedition to me earlier this week," Leslie said. "What's your take on it, Uncle Booker?"

"I also paid a visit to the Archives and spent an hour reviewing the original architectural plans for the State Capitol," Booker said. "The very materials Motherwell inspected, according to initials on the file folders."

"Are you good with Motherwell's explanation it's nothing more than a personal hobby?"

"There's always the chance he was telling the truth," Booker said. "Yet I would have thought he'd be examining the exterior drawings dealing with the building's major architectural elements—the columns, the entrance, and the dome—which give it such a distinctive appearance."

"You're saying he looked at something else?" I asked.

Booker gave us a nod.

"I found his initials on the files concerning the interior details. You must remember the Capitol was built well over 100 years ago when construction was less efficient. Mr. Motherwell seems to have spent his time studying those little-known chaseways and other passages providing access to pipes, ductwork, and mechanical rooms."

"You're telling us he was interested in specific interior features?" Leslie asked.

"He spent no time with the exterior views," Booker said. "I checked, and no one has requested those files in the past 15 months."

As I tried to make sense of Booker's discovery, he lifted the sleeve of his shirt and gazed at his watch. I wondered if he had another appointment later this evening, and then remembered today was Saturday. The weekly drag review at one of Little Rock's popular alternative nightspots would begin in a few hours.

"What will be Monique Monét's attire tonight?" I asked

Reaching into a pants pocket, Booker removed his cell phone.

"I went through a dress rehearsal of my complete outfit earlier this afternoon and took a selfie," he said.

He scrolled down the screen for a moment before handing the phone to me.

In the photograph, he wore a long royal blue sleeveless gown clinging to his small, slender body like a glove. The conservative neckline was more than offset by a slit reaching almost to his hip. With his makeup artfully applied and wearing a blonde wig, Booker was an attractive cross-dresser, hardly looking like himself.

Leslie gestured for the phone and I gave it to her.

"Where did you get those heels, Uncle Booker?" she asked. "They're stunning. I want a pair!"

~ TWENTY-SEVEN ~

Early Tuesday morning following Memorial Day, Leslie and I left Little Rock, heading southwest. We drove around Hot Springs on the bypass and continued west to Lake Ouachita, the huge Corps of Engineers' reservoir. I had an appointment with Charlie Engstrom, Constance Engstrom's younger brother, at his upscale resort located at the southwestern end of the lake. While he and I discussed the ins and outs of Arkansas's tourism industry, Leslie planned to launch her drone at the water's edge and practice tracking boats as they left the resort's marina. She was scheduled to shoot Hillcountry Marine's new line of party barges later in the year and felt the additional experience would work to her advantage.

Once I dropped Leslie off at the marina with a promise to meet her in an hour, I drove up the hill past a complex of stylish condominiums to the resort's office. I grabbed my notepad and stepped inside. With a coffee cup in each hand, Charlie greeted me like a lifelong friend even though our sole interaction had been a five-minute telephone conversation late last week. He gave me a cup, and then led me through the building to a balcony overlooking the deep blue waters and we sat outside at a table with a commanding view. The coffee was excellent.

"Constance tells me your agency will make a run at the state's tourism account," he said.

"Your sister's right," I said. "We've spent the past month developing preliminary plans. I've dreamed of landing this client since I first got into advertising."

"I've known the ABC team for years, and they've delivered good results," he said. "It may be time for a change, although unseating them will be difficult. Your situation will be like taking on an entrenched politician. There's a lot of power in the incumbency."

"No doubt we're facing an uphill battle," I said. "I'm hopeful you're willing to share some strategic insights. Things that have stuck in your mind during your career in the hospitality industry."

Charlie gave me a slight nod and then turned and stared over the thousands of acres of open water stretching before us. I managed to pick out Leslie standing on the shoreline far below, but couldn't spot her drone.

"It's a little over three miles to the opposite side of the lake," he said. "How many occupied boats do you see between here and there?"

I squinted and gazed toward the remote shore.

"There's one leaving your marina," I said, "and at least one—maybe two—more in the distance."

"You're looking at the biggest problem my competitors and I face in the resort business," Charlie said. "We have more customers than we can handle on weekends, but come mid-week—like today—this huge lake is all but empty."

He paused and looked to me.

"It also represents an opportunity."

"Go on," I said.

"The ABC crew has spent decades positioning Arkansas as a wonderful family destination," Charlie said, "and they've been successful. Yet there must be a couple of million households within easy driving distance of Ouachita having no children in their homes, many of them retirees with disposable incomes and all sorts of discretionary time. Since they're not worried about school, soccer games, or jobs, they could visit on weekdays and fill my rooms, eat at my restaurant, and rent my boats."

"And you might even be willing to discount your rates," I said, making a note.

"Damn right."

"Anything else?" I asked.

192

"It seems we've devoted most of our resources to attracting out-of-state tourists," Charlie said. "Rather than watching our fellow Arkansans travel beyond our borders and spend their hard-earned money elsewhere, my recommendation is we develop an aggressive plan to cross-sell the state."

"By that you mean getting people from one corner of Arkansas to experience other regions of the state?"

"Exactly," Charlie said. "Convincing five percent of them to vacation at home would mean millions of dollars in extra sales. Here's an example: I've never been to northeast Arkansas but know tourists can explore the studio where Ernest Hemingway wrote a famous novel and visit the original house where Johnny Cash grew up. And sample a platter of fried catfish or a rack of barbecued ribs along the way."

I jotted down more reminders between sips of coffee. And continued to do so for the next 30 minutes as Charlie and I exchanged thoughts. He liked my idea of recruiting partners among the state's leading corporate entities and expanded upon it, stating it'd be an excellent way to leverage the state's limited advertising funds. Likewise, he felt working with selected automobile dealerships across Arkansas to build a promotional campaign based on a network of driving tours had potential.

"A passport might offer noteworthy possibilities," I said.

"With prizes for those meeting a certain threshold," Charlie added. "Something as simple as a certificate signed by the governor might entice local folks to travel throughout Arkansas."

A glance at my watch confirmed my hour with Charlie was nearing its end.

"One more thing," Charlie said. "I have a cousin who's a single mom, and she's always complaining about how much trouble she has planning a vacation, struggling to find activities her kids will enjoy. This demographic segment might present an attractive niche market for you."

After making another note, I stood and thanked him for sharing his time and observations, telling him how much I appreciated his perspective on the tourism industry.

"Best wishes with your agency's bid," he said. "It's clear your business is much like mine—cutthroat competition at every turn."

We shook hands, and I headed down the hill where Leslie was packing her drone.

"Today couldn't have gone better," she said with a bright smile. "I introduced myself to a pair of fishermen on the dock and explained what I wanted to do, promising them a video clip of the footage if they'd motor back and forth in front of me. They agreed, and I got a series of nice shots from a variety of angles. The drone's capabilities are amazing."

"So, you accomplished your objective?"

"And some," she said. "I now feel confident handling Amelia."

As I placed her box of equipment into the truck, Leslie asked, "How was your conversation with the resort owner?"

"It was far more helpful than I expected," I said. "In addition to convincing me the agency's planning is on the right track, he suggested several promising ideas. I, too, had a productive hour."

"I think we should reward ourselves," Leslie said. "I spotted a Dairy Queen as we drove through Hot Springs. Let's get a pair of milkshakes on the way home."

It was an offer I couldn't refuse. I opted for a chocolate chip cookie dough shake. Large.

* * *

About half an hour outside Little Rock, my cell rang. It was Booker.

"It's not even noon," I said. "Awful early for a call from you. And before you respond, let me warn you my sweet bride is listening in."

"And the top of the morning to you, Ms. Carlisle," he said.

"We've already had a good day, Uncle Booker," she said. "I hope you can add to it."

"That remains to be seen," he said. "However, I did uncover a pair of fascinating developments well after midnight during my latest foray into the underbelly of the internet's dark web."

194

"Items pertaining to the Flyover Family?" I asked.

"Most certainly," Booker said. "First, I located a contractor's update on the construction of the building to house the Francis Marion Memorial Camp for Southern Youth. It's running well ahead of schedule, all but guaranteeing the facility will be ready for both sessions when August comes around."

"No doubt they've already had a handful of campers register," Leslie said.

"Ha!" Booker said. "Enrollment has been open less than a week and the roster is well over half-filled. I also confirmed their order for 35 twin mattresses has been received, with shipment expected within the next month."

"Thirty-five," I said. "I thought the camp's capacity was 30."

"I, too, was confused," Booker said. "In fact, one of the members broached an identical question in their private chat room. It seems 30 mattresses are for campers, and the remainder will be for the director, the camp nurse, and three counselors."

"Did you discover other items of interest?" Leslie asked.

"Yes, dear one," Booker said. "Something taking me by total surprise: an essay contest."

I stared out the windshield, trying to ignore the never-ending and unappealing strip development along I-30. It seemed to grow uglier by the day.

"An essay contest," I said. "I hope you're joking."

"I kid you not," Booker said. "It's still in the planning stages, but indications are it will be open to high school juniors and seniors. A 750-word maximum; typed and double-spaced."

"Any particular topic?" Leslie asked.

"Each essay will address this subject," Booker said. "'What David O. Dodd means to the South.'"

Leslie turned to me, clearly confused.

"Although I cannot see your face, Ms. Carlisle," Booker said, "my intuition tells me you're unfamiliar with the storied history of Mr. Dodd."

"I've never heard of the man," she said.

"I suspect my dear nephew can provide you with appropriate edification."

I took a deep breath and exhaled. "Union troops caught David Owen Dodd spying for the Confederacy during the Civil War. He was hanged in Little Rock two weeks later as a result and is buried in the city's Mount Holly Cemetery. And because of his age—he was 17 at the time—he's known as the 'Boy Martyr' of the Confederacy by certain groups."

"You mean they're asking these students to write about a young man who was, in effect, a traitor to the United States?" Leslie asked.

"It could be their perspective is a bit different from yours," Booker said.

"What's the prize?" Leslie asked.

"A cash award of $1,000," Booker said. "The judges, by the way, are three historians on the faculty at a small evangelical college on the East Coast. I find their academic credentials rather dubious."

"Any other details regarding this contest?" I asked.

"The essay contest will be formally announced at a press conference later this fall," Booker said. "Additional specifics have yet to be determined."

"Thanks for the up—" I began.

"My god!" Booker said, interrupting me. "My avocado toast is burning." The call ended.

We drove a few miles in silence.

"There's another aspect of this story you don't know," I said as we entered Little Rock's city limits.

"It gets worse?" Leslie asked.

"Let's just say it gets more complicated," I said. "Several of my colleagues at the agency have volunteered to help students in the Little Rock School District overcome reading deficiencies. The agency has signed on as a corporate partner to assist the David O. Dodd Elementary School in southwest Little Rock. Over half of its students are Black."

196

Leslie's chin dropped. "You're telling me these young African-American kids attend classes at an elementary school named in honor of a Confederate spy?"

"That's an apt summary," I said. "And Chantille Huxley, my associate who's spearheading the agency's efforts, is a Black mother with two kids enrolled in that very school."

Leslie pointed to a liquor store on the corner ahead of us.

"Pull in here," she said. "We going to need a new bottle of bourbon."

~ TWENTY-EIGHT ~

The month of June flew by. The staff at Lassiter & Associates continued to put in extended hours, not only in behalf of our existing clients but also toward our goal of fine-tuning a strong bid for the advertising account of the Arkansas Department of Parks, Heritage, and Tourism. Although winning this state agency's business remained a long shot, my colleagues and I kept the faith, discussing it almost daily and recording ideas and strategies to explore.

Leslie's schedule was every bit as busy as mine. She spent a full week in northwest Arkansas shooting the Crystal Bridges Museum of American Art in Bentonville, the University of Arkansas campus in Fayetteville, and the historic district of Eureka Springs. She phoned each evening to update her progress.

"Randy," she had said on her latest call, "I can't imagine tackling these assignments without a drone. Amelia has added another dimension to my work. You won't believe the shots I got circling the Christ of the Ozarks statue with downtown Eureka Springs in the background. They're nothing short of amazing."

"Maybe you can put this experience to good use later in the summer," I said. "The agency has scheduled a photo-shoot for Hillcountry Marine's new product line in August, and much of the work will require drone footage over the water. Any chance you'd be interested in this job?"

"Award that assignment to another photographer," she said after a giggle, "and I can guarantee the lifestyle to which you've become accustomed will take a major turn in a negative direction."

"I'll put you down as interested."

* * *

On Monday, July 1, I received a much-anticipated fax from the Arkansas Department of Finance & Administration. It contained complete details on the Request for Proposals (RFP) process for selecting an advertising agency to represent the Arkansas Department of Parks, Heritage and Tourism. After having copies made for my department heads, I spent a full hour reviewing the document.

It was pretty much what I expected. A response would, at a minimum, include: a history of the agency; a list of past and current clients; a five-year summary of annual billings; financial statements from the last three fiscal years; and a list of employees, their relevant experience, and job titles. The concluding portion would be an essay explaining why the team at Lassiter & Associates would provide an ideal match for the needs and expectations of the Department and the State of Arkansas. We'd anticipated what would be required and had been compiling information over the past few months. I grabbed a notepad and began jotting down ideas for the essay, wishing I'd paid more attention in my English composition classes a couple of decades ago.

* * *

Toward the end of the month, Joan Pfeiffer invited Leslie and me to join her and State Senator Somer Smith for dinner. Joan lived on Oakwood Road in the city's fashionable Hillcrest neighborhood. What her home lacked it size, it more than made up for in location, wonderfully situated on a large yet steep corner lot overlooking the forested slopes of Allsopp Park.

We arrived ten minutes past the suggested time—or in Leslie's words, "fashionably late"—and, after a round of hugs, presented

Joan with a jar of homemade strawberry preserves we'd frozen back in the spring as our hostess gift along with a midrange bottle of Chardonay. She led us through the house to a spacious deck where Somer was putting final touches on a tempting charcuterie board. Leslie got another hug and then Somer and I exchanged handshakes, followed by the filling of four wine glasses.

"I'm told the official RFP for the state's tourism contract has been released," Joan said, handing me a drink. "May I assume Lassiter & Associates received a copy?"

"Weeks ago," I said. "We're well into the application process and plan to submit the day of the deadline."

"The rumor among my colleagues in the Senate is it's drawing a lot of attention," Somer said. "In addition to representing a good deal of billings, there's an element of prestige at stake. What some might call bragging rights."

"Randy and his team are hard at it," Leslie said. "He spent two hours last night on the essay to accompany their bid."

"On a different subject," I said and looked to Somer. "Anything more on the disgusting editorial attack you experienced earlier this summer?"

"We got an indirect confirmation on the perpetrator,"Joan said with a smile, shaking her head. "It's almost funny."

"Like most newspapers, my hometown weekly publishes 'letters to the editor' each issue," Somer said. "Two weeks ago, it included one critical of my work in the legislature, calling me Senator Reparations Smith."

"One P or two in reparations?" Leslie asked.

"I had the same question," Somer said, "and phoned the editor, a longtime friend. He admitted they'd corrected the typo before publishing it."

"So, your hunch was right regarding the instigator of your nasty message?" I asked.

"It seems to be the case," Somer said. "American democracy at work."

He passed the cheeses and crackers and I refilled my plate.

"It's reasonably good news," Joan added. "This particular individual has a reputation of being all bark and no bite."

Leslie straightened in her deck chair.

"I should've brought my camera," she whispered.

Raising her hand little by little, she pointed through the balusters under the deck's top railing.

An adult whitetail deer and two speckled fawns grazed on the lawn far below us.

"Those are Joan's pets," Somer said. "She spreads a bucket of corn on the ground every evening."

"I've named them," Joan said. "The mama is Deerlene and her two cute babies are Dottie and Spot."

She stood and walked to the edge of the deck.

"They're not shy," she said. "They're used to us watching them."

Somer, Leslie, and I joined her at the railing and gazed at the browsing trio. While the deer glanced up to us now and then and flicked their tails, they continued to eat, their human observers not worrying them in the least.

"How can you tell the fawns apart?" I asked.

"Well—" she began before Somer interrupted her.

"She can't," he said with a laugh.

"But I can tell our appetizers have disappeared," she said. "Let's go inside for dinner."

And a fine meal it was: lasagna based on a recipe from Joan's grandmother with fresh green beans and a tasty side salad. I was on my second helping of the pasta when Somer cleared his throat.

"I wanted to mention an intriguing meeting I attended the first of this week," he said. "As you may remember, I'm chair of the Senate's City, County, and Local Affairs Committee. Governor Butler invited committee members to the Governor's Mansion for lunch."

"Isn't a meal at the mansion rather unusual?" I asked.

"I suspect so," Somer. "It was a first for me."

Joan shook her head.

"I can assure you none of my House committees have been summoned to the Governor's Mansion for a meeting, much less a meal."

"Your use of the word 'intriguing' caught my attention," Leslie said. "What was the topic?"

"Governor Butler also invited the Director of the State Police to attend," Somer said. "She then introduced the Special Agent in Charge of the FBI's Little Rock Field Office for a presentation."

"I take it this was not your basic PowerPoint on the origin, history, and responsibilities of a venerable federal institution," I said.

He chuckled and gave me a slight nod.

"You are correct. The agent spent the next 25 minutes briefing us on what the agency views as a growing threat: terrorists."

Somer paused for several beats, making eye contact with each of us.

"Not international terrorists, but those operating from our own backyards. Domestic terrorists."

"When Somer first shared this with me," Joan said, "I assumed the FBI's major concern is extremists in large urban areas in other states."

"But that's not the case?" Leslie asked.

"The possibility of sabotage aimed at the country's electrical grid is stressing FBI analysts," Somer said. "Rural states such as Arkansas are viewed as having an abundance of vulnerable targets."

"I seem to recall reading something about attacks on electrical substations somewhere out West," I said. "Maybe during this past winter?"

"You're referring to a series of strikes in Washington state over the Christmas holidays which left thousands in the dark and cold for over 48 hours," Somer said. "Within recent months, similar incidents in rural North Carolina left 40,000 customers without power for days. In both cases, property damages to the electrical substations ran into the millions of dollars."

"Who's doing this?" Leslie asked. "And why?"

"In Washington, the FBI arrested two men, identified in the press as neo-Nazis, and charged them with conspiracy to damage energy facilities, among other offenses. They're still seeking to identify suspects in the North Carolina blackouts."

Somer paused and swallowed a sip of his wine.

"And the why?" I asked.

"FBI profilers continue to debate the motives," Somer said. "Many think these individuals are attempting to sow discord in their communities. Or in the words of our presenter, 'to create civil disorder and inspire further violence.'"

"In short," Joan said, "to cause people to lose faith in their government."

"Exactly," Somer said. "And there are thousands of electric substations throughout the country, all possible targets."

"What's the solution?" I asked. "Armed guards at every facility?"

"Such a response would be prohibitively expensive," Somer said, shaking his head. "Electric utilities in Arkansas have begun installing surveillance equipment at their most susceptible locations. What the FBI recommends is closer cooperation among law enforcement agencies across the state, with special attention to including substations during routine patrols by city and county officers. He also suggested the state consider a public service campaign, asking citizens to report anything suspicious they might notice around their local substations."

"How serious is this threat?" Leslie asked.

"The FBI agent was quite matter-of-fact, saying it's not a question of if but when," Somer said. "It's already happening in several adjacent states. Because of half a dozen unpublicized events, ERCOT, the Electric Reliability Council of Texas, has committed millions of dollars to additional security measures."

"In other words," I said, "damn serious."

That got another nod from Somer.

"The agent added it's one of the rare issues over his 20-year career keeping him awake at nights."

Joan stood and gave us a big smile.

"I believe it's time to change the subject to something a bit more pleasant. I'll be right back."

She returned with four heaping bowls of homemade peach cobbler.

As Leslie and I got to my truck after leaving Joan's house, I reached for the cell phone.

"Surely you're not calling somebody at this hour," she said. "It's 9:30."

"For Booker, it's mid-day. I want to tell him about this development regarding domestic terrorists. Besides, we haven't visited in weeks. He's not returned the last two or three messages I've left."

"Ah," he said, answering on the third ring. "The dear nephew."

"You're alive. I've tried phoning you without success for days."

There was a pause in the conversation.

"Perhaps I failed to divulge my plans for a much-deserved vacation," he finally said. "I've returned from a ten-day jaunt to Mallorca, a fabulous Mediterranean island off the Spanish coast. It provided the perfect hedonistic escape. Exclusive clubs, wild dancing until dawn, and young topless women sunbathing on every—"

"Hello, Uncle Booker," Leslie said, interrupting him. "I'm sure we've heard enough regarding your … uh … latest debauchery. We have an interesting update for you."

"Oh, hello dear," he said after clearing his throat. "I didn't realize my clever nephew had me on speakerphone."

"We had dinner with Representative Pfeiffer and Senator Smith this evening," I said, "and heard a tantalizing tidbit from Somer. He attended a private meeting earlier this week where an FBI agent warned a Senate committee about a rising concern: domestic terrorism."

"Here in our state?" Booker asked, the surprise in his voice evident. "In Arkansas?"

"These homegrown terrorists are becoming more active in the South, and this agent is convinced it's just a matter of time before they strike isolated electrical substations within our borders."

"They're attacking the grid?" Booker asked. "Whatever for?"

"The theory is they hope to disrupt society, giving people reason to lose confidence in their elected officials," Leslie said.

"Basic anarchists, in other words," Booker said.

"Next time you delve into the dark web," I said, "please keep an eye open for anything tying in with this threat."

"I intend to resume my online activities within the hour," Booker said. "I shall be on high alert for this new hazard."

~ TWENTY-NINE ~

During dinner with Joan and Somer, Leslie and the senator had agreed to get together the following week in Osceola, his hometown, for a photo session. Leslie had invited me to accompany her to northeast Arkansas for the day, but work commitments kept me in the office. She returned home about 7:00 as I removed a meat loaf from the oven.

"Something smells delicious," she said from the front hallway. "Let me store my gear and I'll meet you at the table."

A couple of minutes later, I handed her a glass of Merlot and she rewarded me with a kiss.

"What a day," she said, taking her seat. "Long yet productive."

Over dinner, Leslie filled me on her trip to Osceola.

"I met Somer at his mother's house where he introduced me to her and his sisters," she said. "What a gracious family. I took pictures at their home, and then he and I walked to the downtown square where I got portraits of Somer with the historic Mississippi County Courthouse behind him. During the short time we were there, a dozen or more people came by and greeted him, most giving Somer a hug, all of which I recorded. One of his friends was the newspaper editor he'd mentioned last week. They enjoyed a good laugh about the letter he'd published."

"You sound pleased with the day's activities," I said.

"Maybe my best photos were taken south of Osceola at a place called Sans Souci Landing, an overlook and access point on the

Mississippi River. We had a meaningful talk while I shot pictures of Somer with a towboat and string of barges in the background."

"Meaningful?" I asked, passing her the platter of meat loaf. She took another slice. "You've snared my attention."

"During our conversation, I learned Somer has a tragic incident in his past. One week before his sixth birthday, he and a group of cousins were playing on a sandbar a hundred yards upstream from this landing. One of the other boys slipped and fell into the river and the oldest of the lot jumped in to save him. Both were swept away by the current, apparently drowning although neither body was ever found."

"My gosh," I said. "What a horrible thing for anyone to witness, especially at that age. He was just a kid."

"As a consequence, Somer's mother laid down the law, forbidding him to go near the river throughout his youth," Leslie said. "He never learned to swim. And to this day remains petrified by lakes, ponds, and rivers."

Leslie drained her glass of Merlot and I gave her a refill. Same for me.

"However, years afterwards, something positive resulted from this family tragedy," Leslie said. "During Somer's first term in the state legislature, he introduced a bill establishing a program providing small grants to local park and recreation departments for water safety classes. It passed the Senate without a dissenting vote, sailed through the House, and was signed by the governor."

"Surely its enactment gave Somer some sense of accomplishment."

"He's received several letters from youngsters who credit those classes with saving their lives," Leslie said, bobbing her head. "They're hanging in his Senate office."

* * *

Leslie and I left for north Arkansas early Tuesday morning, August 8, so she could photograph Hillcountry Marine's new line of pontoon boats. Megan and Harrison had gone up the previous day to scout locations on nearby Bull Shoals Lake and to select models to use on the shoot. They knew Leslie wanted 10 to 12 individuals, to include two or three children and one baby-boomer couple, all of whom would be willing to take direction and had no fear of water. As for their physical appearance, Leslie had said, "Look for average citizens instead of beautiful people. Our job is to draw attention to the boats, not to a gorgeous goddess in a bikini."

We met our colleagues at a large marina on Bull Shoals well before noon. Megan and Harrison showed us the pair of brand-new party barges at our disposal: one to be photographed and the other to provide a platform for Leslie's work.

"Late yesterday afternoon we scouted potential locations," Megan said. "We found two appearing to offer the settings you requested. One's a small cove bordered by a dense forest and the other is a scenic stretch of shore lined by bluffs."

"And they're close by," Harrison said. "A 15-minute ride at most."

"I'd like to see them," Leslie said.

With Harrison behind the steering console of what we'd dubbed the work boat, we left the dock, cruising at low speed until we cleared the "no-wake" zone. As we headed to the cove, Megan and Harrison updated us on their progress.

"I think you'll be pleased with our models," Megan said. "They're scheduled to meet us at three o'clock. Two of the adults have experience piloting pontoon boats, so we're good there. And they all know to bring colorful outfits appropriate to a lake setting."

Harrison pointed to a hefty box on the deck.

"There's our portable changing room," he said. "Once we get it set up, our talent will be able to switch clothing in privacy. And the ice chests and those other boxes hold our food, drinks, and props."

"We're planning for two shoots, right?" Leslie asked. "One later today and another first thing in the morning?"

"That's correct," Megan said. "If we're lucky, we should be able to hit those 'golden hours' you mentioned."

We'd been in the cove all of five minutes when Leslie said, "This is perfect. It's protected from the wind, so the water should be calm. And the hillside covered with trees will provide an ideal background. Let's take a look at the second location."

That was my cue. I slipped behind the steering wheel and, with Harrison's tutelage, took us to the colorful cliffs. This site also met with Leslie's approval.

"We'll shoot here today, saving the cove for first thing tomorrow morning," she said. "The bluff faces west so we can hope for warm evening lighting."

With Leslie's inspection complete, we cut across the main channel of the lake to the marina. A steady wind had appeared, creating choppy conditions, and Harrison eased back on the throttle. Even so, the boat's pontoons kicked up a spray of water with every wave. I noticed Leslie glancing from one distant shore to the other. She looked serious.

"A penny for your thoughts."

"This is a huge reservoir, isn't it?" she asked. "Among the biggest in the state?"

"I read in one of the tourist brochures it's something on the order of 70 square miles. And up to 200 feet deep in places."

Her reaction was subtle, but I still noticed a slight shudder.

"I was just thinking," she said, "we could never get Somer to join us here."

I swept my eyes over the vast body of water. Leslie was right. This would be a nightmare for our friend.

We grabbed a quick lunch at Gaston's Resort before returning to the marina and transferring Leslie's gear from my truck to the party barge. While Megan began organizing the outfits and various props to be used by the models, Harrison and I assembled the changing station. Working at the other end of the barge, Leslie unpacked Amelia and flew her around and over the docks, confirming her drone was operating properly, before landing it on the boat.

The models arrived on time, much to Leslie's relief. When introductions were completed, she explained the day's assignment, describing the shots she hoped to get, and answered a handful of questions. Leslie then handed a photo release to each individual. Once those signed forms were collected, we motored the two boats from the marina. Half the models were on the barge with Harrison at the helm and the rest joined Megan, Leslie, and me on the other. Leslie launched Amelia, and the drone trailed us across the lake.

As Leslie had hoped, the sky remained clear, and the water in front of the bluff was a vivid blue. After she determined where she wanted the subject boat to be positioned, Harrison dropped anchor. When the first grouping of talent had changed into the proper attire and got into position, the party barge Leslie would shoot from backed away. She spent an hour photographing the boat and its smiling passengers from almost every angle possible with the drone, flying Amelia with confidence and expertise. She next took what seemed like a couple of hundred still photos using her Nikon and an assortment of lenses.

At Leslie's insistence, we enjoyed a short break and tied the boats together. The original set of models came onto our party barge and the next group stepped onto the other pontoon boat, with Megan and Harrison distributing binoculars, beach hats, inner tubes, fishing rods, and other props. Under Leslie's guidance, we relocated the boat to be photographed 50 yards down the shore to give the pictures a different look. Leslie then devoted another hour to shooting, using both the drone and her still camera.

As the afternoon progressed, the light began to warm and soon bathed the party barge and its merry band with a radiant glow. Leslie could hardly contain her excitement, switching between Amelia and the Nikon, and encouraging her charges with shouts of "Beautiful," "Keep those smiles coming," and "Perfect."

Twenty minutes later, the golden hour was finished. As we headed to the marina, Leslie grabbed shots of the party barge ahead of us silhouetted by a spectacular sunset.

At dinner, she shared a selection of still photographs with Harrison, Megan, and me.

"All in all," she said. "It was a good day. We got some great images. Now, if Mother Nature will again cooperate tomorrow."

Good old Mother Nature came through the next morning. The water in the cove was silky smooth, yielding stunning reflections against the blanket of trees in the background. I'd never seen Leslie more enthusiastic as she piloted Amelia over, around, and past the party barge and its smiling talent. An hour into her work, Leslie announced it was time to switch crews. Harrison guided the work boat to the other barge. We lashed the two boats together and, after swapping sets of models, Leslie resumed shooting. At ten o'clock, she announced the need for one final shot: a portrait of the entire assembly.

Upon our return to the marina, Leslie made a point of thanking each person, promising to send everyone a group photograph. Meanwhile, Harrison, Megan, and I disassembled the changing booth and collected and packed the assortment of clothing and props. At eleven o'clock, Harrison and Megan hurried away so Megan could make a late afternoon meeting at the office. Leslie and I loaded her photo gear in my truck and departed 15 minutes later.

* * *

During our lunch stop in Yellville, I phoned Del Boddington at Hill Country Marine and gave him a progress report on the photo shoot and thanked him for having arranged for the pontoon boats. I also said we'd forward several of the agency's recommended ads featuring the new photography for him and Tabitha to review.

Our blue-plate specials of chicken and dumplings had been delivered when Sheriff Hutch Thomas walked in, trailed by a pair of deputies. He gazed across the bustling restaurant and nodded to a handful of customers before his eyes met mine. Thomas waved and walked to our booth, his right hand extended.

"Mr. Lassiter," he said. "What brings you to our fine town?"

"Let me introduce you to my wife Leslie," I said as we exchanged a handshake. "She's the agency's photographer. We came up for a photo session for Del's outfit."

"My pleasure, Mrs. Lassiter," he said, taking her hand in his.

I halfway expected her to correct the sheriff, explaining she'd retained her maiden name, but saw her give me a subtle smile and a faint shake of her head. It was a discussion she could forgo.

Thomas tilted his head toward the table where his colleagues had taken seats.

"I better go join my boys. I know from experience they're not gonna wait on me."

"Sheriff Thomas," I said. "One quick question: is your summer camp off to a good start?"

"Today is the third day for the girls' session," he said, "and it's going great. The young men will be here next week."

He looked to Leslie and gave her a wink.

"We might even need to hire a professional photographer to capture all the activity."

The sheriff turned and walked away, patting backs and squeezing shoulders as he edged through the crowded diner to his deputies.

"He's the dude who held you at gunpoint?" Leslie asked.

"The very one."

"I'm glad he showed some restraint."

"Me, too."

As the waitress began clearing our table, she mentioned the dessert of the day: homemade peanut butter pie. Unable to resist temptation, I ordered a piece, offering to share it with Leslie.

"How far to the Francis Marion Memorial Camp for Southern Youth?" Leslie asked.

"It's 10 or 12 miles south of town," I said. "It wouldn't be much out of the way as we head to Little Rock if you'd like to stop. I'm not sure they'll let us in, but I could show you the entrance."

The peanut butter pie was delicious, even better than I'd hoped. Leslie cleaned the last crumbs of her half, scooted our dessert plate aside, and gave me a clever smile.

"Let's stop by the camp as we head home," she said. "I have an idea."

~ THIRTY ~

Sheriff Hutch Thomas gave Leslie and me a perfunctory smile and wave as we departed the restaurant. Climbing into my Toyota pickup, we left Yellville, driving south on Arkansas 14. I almost missed the turn, but spotted a small roadside sign reading **Francis Marion Camp** at the last moment. Its arrow pointed us onto same rough gravel lane Erin had directed Megan and me to weeks earlier. The thick coating of dust on the trees and bushes along the right of way indicated the narrow, twisting road had hosted a serious amount of traffic in recent days. Riddled with potholes and ruts, it was a rough and bouncy ride.

The Flyover Family had made an effort to improve the first impression for visitors to their property. What had been an over-grown fencerow was now cleared, the rusty gate had been replaced with a new one, now standing wide open, and several loads of chat had been spread across the once-challenging driveway. The **No Trespassing** warnings had been removed, and guests were greeted with an impressive banner stretching above the entrance: **Welcome to the Francis Marion Memorial Camp for Southern Youth!**

Rather than wheeling into the camp, I stopped on the shoulder of the road and we looked onto the property. We saw a handful of vehicles parked in front of the old farmhouse headquarters, although the new dormitory and classroom building was out of sight. I lowered my window and we could hear the laughter and shouts of young women in the distance.

"I believe you mentioned the property line was not too far down this road," Leslie said.

"During one of his online investigations, Booker found the boundaries," I said. "He told me the south side of the compound butts up against the National Park Service acreage."

"Let's drive a bit further."

Within 50 yards we came to a towering white oak with a narrow vertical marker nailed to its massive trunk a good six feet off the ground. It read: **US Boundary—NPS**. What appeared to be an old logging road angled off to the right. Partially obscured by weeds and bushes, it was lined on one side with the remains of an ancient stacked stone fence.

"Let's park here," Leslie said.

I pulled off the county road, nosed my pickup onto the old trace, and turned off the ignition.

"Does this have something to do with the cryptic idea you referred to in the restaurant?"

"It does indeed," she said. "It's time for some discreet aerial surveillance."

Leslie opened her door and started to step to the ground.

I placed a hand on her shoulder.

"Before you go traipsing down this little trail, douse yourself with bug spray from the can in the glove box," I said. "We're in the prime of tick and chigger season, and this brush provides the ideal habitat. When you're done, toss the can to me."

After spraying my arms, ankles, legs, and waist, I met Leslie at the truck's tailgate where she assembled Amelia.

"Didn't I read it's illegal to pilot a drone above national park property?" I asked. "Maybe in the detailed list of restrictions you shared with me?"

"You are correct," Leslie said, giving me an impish grin. "But what are the chances of a ranger stumbling onto us?"

I considered her question for a bit.

"Pretty remote, I'd say. Yet I'd hate to see your substantial investment in Amelia confiscated by an officious federal employee.

And then, of course, there'd be the time-consuming and expensive process of bailing you out of jail."

Hands on her hips, Leslie stared at me, shaking her head.

"Okay, okay," she said, hints of irritation coming through.

She sorted through her bulging camera bag, removed her favorite Nikon, and handed it to me.

"This is my insurance policy. Hang it around your neck and follow me."

Thirty feet ahead of us was a slight clearing. After placing Amelia on a handy flat rock in the middle of the old logging road, Leslie fiddled with the remote-control transmitter in her hands. The four tiny propellers began spinning, and the drone lifted from the ground and was soon above the canopy of trees. In a matter of seconds it disappeared, heading in a northward direction.

"Amelia is now peering down on the Flyover Family's compound," Leslie said, staring at the image on her transmitter. "I can see the—"

"Did you hear something?" I asked, interrupting.

"Hear what?" she asked, her gaze glued to the device in her hands.

"There's a vehicle approaching on the road. It's probably a local, but …" I shrugged.

Leslie turned to face the road, her eyes wide.

"I'll set Amelia to hover," she said and made a few quick adjustments to the control panel.

She glanced at our surroundings before darting to a nearby tree. She slipped the transmitter behind its wide trunk, twice peeking back to make certain it was concealed.

A large pickup truck coasted to a stop adjacent to mine. It was white with oversized tires, had a light bar stretched across the top of the cab, and carried a heavy-duty brush guard mounted in front of the grill. Running the length of the vehicle's body was a thin green stripe, and on the passenger door was a prominent arrowhead-shaped emblem identifying its owner: **National Park Service**. Beside the insignia were the words **U.S. Park Ranger**.

"Randy," Leslie whispered, "please give me the camera."

As I handed her the Nikon, a door slammed. A woman stepped around the truck and began walking to us. Wearing a short-sleeve gray shirt with a badge, green shorts, a wide-brimmed hat, and a pair of scuffed hiking boots, she appeared to be in her mid-40s.

"Good afternoon," she said. "Checking to make sure you folks are okay."

Since I'd seen her give the bed of my truck more than a cursory glance, I had doubts about her interest in our welfare. I figured she'd already called in my license plate to her home base. We began walking toward her.

"Doing fine," Leslie said.

She lifted her camera for the ranger to see.

"As soon as we spotted this old stone wall, I knew I had to get some pictures."

She pivoted and gestured to the relic standing behind us.

"With all the moss and lichens, it should make a fine black and white photograph."

The ranger bobbed her head.

"At one time, this land belonged to a pioneer settler named Jeremiah Dobson," she said. "He and his wife moved here in the late 1840s from Kentucky. They had 11 kids, seven of whom reached adulthood. This short stretch of rock fence is the only remnant of their original 40-acre homestead."

"It's amazing how things revert back to nature," I said, trying to break an awkward pause in the conversation.

"Enjoy yourselves," the ranger said. "Be careful, though. This area's known for producing copperheads. One of my colleagues claims there's a den of 'em under the stone wall."

She gave us a nonchalant salute and returned to her truck. We waved as she drove off, leaving a trail of dust as she continued her journey south on the county road.

I was surprised when Leslie pulled me close and gave me a big kiss.

"Thanks for the warning about a potential visit by a ranger. If I hadn't had this in my hands," she said, holding the camera in front of her, "we might have struggled with an explanation for our stop."

"And you might have found yourself occupying the passenger seat in the ranger's pickup, with me following you to the nearest lockup."

She shook her head, gave me a gentle pat on the cheek, and trotted back to our original spot and reached behind the tree. Retrieving the remote control for Amelia, she began tweaking the knobs.

"Randy," she said. "You need to see this."

Catching up, I peered over her shoulder and studied the screen on her monitor.

"Amelia's cruising at an altitude of 125 feet," she said. "This is the headquarters house."

I looked at the image and saw the group's farmhouse.

Seconds later, she said, "And this must be the new building for the dormitory and classrooms."

"It's big," I said as the structure came into view. I noticed two concrete courts behind it, one for tennis and the other for basketball.

"A pickleball court?" I asked, pointing to an unfamiliar shape near the others.

"I believe so," Leslie said. "And there's a horseshoe pit beyond it."

"Let's check out the pond," I said. "From the sounds of things earlier, I'd guess the campers are swimming."

"Can you direct me there?"

"It's not too far past the new building," I said. "To the northwest, I believe."

Within a few moments, Leslie had Amelia hovering above the pond. It was far bigger than I expected, more on the order of a small lake. We found a beach at one end with the swimming area marked by a string of buoys. Most of the girls were frolicking in the water while four or five sunned themselves on a floating platform.

"They can't hear Amelia, can they?" I asked.

"Not a chance," Leslie said, "and she's little enough she's all but invisible against the bright sky."

As we watched the young women at play, oblivious to our prying eyes, I realized why so many people had concerns regarding the potential loss of privacy with this airborne technology.

"Was there anything else you'd like to see?" Leslie asked, pulling me back to the present.

"Booker mentioned a shooting range," I said. "Let's see if we can find it."

It took a while for Leslie to locate the facility. We counted a dozen firing stations with a series of targets arranged at various intervals. A large earthen berm had been placed behind the most distant targets to catch the shots. A lone pickup was parked adjacent to a building at the shooting range, but we didn't spot a soul.

"If there's nothing else, I'll fly Amelia back," Leslie said.

I continued to stare at the monitor, mesmerized by the ever-changing images. Something caught my attention as the drone passed over a portion of the lake opposite the swimming beach.

"Can you retrace those last few seconds?"

She paused Amelia and then reversed her course.

"There," I said, pointing to the corner of the screen. "What's that?"

Leslie maneuvered the drone above the spot I'd seen.

"I'm not sure," she said. "It resembles a pile of wreckage."

"Can you bring us a bit closer?" I asked.

Leslie zoomed in. The enlarged image revealed a stack of lumber and what appeared to be a pair of pontoon floats or tubes near the edge of the lake.

"Those two long cylinders were donated to the camp by Del Boddington of Hillcountry Marine," I said. "They were dented and he couldn't use them to build a party barge."

"I wonder why they're here?"

My brain was entertaining the same question. "It could be they plan on building another swimming dock," I said. "But this is very near the dam, isn't it? I believe it's a good distance from the beach."

Leslie switched our view of the lake from close-up to wide-angle. The swimming area must have been at least a couple of hundred yards away.

"Maybe they have another project in mind," Leslie said.

She piloted Amelia to the clearing, landing the drone on the big rock at her feet.

While she dissembled the aircraft, I kept thinking about that pair of pontoon floats. Perhaps Uncle Booker could offer his insights.

~ THIRTY-ONE ~

We'd been home no more than 15 minutes when our land line rang.

After Leslie picked up the phone, I heard her say, "Let me put you on speaker-phone. Hang on, and I'll get Randy."

I met her in the hallway.

"Joan Pfeiffer's calling," she said, her voice low. "She sounds upset. Very upset."

We walked into the den and took seats near the phone, Leslie to one side of it and me on the other.

"Good evening, Joan," I said. "What can we do for you?"

"Have you been on Facebook today?" She sounded almost breathless.

I looked at Leslie and she shook her head.

"Neither of us have checked it," I said. "I try to spend as little time there as possible. Too much negativity."

"I have a page on Facebook," Leslie said. "It's just about required in my business, although I make a point of checking it no more than once a day. Often not at all."

"You're smart," Joan said.

We heard her sniff.

"This so-called 'social media' is nothing but a national travesty. A cancerous blot on our formerly civilized society."

"What's happened?" Leslie asked.

220

"I wish Somer were here to give you the complete story," Joan said. "He's driving to Osceola, so you'll have to hear my version."

She paused for a moment.

"First, though, I'm not interrupting dinner, am I?"

"Not at all," I said. "Please fill us in."

Joan took a deep breath.

"I suppose it's best to start at the beginning," she said. "Many years ago, when Somer was still in college."

"During his time at Harvard?" I asked.

"His senior year," Joan said. "He was elected captain of the school's debate team."

"I believe they won some sort of national title that year," I said.

"He's told me on more than one occasion those were the best days of his undergraduate years," Joan said. "Yet all these decades later, one incident has come back to haunt him. He and his fellow students were priming for a debate against Yale."

"Wasn't Yale a bitter opponent?" Leslie asked.

"Their biggest rival," Joan said. "To strengthen their individual presentations, the preparations included filming practice sessions. Afterwards, they evaluated each other's posture, their gestures, their enunciation, their pacing, their eye contact, and, of course, their arguments."

"That's sounds like Somer," I said. "Like the Boy Scout he was. Always prepared."

"Somer claims it was the most arduous training he'd ever experienced," Joan said. "He even compared it to the comprehensive techniques used today by many successful athletic teams."

"No doubt it worked," I said, "given their accomplishments."

"The topic of this particular debate was 'Paying Reparations to Descendants of American Slaves,'" Joan said.

"A timely and controversial subject," Leslie said. "Both then and now."

I recalled our earlier conversation regarding the primitive editorial cartoon identifying Somer as Senator Repparations Smith.

When I looked to Leslie, her knowing nod seemed to indicate the same thought had occurred to her.

"Indeed," Joan with a sigh. "Somer, being as thorough and meticulous then as he is today, prepared arguments both for and against a federal reparations program."

"Let me guess," I said. "He practiced both the pro and con positions."

"Many times," Joan said.

"Let me continue this guessing game," Leslie said. "These practice rounds were filmed back in the day. And somehow the tapes of Somer's practice sessions were released and are now being seen and shared by thousands of viewers on Facebook."

"You're close," Joan said. "The sole video now circulating is a portion of one where Somer argues reparations are owed to millions of descendants of American slaves. It's been edited down to less than two minutes, but Somer's voice is emphatic and crystal clear. The clip reminds me of Dr. Martin Luther King."

"Tell us about the comments on Facebook," I said.

"Overwhelmingly negative," Joan said. "For every positive comment, there must be 20 to 30 in opposition. And many of them are vicious. The animosity and hatred people are willing to express online is frightening, much of it with racial overtones. Some have posted photos of Somer and several have included his addresses—both home and e-mail—along with his phone numbers."

"How is our friend taking this?" I asked.

"At first, he assumed it would blow over," Joan said. "However, I told him he was living in a fantasy world. With the divisiveness in today's political environment, I felt sure this short tape would cause him a great deal of grief."

She paused for a beat.

"And a great deal of grief is what he and his family have experienced in the past 24 hours. Somer's gone to Osceola to calm his mother and sisters down."

"How can we help?" Leslie asked.

"I'm hopeful your sweet husband can offer some assistance," Joan said. "If my memory's correct, Randy and his colleagues have a good deal of expertise in public relations."

While Joan had been sharing this horror story, I'd tried to clear my mind and give some thought to how this unnerving situation could be approached. One thing was for damn certain; it couldn't be contained. To use an old cliché, that horse was out of the barn. But could something be done to minimize the damage? To stem this enormous tide overwhelming Senator Somerset Spartacus Smith and jeopardizing his career? Was there a solution to this predicament?

I saw Leslie staring at me, and realized Joan was awaiting a response.

"Of course," I said, "we'll get to work on this right away. I'll invite a couple of my coworkers here this evening and we'll try to determine how to stop the bleeding."

"My prayers have been answered," Joan said, the relief in her voice obvious. "Thank you so much!"

Shaking my head, I couldn't help but chuckle.

"Joan," I said, "those prayers haven't been answered yet, but we'll think of something. In the meantime, my recommendation is to keep on praying."

* * *

Three-quarters of an hour later, Megan Maloney and Abigail Ahart had joined Leslie and me in our den. These two colleagues had jumped at the chance to help, as I knew they would. Megan suggested I invite Erin Askew to participate.

"She's got good political instincts," she'd said of Erin. "Plus, she's a bit younger than the rest of us and is no doubt more familiar with the intricacies and nuances of social media."

A quick call to Erin and she was on the way, arriving soon after the others.

Leslie and I spent 15 minutes bringing the women up-to-speed on the unpleasant circumstances facing Somer Smith.

"You're right," Erin said. "It's bad. I follow Senator Smith on Facebook, and things blew up earlier today. One of the messiest and most volatile reactions I've witnessed."

"As we might have expected, Fox News is making a big deal out of it," Megan said. "They've been airing the clip once an hour since noon."

I excused myself for a moment, returning with two bottles of wine, one white and the other a red. Anticipating my move, Leslie appeared with a tray of glasses. The women opted for the Chardonay while I chose the Malbec.

Holding my glass high, I said, "Here's to State Senator Somer Smith. May we find a way to extricate him from this dilemma."

A chorus of "hear, hear!" came next.

"Before we delve into this," Megan said, "how's Senator Smith holding up?"

"State Representative Joan Pfeiffer, who alerted us to Somer's predicament, said he's driven home to be with his family in northeast Arkansas," I said. "She indicated he's coping as best could be expected."

"First things first," Abbie said. "Is the tape genuine?"

"Joan said it was," Leslie said. "The problem, of course, is it's taken out of context. The companion tape where Somer argues against reparations hasn't been released."

"I'd suggest we contact the Harvard University administration, asking for help in setting the record straight," Megan said. "The second tape where the senator speaks against these payments must be made public."

"I suspect there are prominent Harvard graduates in Arkansas who might be willing to act in his behalf," I said. "My Uncle Booker can ferret out the possible candidates."

Erin snapped her fingers.

"As you know, I'm a sports groupie. Here's a wild idea, perhaps too wild."

She hesitated, shaking her head.

"Never mind; it's too bizarre."

"Let's hear it," I said. "We're desperate."

224

"The state's top high school basketball recruit lives in Somer's district," she said. "The head coach of the Razorbacks has spent a lot of time in the area. Maybe he'd speak out for Somer."

Before anybody could react to Erin's suggestion, the phone rang, startling us all. Late evening calls were seldom good in my experience, but this wasn't a typical night. Leslie answered it, and then gestured for me.

"It's Joan," she said.

Her message was brief. Somer had called Governor Patricia Butler at the mansion, asking for an appointment for me with one of her key staffers. Joan said he'd given the governor our phone number, and I should expect a call later in the evening.

"Somer and I appreciate your help more than you can imagine," she said and ended the conversation.

After I shared this latest development with our guests, we continued to discuss options for salvaging Somer's reputation. The consensus seemed to be we hold a news conference in the immediate future to set the record straight. Who would speak and where were the operative questions. And would the media attend?

This conversation was interrupted by another phone call. Leslie again picked up the phone, listened for a moment, and motioned for me.

"It's a man," she said, placing a hand over the mouthpiece. "He's identified himself as Governor Butler's chief-of-staff."

"This is Randy Lassiter," I said, taking the phone's receiver.

"Mort Sensabaugh here," he said. "Sorry for disturbing you at this hour, but Governor Butler asked me to give you a call. Can you be in my office in the State Capitol at 7:30 in the morning?"

"Yes sir," I said. "What—"

"We'll be addressing Senator Somer Smith's unfortunate situation," he said.

"See you tomorrow."

The line went dead.

I turned and saw four faces staring at me.

"That was Mort Sensabaugh from Governor Butler's staff," I said. "I'm to be in his office first thing in the morning."

~ THIRTY-TWO ~

After I refilled everyone's glass, our little group talked for another hour while I took three pages of notes. The last couple of ideas we discussed had marginal merit, indicating we'd reached the point of diminishing returns.

"Gosh, it's well past midnight," Abbie said as the conversation dwindled. "I don't think I can contribute much more."

Megan and Erin seemed to have come to the same conclusion, for our three guests stood as a group and began gathering their purses and notepads.

"Best wishes with tomorrow's appointment," Megan said as the others nodded.

"I'll keep you posted," I said. "It should be an interesting day."

Leslie and I showed everyone to the door, thanking them for their help from the front porch.

"I'm ready to crash," Leslie said once we were back inside. "It's going to be a short night."

"First though," I said, "I need to give Booker a call."

He picked up on the second ring.

"My god, dear nephew," he said. "What are you doing up at this hour?"

"It concerns our friend Senator Somer Smith," I said. "His political career is in jeopardy, and we're trying to assist him."

"May I be of aid?"

"Your unique expertise is the reason for this call," I said. "Somer's a Harvard University graduate. Can you track down a handful of prominent Arkansas residents who are also alumni of that fine institution who might be willing to do a favor in his behalf? If they're major donors to the university, even better."

"What kind of favor, to use your word, do you have in mind?" Booker asked.

"We need an influential individual or two who would be willing to personally contact Harvard's president, asking him or her to release a video tape of Somer produced in a debate class years ago."

"Does this have anything to do with the clip now circulating on Facebook?"

"Everything," I said. "It's the counterpunch to the one you mentioned."

"I'm on it," he said. "May I assume you require these names rather soon?"

"By seven o'clock," I said and glanced at my watch. "In six hours."

The line went dead.

* * *

Twenty or thirty minutes later, I was still wide awake, tossing and turning in bed while my mind continued to race.

"Having trouble dozing off?" Leslie whispered.

"Too much to think about," I said. "And you?"

"Same here," she said. "But I have an idea if you're agreeable. In the past, it's helped us get to sleep."

"Let's hear it."

Instead, I felt her hand slide across my bare chest and then further down onto my groin.

It worked. Almost too well as it turned out.

While I'm normally able to set my own mental alarm clock, it came close to failing me this time. I woke up 45 minutes prior to my appointment with Mort Sensabaugh. Showered and shaved, I skipped breakfast and gave Leslie a quick but sincere kiss as I hurried to the door, tightening my necktie on the way.

"Don't forget this," she said, waving a sheet of paper in my direction. "It's the list of selected Harvard University graduates Booker compiled overnight. I printed a copy while you showered."

I found a parking space within a block of the State Capitol, cleared the security checkpoint, and dashed up the long marble staircase at the north end of the building. The Governor's Office was to my right at the top of the steps. The smiling receptionist took my name and made a brief call.

Remembering the printout Leslie had handed me, I removed it from my pocket and studied the list. Booker had found seven Harvard alumni living in Arkansas who'd each made substantial donations in the six-figure range and above to the university in recent years. Booker had done a thorough job, including home and e-mail addresses and telephone numbers for all seven. I recognized the names of four of the people, but the others were unknown to me. Two minutes later, a short, heavyset man entered the lobby and extended his hand.

"Mr. Lassiter," he said, "I'm Mort Sensabaugh. Come on back."

I followed him through a maze of cubicles before he led me into a compact office. Sagging under a towering stack of files, a small credenza behind his desk appeared ready for an imminent collapse. Above it was a bulletin board covered with notes pinned two and three deep. Not a single square inch of the original surface of his desk was visible under the mounds of paper.

"Would you like a cup of coffee?" he asked.

What I wanted was a doughnut. However, that didn't seem to be in the offing.

"Sure," I said. "Black."

He returned a minute later carrying two cups of the steaming beverage and handed one to me.

"Our friend Senator Smith is in one hell of a mess," Mort said. "Through none of his own doing. But nevertheless, a damn mess."

There was a slight pause as he took a sip of coffee.

228

"I understand from the senator you've given some thought to this unfortunate situation."

"Three of my colleagues, my wife, and I spent several hours last night brainstorming various possibilities," I said, as a door opened behind me.

Staring over my shoulder, Mort rose from his chair.

"Randy Lassiter," he said, "let me introduce you to Governor Patricia Butler."

I turned and there she was, big as life. Arkansas's second female governor. Almost matching me in height, she gave me a pleasant smile as I stumbled to my feet.

"My pleasure," she said as we shook hands. "So, you're the man Somer holds in such high regard. Let's hear those brainstorming ideas you were going to mention as I walked in."

"We're hopeful somebody on this list might be willing to call the president of Harvard University," I said, handing her the sheet of paper from my pocket. "These alumni, all Arkansas residents, are major financial contributors to the school. Maybe one of them can convince Harvard's president to release the companion tape to the one doing the damage on Facebook."

Governor Butler's eyes skipped down the page. Finished, she handed it to her colleague, giving him a subtle nod.

"I think we have a winner with number five," she said, arching her eyebrows.

I attempted to recall the names Booker had uncovered. If my memory was correct, the fifth one down the list was an entrepreneur in south Arkansas who'd made a fortune in the lithium extraction business.

Mort studied the sheet for a few seconds before returning it to the governor, smiling as he did so.

"I believe he's requested a big favor from you," he said.

"If you'll excuse me," she said, "I have a call to make."

When she left the room, Mort and I returned to our seats.

"Well, Mr. Lassiter," he said, "you're one for one. Let's hear the rest of your ideas."

"Please call me Randy," I said. "We're thinking a news conference could be an effective option. The sooner the better. Governor Butler would speak, of course, along with Senator Smith and others."

"The others," he said. "Who are they?"

"One name we've considered is Rollie Waymack, the head basketball coach at the University of Arkansas."

Mort scowled, not the reaction I'd anticipated.

"How in hell could a basketball coach help with this?"

"We've learned Arkansas's number-one-rated high school point guard lives in Somer's senate district. This kid is a top priority for the Razorbacks, and Coach Waymack has been spending hours in northeast Arkansas, hoping to recruit him."

"And you think this coach might be willing to speak in Senator Smith's behalf?"

"Don't forget the Razorbacks seem to have a unifying effect in this state," I said. "Everybody loves them. Democrats, Republicans, Independents."

Mort snorted.

"I'm from Texas, and don't understand this strange fascination."

"There's more," I said. "We're told this young basketball superstar is related to Somer. Not yet sure of the exact ties, although there's a connection. So, yeah, we figure it'd be worth a shot. We found two photographs on the Internet where Coach Waymack and Somer are posing together."

As Mort scribbled something on his notepad, his telephone rang. He shook his head and took the call.

"Sensabaugh here," he said.

"Senator Smith," he said seconds later. "Good morning."

After a short while, he said, "Yes, Mr. Lassiter—Randy, that is—is with me and we're making progress."

Following a short pause, he continued, "I'm glad to hear you're headed this way. I'll call soon with an update on the day's plans."

He'd hardly put the receiver down when the phone rang again.

"Yes, ma'am," he said. "We're on the way."

230

Mort grabbed his notepad and pen, got to his feet, and stepped from behind his messy desk.

"We're going down the hall," he said. "The boss has beckoned."

I trailed him through a cramped corridor and past half a dozen desks where his colleagues tended to the affairs of state government. We went through one last door, entering Governor Butler's private suite.

Her office was the opposite of Mort's. Spacious and uncluttered with a large window facing the downtown skyscrapers, it featured a matched pair of handsome leather chairs and several original paintings. A collection of photographs hung from one wall. I noticed one of Governor Butler with the President taken in the Oval Office.

Governor Butler sat behind a clean desk and seemed to be concluding a telephone conversation. She nodded at us and gestured toward the captain's chairs in front of the desk. Mort and I took our seats.

"It's not quite eight o'clock," she said after ending the call, "and we've already had a productive morning. Not a bad start for the day."

"I take it our Harvard alumnus in south Arkansas has agreed to help?" Mort asked.

Governor Butler gave him a knowing smile.

"He jumped at the chance. He's a personal friend of the university's president and promised to call her within the hour, all but guaranteeing the release of the second tape."

"If I'm not overstepping my bounds," Mort said, "may I ask what was required for his cooperation?"

Governor Butler shrugged.

"Just a little quid pro quo," she said. "He desperately wants to be named to the state's oil and gas commission. What he doesn't know is one of the members confided to me last month she plans to resign. So, I'll announce his appointment in another week or two. He also pledged to send a generous campaign contribution when the timing is right."

"Randy's team generated another idea I want him to share with you," Mort said. "Even though it's a little unorthodox, it could have legs."

"Unorthodox," she said. "I like it already."

I explained our interest in getting Rollie Waymack, head coach of the University of Arkansas Razorback basketball team, to speak in defense of Senator Smith.

The governor listened attentively, nodding now and then as I spoke.

"Arkansas's coaches tend to shy away from politics," she said. "For good reason. However, I remember my grandfather mentioning a former University of Arkansas football coach named Lou Holtz who took a publicized stand on a political issue of some sort years ago. The precedent's been set. I'd say we give it a shot."

Mort jotted something down on his notepad.

"How should we pursue this?" he asked.

"Call the Secretary of Higher Education," she said. "Ask her to phone the Chancellor of the University of Arkansas at once who can then make this request of Coach Waymack."

"What's our time frame?" Mort asked.

"I want this news conference to happen today," the Governor said. "Somer should be here by late morning. Let's schedule it for one o'clock. Coach Waymack has better access to planes than we do. He can get down here without a problem."

She turned to me.

"Any other aces up your sleeve?"

"Would you consider asking the pro tem of the Senate to speak in Somer's behalf?"

"Senator Rufus Henshaw?" the governor asked, the pitch in her voice an octave higher.

I noticed she'd also elevated her eyebrows.

"You're serious, right?"

Mort had bolted upright.

"Are you fricking kidding me? The SOB has been a complete pain in the ass for this administration since day one. He belongs to the other party, for God's sake."

232

He continued to stare at me as his face reddened.

"I'll have to admit, my initial reaction is similar to Mort's," the governor said. "Maybe you can explain your rationale."

"I realize this man is about as right wing as they get," I said. "A card-carrying conservative. Yet despite the odds, he and Somer have developed a cordial relationship, one of mutual respect."

"But what's it going to take for him to publicly come out in support of Somer," Mort asked. "Such a move could alienate his base."

"Randy may have something here," Butler said, leaning back in her chair. "A week or two ago, Senator Henshaw caught me in the senate chambers, pulled me aside, and said he wanted to visit privately on what he described as a delicate matter. Given our past history, I more or less blew him off. With the situation we're facing, this might be the time to see what he wanted."

"For the record," Mort said, "I think this is a terrible idea."

Governor Butler picked up her phone.

"Liza," she said, "please get Senator Rufus Henshaw on the phone."

She placed the receiver back in the cradle and took a sip of her coffee.

"Be careful with Henshaw," Mort said. "This dude is nothing but bad news."

"He's bound to have a few redeeming qualities," the governor said. "Most men do."

Her telephone rang.

"Here goes," Governor Butler said and reached for it.

~ THIRTY-THREE ~

"Senator Henshaw," Governor Butler said into her telephone. "Good morning to you. How's my favorite member of the loyal opposition?" she asked, her tone light and cheerful.

She winked at Mort and me.

She listened to the senate pro tem for a bit, bobbing her head as he replied.

"I know what you mean, Senator," she said. "I have the same problem almost daily. The press never seems to get it right."

Glancing at us, she shook her head and then rolled her eyes, again surprising me. First a wink and now this. I didn't realize governors did those sorts of things.

"No, sir," she said. "I don't believe the timing is right to amend the state's transparency act. You'd sure enough get vilified by the media if you attempted such a move. Maybe even hung in effigy by an aroused public. The fact is, Senator, I'd have to come after you, too."

There was another quiet spell while the man at the other end of the line responded.

"The reason for my call?" she asked. "I remembered you mentioning something in the senate a few days ago regarding a matter you wanted to discuss. Maybe we can astound the world and initiate a round of bipartisanship in this state."

She rolled her eyes once more.

Governor Butler reached for a pen and began taking notes. A full minute passed, and she looked up to Mort and me, giving us a nod and a slight grin.

"Let's make sure I have this straight," she said. "Your wife's sister has a lazy, worthless son who's at Cummins for drug possession. Not dealing, but simple possession. You're sure?"

Cummins, I knew, was an exclusive gated community—otherwise known as a state prison—in southeastern Arkansas.

"If he's innocent, Senator, explain to me a second time why he pleaded guilty."

She scribbled a series of words on her notepad.

"And you'd like me to ask the state board of corrections to release him early based on good behavior, right? Give me his name again."

She jotted down a few more details.

"I'll see what I can do," Governor Butler said. "You're respected among your colleague in the General Assembly as an honorable horse trader, Senator. You're a veteran legislator and understand how things work. You scratch my back, and I'll scratch yours."

She chuckled at something she'd heard.

"Of course, I'll expect a favor in return," she said. "That's the way this political system of ours works. Truth is, it'll be a kind gesture for a good friend of yours. Senator Somer Smith."

I was curious about Henshaw's reaction to her remarks. Unfortunately, I had no choice other than to observe as she carried on the conversation, only half of which I could hear.

"But you know he's a fine man," she said. "As respectable as they come. The video clip on Facebook was a portion of a rehearsal from years ago at Harvard. There's another tape recorded at the same session where he argues against the idea of compensation. We intend to produce it this afternoon for the media."

She leaned back in her chair and listened for a bit.

"Yes, Senator Henshaw. You have my word," she said. "Let me cut to the chase. There'll be a news conference at one o'clock in the Governor's Conference Room to set the record straight, to refute these ill-advised allegations regarding Senator Smith. I want you to stand up and say a few words in support of Somer."

There was another period of silence, longer than the others.

"You don't even need to use the word reparations in your remarks," Governor Butler said. "Speak from the heart, telling those in attendance of your high regard for Senator Smith and your knowledge of his years of excellent work in our legislative body. I'm asking you for nothing more than to express your total faith in him doing the right thing."

Her next pause was shorter.

"Thank you," she said, giving us a thumbs up. "We'll see you at one. And I promise I'll do my best to intervene in behalf of your wife's sorry nephew."

Ending the call, Governor Butler placed the phone's receiver to its cradle.

She looked to me, a wry grin on her face. "Well, Mr. Lassiter," she said. "Our efforts to salvage Senator Somer Smith's career are underway. Let's hope we succeed. It's going to be an interesting day."

* * *

I drove to Lassiter & Associates and managed to get in a couple of hours of work before returning to the State Capitol for the one o'clock media event. Three or four dozen protestors milling around on the building's front lawn surprised me. As I got closer, I realized I was viewing two distinct factions, more or less equal in number, with an even mixture of black and white faces. One group supported the tape they'd seen of Somer Smith on Facebook, waving signs and placards reading "Hell Yes! Reparations Now!" and "Pay for Slave Labor!" and others of a similar ilk. Posters carried by the second cluster of demonstrators featured opposing messages, ranging from "Impeach Somer Smith" to "Lock Him Up!" A squad car from the Little Rock Police Department separated them, its two officers keeping the peace. So far, at least.

Stepping into the Governor's Conference Room at 12:25, I was pleased to see an AV team positioning a monitor and testing a laptop. It was a good sign.

Mort Sensabaugh walked in and gave me a thumbs-up.

"The president of Harvard came through," he said. "In addition to arranging for us to get a copy of the other rehearsal tape, she sent a short video clip where she praises Senator Smith as a distinguished Harvard alumnus. Want a quick preview as soon as the equipment's ready to go?"

"You bet."

"While we wait, here's an update," Mort said. "Senator Smith got into town a quarter of an hour ago and went to see Governor Butler. And Coach Waymack jetted in a bit earlier. I retrieved him at the airport and escorted him into the governor's inner sanctum less than five minutes ago."

"Are things okay with Senator Henshaw?" I asked. "He hasn't bailed on us, has he?"

Mort shook his head. "Last I heard, he was rehearsing his remarks in one of the back offices in the senate."

"Everything's falling into place?"

"So far, so good. We've been told Fox has sent a reporter into town to cover this story." He shrugged. "We'll find out soon enough."

"The equipment's ready," one of the technicians said. "Did y'all want to see the recordings?"

"Yes sir," Mort replied.

I slipped into a seat across from him at the long conference table. The first tape, not much more than a minute and a half long, showed the president of Harvard sitting at her antique desk. Describing Senator Somer Smith as one of the university's most illustrious graduates, she expressed her sincere regret for the damage done to his reputation while insisting the next tape would set the record straight, that Somer Smith had prepared arguments both for and against reparations.

Like the tape circulating on Facebook, the second video clip showed Somer's drive and intensity and total grasp of the subject. Cash payments to descendants of slaves would be little more than a federal bribe and an insult to hard-working African-Americans across the land, Somer argued. He concluded by stating the ultimate solution to America's racial injustices required an unwavering commitment from our society to fully honor, respect, and implement the Civil Rights Act of 1964 and subsequent laws Congress had enacted. It was a powerful and persuasive statement against reparations. Joan had been right; Somer's dynamic presentation reminded me of the orations given by Dr. Martin Luther King at his peak.

"Wow," I said. "I would hate to debate him on any subject."

"No kidding," Mort said. "The man can deliver a speech."

He shook my hand and returned to the governor's office, saying he needed to confirm Governor Butler was comfortable with the upcoming event.

The doors of the conference room soon opened and members of the media and interested citizens began streaming in. Within minutes, all four of Little Rock's television stations were represented, and their crews arranged a bevy of tripods and cameras near the podium. Leslie and Joan appeared, and I got hugs from each. When Megan, Abbie, and Erin arrived, I introduced them to Joan, explaining their role in preparing Somer's defense. With tears in her eyes, Joan thanked my colleagues for their help.

The crowd continued to grow, with many in the group Somer's fellow legislators. The room was nearing capacity when people gathered at the main entrance parted to allow another media team into the space. A man wearing a Fox News jacket made his way to the front of the room, careful not to KO anyone with his camera. He was followed by an attractive young woman, a blonde who flashed an engaging smile while working her way through the horde. As her cameraman positioned his gear, she took a seat at the media table.

Governor Patricia Butler walked into the conference room at 1:00 on the dot, entering from the private door opening into the governor's office complex. Behind her came Senator Somer Smith, Senator Rufus Henshaw, Razorback basketball coach Rollie Waymack, and Mort Sensabaugh. All but Sensabaugh flanked the governor, opposite the large monitor. Mort eased into the throng, coming to a stop beside me, as Governor Butler approached the podium.

"It's showtime," he whispered, giving me a gentle jab me in the ribs with his knuckles. "Thanks for your help making this come together."

"It's a privilege to serve as Arkansas's governor," Governor Butler said. "Yet today's news conference truly embarrasses me. Because of a small group of irresponsible individuals on social media, we're forced to hold this event to clear the name of one of the most respected members of the Arkansas General Assembly, State Senator Somer Smith."

Governor Butler paused and looked over the gathering. "I see the senator's mother and sisters in the back of the room," she said, extending an open hand toward the women. "I am so sorry for the pain and suffering this incident has caused the Smith family. You deserve so much better."

A few people began to clap, but Governor Butler raised a hand to silence them. "Yesterday, a video showing Senator Smith during his collegiate days at Harvard began circulating on one of the social media platforms. Captain of the school's debate team, Somer was charged with preparing for an upcoming debate on the controversial issue of reparations. Being as thorough then as he is today, Somer practiced his arguments both for and against these payments. His rehearsals were recorded to help him improve his debating skills. The tape making the rounds during the past 24 hours was the one in favor of reparations. The companion video, the one where Somer Smith forcefully opposed such payments, wasn't posted on Facebook."

The governor gazed over the one hundred or so people in the room. "Many individuals have come forward in Somer's defense. One of those is Dr. Hannah Brewster, president of Harvard University. She's joining us via a prerecorded video message."

At the end of Dr. Brewster's short yet heartfelt remarks, the audience burst into applause, stopping when Governor Butler returned to the podium.

"Dr. Brewster mentioned the all-important second practice tape, the one where a young Somer Smith challenged the very concept of reparations. And, I might add, the video the reckless rene-gades on Facebook chose not to share. Let's watch it now, courtesy of Dr. Brewster and her Harvard colleagues."

People in the room viewed the tape in complete silence, spell-bound as Somer eloquently made his points against a national rep-arations program. At its conclusion, the crowd erupted in prolonged applause.

I thought back to the protestors I'd encountered in front of the building. Maybe the two groups could swap signs and continue their demonstrations.

Again stepping to the podium, Governor Butler stared at the reporters assembled before her. "I hope our friends in the media can help correct this terrible travesty."

I noticed her stern gaze had settled on the woman from Fox News.

"I've taken the liberty of inviting several others to speak in Senator Smith's behalf," the governor said. "First, we'll hear from Senator Rufus Henshaw."

Henshaw made his way to the microphone, removed a folded sheet of paper from his suit pocket, and cleared his throat.

"Senator Smith and I are known to have our disagreements," he said, placing the paper on the lectern. "Somer often leans one way and me the other. Despite our differences, I have found him to be an upright and worthy colleague, year in and year out. There's nobody in the Arkansas Senate more devoted to this state than Somer Smith. I suspect many of my supporters will be sur-prised seeing me here today, and some of 'em are likely to give me heck. What I'll tell them is this: if they knew Somer like I do, they'd realize all this internet commotion is nothing but ..." Henshaw hesitated and a grin emerged on his face as he settled on better wording, continuing with, "bull hockey."

After he stepped aside to loud applause, the Governor whis-pered something in his ear and patted him on the shoulder. As she returned to the podium, I would have sworn she looked my way and gave me a subtle nod.

240

"Thank you, senator. We'll now hear from Arkansas Razorback basketball coach Rollie Waymack."

Waymack walked to the microphone and nodded to the crowd. "Most of the time us coaches try to avoid politics. Mixing sports with politics is generally bad for one's career. But I've taken this situation with Senator Smith as a personal blow. I've got to know Somer in recent months as I've traveled time and again to northeast Arkansas, hoping to recruit his nephew to play ball for me. I've found Somer to be kind and fair, loyal to this state. I've learned from my own experiences how vicious social media attacks can be. I also know Senator Somer Smith is a uniter, not a divider. I'm proud to call him a friend. And I hope to see him in Fayetteville this fall, watching his nephew play ball for me."

Waymack waved to the audience and got a handshake and a smile from the governor as he stepped away to a round of applause.

"Thank you, Coach Waymack," she said. "And now, let's hear from Senator Smith himself."

Somer came forward, receiving a lengthy hug from Governor Butler as he approached the podium. Using a handkerchief, he dabbed the moisture from his eyes, and stared across the room.

"The past two days have been the most challenging of my life," he said. "However, seeing you all here this afternoon and hearing those earlier remarks, I'm feeling recharged. And blessed."

Somer pivoted and glanced back to Governor Butler.

"Governor, I cannot thank you enough for your support and for organizing this news conference."

He gestured toward Senator Henshaw.

"And Rufus, you know I love you like a brother."

Turning to Waymack, he said, "As you're well aware, Coach, the youth of today are independent. But you have my promise I will do my best to encourage my young nephew to become a Hog."

Looking across the room of smiling faces, Somer paused to gather himself.

"Let me leave you with this final thought, one of my favorite quotes from Dr. King: 'We must learn to live together as brothers or perish together as fools.'"

~ THIRTY-FOUR ~

Senator Somer Smith's closing statement was greeted with a rousing ovation. He turned away from the crowd and was enveloped in a tight hug from Governor Patricia Butler. Senator Henshaw followed with a gentler, briefer embrace before Coach Rollie Waymack draped a long arm across Somer's shoulders.

Composing herself, Governor Butler stepped to the podium.

"If members of the media have questions for any of us, now's the time to ask."

A man seated at the front of the table lifted his hand. I recognized him as chief of the local AP bureau.

"This is for Senator Smith," he said. "Have you or your family received threats since the release of the tape?"

Governor Butler moved to the side as Somer came forward. Grasping the edges of the podium with both hands, he looked straight at the reporter, his stare direct and unrelenting.

"My mailbox has been knocked down and destroyed, my truck has been vandalized, and vile and disgusting messages have been spray-painted onto both my house and my mother's home. Not to mention hundreds of nasty e-mails and phone messages."

His voice breaking, Somer hesitated a moment, seeming to gather his poise.

"By seven o'clock this morning, I'd gotten 53 death threats and a couple dozen more had been aimed at my family. I have no doubt others have accumulated since."

Somer paused for a beat.

"So, yeah, you could say I've received some threats."

Governor Butler leaned toward the microphone.

"Because of the potential dangers facing Senator Smith and members of his family, I've asked the Arkansas State Police director to assign a team to provide around-the-clock security."

Another hand shot up, and Governor Butler acknowledged the reporter. It was the woman from Fox News.

"This question is for Senator Henshaw," she said.

The governor and Somer scooted aside, making room for Henshaw at the microphone.

"Senator Henshaw," she began, "how can you justify your support of Senator Smith, given his wishy-washy history on the reparations issue? Don't you worry your base will turn on you? You are, after all, one of the state's leading legislators and chair of the conservative caucus."

Henshaw glared at her, shaking his big head. The seconds dragged on.

"Young lady," he said. "Didn't you hear what Senator Smith shared with us not five minutes ago?"

He glanced at the sheet of paper in his left hand.

"I wrote those words down to remember them. You might do the same."

He again looked at the page and read aloud: "'We must learn to live together as brothers or perish together as fools.'"

Training his gaze once again at the reporter, he said, "You and your network cronies are just trying to stir things up. And it's starting to rub me the wrong way."

As few people in the back of the room began to clap and others joined in, Governor Butler returned to the podium and gestured for quiet.

"Are there any other questions from the media?" she asked.

A third hand rose. A closer look revealed the woman was the longtime evening news anchor for Little Rock's top-rated television station.

"Another question for Senator Smith," she said. "I'll go ahead and acknowledge the elephant in the room. What is your personal opinion on the reparations issue? Not 30 years ago, but today?"

Somer came forward and looked over the crowded yet absolutely quiet chamber.

"Ours is an imperfect society. Injustices exist. But I cannot support the concept of reparations. To me, paying people today for the slave labor of their distant ancestors makes no sense. Are we going to offer payments to descendants of the Native Americans whose lands were stolen time and time again? To the countless indentured servants who suffered decades of hardship during America's formative years?"

He paused, moving his eyes across the spectators.

"My position won't be popular with some of my constituents; so be it. However, I'm convinced a reparations program would do our country far more harm than good. It would further divide us, something we can ill afford to do."

A handful of folks started to clap, but Somer raised a hand, asking for silence.

"That said, we must strive each and every day to reach the key objective our forefathers wisely and deliberately placed in the preamble of the U.S. Constitution: to form a 'more perfect union.'"

As Somer backed away from the podium, the room erupted in applause. Mort got my attention and we exchanged a firm handshake. I saw Leslie waving goodbye from the back of the crowd, and she blew me a kiss. Struggling to be heard over the clamor, Governor Butler thanked the media for their participation and announced the event had concluded.

* * *

Mort pulled me into Governor Butler's suite following the news conference. A dozen or so people had congregated in the space, talking in small groups. Somer saw me enter the room and made a beeline in my direction, dragging Senator Henshaw behind him.

"Rufus," he said. "I want you to meet my good friend Randy Lassiter. He helped organize this event."

"Pleased to meet you, sir," I said, shaking Henshaw's massive hand. "I loved your 'bull hockey' comment."

"Gosh, but if I didn't almost say the wrong thing," he said, giving me a big grin. "I sure didn't want to embarrass the governor. Or be bleeped on television. My wife would have read me the riot act. Not to mention the granddaughter."

Somer gave me a hug.

"Thanks so much, young man," he whispered into my ear. "I'll be forever in your debt."

"It was a joint effort," I said. "Our mutual friend is the one who got things going."

"Don't I know it," Somer said, his eyes moist. "She's a special woman."

Joan walked in at that moment and made her way to Somer's side, wrapping her arms around him. She kissed him on the cheek.

"I'll deal with you another day," she said, giving me a wink.

I introduced myself to Coach Waymack and handed him a business card, telling him to call if I could ever be of service. When he reached for his wallet to reciprocate, I asked him to sign his card.

"One of my coworkers is a sports groupie," I said. "This will make her day. In fact, she's the one who suggested we recruit you to speak today."

"What's her name?" he asked, searching through his jacket for a pen. "The least I can do is personalize it."

He handed me the card a minute or so later, patted me on the shoulder, and turned toward the door.

"Nice to meet you," he said. "If you'll excuse me, I've got a recruiting trip to take."

As I placed his autographed card in a pocket, Governor Butler caught my attention and motioned for me to join her and Mort in a corner behind her desk.

"Somer Smith is a rare beacon of light in Arkansas politics," she said. "This state needs him more than ever. Mort and I recognize the crucial role you and your colleagues filled to protect his career. Finding an entrée to Harvard's president was a masterstroke."

"Thanks," I said, "although you've given us too much credit. I think Somer himself rose to the occasion half an hour ago and saved his own hide."

"With Senator Henshaw's able assistance," the governor added.

"And I'll admit the basketball coach surprised me with his comments," Mort said. "Including him was a good touch."

"But it's not over, is it?" I asked.

Governor Butler pursed her lips and shook her head.

"In today's political environment, it's never over," she said. "No doubt Somer's rejection of the reparations issue will generate animosity from a yet-unidentified group."

Great, I thought. Just great.

* * *

Needless to say, the afternoon was anti-climactic. Once I caught up on phone calls and e-mails, I invited Erin, Megan, and Abbie into my office and told them how grateful Senator Somer Smith and Governor Patricia Butler were for their help.

"I've never been prouder of Lassiter & Associates than I was earlier today," I said. "Flying under the radar, we helped set the record straight for a good person who'd been victimized by social media. I appreciate your work into the early hours this morning during our brainstorming session. Each of you went above and beyond the call of duty."

"To be honest, I enjoyed it," Megan said. "It reminded me of my college days pulling the occasional all-nighter."

"I'm embarrassed to admit I've paid little attention to politics," Abbie said. "I'm thinking it's time to change my ways. The energy in that conference room today was palpable."

"And I have something special for the newest member of our team," I said.

I reached into my pocket and handed Coach Waymack's business card to Erin.

As Erin flipped the card over and began reading the back, a smile broke over her face.

"I can't believe this," she said.

"What does it say?" Megan asked.

I, too, was curious since I hadn't bothered to examine the coach's message, assuming he'd done nothing more than autograph the blank side of his business card.

Erin cleared her throat.

"He wrote, 'Dear Erin—I understand you're to blame for involving me in this political situation. I'll get even!' It's signed, 'Coach Rollie Waymack.' And there's a PS: 'Call my number, ask for Ginny, and she'll send you a pair of Razorback basketball tickets.'"

I noticed a mischievous glint in Erin's eyes.

"I believe I'll have to check the schedule," she said, "and ask for tickets when my beloved Tennessee Volunteers are visiting Fayetteville."

* * *

I got home about 5:30, made myself a bourbon, and was reading the mail when Leslie stepped inside.

"Quite the day," she said, giving me a kiss on the lips. "And I'll take a glass of Chardonay. You have my permission to make it a generous pour."

We met in the den a few minutes later to watch the evening news. An escalation in an on-going squabble between the President and the Speaker of the House was the lead story from Washington. When this piece was completed, a teaser on the screen read: "Next: State Senator Smith Addresses Reparations Issue."

Halfway through the commercial break, the station aired one of the 30-second spots Lassiter & Associates had produced for the Isla del Sol Casino & Resort in Tunica, Mississippi.

"Not bad," Leslie said at its end. "Your team almost made that den of iniquity seem appealing."

At least she said it with a grin.

"Fact is, this girl is going to need a break soon, and I'd be willing to let you take me there. Especially if a spa package is included. Besides, I haven't crossed the Mississippi in ages."

As I made a mental note to schedule such a trip, Senator Somer Smith appeared on the television. The video footage showed him speaking inside the Governor's Conference Room earlier in the day. The voice-over reported Senator Smith had addressed a social media furor based on a videotape recorded years earlier and taken out of context. The piece ended with Somer's statement, "I'm convinced a reparations program would do our country far more harm than good," and then cut to his closing quote from the Constitution, imploring Arkansans to work together "to form a more perfect union."

"The coverage was both fair and favorable," Leslie said with a nod. "Brief, but still better than I expected."

In my opinion, it was one of the best sound bites in recent memory. Before I could comment, the telephone rang. The screen indicated it was a call from my favorite uncle.

"It's Booker," I said to Leslie. "Let's hear what's on his mind."

"Good evening," I said into the phone. "Once again you're on the speaker, so try to minimize your misogynistic comments for Leslie's sake."

"I'm offended, dear nephew," Booker said. "Deeply offended. You of all people know I love women. How many times is it I've been married? My mind's gone blank."

Four or five, I thought, although I wasn't certain. "Several," I said. "Maybe more than several."

"And each one a loving relationship," Booker said. "At least in the beginning."

"Hello, Uncle Booker," Leslie said. "We've been watching coverage of Senator Smith's news conference."

"Thanks again for tracking down those Harvard graduates," I said. "You helped turn the tide in Senator Smith's favor."

"All in an evening's work," he said. "You may call me the bulwark of democracy."

"I haven't seen you in days," Leslie said. "We'll have to get together soon."

"I've been patiently waiting for another dinner invitation," Booker said. "Vegan, of course."

Leslie looked at me and made a face.

"Of course," she said. "Perhaps this fall when things settle down."

This would cost me, and I'd be lucky to get away with a weekend at a resort, even with an all-inclusive spa treatment. After the last vegan meal with Uncle Booker, I'd rewarded Leslie with a diamond bracelet. Quite nice, to be a bit more precise. Maybe even extravagantly nice.

"As for the purpose of this call," Booker said, "I've uncovered an interesting and unsettling development."

"More gleanings from the dark recesses of the internet?" I asked.

"Exactly so," Booker said. "The FBI's field office in Little Rock has issued a confidential advisory to law enforcement officials throughout the state, warning them of an uptick in chatter among hate groups within our borders."

"'An uptick in chatter,'" Leslie repeated. "A rather vague phrase, I'd say."

"My best interpretation," Booker said, "is the federal authorities have observed more action than usual among these organizations. A surge in phone calls, e-mails, and the like. In short, the FBI says there are indications an incident of some sort may be in the works, but they don't yet have any details."

"This increased activity," I said. "When did it first come to their attention?"

"As best I can determine, this all happened in the last 24 hours," Booker said. "I know for a certainty their alert was posted in the past 15 minutes."

"Methinks something's afoot," I said.

Leslie rolled her eyes.

~ THIRTY-FIVE ~

I spent much of the next week reviewing and fine-tuning the comprehensive response from Lassiter & Associates to the official "Request for Proposals" regarding the state's tourism account. My colleagues and I had devoted hours to the thick document, making sure each *i* was dotted and every *t* crossed.

The dog-eared draft copy accompanied me home Friday evening for a final markup. I'd poured myself an adult libation and was rereading it for maybe the sixth time when Leslie joined me in the den.

"You'll be submitting the agency's RFP soon, right?"

"The deadline is the first of September," I said. "Two weeks off. My plan is to deliver it in person on the afternoon of the cut-off date."

"I'll be glad to look it over if you'd like," Leslie said. "With a fresh set of eyes."

Proofreading was among her many skills. She'd helped on more than one occasion with bid proposals the agency had prepared, always catching one or two things we'd somehow missed.

"I believe our response is in great shape, but I'd be foolish to decline your offer," I said. "Erin and I dedicated most of the morning to a line-by-line examination."

Leslie stepped away, soon returning with a glass of wine.

"How's Erin doing?" she asked. "You haven't mentioned her much in recent days."

"As you know, she played a key role in our efforts regarding Somer's recent troubles," I said. "But she seemed different today, a bit out of sorts."

Leslie grinned at me, shaking her head.

"Don't tell me she and her twin sister have reverted to their former tricks. You know, pulling the old switcheroo on an unsuspecting Randy Lassiter."

"Nope; there's no question she's the original Erin. Yet her usual vibrant personality seemed a little subdued."

"There may be something to your concern," Leslie said. "She called me the first of this week, saying her weekends were now open and hoping there might be an opportunity for a bit of modeling work."

"Do you have anything scheduled she can help with?" I asked.

"As a matter of fact, I do," Leslie said. "First thing tomorrow morning, I'll be working with her and another girl. I got a last-minute assignment from Dillard's to shoot jewelry at their corporate headquarters for the Christmas catalog, and Erin agreed to come in for a couple of hours. I'll see if I can uncover anything."

I recalled approving Erin's request for two hours of leave.

* * *

At breakfast the following day, Leslie handed me the RFP draft. She'd risen early to proof it over a couple of cups of coffee. I noticed four or five bright tabs dangling from the margins.

"Problems?" I asked, shocked to see the unwanted markers decorating my precious document.

Leslie shrugged.

"I like the agency's recommendation to make the state a mecca for folks wanting to trace their family trees. But don't forget there's an 'a' rather than an 'o' in the middle of genealogy. And if millennials are a priority, make sure to nail the spelling."

She gave me a hug and scooted out the door as I struggled to put my chin back in place.

While Leslie photographed necklaces, bracelets, and earrings, I phoned the general manager at the Isla del Sol Casino & Resort in

Tunica. Lassiter & Associates had held the advertising account for several years now, and she and I had developed a good relationship.

"How's business?" I asked.

"I've been meaning to call you," she said. "The summer season's been nothing less than incredible and fall bookings are running strong. Our IT team tells me website visitation is off the charts. And I should add our gross revenues are up nearly 18% for the year."

"The big bosses are happy?" I asked, referring to the resort's Las Vegas owners.

"For now," she said with a chuckle. "What they'll expect is for these gains to become routine."

"We'll do our best," I said. "But the real reason I called is I want to make a weekend reservation for late September. With a deluxe treatment at the resort's spa."

"This spa experience," she said. "Is it for your wife, or would you like to make it for a couple?"

I'd never had a massage, not sure about … something. Maybe I didn't want to risk embarrassing myself.

"You'd both enjoy it, Randy," she said. "Lots of candles, warm oils, exotic incense, and soothing music."

There was a pause in the conversation while I considered her suggestion.

"I'll tell you what," she said. "We'll put the two of you down for the couple's luxury spa package. If either of you are disappointed in the slightest, I'll refund your money."

"Deal."

I went home for lunch. Leslie returned a few minutes after noon and I met her at the front door.

"Your mystery has been solved," she said, giving me a peck on the lips.

"What mystery?" I asked, clearly confused.

"The why-is-Erin-acting-weird mystery."

"Let me guess," I said. "She and her sister are squabbling."

"It's the boyfriend. Alex."

"Don't tell me he's back with her twin again."

Leslie shook her head.

"After we'd finished shooting and the other girl had left, I mentioned to Erin she seemed distant, troubled even. I told her I had a shoulder if she needed someone to lean on."

"And she accepted?"

"For a full 30 minutes," Leslie said, "much of it tearful. We sat in my car and she explained how Alex had withdrawn. According to Erin, he's completely preoccupied with Flyover Family dealings. I believe she's just now come to the realization that it's a serious militia group and not just an organization to perpetuate Southern culture and traditions."

"Did she share any details about Alex's activities?"

"Plenty," Leslie said, giving her head a quick nod. "It seems he's spending every spare hour at the Flyover Family compound."

"Doing what?"

"Erin recited a long list of projects Alex was working on rather than finding time for her. Expanding the firing range, clearing brush, installing a solar power system, building a new swimming platform, and so on."

"So, there's an explanation for her recent behavior."

"Here's the straw breaking the camel's back," Leslie said. "As you know, Erin's a huge sports fan. She'd gone online and paid a small fortune for a pair of tickets to a crucial Cowboys game in Dallas later this fall. Against the Kansas City Chiefs, I think. And booked them a suite in a boutique hotel and made dinner reservations at one of the city's trendiest restaurants. She described it as her idea of a 'perfect romantic weekend'."

"And Alex turned her down?"

"What's worse, he said he no longer had time for frivolous things such as sports."

I stared at Leslie, shaking my head.

"In other words," I said, "no time for her."

"Erin told Alex they were done. She's going to the game with Erica who lives in Fort Worth."

* * *

On the afternoon of the September 1 deadline, I carried a box to the Office of State Purchasing and hand-delivered five copies of Lassiter & Associates' response to the RFP for the Arkansas tourism account. The helpful clerk reminded me the three top-scoring advertising agencies, based on a thorough review, would be invited to submit actual bids for the state contract. I gave her a wink and said I'd be awaiting the official invitation.

When I returned to the office, I called a staff meeting for the entire crew and thanked them for their long hours of work during the grueling RFP process. As a reward, I said the office would close at noon on Friday and encouraged everyone to enjoy the long weekend.

A few weeks later, I went to the Arkansas State Fair with Megan to view the Hillcountry Marine booth in the Hall of Industry Building. It was an attractive exhibit with bright posters along with a dynamic video clip of footage Leslie had compiled running on a monitor. Harrison Davies of my staff and Tabitha Boddington stood behind a table, both busy answering questions and distributing brochures.

I felt a tap on my shoulder and turned to see Del Boddington behind standing behind us. He shook Megan's hand and then mine, a wide smile on his face.

"Your display looks great," I said. "Hope you're pleased with it."

"Tabitha tells me she's already identified at least seven solid prospects," he said. "And this is the first day of the fair. She's afraid they'll run out of brochures."

"There's more in the office," Megan said. "We've got you covered."

"You just missed Sheriff Hutch Thomas," Del said. He nodded to the adjacent booth.

I'd failed to notice the space next to Hillcountry Marine had been assigned to The Flyover Family. A young man and middle-aged woman were seated at a table covered with pamphlets and decals. Behind them stood two flags: one a traditional US stars and stripes and the other the distinctive Confederate battle flag.

254

Between the flags was a collection of enlarged photographs, most of them taken during the camps held earlier this summer: boys and girls swimming, playing ball, performing skits, and attending classes.

Spotting my gaze, Megan stepped to the booth and picked up copies of the materials on display. The woman smiled and they began talking.

"What's going on with Sheriff Thomas?" I asked.

"He's one busy man," Del said. "In addition to maintaining the peace in Marion County, he's spending time on his group's property south of town. And, of course, he's making the rounds as a candidate for the state legislature."

"Any scuttlebutt you can share?"

"I've been told the incumbent, a personal friend of mine, won't run for reelection. He's seen the writing on the wall. And it's a shame because he's served us well."

Megan shook the woman's hand and began walking toward us.

"We'll head back to the office," I said to Del. "Good luck with the rest of the fair."

"It's already been worth our money," he said. "I'll call if we need more brochures."

As Megan and I returned to my truck, she handed me the items she'd gathered at the Flyover Family booth: a colorful decal with both the Arkansas and Confederate flags; a pencil featuring the Flyover Family logo; a pamphlet describing the group and its mission, complete with an application for membership; and a registration form for next year's summer camps for boys and girls.

"Good stuff for your archives," she said, giving me a mischievous grin.

When Megan and I returned to the office a quarter of an hour later, Erin greeted us with a beaming smile.

"Great news," she said. "The Office of State Purchasing called not five minutes ago. Lassiter & Associates has been invited to bid on the state's tourism account."

Megan and I exchanged high fives.

Leslie and I left Little Rock on a Friday afternoon in late September, heading almost due east for Tunica's Isla del Sol Casino & Resort. At the registration desk, we got a pleasant surprise: the hotel's general manager had upgraded our accommodations, placing us in the Presidential Suite on the building's top floor. We enjoyed a fine dinner and then spent an hour in the casino where I had no trouble exhausting my $100 limit playing blackjack. But Leslie hit a hot streak at the slots, carrying on like one of the models in the agency's TV commercials and winning $650 before cashing out. Following a nightcap in the hotel bar, we returned to the suite where we soaked in our private hot tub while watching the moonlight reflect off the Mississippi River.

At breakfast the next morning, Leslie squeezed my hand and gave me a clever grin.

"Today's session at the spa is making you nervous, right?"

"Why would you say that?" I asked.

"You barely touched your French toast and you've ignored your coffee."

I shook my head.

"Nah," I said. "I'm mentally replaying my blackjack hands from last night. I still can't believe I did so poorly."

"You're not fooling me," she said. "As you know, I schedule a massage every month to six weeks. Let me give you some pointers."

I shrugged. "Okay."

"Once finished here, we'll return to our suite, shower, and then change into loose-fitting outfits. Got it?"

I gave her a nod.

"And then we'll ride the special elevator down to the spa."

I took a sip of lukewarm coffee.

"In the spa, we'll remove our clothes and—"

"Everything?" I asked, interrupting her.

"Of course," she said with a giggle. "Our private regions, shall we say, will be covered by towels."

"What if a woman's assigned to me?"

"Would you prefer a masseur?" she asked.

"Well, no," I mumbled after thinking about it for a minute.

Much to my amazement, I survived my first massage. In fact, it proved to be one of the most relaxing experiences of my life.

Leslie took my hand in hers as we returned to our room.

"Tell me the truth," she said. "That wasn't so bad, was it?"

"I feel like a new man."

"With the big presentation coming up, we may need to make a massage a part of your weekly routine."

I could live with it.

~ THIRTY-SIX ~

We conducted two focus groups during the initial week of October, one in Dallas and the other in Memphis. The two-hour sessions, both held at night to accommodate the employed among those invited to attend, revealed no great surprises to the half dozen representatives from Lassiter & Associates observing behind the mirrored walls. Participants who'd traveled to Arkansas in the past were often positive, and some were almost effusive in the descriptions of their experiences. For the most part, those who'd never visited the state knew little about Arkansas, and expressed indifference to skepticism its attractions offered much to interest them and their families.

However, we picked up one key insight from those two evenings. Several of those who'd vacationed in the state kept using the word "authentic" to explain why they'd enjoyed their time in Arkansas. Describing the state's people, communities, culture, and hospitality as genuine, they said Arkansas was a welcome change from Branson, Myrtle Beach, Gatlinburg, and other highly commercialized tourist haunts.

At a meeting of the agency's department heads on the morning after the Memphis session, I instructed my colleagues to begin development of a comprehensive marketing campaign capitalizing on this crucial distinction, stating "authenticity" would form the foundation of our creative approach. I reminded them we had three weeks to do it, and we'd convene every other day at 5:00 PM to monitor our progress. The excitement in the room was almost palpable as the gathering adjourned.

The Lassiter & Associates crew responded to the challenge. I was soon receiving a slew of proposed print ads, TV spots, and online components touting the state's authentic hospitality, food, arts, music, crafts, and festivals. The agency's department heads and I dedicated hours to critiquing these submissions, winnowing the concepts down and feeling more confident by the day.

One evening a week prior to our scheduled presentation before the committee of official reviewers, Booker telephoned. I was relaxing at home with Leslie after a stressful yet productive day at the office when the call came through.

"I trust you have me on speakerphone," he said.

"We're both here, Uncle Booker," Leslie said. "How are things in your world?"

"Precisely the reason I've called," he said. "My latest browsings on the dark web have uncovered a confidential advisory from the FBI's Little Rock Field Office."

"Is it similar to the one you mentioned a week or two ago?" I asked.

"Tonight's alert is a refinement of the earlier release," he said. "Its wording is more ominous, warning of a major incident from an undetermined right-wing hate group."

"Anything specific regarding a location or timing?" Leslie asked.

"No details at all," Booker said. "Just a stern reminder to the state's law enforcement community from their federal cohorts to be especially vigilant. But given the severe tone of this missive, my estimate is the next ten days will be critical. The alarm smacks of urgency."

* * *

The succeeding days found the Lassiter & Associates team fine-tuning our hour-long sales pitch. Once we finished the final rehearsal for the presentation a full day before our scheduled appearance, Megan and I drove to the Statehouse Convention

Center in the city's downtown district and inspected the room where we'd do our dead level best to convince the reviewers our proposal was the preferred choice for Arkansas.

I'd been notified earlier a random drawing had placed our agency in the middle position for the following day's activities. The Andrews Bingham Carter group would have an hour beginning at 8:00 AM with another 30 minutes set aside for questions and clarifications. The room would then be cleared and we'd set up for our 10:30 slot. The concluding presentation by the Richmond Kefauver firm out of Dallas would take place at 2:00 PM. The media and the public, of course, had the option of attending any and all presentations. At 4:00 PM, representatives from the three competing advertising agencies, the media, and interested citizens would be allowed into the room to hear the decision of the independent judges.

I'm not sure I ever went to sleep the night prior to the big day. I showered, managed to shave without nicking myself, and had a breakfast of oatmeal and a banana. Along with two cups of coffee. And a handful of antacid tablets. Leslie straightened my tie and gave me a kiss as I left.

"I'll catch up with you mid-morning," she said. "I want to see how the agency's artists have used my photography."

I felt certain she'd be pleased with what she saw. Leslie's images, both still and from the drone, represented a substantial part of our overall campaign, appearing in the proposed magazine ads, television commercials, and internet postings.

Arriving at Lassiter & Associates at 6:45, I made a pot of coffee and began one last pass through my prepared remarks. An hour later, Megan and Erin stepped into my office, each offering any assistance they might provide.

"We're good to go," I said. "Let's hope the god of advertising favors us today."

"An advertising god?" Erin asked, raising her eyebrows. "Surely you jest."

"It's Janus," Megan said. "I've read he's the god of marketing."

"Isn't Janus the two-faced deity?" Erin asked.

"No problem," I said with a shrug, "as long as one of 'em smiles on us."

At 10:00, the Lassiter delegation drove to the convention center in a small convoy. We entered the designated room as the Andrews Bingham Carter group was exiting. My "good morning" to our competitors got a halfhearted nod or two.

"The ABC staff didn't look very happy," Megan said as the last of them left.

"Maybe their sense of entitlement has been offended," I said. "This is the first time in decades they've gone through an actual review."

By 10:20, we had our PowerPoint presentation queued up, the easels were in place, and I'd made a final visit to the men's room. Along the way, I'd spotted name plates at the long table reserved for the judges. Three of the five appeared to represent females.

This could work to our advantage, I thought. Megan and I had discussed an option a day or two ago that might resonate with the women who'd evaluate our proposal. I'd have to play it by ear.

At 10:25, Ms. Steele Parker, secretary of the Arkansas Department of Parks, Heritage & Tourism, escorted five individuals into the room and they took seats behind the table. After Ms. Parker welcomed everyone, she introduced her panel of judges. Two were tourism directors, one from the state of West Virginia and the other from the city of Colorado Springs. The remaining three included a museum administrator from Indianapolis, a state senator from Georgia, and a travel marketing executive from American Express Corporation.

"We'll now hear from the second of our three finalists, Lassiter & Associates," she said. "Mr. Lassiter, the floor is yours."

I began by thanking Ms. Parker for the opportunity to bid on the state's account and next welcomed the visiting judges to Arkansas.

"I suspect Ms. Parker has convinced you this is a special state," I said. "It's a message my colleagues and I are eager to deliver to the rest of the nation."

For 45 minutes, my team and I shared our proposed plan for inviting travelers to a destination where they could enjoy authentic vacation experiences—Arkansas. We showed not only video clips from our focus groups, but examples of how we'd position the state with print, broadcast, and the internet. I revealed our strategy to recruit the state's leading corporate entities to the cause, leveraging Arkansas's limited promotional budget. After Megan delved into the idea of cross-selling the state, Abbie addressed making the most of the 37 million retirees living within a day's drive of Arkansas, enticing them to the state with attractive pricing for midweek visits.

As we neared the end of our allotted time, I decided to take a risk.

"My associates and I've spent hours examining successful examples from other states," I said. "We were impressed with the media exposure and additional visitation Alabama has enjoyed with the Year of Alabama Music, the Year of Alabama Food, and others."

I spotted a nod from the West Virginia tourism director.

"We like the idea of promoting the Year of the Tourist Mom," I said, pausing to let the phrase soak in.

"The Year of the Tourist Mom will be a promotional campaign acknowledging the vital role women have in making vacation decisions, rewarding them with a series of special offers and incentives leading to authentic experiences for them and their families. And we'd develop a program of distinctive tools to help single mothers plan trips with their children."

I'd gone off script, as evidenced by expressions on the faces of several of my colleagues. But I caught subtle nods from two of the three female judges.

"The Year of the Tourist Mom would, of course, be followed by the Year of the Tourist Dad," I said. "We're convinced such recognition would mesh perfectly with our commitment to authenticity."

I paused a moment and directed my open palm to the group of Lassiter & Associates seated to the side of the room.

"Our organization wants this account so bad we can almost taste it. Although we're not the biggest agency in town, I can guarantee nobody will outwork us."

I returned my gaze to the judges.

"That concludes our proposed plan of action. We'll be happy to answer any questions you might have."

Steele Parker stood, gave me a smile, and said, "Let me congratulate Lassiter & Associates for a fine presentation."

She turned to her panel.

"We'll now hear comments and questions from our judges."

A hand went up. It was the woman from American Express.

"I'm intrigued by your focus on the role of women in the vacation planning process. Our emphasis on the female component of the travel industry has paid big dividends for AmEx."

The West Virginia tourism director reached for the microphone.

"I also like the idea of using the state's corporate entities to become, in effect, your marketing partners. Have any committed to this concept?"

"One of Arkansas's leading boat manufacturers is already on board," I said, thankful I'd broached the idea with Del Boddington of Hillcountry Marine during our last visit.

"As for others, we're counting on Governor Butler's close ties with the private sector to open additional doors for us."

I spotted a smile from Steele Parker.

"I have a question," said the museum administrator. "Or rather a comment. We also have struggled with too many visitors on weekends and too few on weekdays at our galleries in Indianapolis. Offering midweek incentives for senior travelers makes sense."

The legislator from Georgia raised an arm to get my attention.

"I noticed your current accounts include a casino and resort client in Mississippi," he said. "Will this present a conflict of interest?"

We'd anticipated the question and had spent a good deal of time discussing it during one staff meeting. And I'd asked at attorney friend of mine who specialized in state contracts for her opinion, and she felt it wouldn't be an issue.

"The agency has one person assigned full-time to the casino," I said. "For the potential new account we're discussing today, Lassiter & Associates will have a complete team devoted to servicing it. The two will work independently of each other. So, no, we don't envision a conflict of any sort."

Steele Parker again stood and, glancing at her watch, announced it was time to clear the room.

"Our third presentation will begin here at 2:00."

As the panel walked past, the Georgia legislator stuck out his hand.

"Excellent plan," he said. "Your business-like approach is refreshing."

The Lassiter team packed our gear and materials and returned to the agency's conference room where a lunch buffet of pizza and salad awaited us. It was a jovial meal. Those who had attended the presentation shared their observations with those who'd remained to cover the phones.

As we cleaned the mess, I was asked for a prediction. The room grew quiet.

"The odds aren't in our favor," I said, "going against an entrenched incumbent. However, I think Governor Butler was sincere with her promise to provide an honest and open review. We'll know soon enough."

I then swept my gaze across the attentive faces. "But I do know this: I've never been prouder of this group. Thank you so much."

With my thoughts on the 4:00 PM decision, the day seemed to drag by. After I'd dealt with a batch of e-mails, Erin routed a call to me. It was from the owner of the city's largest pawn shop, the man who weeks ago had cancelled our business relationship before it even began.

"Mr. Lassiter," he said. "Things have changed. Are you ready to take over our account?"

"I thought your new wife handled your marketing."

"She's no longer with the firm," he said. "Or with me, for that matter. How soon can you start?"

264

Surprising myself, I abandoned my initial reaction and said, "You're kind to call, but our plate is full. You'll need to go elsewhere."

The Lassiter convoy made the short drive to the convention center, arriving at 3:45. We'd gathered around a pair of tables when Steele Parker and the panel of judges returned, taking their places at the head of the room.

Ms. Parker stood and faced the one hundred or so spectators in the audience.

"We've had a stimulating day," she said. "First, let me thank our judges for your attention."

She began clapping and those of us in the crowd followed her lead.

"I'd also like to express my sincere appreciation to our three finalists: the Andrews Carter Bingham Group, Lassiter & Associates, and Richmond Kefauver."

Those words led to another short burst of applause.

"We'll now turn it over to our judges for an open discussion," she said. "Once they've concluded their deliberations, I'll entertain a motion from the panel." Ms. Parker then slipped back into her chair.

There was an awkward pause before the Georgia legislator cleared his throat and spoke.

"This has been a fascinating experience," he said. "Three fine pitches have left me in a dilemma. I liked them all."

While the others nodded in agreement, the woman from American Express said, "I feel the same. Whatever direction we go, the people of Arkansas will benefit."

For the next ten minutes, the panelists reviewed the high points of each presentation, commenting on the work of all three advertising agencies. I was unable to detect a trend in their remarks.

"Based on our instructions from Director Steele," the museum administrator said, "we're expected to make a recommendation at this time."

After a moment's hesitation, she said, "My scoring has resulted in a slight edge for the incumbent agency. Given its history with the state, I propose we endorse Andrews Carter Bingham for the new contract."

I felt my heart lurch.

The room remained strangely quiet. Faces down, the other judges studied their notes. Seconds passed.

Steele Parker stood and addressed the panel.

"For the lack of a second, I'll ask if there's another recommendation."

The man from Colorado raised a hand.

"I'll move we select the Richmond Kefauver firm. My scores are almost identical for all three presenters, but their creative caught my eye."

Again, my chest tightened and my fists were clinched.

Once more, quietness surrounded me. Steele Parker looked at the judges.

The American Express representative gestured to get Parker's attention.

"I feel the proposal offered by Lassiter & Associates will best serve the people of Arkansas," she said. "I like their energy level and their complete package. They got my top rating."

"I'm pleased to second her motion," said the Georgia legislator. "It was a total effort."

Director Parker stood and faced the crowd.

"We have a motion and a second," she said. "Is there any additional discussion?"

"I'm in full agreement with my colleagues," said the West Virginia tourism director. "The Lassiter group's plan is data-driven, comprehensive, and exciting."

"In that case, I'll switch my vote," said the Colorado man.

"I would like to change mine as well," said the lady from the Indianapolis, "to make it unanimous."

Director Parker faced the judges. "To make this official, I will need to see a show of hands. Those in favor of recommending Lassiter & Associates as the next advertising agency for the Arkansas Department of Parks, Heritage & Tourism will be Lassiter & Associates, please indicate by raising your hand."

Five hands lifted.

"There we have it," she said to the crowd. "Pending legislative approval, Lassiter & Associates will be the official agency for the Department."

She turned in my direction with a smile.

"Mr. Lassiter," she said, "congratulations to you and your colleagues for an outstanding presentation. Welcome aboard."

A round of applause greeted her announcement.

I stared at the Director Parker and her panel, scarcely believing my ears. We'd beaten the odds! Lassiter & Associates had been chosen to represent State of Arkansas.

Leslie appeared out of the crowd and wrapped her arms around me. "I knew you could do it," she said. "I'm so proud of you and the entire Lassiter team."

Megan, Abbie, Chantille, Harrison and half a dozen others gathered around, their faces beaming. Megan's eyes sparkled in delight. As I reached to give her a hug, I caught another familiar face moving my way.

It was Joan Pfeiffer, my dear friend in the Arkansas House of Representatives. But she wasn't smiling. Hardly. She marched toward me, a look of panic and fright on her face. She leaned forward, almost seeming to faint into my arms.

"They've got him," she whispered into my ear. "They've kidnapped Somer."

~ THIRTY-SEVEN ~

I placed both hands on Joan's shoulders and drew closer. Her eyes moist and puffy, she'd been crying.

"What did you say?" I asked, my voice low.

"Somer has been kidnapped," she whispered. "It happened yesterday."

Out of the corner of my eye, I saw Steele Parker's subtle gesture to get my attention. I gave her a quick nod.

I motioned for Leslie to join Joan and me. Pulling her near, I said, "Please take Joan across the street and grab us a table at the Capital Hotel Bar. I'll meet you there as soon as I can."

As they walked to the room's exit, I hurried to Ms. Parker. She stood between two people I didn't recognize.

"Randy," she said, surprising me with use of my given name. "These folks are from *Arkansas Business* and hope you might have time to pose for a photo and answer a few questions. While you visit with them, I'll thank our judges once more before they're driven to the airport."

"Certainly," I said, and approached the duo.

Within fifteen minutes, the photographer had gotten her photos and the reporter had recorded my responses to his questions. Lucky for me, they were of the softball variety.

Megan was boxing the last of our materials at the interview's conclusion. She came over and gave me a hug.

"I still can't believe it," she said, a grin stretching across her face. "We did it!"

Our loud high-five didn't go unnoticed.

"I want you to do me a favor. Call the office and state that Lassiter & Associates will be closed Monday," I said. "Tell everyone to take the day off as a reward for their hours and hours of work for this victory."

She looked me hard in the eyes.

"Something's up, Randy," she said. "You're in another world."

"There's an unexpected situation requiring my immediate attention," I said. "You and I and our colleagues will celebrate later."

I squeezed her shoulder.

"Today could never have happened without Megan Maloney. I appreciate you so much."

Nearing the convention center's exit, I again encountered Steele Parker. She smiled and extended a hand.

"I don't believe I've personally congratulated you," she said. "You and your coworkers did an outstanding job."

"Thank you, Ms. Parker—"

She held up her hand to interrupt me.

"It's Steele," she said. "We're now on the same team."

"I like the sound of that," I said. "My associates and I are eager to meet your staff. Any chance we can schedule a meeting sometime next week?"

She handed me a business card.

"My personal cell is listed on the back. Give me a call and we'll get it on the calendar."

I excused myself and turned to leave.

"Randy," she said, "there's one more thing. I called Governor Butler to report the committee's decision. She was delighted with the outcome and asked me to pass along her best wishes." She paused a moment, and added, "I got the impression she already knows you."

Nodding, I shrugged and said, "We recently worked together on another matter."

I dashed across the street to the Capital Hotel Bar. Leslie and Joan sat at a corner table, talking quietly, their heads almost touching. Once I'd slipped into a chair, a waiter appeared at my side.

"May I get you a drink?" she asked.

I looked at the pair of glasses in front of Leslie and Joan. Bourbons on the rocks.

"I'll take what they're having," I said, "but make mine a double."

After the waiter left, I scooted my chair closer to the table and leaned toward Joan.

"Did I understand correctly?" I asked. "Somer's been kidnapped?"

She gave her head a slight bob and wiped her eyes with a tissue.

"It must've occurred last evening. Following dinner at my home, I'd invited Somer to spend the night. Stating he had a committee meeting first thing this morning, he opted to stay at his place in the Capitol Hill Apartments."

Joan was referring to an old yet handsome seven-story brick building a block north of the State Capitol that had housed legislators for decades. I'd attended the occasional reception there earlier in my career.

"We'd made plans to meet in the capitol cafeteria for lunch today," Joan said. "When he didn't appear and I couldn't reach him on his phone, I walked to his apartment and used the key he'd given me. Somer wasn't there. I looked out the window and saw his car on the lot below."

"Did his apartment seem normal?" Leslie asked.

"Nice and tidy," Joan said. "Bed made and everything in order. Typical of Somer."

"At what point did you realize he'd been kidnapped?" I asked.

"I left Somer's apartment and returned to the Capitol," Joan said, dabbing at her eyes again. "Once I entered the building, a state trooper saw me and got my attention, saying I was needed in Governor Butler's office."

As the waiter neared with my bourbon, I asked Joan if she'd eaten any lunch. Learning she hadn't had anything since breakfast, I asked the waiter to bring us menus.

"I was ushered into Governor Butler's private office," Joan said. "Three or four people were there in addition to the governor. One was the director of Arkansas State Police."

The waiter reappeared, handing menus to the three of us. Before she turned to leave, I asked if she could wait a moment and we'd give her our selections. While the women perused the options, I ordered the pimento cheese and homemade soda crackers for our appetizer, and the 14 oz rib eye—medium rare— for my dinner. The women chose salads, one a Cobb and the other a Caesar. I finally took a swallow of my drink.

"Now," Joan said, "where were we?"

"You'd just gotten to the governor's office," Leslie said, "and spotted the state police director."

"At first, I assumed Somer had been involved in an accident of some sort," Joan said. "But I remembered seeing his car parked in the lot below his apartment. I was so confused."

She paused and reached for her drink, taking a small sip.

A movement in my peripheral vision caught my attention. I noticed a large man approaching our table. He seemed a bit wobbly. I glanced up and saw one of the founding partners in the Andrews Bingham Carter group come to a stop at my side.

I stood and we shook hands. He was definitely unsteady.

"So, Lassiter's already celebrating?" he asked, slurring his words. "Congratulations. We had a good run and I reckon it's time for an infusion of new blood."

"Thanks," I said, unsure how to respond. "You can be proud of your agency's work over the years."

"Whatever," he said. "Break a leg."

He patted me on the shoulder, slowly pivoted, and began tottering in the direction of a crowded table in the opposite end of the noisy room.

"A close friend?" Leslie whispered.

"Not exactly. He's the B in the ABC outfit," I said. "But back to Joan. What did you learn in Governor Butler's office?"

"After we'd taken seats around a small conference table, I was asked if I'd heard anything from Somer," she said. "I shook my head, demanding to know what the hell was going on. The state police director told me Senator Smith had apparently been kidnapped."

"Apparently?" Leslie asked. "Don't they know for sure?"

"Governor Butler spoke next," Joan said. "She said her office had received a call at eight this morning. The man on the phone demanded he speak to, quote, the governor herself, unquote. She had a breakfast meeting first thing today and hadn't yet arrived. Her receptionist explained this to the caller and offered to take a message, but he insisted on the cell number of the governor's chief-of-staff. The receptionist was then told Senator Somerset Smith had been kidnapped and instructions would be forthcoming at eight o'clock tomorrow morning. The call ended."

"Kidnapped," I said, shaking my head. "I didn't realize political kidnappings happened in our country." I took a hearty sip of bourbon.

"The director says they occur more often than we know, most never making the news," Joan said. "As for this situation, I was told it appears to be a political kidnapping, similar to the wild scheme targeting the Michigan governor several years ago."

"Were they able to trace the call?" Leslie asked.

"I asked the same question," Joan said. "The governor's office has an electronic record of all calls, both incoming and outbound. Somehow, they determined it was a burner phone, one of those disposable devices available in any big-box retailer. No way to track it down."

"Any explanation of why they wanted Mort Sensabaugh's cell number?" I asked.

"Mort was among those in the room," Joan said. "When I posed the same question, he opened his phone and showed me a photo. It was Somer."

Our waiter appeared with the grill's famous pimento cheese and crackers. After placing three small plates around the table, she said the entrées would be served soon. Bobbing our heads, we thanked her.

"Tell us about this photograph," Leslie said. "I didn't know burner phones could take and transmit pictures."

"I, too, was surprised," Joan said. "Although the image wasn't sharp, there was no doubt the man was Somer. Standing and holding a copy of today's newspaper, he appeared expressionless."

272

"Joan," I said, pointing to the appetizer, "we need to get food in your belly."

She placed a scoop of the cheese and a handful of crackers onto her plate, and Leslie and I did likewise.

"I assume the troopers checked his office in the State Capitol," I said.

"Locked tight," Joan said. "His iPad was on the desk, which was unusual. He seldom goes anywhere without it."

"And they checked security cameras?" Leslie asked.

"Footage from the entrance to his apartment building showed nothing. There's also a video camera at the edge of the parking lot," Joan said, "but they learned it hasn't worked in years. Vandals have even painted graffiti over the 'Security Cameras in Use' signs. One of the tenants told the trooper it was common knowledge the camera was broken."

"What's next?" I asked.

"I've been told to be in Governor Butler's office by 7:45 tomorrow morning," she said. "I'm sure the state police have a plan, but they didn't share anything with me."

"What can we do?" Leslie asked.

"Being here with me means more than you can imagine," Joan said, and wiped a tear from her face.

As the waiter served our meals, I requested another round of drinks. I was ready to cut into my rib eye when I felt my cell vibrate.

It was a text from Booker: "Something significant must be underway," he wrote. "Local chatter on the dark web has exploded."

Leslie caught me glancing at my phone. "Everything okay?"

"Just an update from Uncle Booker," I said.

Her eyes widened.

"Nothing to worry about," I said.

Or could all the commotion on the internet's underbelly be somehow related to Somer's disappearance?

We ate our dinner, for the most part avoiding any additional comments regarding Somer's kidnapping. After concluding the evening with a round of coffee, Leslie and I escorted Joan to her car, each of us giving her a tight hug before she left.

"The text you got from Booker," Leslie said as we drove home. "Anything to it?"

"He said activity on the dark web was hopping," I said.

"My bet is it's tied in with the kidnapping."

I wasn't going to argue with her.

Leslie and I'd been home half an hour and our telephone rang. It was Mort Sensabaugh from Governor Butler's office.

"Representative Joan Pfeiffer phoned," he said. "She wants you and your wife to be in attendance tomorrow morning for the call from Senator Smith's kidnappers. 'For moral support' is how she put it."

This was unexpected.

"You're sure?" I asked.

"Tomorrow's Saturday, so you shouldn't have any trouble finding a parking space near the Capitol," he said. "The call is supposed to be placed at eight, so please arrive in plenty of time."

It was another restless night.

~ THIRTY-EIGHT ~

Leslie and I cleared security at the State Capitol a little before 7:30 the next morning, made the long climb up the deserted marble staircase to the second floor, and stepped into the reception area of Governor Butler's office. Joan walked in minutes after we'd taken our seats, giving each of us a kiss on the cheek

"God, I didn't sleep a wink," she said. "I'm a total wreck worrying about Somer."

The usual sparkle in her eyes had vanished.

Leslie had an arm wrapped around Joan when the door to the inner sanctum opened and Mort Sensabaugh entered the room.

"Good morning to all," he said. He stepped to Joan and gave her a hug.

"And you must be Leslie," he said, introducing himself and extending a hand. Once that exchange was complete, he said, "Now, if the three of you will come with me."

We trailed him through the quiet maze of desks and cubicles to Governor Patricia Butler's private suite. Half a dozen chairs were arranged around a long rectangular table. At one end of the table sat a standard telephone and near it were several electronic devices requiring the full attention of man and a woman. Pens and pads of paper had been positioned in front of two of the chairs.

After introducing Leslie and me to State Police Director Leroy Yeargan, Mort pointed to a pair of chairs placed against the wall.

"There's where you two will sit."

Governor Butler stepped in moments later and made a beeline for Leslie.

"You must be Randy's wife," she said. "I'm Patricia Butler. Representative Pfeiffer has said so much about you."

Blushing as they shook hands, Leslie said, "I'm pleased to meet you, though I wish it were under better circumstances."

Her lips pursed, the governor nodded in agreement before turning to embrace Joan.

Glancing at his watch, Director Yeargan cleared his throat, getting our attention.

"The call from Senator Smith's kidnappers should come through soon," Yeargan said. "We're fortunate to have two experienced professionals with us this morning who will handle the technical details. They are Lieutenant Angela Russo from my criminal investigative division, and Special Agent Allen Mayne with the FBI's Little Rock Field Office."

The pair looked up, acknowledged us with perfunctory nods, and then resumed their duties.

"While they complete their tasks, please take your seats," he said. "I'll confirm our ground rules."

Governor Butler, Joan, and Mort gathered around the table, leaving chairs open for the director and the two specialists. Leslie and I slipped into our assigned spots.

"First and foremost, what happens in this room stays in this room," Yeargan said. "We don't want to take this situation public unless we have no other choice."

"Representative Pfeiffer and I have discussed this matter at length with Director Yeargan," the governor said. "We're convinced keeping it on the q.t. is our best course of action. At least for the present."

"Let me remind you no one other that Governor Butler speaks; the room must be silent," Yeargan said. He moved his eyes from face to face, making certain everyone understood. "If necessary, she and I will communicate by written form. The speaker system should allow all of us to hear the entire conversation. Any questions?"

"Will you be able to trace this call?" Joan asked.

"We hope to have the chance," the director said. "Unfortunately, there are no guarantees."

Lieutenant Russo looked to her boss.

"We're good to go," she said, as she and Special Agent Mayne slid into their chairs.

"Back to Representative Pfeiffer's question," Yeargan said. "It's true tracking calls is less difficult than it was a decade ago. The proliferation of cell towers has changed the game, although narrowing the site of a call down to a specific location at once is something you're more likely to see on TV than in real—"

The sharp jangling of the telephone in front of Governor Butler interrupted his remarks. I took a peek at my watch, noting the caller was two minutes ahead of schedule. The governor reached for it but didn't lift the receiver until she got a thumbs-up from Director Yeargan.

"This is Patricia Butler."

"Good morning, Governor," a male voice said. "You'll be pleased to hear Senator Somerset Smith had a restful night. He's assured us he is eager to resume his usual routine."

"How can we make that happen?" the governor asked.

"It's Saturday," the caller said. "Your assignment is to immediately call a special session of the Arkansas General Assembly. It will begin at 9:00 AM Tuesday."

There was a pause.

"Again, use your gubernatorial power to convene a special session for the Arkansas legislature. It will begin in 73 hours. Next Tuesday morning. Stay tuned for details."

"Surely you're not—"

The line went dead.

Shaking her head, Governor Butler stared at the handset for a moment before returning it to its cradle.

"A special session," she said. "Whatever for?"

Joan and Mort exchanged shrugs.

Staring at his watch, Director Yeargan said, "Damn. The call took all of 15 seconds."

He then looked to his technical team.

"Get anything?"

"It originated somewhere south of Helena," Russo said, her eyes glued to a computer screen.

"Within the town of Elaine," Mayne said, placing the accent on the first syllable instead of pronouncing it like a woman's name.

He must be a local, I thought. Folks unfamiliar with the community always said it wrong.

"Why Elaine?" the governor asked. "It's a small farming town in the Delta."

"It's isolated," Director Yeargan said. "Not overrun with law enforcement personnel."

"There is another possibility," I said, recalling a feature article I'd read months ago. "Perhaps they're trying to make a statement."

"What kind of statement?" Mort asked.

"Elaine was the site of a major race riot over a century ago," I said. "Some historians insist it was a massacre, resulting in the deaths of dozens—maybe hundreds—of African-Americans."

Given the stares aimed in my direction, none of the others in the room were familiar with this neglected footnote in the state's past.

The jarring ring of the telephone swung everyone's attention back to the table.

"Governor Patricia Butler speaking."

"Regarding the forthcoming special session, Governor Butler," said a female voice. "Your agenda must include a bill to prohibit any sort of reparations program in Arkansas dealing with slavery. Feel free to add other topics, but legislation prohibiting reparations must be included. Understand?"

"A reparations program?" the governor said, incredulous. "We've never even considered such legislation."

"And your signature on the bill will prevent reparations efforts in future years."

Following a pause, she was told, "Expect one more call."

The next thing we heard was a loud dial tone.

"Any luck?" Yeargan asked his experts.

The room remained silent for half a minute.

"This call came from outside Hope," Mayne said.

"From the community of Washington," Russo added.

"There's a nice state park down there," Mort said. "Chock full of historic buildings."

"Yet what's the significance of this particular town?" Joan asked. "My gut tells me these are not random locations drawn from a hat."

When no one else offered an idea, I raised a hand. "I doubt it's a coincidence Washington served as Arkansas's confederate state capital during the Civil War."

The others in the room seemed to be mulling this over when Yeargan spoke.

"I get the distinct impression our callers were reading from prepared statements," he said. "Almost a monotone in both cases."

"We'll know more after we run the tapes through our voice modulation system," said agent Mayne, nodding to Yeargan.

"One thing is clear: they didn't want to engage in a conversation with the governor."

The room grew quiet as eight sets of eyes settled on the phone. Finally, it rang.

"This is Governor Butler."

"Our concluding call," said a third voice, deeper than the other callers.

"As soon as your office gets the anti-reparations bill drafted, post it on your official website. Our technical staff—to include a trio of lawyers—will review it at once. Senator Smith will remain in our care until the approved bill receives your signature and becomes law. For his sake, do a good job. Goodbye."

Director Yeargan shook his head.

"The last call was the shortest of the three. We needed more time."

The room was quiet as the experts examined their equipment. After maybe 20 seconds had passed, Agent Mayne snorted and pointed at his monitor.

"You're kidding me," he said.

"Unbelievable," said Russo, shaking her head. "But that seems to be the case."

"What do you mean?" Yeargan asked.

"It appears the last call was placed within 200 yards of this very office," Mayne said. "A short distance to the north of us."

Mort pushed away from the table, got to his feet, and strode to the door leading into the Governor's Conference Room. The rest of us fell in line behind him. He walked past the ornate marble fireplace, coming to a stop in front of the bank of tall windows at the room's north end. As Mort shoved the heavy curtains open and gazed outside, the rest of us crowded around him.

"Are you saying they called within sight of this memorial?" he asked, gesturing toward the monument to the Little Rock Nine.

The large bronze sculpture, a popular photo op on the State Capitol grounds, honored nine young black students who'd desegrated Little Rock Central High School in 1957.

"I think that's exactly what happened," Russo said.

"Damn" was Yeargan's sole comment.

From the expression on her face, Governor Patricia Butler felt the same.

"The Elaine race riot, the Confederate Capitol, and now the Little Rock Nine," said Joan. "Quite the trifecta. We're dealing with people who have some understanding of history."

"Or at least their version of it," Mort said.

"And by kidnapping Senator Smith, perhaps the most prominent African-American in Arkansas, they're letting us know they're serious," Governor Butler said.

As we stepped from the window, Mort reached into his pocket and removed his cell phone.

"Another photograph from the kidnappers has arrived," he said a moment later.

He glanced at the image for a few seconds and handed his phone to Governor Butler. She studied it for a moment and then gave it to Joan.

"Somer's alive," she said, the relief apparent in her voice. "The newspaper he's holding is today's edition."

Once Yeargan and his colleagues viewed the picture, Leslie and I had a chance to see it.

"He's wearing a jacket," Leslie said. "It must have been taken outside."

Yeargan gestured for the phone, and Leslie returned it to him. "Interesting," he said. "Very interesting."

* * *

Joan insisted on taking Leslie and me to dinner that evening, reserving a table in a quiet corner of a restaurant in Little Rock's River District.

"I spent the rest of the morning with Governor Butler," she said. "It required a lot of effort, but she managed to convince the legislative leadership to agree to a special session, which has now been officially called."

"Did she have to divulge the reason?" I asked.

"Yes, but only after swearing them to secrecy," Joan said. "They ginned up a couple of other items to include on the legislative agenda. One dealing with medical coverage for at-risk children and the other something to do with state prisons."

"The reparations bill," I said. "How will it be presented?"

"Good question," Joan said. "She had to hide it in a shell bill with a rather ambiguous title. At this time, of course, there's no substance to it. As you might expect, it's aroused the curiosity of one persistent reporter who's pressing for details."

"What's next?" Leslie asked.

"We pray Somer is rescued before the legislature convenes," Joan said. "While his safe return is her primary concern, Governor Butler plans to move slowly with the reparations matter, buying time for the State Police and FBI to find Somer."

"Have they developed any leads?" I asked.

Joan hesitated and then shook her head.

"They're struggling," she said. "No real breakthroughs yet."

I got the waiter's attention and asked for another round of drinks.

~ THIRTY-NINE ~

My cell phone rang as Leslie and I drove home after our dinner with Joan. It was Booker.

"Good evening, favorite uncle," I said, activating the speakerphone function.

Much to my surprise, this impertinent greeting failed to generate his usual rebuke. In fact, all I heard was silence.

"How are things in your world?" I asked, trying another approach.

"Confusing, dear nephew," he said at last. "Yesterday, chatter on the portion of the dark web I monitor was unbelievable, as active as I've ever witnessed. And tonight? Things are strangely serene. Too calm."

I caught Leslie's glance. She and I had agreed earlier we couldn't share news of Somer's kidnapping with Uncle Booker. It was a point made crystal clear by State Police Director Leroy Yeargan.

"It's the weekend," I said. "Perhaps everyone's taking a break from the internet. Didn't the Razorbacks have a big game earlier today?"

"Are you referring to American football?" he asked, the disdain apparent in his question. "As you know, I hold that alleged sport in the lowest possible regard. Now, if you're open to a discussion on the nuances of soccer, I would relish such a conversation."

"Another time," I said. "Thanks for the update on the dark web. Anything else?"

"The feisty tribe I monitor has grown inexplicably quiet, convincing me something significant is underway. The FBI did, of course, distribute a cautionary warning mere days ago."

"Here's a possibility," I said. "Perhaps word is out about the David O. Dodd essay contest, and they're all home, helping their children draft those heartfelt compositions."

Booker snorted.

"I could only wish such a scenario was the case."

He paused for a moment. "Also, I believe congratulations are in order. I recall seeing a posting on Facebook about Lassiter & Associates winning an esteemed account."

"It was a team effort," I said. "The research you conducted on tourism websites many weeks ago was helpful."

Seconds passed. I wondered if the call had been dropped.

"I must comb my wig and determine which heels I shall wear for tonight's pageant," Booker finally said.

"Break a leg," Leslie said.

"Thank you. Cheerio."

* * *

Joan phoned while we ate breakfast Sunday.

"Good news," she said. "Mort Sensabaugh received another photograph of Somer this morning holding a copy of today's newspaper."

"Any message with it?" I asked.

"It seems the picture was the message," Joan said. "We know he's still alive."

We'd been home from church less than an hour when Del Boddington called.

"Randy," he said. "Any chance you and Leslie can drive up tomorrow morning? We found a small cove on the lake lined with the best fall foliage I've ever seen, like what you might expect in New England. It's perfect for a quick and easy photo-shoot. A cold front is predicted to blast through late tomorrow, and wind gusts should knock down most of the leaves."

"It might work," I said. "We've closed the agency for the day. Give me a second and let me check with my bride."

I muted the phone and told Leslie about Del's proposal.

"We can sit here and worry ourselves to death over Somer," she said, "or we can spend a productive day in the Ozarks. We both love Somer, yet there's nothing we can do to help him."

I told Del we'd meet him at the marina at 10:00 AM.

"We'll have a party barge anchored in place," he said, "with Tabitha and three or four of her friends onboard to provide talent with all the props. I'll ferry you and your wife to and from the cove. She should be able to complete the job in an hour, two at most."

While I prepared a pasta dinner that evening, Leslie assembled her photo gear and charged batteries for both Amelia, the drone, and her still cameras.

We phoned Joan following the meal for an update.

"I'm glad you called," she said. "I had a conversation with Director Yeargan late this afternoon, but his words weren't encouraging."

"Did he have any developments to report?" Leslie asked.

"Not much," she said. "First, there's a limited number of security cameras on the state capitol grounds. Except for catching one of our freshman legislators urinating behind a bush, a review of the footage revealed nothing of interest. Usual activities at the loading dock and so on."

"Not even around the sculpture of the Little Rock Nine?" I asked. "For the last call yesterday morning?"

"There's a camera there," Joan said. "The bad news is it's aimed at the statues of the nine students rather than their surroundings. In other words, no help at all."

I stared at the telephone positioned between us, growing frustrated by the lack of good news.

"Did he have anything positive to report?" Leslie asked as the same question ricocheted through my mind.

"There were a couple of things," Joan said after a pause. "The experts have spent hours examining those two earlier pictures and the one Mort got this morning. As you noticed, the shots we saw were pretty grainy. However, Director Yeargan said there may be a clue in the third photograph."

Finally, I thought, maybe something to give us some hope.

"They think Somer might have been standing near water for today's picture," she said. "Although it's another tight shot, there's what could be the hint of water reflecting over his shoulder. Nothing definite, Yeargan stressed, but a 50/50 chance."

"That's a bit of progress," Leslie said.

"One more thing," Joan said. "All three photographs came with a time stamp indicating the exact instance they were taken. The last two were shot outdoors. Measuring the angle of shadows on his face, they were able to narrow down the location of these pictures to the central third of the state. Essentially from the Mountain Home area on the north to El Dorado and vicinity to the south."

Leslie looked at me, raised her eyebrows, and shrugged.

"I don't want to sound negative," I said, "but I'm not sure how much that tells us."

"I had a similar reaction and expressed it in rather crude terms to Director Yeargan," Joan said. "He explained this determination rules out the likelihood of people in Somer's hometown of Osceola, where he has known detractors, holding him nearby."

"What's the status of the Governor's work on the anti-reparations bill?" I asked.

"She's scheduled to confer with her key advisors first thing tomorrow morning," Joan said. "Along with the Speaker of the House, the Pro Tem of the Senate, and the state's Attorney General."

No doubt it would be a fascinating meeting. I didn't envy Governor Butler's challenge to explain the circumstances to those in attendance.

* * *

We departed Little Rock at 6:00 AM Monday for our rendezvous with the Hillcountry Marine group, stopping at Ferguson's Country Store around the halfway point for coffee and their famous homemade cinnamon rolls. At 9:45, we pulled into the parking lot at the marina on Bull Shoals Lake. Del met us at the foot of the long walkway leading onto the massive dock.

"Tabitha and her buddies left with their boat a quarter of an hour ago," he said. "Once we load your gear, we'll be on our way."

The three of us managed to get Leslie's equipment transported onto Del's party barge in one trip. Ten minutes after we'd arrived, we were motoring across open water, noting the calm conditions and bright blue sky. When we arrived at the secluded cove, it was every bit as scenic as Del had described. The brilliant maple and hickory leaves provided a spectacular backdrop for the party barge holding Tabitha and her friends.

Leslie went to work, beginning with a series of drone shots. She seemed pleased with the results, time and again praising the models for their smiles and cooperation. Telling them to enjoy a 10-minute break, Leslie packed Amelia in her carrying case and tinkered with her digital Nikon camera, preparing it for action.

Directing Del as he navigated our pontoon boat around the anchored barge, Leslie must have fired off at least a hundred frames. Twenty minutes later, she announced the photo-shoot was done, that she'd gotten the images she needed. After Leslie had thanked the talent for their willing assistance, Del returned us to the dock.

"I appreciate y'all coming here on such short notice," he said.

"It was a treat to get on the lake again," Leslie said. "I'll forward the best shots to you later this week. And I'll make sure the graphic artists at the agency get a complete set."

Following a round of handshakes with Del, we left the marina, aiming for Little Rock. Driving back through Yellville, we stopped at a local dairy bar for lunch, dining in the truck's cab. Not the healthiest meal, it was speedy and tasty.

"Would you be willing to consider a little detour to the Flyover Family's neighborhood?" Leslie asked, eating the last of our fries. "Maybe to include a bit of discreet surveillance?"

"It'll allow us to update Booker on the project he mentioned," I said. "Something regarding an expansion of their firing range if my memory's correct."

Heading south out of Yellville on Arkansas Highway 14, we turned onto the county road leading to the compound. I slowed as we passed its entrance. Two vehicles could be seen beyond the closed gate, parked in front of the restored homeplace.

"Let's go to the same spot we used earlier," Leslie said.

Less than a minute later, I pulled off the gravel road and parked at the edge of the old trace we'd discovered on our previous outing.

"What are the odds of us encountering a Park Service ranger again?" Leslie asked with a grin.

"Nil," I said. "Perhaps less than nil."

"But I learned a lesson," she said. "We're going to play it safe today."

She retrieved her tripod from the backseat of my pickup. Extending its legs as she walked, Leslie placed it in front of the ancient rock wall 15 to 20 yards beyond the truck. Mounting her Nikon camera on the tripod, she aimed its lens at the moss-covered stones.

"This composition's not bad," Leslie said as she studied the image through her viewfinder.

I heard her shutter fire. And then a couple more times.

"Better than decent. The contrast between the rocks and the surrounding foliage, backlit by the sun, is amazing."

She scooted the tripod down a few feet, moved it closer to the stacked stones, and took another dozen or so photographs.

"I assume your plan is to leave the Nikon here while you're flying the drone?" I asked. "In case, a certain unlikely situation should arise?"

"Exactly so," she said.

Leslie wrapped her arms around my neck and gave me a big kiss.

"And now, we'll prepare to launch Amelia for her second reconnaissance flight above the Flyover Family's sovereign territory."

We returned to the truck where Leslie placed the case holding the drone and its array of assorted paraphernalia in its bed. After asking me to carry the remote-control unit, she lifted the drone from its case, and we walked past her tripod to the large flat stone we'd used weeks ago as Amelia's launching pad. When she'd positioned the drone to her satisfaction, Leslie took the flight controller from my hands.

"Are we good to go?" she asked.

I gave her a nod. Amelia soon rose through the clearing and disappeared beyond the trees as Leslie piloted her north above the Flyover Family property.

"We're now looking down on the frame house," she said, staring at the device in her hands. "I can see the new dormitory and classroom building at the edge of my screen."

Hearing an unexpected noise in the background, I took a few hurried steps away from Leslie, pausing near the edge of the county road. A vehicle was approaching, no question about it. I ran to Leslie and touched her on the shoulder.

"There's a car or truck coming this way," I said. "We can hope it's just someone passing through."

"I'll set Amelia to hover in place," Leslie said, making adjustments on the control panel. She then darted behind the trunk of a large tree next to the old roadway where she stashed the unit out of sight.

As I jogged toward my truck, Leslie scurried to her Nikon and crouched behind the tripod.

Kicking up a cloud of dust, a pickup truck appeared, coasting to a stop next to mine. But it wasn't a random motorist out for a pleasure drive. Nor was it the National Park Ranger we'd met on our last visit here.

The decal on the door had four words: **Marion County Sheriff's Department**. The driver's door opened and Sheriff Hutch Thomas emerged from the truck and began walking in our direction.

288

~ FORTY ~

Tossing a toothpick to the ground as he approached, Sheriff Hutch Thomas then slipped his aviator sunglasses into a shirt pocket. Leslie stepped from behind her tripod and began walking toward us from the opposite direction.

"Mr. Lassiter," he said. "What brings you and your pretty little wife to our parts again?"

After a lingering look into my truck, he stopped ten feet or so in front of me, not interested in exchanging a handshake.

"Leslie had another photo-shoot on the lake with Del and his daughter this morning," I said before turning and gesturing to the rock wall over my shoulder. "We'd stopped at this stacked stone fence on our last trip up here."

"I got several nice shots here during the summer," Leslie said, "and thought it would be a worthwhile location to visit again in the fall. As you can see, the foliage is brilliant."

Seconds passed as the sheriff gazed in the direction of Leslie's tripod.

"This spot's mighty obscure," he said. "How did it come to your attention?"

My heart skipped a beat. Sheriff Hutch Thomas was right. Almost hidden by the undergrowth, it was all but invisible from the road.

But Leslie came through.

"When we ran into a National Park Service ranger earlier this year, I asked for leads on unusual photo ops, telling her I was a professional photographer. She mentioned this and gave us directions, saying it was settled by the Dobson family generations ago."

How she remembered the name Dobson was beyond me.

The sheriff smiled and gave Leslie a nod.

"There's still a handful of Dobsons scattered across these here hills," he said. "One of 'em worked for me during my first term as sheriff. A decent bunch."

"How goes your campaign?" I asked.

"So far, so good," he said. "I'm making the circuit from one corner of the district to the next, eating more fried chicken than I can shake a stick at."

Giving us a slight wave, he took a couple of steps back.

"I reckon it's time for me to continue on my afternoon rounds. Hope you get some nice pictures."

He slipped on his sunglasses, returned to his truck, and drove away, leaving a trail of dust as he left.

"I have a question," I said, "for my pretty little wife." I waggled my eyebrows.

"Watch it buster," she said with a clever grin. "You don't want to jeopardize a good thing."

"Point taken," I said. "But how in the world did you manage to recall the name of the clan homesteading this property? I'm pretty sure your response saved us from a stern interrogation by the sheriff."

"It came to me when I saw Sheriff Thomas," she said with a shrug. "Popped into my head like magic, sort of an epiphany."

"Speaking of magic, we'd better check on Amelia."

I followed Leslie to the base of the tree where she'd stashed the drone's remote-control unit. She retrieved the device and studied the screen.

"She's just as we left her," Leslie said. "Quietly loitering 150 feet above the farmhouse."

"Anything going on?" I asked.

"I don't see any people moving around," she said, fiddling with the joystick. "Here's something though; more construction near the new building. A series of forms has been arranged in a repetitive pattern in the dirt."

I peered over her shoulder at the monitor as she zoomed in on the site.

"It resembles the outline of an amphitheater," I said. "Sounds logical for a kids' summer camp."

Leslie then flew Amelia northward, and the shooting range came into view. A bulldozer had been parked at one end of the long complex. Leslie pointed to a large mass of smoldering debris visible on the screen.

"They must have knocked down a stand of trees to expand the range," she said. "There's plenty of room to add another group of firing stations."

"Does this complete our assignment?" I asked.

"I believe we're good to go," Leslie said. "I will fly our little baby home."

"Little baby?" I asked.

"I've spent hours bonding with Amelia," she said. "This drone isn't merely another camera. In certain ways, it's an extension of me. Thus, little baby."

I kept my eye on the monitor while the drone, or our little baby, flew closer.

"I think she's nearing the big pond," I said. "Can you bring her back over the west side of the water near the dam? Let's check on those pontoon floats and what we assumed was a pile of building materials."

"We're cruising at 75 feet," Leslie said as a great blue heron glided beneath the drone. "The collection of supplies should appear soon."

But it didn't. When the drone hovered above the place I'd mentioned, all we saw was a slight depression in the ground and a patch of yellowish grass where the lumber and pontoon tubes had been stacked on our previous flyover. Nearby vehicular tracks in the pasture led in the direction of the original farmhouse.

"Those tire marks indicate there's been a good deal of traffic to this location," I said. "What could have happened to those floats and boards?"

"We'll gain a bit of altitude and get a better look at the pond," Leslie said, working the joystick.

As Amelia flew upwards, more and more water became evident on the monitor. Leslie spotted a flock of ducks bobbing on the pond.

"What are we looking at?" I asked as an object floating on the water came into view.

"I'm not sure," Leslie said. "Is it some sort of weird boat?"

She piloted the drone to a higher altitude, zooming out so we could see the entire body of water.

"It seems to be positioned almost exactly in the center of the pond."

"Can you dip down for a closer inspection?"

Within seconds Amelia was a dozen or so feet above the water's surface, circling this unexpected thing piquing our curiosity.

"It's a UFO," I said. "An Unidentified Floating Object."

"Whatever it is," Leslie said, "it looks to be built on those pontoon tubes we discovered last time we were here. It reminds me of a primitive raft. Something a modern-day Tom Sawyer might make."

A wooden deck stretched from one end to the other, and in the middle was a small shack, also made of wood, maybe ten feet square and some eight feet tall. Roofed with corrugated tin, it had a pair of tiny windows on opposite sides and a single wooden door secured with a padlock.

"Could this be a swimming platform of some sort?" Leslie asked

"I noticed a chain disappearing into the water at one end," I said. "If it's a swimming dock, why is it anchored 200 yards from the swimming beach? And it lacks a ladder allowing access from the water for swimmers."

Leslie circled the drone around the peculiar structure once more.

"There's an interesting item," I said, pointing to the image on the monitor. "It's a cleat for tying boats on the edge of the wooden deck."

"We saw ducks a little earlier," Leslie said. "Maybe the group plans to ferry hunters out to this raft. I believe duck season is getting close."

I shook my head.

"Although they could stretch camouflage netting across it, I doubt if it would work. I've never seen a duck blind resembling anything like this."

"I can't imagine any self-respecting hunter leaving his equipment out here," Leslie said. "But why is the door padlocked?"

I didn't have an answer.

"Will you take her up to give us a wider perspective?" I asked. "Something on the shoreline near the swimming beach caught my attention a moment ago."

When Leslie piloted Amelia up and away from the raft-like object, the camp's swimming area, marked by buoys and ropes, came into view.

"What's that toward the bottom of your screen?" I asked.

Leslie zoomed in. We saw a fishing boat with a small outboard motor pulled to the shore.

"Do you remember this boat from our last visit?" Leslie asked.

"I don't recall seeing it," I said. "They probably use it to get people out to the raft."

"Ready for me to bring Amelia in?"

"Before we call it a day," I said, "let's take one more peek at our strange watercraft."

"The pond is so smooth," Leslie said as she steered Amelia away from the shoreline. "It's like flying over a sheet of blue glass."

She was right. From our vantage point, the unusual contraption floated on a calm, mirror-like surface. But as the drone descended, a small ripple materialized on the water, originating from one corner of the raft and expanding outward in ever-enlarging concentric circles.

"Did you see that?" I asked, my pulse quickening.

"See what?" she said. "I'm not sure where to look."

"Watch the water at the lower right corner near the cleat."

Seconds passed.

"What are we looking for?"

"Be patient," I said, wondering if I was imagining things.

More seconds passed.

Another ripple appeared. And then another, much larger.

Leslie gasped.

"Do those little waves mean what I think they mean? That something—or someone—is moving on that makeshift boat? Locked in place?"

"No, it means nothing of the sort," said a voice from behind us.

Leslie and I spun around.

Sheriff Hutch Thomas had returned.

~ FORTY-ONE ~

"Fly your damn drone back and land it at my feet," Sheriff Thomas said, almost shouting. "Right now."

"We're standing on public property owned by the National Park Service," I said. "You have no authority to—"

"You can save your righteous indignation for later," the sheriff said, interrupting me. "You two are under arrest for willfully and unlawfully violating the airspace of a private landowner. I'll read your rights to you when we get to the county jail in Yellville. Now, Mrs. Lassiter, I want you to bring the aircraft to the ground at once."

Staring at her feet, Leslie ignored him.

"Mrs. Lassiter," he said, his voice rising in pitch, "I've given you an order."

Leslie looked up and met his gaze. "I don't believe there's a Mrs. Lassiter here."

"She's your wife, isn't she?" he asked, glancing over his shoulder to me.

"But she's not a Lassiter," I said. "Her name is Carlisle. Leslie Carlisle."

"Now that we have that settled," he said, "Ms. Carlisle, you must return your drone without delay."

Her eyes glued to the remote-control panel in her hands, Leslie piloted Amelia to a gentle landing on the rock at her feet.

Before she could reach for Amelia, Sheriff Thomas extended an arm and stepped in front of her.

"I believe you've given me no choice but to seize this aircraft for evidence," he said and grabbed the drone. "I'll also need each of you to give me your cell phones."

"You've got to be kidding," I said.

"Not at all," he said.

Cradling Amelia in the crook of an arm, he held out a hand. "Your phones, please."

After Leslie gave him her cell, I handed him mine

"Collect all your stuff and load it into your truck.".

We retrieved the control unit for the drone and Leslie's Nikon camera and tripod and followed the sheriff to my Toyota. As we placed the gear in the backseat, I noticed the drone's empty case in plain sight in the truck's bed. There it was; an explanation of how Sheriff Thomas knew what was happening. He must have spotted it when he walked past my truck during his initial stop. And decided to sneak back to see what we were doing.

"As for the movement from our little houseboat you claim to have seen, let me assure you there's nothing aboard," he said. "The slightest breeze will set it rocking. Understand?"

I gave him a nod, but avoided any eye contact. I knew what I'd seen.

"I'm going to hike down the road to get my truck," he said. "I'll return in a couple of minutes. First, though, give me your keys so you two won't be tempted to run off."

He walked away, carrying Amelia, our cell phones, and my key ring.

"Do you believe him regarding the raft?" Leslie asked. "That those ripples are meaningless?"

"If they're of no consequence, why is he making such a big deal out of them?" I asked. "More than ever, I'm convinced Senator Somer Smith is held hostage out there."

"It's well known the senator is terrified of water," Leslie said. "Can you think of a better place to hold him captive than in the middle of a lake?"

We heard a vehicle approaching. It was Sheriff Thomas. He coasted to a stop, rolled down the pickup's window, and tossed me my keys.

"We're going to make a quick drive to Yellville in a two-vehicle convoy, my truck in the lead," he said. "Mr. Lassiter, I want you to follow me straight to our county jail where you and Ms. Carlisle will be booked. Do not try to escape. Do not attempt anything stupid. You realize you cannot outrun this?"

Sheriff Thomas held the microphone of his police radio for us to see. He paused, staring at me and waiting for a reply.

I bobbed my head.

"Let's go."

After Leslie and I climbed into my Toyota, Sheriff Thomas pulled onto the county road and we fell in behind his dust.

"Damn," Leslie said. "I wish we had a phone."

"We do," I said. "It's in the glove box."

"You have a spare?" Her eyes were big.

"The agency bought cell phones for every employee," I said. "For business use."

Leslie rustled through the glove compartment

"I found it!"

"I've made a practice of keeping it charged," I said, "but have never used it, preferring my personal cell. In fact, there's not a contact in the directory. Not one."

"And I can't recall a single number other than my own," she said, shaking her head. "And yours."

"First off," I said, "we can't allow the sheriff to see us talking on it."

"Got it."

"Please call my office," I said, and gave her the number. "And ask—"

"But isn't your office closed?"

I'd forgotten about shutting down Lassiter & Associates for the day. Muttering a few choice obscenities, I pounded the steering wheel with my fist.

"And dialing 911 will connect us with the Marion County Sheriff's Office, right?" Leslie asked.

"Probably not our best option," I said.

When we came to a stop behind the sheriff at the junction with the state highway, I leaned toward the dash, removed my wallet from a rear pocket, and handed it to Leslie.

"Mort Sensabaugh's business card is in there somewhere," I said as we pulled onto the pavement. "Dial his direct number, keeping the phone out of sight in your lap, and place it in speaker mode."

Seconds later I heard a familiar voice.

"This is Mort Sensabaugh. Sorry; I'm unable to take your call. Please leave a message, and I'll get back as soon as I can."

"Mort," I said. "This is Randy Lassiter. Call me immediately, using this number. It's extremely urgent."

"Is there anyone else we can contact?" Leslie asked.

"We don't have many choices," I said. "See if other numbers are listed on Mort's business card. Maybe a general number for the governor's office?"

As Leslie was examining the card, the phone rang.

"Mort," I said. "Leslie and—"

"Hey dude," he said, interrupting me. "Got your—"

"Mort," I said. "We have an emergency."

He was silent for a moment.

"An emergency?" he asked. "What's going on? How can I help?"

"Listen carefully," I said. "Leslie and I think we've stumbled onto the site where Senator Somer Smith is being held hostage."

"How did—"

"But we've been arrested and we're on the way to the Marion County Jail in Yellville."

"What?"

"We believe the local sheriff might be involved with the kidnapping. You need to call State Police Director Yeargan right now, telling him to organize a raid on the Flyover Family compound in southern Marion County."

"The Flyover Family compound in southern Marion County," Mort repeated. "I'm writing this down."

"Tell him it appears Senator Smith is imprisoned in a home-made houseboat anchored in the middle of a small lake on the group's property."

"Randy," he said. "This is beginning to sound pretty sketchy. How are you able to call me if you've been arrested?"

"It's a long story," I said, "and we don't have much time. Leslie and I are in my truck and we've been ordered to follow the sheriff into town after he nabbed us checking out the lake I mentioned."

Leslie gave me a nudge and pointed through the windshield.

"We've now entered Yellville's city limits," I said. "The jail can't be far."

"Why don't you call Yeargan and give him this information firsthand?" Mort asked.

"Because we're going to get tossed into jail within the next few minutes."

Sheriff Thomas drove past the Marion County Courthouse, an impressive three-story stone building, with Leslie and me trailing three or four car lengths behind him.

"Our concern is the senator's captors may move him to another remote location," I said. "Please call Director Yeargan. I'm sure he has troopers stationed nearby."

"Okay," he said. "I'll phone him. But this better not be a wild goose chase."

Sheriff Thomas turned into a parking lot behind the jail, coming to a stop under a sign labeled: **Reserved—Marion County Sheriff**. We pulled in near him where visitor parking was allowed.

"Thanks, Mort," I said. "Gotta go."

Leslie stashed the phone under the passenger seat as Sheriff Thomas motioned for us to follow him. She then slipped Mort's business card into my shirt pocket.

The sheriff took us into a small conference room where a deputy witnessed him reading our Miranda rights. Leslie and I stared at each other, shaking our heads.

"Just like on TV," she whispered as the sheriff completed his recitation.

The deputy booked us on charges the sheriff had stated earlier, adding the federal offense of illegal and unauthorized flights over National Park Service property. After getting fingerprinted, we were led into another room where we posed for mug shots.

"Don't we get to make a phone call?" I asked.

The deputy returned us to the receiving area of the jail and directed me to a wooden desk on the far side of the room. It was bare except for a grungy landline telephone and an old and tattered copy of the Yellville directory.

"One call," he said, taking a seat behind another desk.

I gazed at Leslie, at a loss of who to call, given all the numbers of my friends and acquaintances were stored in my personal cell phone, wherever it was.

"Mort?" she suggested.

I reached into my shirt pocket, removed the business card Mort had given me days earlier, and dialed his number.

He answered on the first ring, surprising me.

"Mort," I said. "It's Randy. Again."

"I did as you asked—"

"If you will, let me do most of the talking," I said, worried the line wasn't secure. "Leslie and I have been booked at the Marion County Jail in Yellville, and you're our one call."

Gesturing at the deputy to get his attention, I said, "I think we'll soon be escorted to our cells."

The deputy nodded.

"Will you call State Representative Joan Pfeiffer, tell her our situation, and ask if she can find one of her contacts in this area who can bail us out?"

I again turned to the deputy.

"Maybe I can get an idea of our bail."

The deputy showed me his right hand, all five fingers extended.

"I think it'll be $500."

Waving an arm in my direction, the deputy mouthed, "Each."

"Make it $500 each," I said.

"Got it," Mort said.

"Now, I have a question for you," I said. "Did you have any luck on the other matter I mentioned?"

Mort hesitated before responding.

"Are you referring to Leroy?"

"Yep."

"Leroy was very interested."

The deputy gestured to his watch.

"Time's up, Mort."

I thanked him and ended the call.

Standing, the deputy pointed to a closed door.

"You two come with me."

Five minutes later, Leslie and I found ourselves in adjacent cells. We'd somehow been spared the indignity of changing into prison uniforms. She was alone in her lockup, but I had a cellmate, an elderly man occupying a bunk and reeking of alcohol. So far, he hadn't moved, much less said a word, but his snoring went on nonstop.

Leslie and I stood next to each other, separated by cold iron bars, quietly talking to pass the time.

"Oh," she said, giving me a wry smile. "I remembered a bit of good news."

"I could use a shot of something positive."

"I switched memory cards in the drone before Amelia's flight over the compound," she said. "If the sheriff decides to keep the images recorded in the drone, we still have the footage from our Hillcountry Marine shoot."

"My worry is he might accidentally destroy the memory card or misplace Amelia," I said, making quote marks in the air with my fingers as I used the word 'accidentally.' "Stranger things have been known to happen."

We'd been confined almost two hours before the same deputy appeared and opened our cell doors.

"You've been bailed out," he said, and led us to the booking area.

A middle-aged woman got to her feet when we walked into the room.

Smiling, she said, "You must be Leslie and Randy. I'm Nita Breckenridge, one of Joan's attorney friends."

Seeing our nods, she fiddled with a cell phone for a moment before handing it to Leslie.

"I'm following instructions," Ms. Breckenridge said. "Joan told me to get you on the line at once."

"Joan," Leslie said. "Nita Breckenridge has come to our rescue."

She paused, and a frown appeared.

"Are you sure?"

Leslie turned to me and whispered, "Somer's wasn't there. He's still missing."

~ FORTY-TWO ~

Leslie handed me the phone, leaning in close so she could listen.

"Joan," I said, "what's happened?"

"A State Police SWAT team conducted a raid in Marion County," she said. "They found a homemade houseboat pulled to the shore, partially destroyed by fire and still smoldering."

There was a pause before she continued. "Somer wasn't there."

"My guess is they're moving him to another place," I said. "Equally remote."

"Leroy feels the same," she said. "According to him, the SWAT team leader has no doubt someone was held captive on this boat. They found a cot, sleeping bag, space heater, ice chest, something called a 'camping toilet,' and two recent editions of the *Arkansas Democrat-Gazette*. Also, there was a hasp on the outside of the door, meaning it could be secured with an exterior lock."

"What's the latest?" Leslie asked.

"The Director is certain they missed rescuing Somer by only minutes," she said. "Although they're concentrating their efforts in northern Arkansas, there's now a statewide alert in place."

"I know you're devastated," I said, "but this is good news. Somer's alive. And my bet is the State Police will locate him by the end of the day."

"Keep the faith," Leslie said. "You'll see Somer soon."

"I appreciate your confidence and support so much," Joan said, "and most of all your love. Now, if you'll let me speak with Nita for a moment."

We gave the cell phone to Nita and walked to the desk where the deputy had arranged the items he'd confiscated from us: watches, wallets, telephones, and keys.

"Where's my drone?" Leslie asked.

"The aircraft will remain in our evidence room," the deputy said. "You can get it following the trial."

"Trial?" we asked at once.

"Those charges don't just go away," he said, not bothering to hide a smirk. "The circuit judge has to rule. You'll be notified when the date is set."

"Sheriff Thomas isn't here to send us off?" I asked, feeling a bit defiant.

"I believe he has more important things to do," the deputy said.

He placed a sheet of paper in front of each of us along with a pen. "Sign these."

After initialing receipts confirming we'd received our personal effects, we returned to Nita who'd completed her conversation with Joan.

"Thanks so much for coming to our rescue," Leslie said.

Nita shrugged.

"Joan's helped me more times than I can count over the years," she said, "and I'm always happy to repay the favors. Yet visiting a jail to bail out a pair of her friends is a first."

I removed a business card from my wallet.

"Take this," I said, "and forward an invoice. I'll get a check headed your way soon."

"Will do," she said. "And please give our mutual friend a hug next time you see her. If you'd like for me to represent you at the forthcoming trial, let me know. We should be able to get the charges dismissed or at least reduced to a minor offense such as trespassing."

We shook hands and left the jail, Nita going one way and Leslie and me the other.

As we walked to the truck, Leslie wrapped an arm around my waist.

"Well, Randy Lassiter," she said, "I think we should do something special to celebrate this occasion. It's not every day we're released from jail."

"Perhaps you have something in mind?"

"How 'bout a pair of thick, creamy milkshakes?" she asked. "Our route to Little Rock will take us right past the same dairy bar where we had our nutritious lunch hours ago."

We bought the shakes and then headed home, calling Mort Sensabaugh en route.

"Sorry I was skeptical earlier," he said, "but I had trouble imagining your situation. I pride myself on constituent services, although today's request went a little beyond the norm. Please accept my humble apology."

"Not a problem," I said. "Any news concerning Senator Smith?"

"Governor Butler remains in constant contact with Director Yeargan," he said. "And Leroy is convinced his colleagues will find the senator before the day's over. Tips have trickled in, a few of which are promising."

We pulled into our driveway at 9:45. Once we'd stored Leslie's gear—minus the drone—I prepared two bourbons. A bit stiffer than our usual.

I was considering a refill when the telephone rang at 10:30. The caller ID indicated it was Joan. I motioned for Leslie to join me, and then activated the speakerphone.

"What's the word?" I asked.

We heard Joan crying. Seconds passed, and I expected the worst. Leslie gasped, her fingers squeezing my shoulder.

"He's alive," Joan finally said, almost breathless. "Somer was found alive, and he's unharmed!"

"Wonderful," Leslie said. "Our prayers have been answered."

"Director Yeargan had flown to the northern part of the state earlier this evening," Joan said. "He's bringing Somer back to Little

Rock tonight on the State Police plane. In fact, they should be landing in the next 35 minutes."

"Any information on his release?" I asked.

"I was told Somer was discovered in a vehicle during a State Police roadblock," she said. "I have no other details."

"Are you going to meet him at the airport?" Leslie asked.

"Of course!" Joan said. "I'm heading out the door as soon as we end this call."

* * *

At noon the next day, Leslie and I met for lunch at home and watched a live news conference from the Governor's Conference Room in the State Capitol. I saw Mort Sensabaugh do a mic check moments before Governor Patricia Butler strode into the room, trailed by Arkansas State Police Director Leroy Yeargan and then State Senator Somer Smith. Walking at a deliberate pace, Somer looked exhausted.

"Good afternoon," the governor began. "I'm pleased to announce a bizarre scheme involving the kidnapping of State Senator Somer Smith ended with the successful release of Senator Smith last evening outside Mountain Home. I want to thank Arkansas State Police Director Leroy Yeargan for his leadership during this difficult time. He and his team performed admirably, managing a difficult situation with the utmost professionalism. At this time, I'll ask Director Yeargan to share details."

As she stepped back to join Senator Smith, Director Yeargan moved to the podium.

"The governor's office received an anonymous call Friday morning asserting Senator Somer Smith had been kidnapped," Yeargan said. "The caller claimed further details would be forthcoming with another call at eight o'clock Saturday morning."

Yeargan paused to gaze across the crowd. "The call came through as promised on Saturday. We had experts with us using sophisticated technology to attempt to trace the call, but it concluded before anything definite could be determined.

"On this call, Governor Butler was told to schedule a special session of the Arkansas General Assembly that would have begun this morning. Again, we were unable to trace the call due to the brevity of the conversation," he said, glancing at his notes. "A photograph of Senator Smith was also transmitted to a member of the governor's staff to confirm he was unharmed."

Director Yeargan cleared his throat and took a sip of water. "We found ourselves dealing with individuals who'd put a great deal of thought into making their demands clear while foiling our attempts to track them. The first call on Saturday morning lasted well less than a minute, and the next two were even shorter. All three were placed from three widely-spaced communities."

Yeargan again referred to his notes. "The second call, occurring some five minutes after the first, instructed Governor Butler to have her staff draft legislation to prohibit enactment of a state reparations program dealing with slavery.

"The third and final call commanded the governor to post this proposed legislation on her official website where the kidnappers would have the opportunity to review it."

Governor Butler stepped next to Director Yeargan and touched his shoulder. He shifted to the side so she could stand in front of the microphone.

"I realize there were concerns from the media questioning the need for this unexpected special session," she said. "You now know why it was scheduled so quickly and why so little information was forthcoming."

She returned to stand beside Senator Smith.

Director Yeargan moved back to the podium. "While Governor Butler and her advisors were drafting the legislation, we were working closing with the FBI's Little Rock Field Office to find Senator Smith. Frankly, we weren't having much success until we received an anonymous tip regarding an unusual situation south of Yellville in Marion County."

"Anonymous?" Leslie asked, shaking her head. She gave my knee a squeeze.

"Accompanied by FBI agents, our SWAT unit raided this site and found evidence a person had been held captive on a houseboat," Yeargan said. "It appears Senator Smith had been removed from this location moments prior to our team's arrival.

"We issued a statewide alert, and a police roadblock near Mountain Home resulted in the successful release of Senator Smith," Yeargan said. "Two men in the vehicle with the senator were arrested and will be charged with kidnapping. I suspect other charges will be filed soon."

He looked up from his notes and eyed the group of reporters seated around the table in front of him. "Before we hear from Senator Smith, are there questions?"

As Director Yeargan stared over the waving hands, the camera panned across the assembled reporters. I recognized a few among them as representatives of the local media, but most of the faces were unfamiliar to me. I assumed they were affiliated with national news organizations.

Yeargan pointed to a woman at the head of the table.

"The two men under arrest," she said. "Are they tied in with any particular group?"

"We're still attempting to sort things out," Yeargan said. "To this point, the men we apprehended have said little. However, if we discover any reason to suspect this was a hate crime, we'll inform the media at once."

A reporter seated near the end of the table got Yeargan's attention.

"What can you tell us about the kidnapping itself?" he asked. "Did it occur in this building?"

"Senator Smith was working late Thursday evening in his office on the third floor," Yeargan said. "He had his back to the door when two men surprised him, binding his wrists and blindfolding and gagging him. Senator Smith was then led to the basement on a circuitous route, evidently through chaseways and little-known stairways. Once in the basement, Senator Smith was confined in a large cardboard box and wheeled outside. When we learned these details from the senator last evening, we reviewed video footage from the Capitol's loading dock. Two men are seen moving a box labeled '4-Drawer Filing Cabinet' onto a truck. Wearing ball-caps, their faces are never visible. We were able to discern the truck's license, but determined hours ago it was a stolen plate."

I remembered Booker's comments regarding Alex Motherwell's unusual research in the Arkansas State Archives. When I looked to Leslie, she gave me a knowing nod.

Yeargan answered a slew of additional questions, but deferred to Governor Butler when asked about the reparations legislation.

"To ensure Senator Smith's safety, we drafted the legislation as demanded," the governor said. "Had the senator not been found, we would have met the kidnappers' demands and posted it on our website. Whether or not we could have gotten it passed by the General Assembly is a moot point."

Another arm went up.

"Has your administration considered such a bill?" asked a reporter from the middle of the media table.

"We have not," Governor Butler said, shaking her head. "And will not."

She glanced over her shoulder to Somer who gave her a subtle bob of his head.

"Now, we'll hear from State Senator Somer Smith."

Looking straight ahead, Somer walked to the podium, gripping its sides with both hands.

"First, let me thank Director Yeargan and his outstanding team of law enforcement personnel who came to my rescue. And a special thanks to the anonymous tipsters who made it possible."

Leslie leaned my way and kissed me on the cheek.

Somer paused and cleared his throat.

"I stood at this very spot only days ago, imploring our society to accept our differences while respecting our collective strengths. Again today, that is my message."

Ignoring the throng of arms waving to get his attention, Senator Smith stepped away, and, with Governor Butler and Director Yeargan following, returned to the governor's private suite.

~ FORTY-THREE ~

When I returned to work after lunch, Erin trailed me into my office and shut the door. As she took a seat in front of my desk, she wiped her nose with a wrinkled handkerchief.

I hung my sport coat on the rack and placed a tissue box near her before slipping into the chair behind my desk. This can't be good, I thought.

"You won't believe the call I got not five minutes ago," she said, shaking her head.

She grabbed a tissue.

Before I could even consider a reply, she stood and began marching across the room.

"Alex Motherwell," she said, almost spitting the words from her mouth. Reaching the far wall, she turned and retraced her steps. "That worthless, no-good SOB phoned, asking if I'd bail him out!"

She stared at me, her eyes narrow slits. "Can you believe it? After all the grief he's caused me?"

"Bail him out?" I asked. "He's in jail?"

I had a hunch where this conversation was headed, but wanted to hear it from her.

"Maybe you've seen something in the media about the kidnapping of a politician," she said.

She neared the wall, pivoted, and began striding in the opposite direction. "I had no idea what he was even referring to."

"I watched a news conference from the State Capitol regarding the kidnapping when I went home for lunch," I said. "The victim was Senator Somer Smith—"

"Our Senator Smith?" she asked, interrupting me. "The man dealing with the Facebook controversy?"

"He was released unharmed. However, the State Police Director didn't divulge any details concerning suspects or arrests."

Coming to a stop behind her chair, Erin grasped it with both hands, her fingers clinching the top rail.

"Apparently Alex, my former fiancé, and Jordan somebody or other, one of his old Army buddies, have been charged with kidnapping the senator," she said. "Alex told me over the phone he didn't do it."

"Was Motherwell arrested in a roadblock?" I asked.

"He was," Erin said, nodding, "although he claimed he and his friend were doing nothing more than transferring a van from one location to another. Alex insisted he didn't know there was prisoner in the rear of the truck."

"Do you believe him?"

"Alex is not stupid," she said, clearly exasperated. "He earned a difficult degree in engineering, graduating with honors. He compiled an exemplary record in the military, serving as an officer. Alex has an important job with a growing company. He received his private pilot license in the past year."

She paused and took a breath. "Alex is intelligent, intuitive, and careful. So, no, I don't believe him for a second. How could he not know there was a man in the back of his van?"

I didn't have an answer.

"And I'm so disgusted with myself, making the big donation to his special project without vetting it. I naively thought it was truly for 'education,'" she said, making air quotes when she got to the last word.

Again, I failed to have a response.

"Thanks for letting me vent," she said.

Erin pulled another tissue from the box, turned, and left my office.

Leslie and I watched the six o'clock news before dinner. The lead story focused on the successful liberation of State Senator Somer Smith from kidnappers in northern Arkansas. After airing a short video clip with Governor Butler, Senator Smith, and State Police Director Yeargan from the noon media event, the report identified the two men arrested in the case—Alex Motherwell and Jordan Engelhart—and showed their mug shots. Both were said to belong to a secretive paramilitary organization based in the Ozarks, although there was no mention of the Flyover Family or its compound. Nor was there any reference to the senator's captivity on a houseboat.

* * *

My department heads and I left the office the next morning for a nine o'clock meeting with Steele Parker, secretary of the Arkansas Department of Parks, Heritage, and Tourism, and key members of her staff. This was the much-anticipated get-together designed to accomplish two objectives. First, Steele and I signed copies of the official contract formalizing the business relationship, beginning on January 1, between her department and Lassiter & Associates. And it provided an excellent opportunity for everyone involved to exchange business cards, put names with faces, and confirm roles and responsibilities. Also, I took the occasion to announce Megan Maloney, my longtime associate, would be the senior account executive, handling the day-to-day activities.

Leslie and I were enjoying a fine takeout dinner of Chinese food after work when my cell rang.

"It's Booker," I said, glancing at the phone. "Let's see what my favorite uncle wants."

"Good evening," he said. "I shall arrive at your domicile at 12:50 tomorrow afternoon. I'll expect you both to be prepared for a brief excursion of the most extraordinary nature. It will transpire in an informal outdoor environment, so please dress accordingly."

"Where will we be going?" I asked. "And—?"

The line went dead.

"Is this something Booker often does?" Leslie asked, having heard the short conversation.

"I'm afraid this will be a first."

I refilled her glass of wine, and decided to top mine off as well.

"Perhaps he wants us to preview his winter incarnation of Monique Monét," I said. "It's November. Maybe he's ready to share her latest seasonal wardrobe."

"Booker's fashion show could be entertaining," Leslie said. "I can't wait to see his shoes."

She picked up one fortune cookie from the dinner table for herself and handed me the other.

"Let's check our predictions," she said. "You go first."

I unfolded the tiny slip of paper, read "'*New project will yield wonderful results*'" aloud, and then slipped the cookie into my mouth.

Leslie broke into a big smile.

"It must be a reference to the agency's state tourism account," I said.

She leaned forward and gave me a kiss.

"Of course," she said. "Indubitably."

I stared at my bride.

"Just how long have you been waiting to use that word?" I asked. "Days? Weeks? Months?"

She winked.

"Now," Leslie said, "for mine,".

She cracked open her cookie and removed the fortune.

"'*You will find enlightenment at a cemetery*,'" she read.

"How unusual," I said. "A cemetery?"

"I've had worse."

* * *

The next morning's newspaper had a lengthy follow-up piece on the rescue of State Senator Somer Smith, noting the prominent politician was allegedly held captive at a rural farmstead in southern Marion County. Much of the piece was devoted to backgrounds of the two men charged in his kidnapping. I was familiar with much of Motherwell's history, and learned Engelhart, a Texas native, had been assigned to the same Army unit as Motherwell. Also a college graduate, he was said to be president of a conservative political consulting outfit based in Baton Rouge, Louisiana. Up until now, neither had a criminal record.

"Any mention of the Flyover Family or Sheriff Hutch Thomas in the article?" Leslie asked.

"Nary a word," I said. "One unnamed law enforcement source close to the investigation said the two men in custody were not cooperating with authorities."

First thing upon my arrival at Lassiter & Associates, I composed an e-mail to Steele Parker, thanking her for hosting yesterday's get-acquainted session. As I pressed the "send" key, Erin strolled into my office. She seemed to be in a better mood this morning.

"Sorry about yesterday," she said. "In retrospect, it appears I'd reached the end of my rope."

"I thought you were reasonably calm and composed," I said with a shrug, "given the circumstances."

She smiled.

"With your permission, I plan to fly to Fort Worth this evening and spend an extended weekend with Erica."

"Permission granted," I said. "But let me encourage you and your twin sister to ... uh ... operate within the general constraints of our society. Or at least to make a serious attempt. And I will be extra vigilant upon your return on Monday. No tricks."

Erin smiled again, said "Of course," and left the room.

Leslie and I met at home for an early lunch. After eating, we slipped on light jackets and walked to the curb at 12:45. Booker showed up as promised, exactly at 12:50, parking his classic 1959 Cadillac sedan with its distinctive tail fins in front of our house. I opened Cruella's front door for Leslie before climbing onto the huge rear seat.

Booker, I noticed, had prepared himself for exposure to the sun. Wearing what he called driving gloves, a dapper fedora, and a bright scarf wrapped around his neck, the only visible skin was on his face, and it was streaked with zinc oxide.

"Did either of you catch the news over the noon hour?" he asked.

"What's happened?" I asked.

"As I entered your neighborhood, I had the radio on and heard the conclusion of a report on another attack on the electrical grid," he said. "I believe it occurred in southwest Arkansas."

Leslie got on her phone and soon found the story.

"Here's the latest," she said and began reading. "'An electrical substation six miles north of Texarkana was damaged last night, causing an extensive blackout lasting up to eight hours in parts of the city. Using high-powered rifles, vandals disabled key pieces of equipment and—'"

"Ha!" Booker snorted. "Vandals spray-paint picnic table and overturn porta-potties. These aren't vandals, but are knowledge-able saboteurs with specific targets."

"Isn't this what the FBI agent warned Senator Smith's committee about?" Leslie asked. "Domestic terrorists?"

"He indicated it was only a matter of time before Arkansas was hit," I said. "It seems as if that day has come."

"Yet another example of America's continuing decline," Booker said. "As for today's outing, our destination is but a short jaunt away. To one of our fair city's finest points of interest. Based on my latest foray into the dark web, I predict we can expect, shall we say, a fascinating occasion."

"A point of interest?" Leslie asked. "Can you share details?"

"The Westminster Abbey of Arkansas, at least in the minds of some," Booker said. "More commonly known as Mount Holly Cemetery."

Leslie twisted in her seat, made eye contact with me, and mouthed, "My fortune cookie."

Booker parked Cruella on a side street adjacent to the historic graveyard. After slipping on a topcoat, he led us through an ornate iron gate. In the distance, we spotted a sparse crowd, many of them appearing to be adolescents. As we made our way toward the assembly, Leslie commented on the brilliant fall foliage, wishing she'd brought her camera. In the background, we heard the roar of traffic on I-630 and then the wailing of a distant siren.

"Do either of you recall the significance of today's date?" Booker asked. "November 10."

I was clueless.

Leslie, however, raised an arm and began waving it back and forth.

"I do," she said. "I do."

Booker gave her a skeptical look.

"Okay, dear," he said. "Please share your exciting insight with us."

"One of my phone apps provides an 'On this day in history' factoid every morning," she said. "If I'm recalling it correctly, 'Sesame Street' premiered on this day in 1969 on PBS. Or was it 1968?"

Booker shook his head, sort of smiled, and patted her on the shoulder.

"A valiant effort, dear," he said, "but not the appropriate answer. It was on this date, November 10, when David O. Dodd was born in 1846."

Leslie turned to me, a puzzled expression on her pretty face.

"I've heard that name somewhere."

"He was the young man executed by Union troops in Little Rock during the Civil War," I said. "Charged with spying for the Confederacy, Dodd was hanged in what's now MacArthur Park. And his body was interred in this very cemetery."

"He's also a hero, dare I say saint, to certain splinter groups of our society," Booker said. "Perhaps in particular to those we see gathered before us."

We'd closed to within 50 feet of the thin crowd when I recognized a familiar voice.

"It's an honor for me to welcome everyone to today's announcement."

316

I gazed across the tops of heads and was surprised to spot Marion County Sheriff Hutch Thomas. He stood behind a portable lectern and was flanked by a pair of flags: one US, the other Confederate.

I extended my arms, blocking both Leslie and Booker.

"This is close enough," I said.

"We're here today to promote an exciting opportunity for Arkansas's high school students," Thomas said. "An essay contest. Our future patriots will be asked to dig down deep into their souls and answer one simple question: What does David O. Dodd mean to the South?

"As most of you know, choosing today for this announcement was not an accident. David Owen Dodd was born on this date in 1846. Nor is our location an accident, for to my right is the grave-site of this brave 'Boy Martyr of the Confederacy.'"

I glanced to his right and saw a handsome marble obelisk eight or nine feet tall. Freshly scrubbed, it had been topped by an enormous wreath of red roses.

"Complete details on the essay contest, including entry forms, will be found at the table to my left," Thomas said. "Entries must be postmarked no later than January 8."

He paused and again looked over the crowd. "Does this date—January 8—mean anything?"

A few seconds of silence passed before an older man standing near us waved an arm and shouted, "Hell, yes! It's the date the damn Yankees killed the innocent boy."

His response drew a mild round of applause mixed with a scattering of boos.

Thomas held up an open palm to quieten the group.

"And our winner will be announced on May 18."

Another pause.

"Does this date ring a bell with anyone?"

The same man raised a hand.

"Hell, yes," he said. "It's the day Arkansas was admitted into the Confederacy in 1861."

Thomas grinned and gestured to the vocal quasi-historian.

"Let me thank my older brother Ardis Thomas III for sharing his intimate knowledge of our southern heritage with us today."

The elder brother tipped his ball cap to the sheriff.

"The winner of this essay contest will be determined by three eminent historians," Hutch Thomas said, "all experts in the real causes of the Civil War."

I felt a nudge in my ribs. Booker leaned toward me, rolling his eyes.

"More likely a trio of third-rate graduate student who failed to complete their dissertations," he whispered.

Thomas paused a moment and took a peek at his notes.

"I don't need to remind this group slavery was not the cause of that brutal conflict. No, not slavery."

This generated another burst of applause.

"The root cause of the War of Northern Aggression was a fundamental difference in states' sovereignty and states' rights," Thomas said. "It led to the tragic and criminal death of a true southern hero, David Owen Dodd."

At this point, most of the crowd clapped enthusiastically and a few pumped their fists in the air.

"I'm quite certain this eye-opening event is evolving into a rally for states' rights," Booker said. "A salutation to the Lost Cause of the Confederacy. Shall we go?"

"My thoughts exactly," I said. "I'd prefer to avoid another encounter with Sheriff Thomas."

~ FORTY-FOUR ~

Uncle Booker turned and began strolling toward Cruella. Leslie and I walked beside him, Leslie to his left and me to the right.

"Seeing Sheriff Thomas emceeing this event surprised me," Leslie said. "And bothers me. Why hasn't he been arrested?"

Booker grunted.

"Do you really expect to see Hutch Thomas in custody?" he asked.

"Damn right," I said.

"Let me share with you what I uncovered late last evening in the deep and troublesome recesses of the dark web," Booker said. "Several years ago, certain powers that be identified Sheriff Hutch Thomas as a preferred candidate for much higher office. Their plan is he'll serve in the Arkansas legislature, advancing to Speaker of the House in his second term. From there, he'll rise to secretary of state or lieutenant governor, and then to governor within 10 to 12 years."

"You're kidding, aren't you?" Leslie asked.

"If only it were so," Booker said. "Unfortunately, it gets worse."

"How could it get worse?" I asked as we entered Booker's car. "He'd be a terrible governor."

"This situation is not isolated to Arkansas," Booker said. "Not by any means. I learned Sheriff Thomas is but one of a select assembly of 75 to 80 local politicians across the country being groomed for higher office, with the eventual goal of installing them in the U.S. Congress, in Cabinet-level positions, or maybe even in the Presidency itself."

"Who or what organization is orchestrating this blueprint or project or whatever you want to call it?" I asked, stunned by his disclosure.

"These anonymous backers, a small yet extremely forceful group of men and women, studied Newt Gingrich's 'Contract with America' that decades ago guided the Republican Party to great success," Booker said. "However, the Gingrich strategy pales in comparison with what's now in progress. To be sure, it is comprehensive and exceedingly well-funded, but they've taken their scheme to another level, packing judicial districts and gerrymandering almost beyond belief. Yet their greatest strength is an unfailing commitment to their vision. They are experts at playing the long game, patiently working the system, making adjustments as necessary, and slowly advancing their pieces."

"Pieces?" Leslie asked. "You make this sound like it's some sort of giant chess match."

"And that, my dear, is precisely what it is," Booker said. "We have our library boards, planning commissions, county officials such as Sheriff Hutch Thomsas, mayors, and similar low-level positions. Thousands of them scattered throughout the country. You can equate those to the pawns in this larger game. Follow me so far?"

Leslie and I nodded.

"Next in the hierarchy of chess pieces are bishops and knights, right?" Booker asked.

I'd played a little chess as a youth, and it sounded correct to me.

"In our scenario, elected members of the legislatures or general assemblies of the 50 states are, in effect, the bishops," Booker said.

"And representatives and senators in Congress could be viewed as knights?" Leslie asked.

"Exactly so," Booker said. "And governors as well. Anybody care to offer a guess about the rooks?"

I considered his question for a moment. A class or entity commanding more value than the governors or members of Congress ...

"Maybe the Supreme Court?" I offered.

"Bingo," said Booker. "As we've seen in recent years, SCOTUS has flexed its muscle, going beyond—in the opinion of more than a few legal scholars—what framers of the Constitution anticipated. And once confirmed, the justices are ensconced for years, for life if they so choose."

"Which leaves us with the queen and king in your clever chessboard analogy," Leslie said. "I suspect the President would be the King."

"But who's the all-powerful queen?" I asked. "Surely not the Vice President?"

"Our queen is none other than the Speaker of the House of Representatives," Booker said, "second to the Vice President in terms of presidential succession but far more formidable in the matter of raw influence. Never forget the speaker is the consequential player who controls committee assignments, sets the legislative body's calendar, determines which bills are brought to the floor, and oversees the budgeting process. The Speaker of the House can make—or break—a president."

Booker started Cruella and we pulled away from the cemetery.

"Let's skip past the national picture for a moment," I said. "Back to Sheriff Thomas. Are you convinced he can skate on the kidnapping incident involving Senator Smith?"

Booker wasted no time nodding his head.

"Sheriff Hutch Thomas is well protected. Even if Senator Smith was held hostage on property affiliated with the sheriff's club, as I've heard rumored, the challenge will be to discover compelling evidence implicating Thomas with the senator's kidnapping." After a pause, Booker continued. "Let the record show I predict such proof will be nigh impossible to find."

"But what if such links were to be unearthed?" Leslie asked.

"A trial in his own backyard would not be a threat to Sheriff Thomas," Booker said. "His family goes back five generations, and I suspect he's safe from any and all legal actions."

"Let's say charges are brought and the prosecution seeks to hold the trial someplace else," I said. "A setting where the Thomas family wields less authority."

"I believe you're referring to a legal term known as 'change of venue,'" Booker said. "Such requests seldom appear before the courts. I have sincere doubts any motion to relocate his trial would be entertained, much less allowed."

He glanced over the seat at me.

"Don't forget Sheriff Thomas has a strong network of allies protecting him," he said. "Some of them live in his home community, of course, and others beyond the state's borders. These people are dedicated to shepherding his gradual rise through the ranks to higher and more significant roles. The same for the other chosen individuals on their list."

I noticed Booker had steered us toward the Arkansas State Capitol.

"Did I mention the group's ultimate goal?" Booker asked.

"Beyond placing their hand-picked people in crucial positions?" I asked.

"That's the means to the end," Booker said. "The definitive prize is conversion of the United States to a Christian nation."

I looked at Booker, wondering if I'd heard him correctly.

"Surely you're not serious," Leslie said, her eyes growing wide.

"The process has been underway for years, predating the current efforts," Booker said. "You may remember reciting the Pledge of Allegiance during your youth. The words 'under God' are a fairly recent addition to the pledge as is the phrase 'In God We Trust' on our coins and currency. Neither were part of the legacy left us by our founding fathers."

It took a couple of attempts, but Booker somehow managed to park Cruella in a standard-sized parking space near the southwest corner of the Capitol.

322

"Please follow me," he said, stepping from the car. He led us down a sidewalk a short distance to a large granite slab perpendicular to the ground. Etched across its top were these words: The Ten Commandments. Shown below was the list of familiar decrees straight from the Book of Exodus.

I realized it was here, but this was the first time I'd seen the actual marker.

"In their infinite wisdom, members of the Arkansas General Assembly chose to erect this shrine on our hallowed Capitol grounds a decade or so ago," Booker asked. "Prominently located on the front lawn of the Capitol are two other state-sanctioned memorials pertinent to today's discussion. One honoring Confederate Soldiers and another commemorating Confederate Women."

"I have a question," Leslie said, staring at the monument. "Doesn't the First Amendment to the Constitution guarantee separation of church and state?"

"I believe that was its intent," Booker said. "To provide a wall between government and religion."

"But doesn't placement of these Biblical commandments in the literal shadow of the State Capitol imply an official endorsement of Christianity?" she asked. "Seems to me it sends a message to anybody who's not a Christian they're … I don't know … out of favor."

"I believe you've hit the proverbial nail on the head," Booker said.

"Likewise," I said, "I thought the idea of state sovereignty or states' rights was settled by the Civil War. Isn't the spread of white nationalism a threat to our country?"

"I could not agree more," Booker said. "I am both ashamed and alarmed by what I see."

"When will all this foolishness end?" Leslie asked.

"What do you mean by 'foolishness'?"

Leslie gestured to the shrine in front of us. "Stuff like this. And those nearby alters to the Confederacy."

"I continue to be astounded by the delightful innocence of those of you in the younger generation," Booker said, shaking his head. "It is … ah … refreshing."

"I'm not sure what you mean by that," Leslie said, "although I'm pretty sure I don't like it."

"No offense intended," Booker said with a chuckle. "You asked when this foolishness, as you described what we've just observed, will end, right?"

She gave him a nod.

"It will never end," he said, "but will continue to expand. Our society is doomed."

~ FORTY-FIVE ~

In late spring of the next year, immediately following Lassiter & Associates' annual Cinco de Mayo potluck luncheon, I rinsed the empty bowl that had held my homemade guacamole, slipped into my office, and shut the door. Leaning back in my chair, I placed my feet on the desk and reflected on changes of the past 12 months.

Things at the advertising agency were going well. Two of the three latest pitches we'd made had generated new clients. Their modest billings should be more than offset by the potential for growth. Representatives of our two pro bono accounts—Habitat for Humanity and the Little Rock Zoo—had thanked the staff for their volunteer work, presenting the agency with a pair of handsome plaques now on display in our lobby. And owners of the Isla del Sol Casino and Resort agreed to a renewed contract, extending our business relationship for another two years.

As expected, overseeing the state's tourism account proved to be a challenge, but my colleagues and I eagerly put in the hours, delivering goods and services—and results. Anecdotal reports from across Arkansas indicated the hospitality community was largely pleased, with record visitation numbers for the first quarter of the year. Charlie Engstrom, who phoned at least once a month to share his latest insights, was euphoric about the 23% increase in his midweek bookings. On a recent visit, Cabinet Secretary Anne Parker told me Governor Patricia Butler was delighted to learn the agency's "Authentic Arkansas" campaign had swept the top awards in a national competition, winning "Best Overall Campaign." She also hinted I could expect an invitation to join her and the governor for lunch in the near future.

Hillcountry Marine's line of luxury party barges became the talk of the industry. Due to unprecedented demand, customers found themselves on a waiting list now approaching six weeks. Junior Judson was a popular draw at trade shows, enthusiastically signing autographs and posing for pictures. One unexpected development was the romance between Tabitha Boddington and Harrison Davies, the Lassiter & Associates employee handling the Hillcountry Marine account. Their engagement had been made public last week.

Meanwhile, Erin Askew had invested a portion of her sweepstakes winnings in a cute bungalow in Hillcrest, one of Little Rock's chic neighborhoods, and was dating the real estate agent who'd sold her the property. Three days ago, on her one-year anniversary, Erin received a well-deserved promotion at Lassiter & Associates, meaning another round of dreaded interviews was on my horizon.

Erin told me her twin sister Erica had been selected for the Dallas Cowboys' cheerleading squad following an extensive series of conversations and tryouts. Although the NFL season was months away, she and her fellow sideline dancers were busy practicing their routines three times a week.

State Representative Joan Pfeiffer simultaneously announced her retirement from the legislature and her pending marriage to State Senator Somerset Smith. According to State Capitol scuttlebutt, Senator Smith was quietly testing the water for a run for the post of attorney general. I knew he'd contacted Leslie within the past few days to schedule a photo shoot. Speculation had Senator Rufus Hinshaw serving as Smith's campaign chairman.

Joan's close friend Nita Breckenridge had represented Leslie and me when we appeared before the circuit judge in Yellville. Finding us guilty of "disturbing the peace," a misdemeanor, he fined us $100 each. While expecting a hit to my wallet, I didn't appreciate his lengthy and patronizing lecture on citizenship.

Noticing my growing irritation, Nita squeezed my arm and mouthed "Don't say a word." It may have been the longest ten minutes of my life, but I bit my tongue and tried to divert my attention by recalling the 50 states (remembering all but three). With Amelia again safely in her custody, Leslie and I celebrated with milkshakes as we left town.

Hutch Thomas won his election to the Arkansas General Assembly by a landslide—with the majority of his campaign funds arriving from out-of-state donors. Refusing to dismiss assertions from media pundits that he'd already set his sights on higher office, Thomas insisted his political future was "in the good Lord's capable hands." Two weekends a month, Thomas could be found on the speaking circuit, appearing at conservative rallies throughout the South. His message to the fanatical crowds was simple: the country needed more people like him in office to combat the escalating threat of "the liberal elite deep state."

Random attacks at electrical substations in rural Arkansas had become almost commonplace, occurring every month or so. Describing them as cowardly acts of domestic terrorists, the FBI had brought in additional agents to assist in the investigations, but had yet to identify any suspects or make an arrest. In a media event conducted on the front steps of the Capitol last week, State Representative Hutch Thomas vowed to hold a televised hearing to "expose the FBI's colossal failure to protect the Arkansas way of life."

Charged with kidnapping State Senator Somer Smith, Alex Motherwell and Jordan Englehart went to trial in Yellville. When cross-examined by the defense attorney, the senator admitted he'd never actually seen the two accused men until the day of the trial. He'd been blindfolded both during the kidnapping and while transported in the van. Another man, still unidentified, had tended to him during his confinement in the small houseboat. The jury deliberated for half an hour before issuing a "Not Guilty" verdict. It was later revealed the jury's foreman was the husband of a niece of State Representative Hutch Thomas.

The Francis Marion Memorial Camp for Southern Youth had scheduled eight sessions for this coming summer, four for girls and another four for boys. Every slot had been reserved, and the standby list was reported to number in the dozens. In an interview published by *Arkansas Business*, a spokesman for The Flyover Family said the group was considering a major expansion to accommodate burgeoning interest in the camp—with rumors circulating the Koch organization would fund the additional facilities.

Spending hour upon hour exploring the deep recesses of the dark web, Uncle Booker continued to monitor the Flyover Family's activities. He'd discovered their David O. Dodd essay contest had garnered responses from well over one thousand high school students. The winner would be recognized at Dodd's gravesite in Mount Holly Cemetery in less than two weeks on May 18, the day Arkansas joined the Confederacy. Booker learned Fox News had agreed to send a journalist to Little Rock to cover the occasion.

Chantelle Huxley and her small team of Lassiter & Associates colleagues continued their tutoring sessions with students at David O. Dodd Elementary. Reading scores had shown marked improvement over the past 12 months. The framed "Certificate of Appreciation" Chantelle received from the superintendent of the Little Rock School District hung on her office wall.

Demand for Leslie's photographic expertise continued to grow, so much so she was giving serious thought to hiring an assistant. Many of her assignments now required aerial shots, making Amelia an indispensable tool. Leslie promised to let me pilot her drone on a short flight later this year, but only after I'd watched a tutorial on YouTube. And I began accompanying her to twice-monthly massage sessions.

At dinner over the weekend, my sister Ellen and Gib, her infuriating husband, told us a sibling for their young son was in the works, with an expected arrival date late in the summer. For the first time in recent memory, my brother-in-law didn't torment me with an attempt at a pun.

Last evening, Uncle Booker had stopped by the house, surprising Leslie and me by stating he'd sold his classic 1959 Cadillac Coupe de Ville.

"This is our penultimate stop," he said, glancing out the window to the curb where he'd parked the fabulous car. "I'm delivering Cruella to her new owner in a quarter of an hour."

Booker then told us he was relocating to Portugal within the month.

Shocked by these revelations, we stared at him, unable to process what we'd heard.

"I enrolled in the Rosetta Stone program earlier this year and have made significant strides with my Portuguese," he said. "Bom dia!"

Leslie squeezed my hand.

"That means 'good day,'" he said. "A broker has purchased a restored 18th-century villa in the historic walled city of Evora in my behalf. She's also arranged for a housekeeper and gardener."

This was too much to absorb. And it made no sense.

"Why Portugal?" I finally asked.

"I must admit to experiencing a great deal of angst choosing between Costa Rica and Portugal," he said. "My vegan lifestyle could be easily accommodated in either. The convenient access to London, Rome, and Paris from Lisbon was the deciding factor."

"Let me rephrase my question," I said, trying to mask my impatience. "Why are you leaving the United States?"

Seconds passed as Booker looked at his feet. "This country is no longer the republic I remember," he eventually said, raising his head and making eye contact. "Things I see on the dark web have convinced me it's time to depart."

Leslie and I gazed at him, our mouths gaping.

After another pause, Uncle Booker shook his head. "America is now The Lost Cause. You two might want to join me."

With that, Booker gave us each a tight hug before leaving through the front door. Leslie and I followed, watching him walk down the porch steps and climb into Cruella DeVille. At the end of the block, the big car slowed down and turned the corner, its bright red brake lights disappearing in the night for the last time.

"Do you think Uncle Booker is right?" Leslie asked. "That America is The Lost Cause?"

"Not if we do our part," I said, reaching for her hand. "Not if we do our part."

The End

ABOUT THE AUTHOR

A former partner in a canoe outfitting business on the Buffalo River, Joe David Rice spent a good deal of time roaming the Ozarks during his younger days. And, as Arkansas's tourism director for over 30 years, he gained an unequaled familiarity with the state, its people, and Arkansas's intriguing nuances. A prize-winner in the Ozark Creative Writers Conference, he's also the author of the two-volume *Arkansas Backstories: Quirks, Characters, and Curiosities of the Natural State*. He and his wife Tracey enjoy their remote cabin in Newton County which backs up to the Buffalo National River's Ponca Wilderness.

The Lost Cause is the fourth novel in the Randy Lassiter/Leslie Carlisle series. These engaging characters meet in the first book, *An Undercurrent of Murder*. Randy and Dr. Gib Yarberry, his annoying brother-in-law, are on an Ozark hiking getaway in the Buffalo River country and stumble into Leslie, a professional photographer sent to the area on assignment, during their October trek. A chance encounter with a group of desperate drug-runners soon has them fleeing for their lives, battling both Mother Nature and some very bad dudes.

The second book, *A Nasty Way to Die*, finds Leslie and Randy searching for Dr. J.J. Newell, Randy's close friend, former college roommate, and soon-to-be best man. Newell, a popular instructor at the local university, has strangely vanished. The hunt for the missing professor leads them to something far beyond what either could have imagined.

The third novel in the Randy Lassiter/Leslie Carlisle series, titled *A Piece of Paradise*, finds them honeymooning on Eleuthera, one of the Out Islands of the Bahamas, where they inadvertently witness a drug drop on a deserted beach early one morning. Their host, owner of a B & B, soon disappears about the time a mysterious yacht, rumored to be chartered by a notorious international drug trafficker, anchors in Governor's Harbor. As Randy and Leslie seek answers, an approaching hurricane adds to an already difficult situation.

Made in the USA
Columbia, SC
01 May 2025

57409842R00183